DESTINY LOST

THE ORION WAR – BOOK 1

M. D. COOPER

ACKNOWLEDGEMENTS

This book is in your hands today in no small part because of you, the readers. Your emails and excitement for the series always inspires me to keep writing.

In addition, the author community, with whom I have found companionship, has helped me hone my craft, and shared stories of encouragement—as I have with them.

Beyond them are the hard-working folks in the aero-space industry, who are working day and night to bring our species to space in a meaningful way. Their dedication and advances are what gives me hope for our future.

Lastly, as I've mentioned before, this book stands on the shoulders of giants. Writers whose stories and imaginations have forged a shared vision of the future, and our destiny, that we call Science Fiction.

CONTENTS

THE WORLD OF AEON 14

For the seasoned science fiction reader, there will be little here which they have not seen in another story, be it planetary rings, nano technology, AI, or mind-to-mind communication.

However, for those who may not know what a HUD is, understand the properties of deuterium, or cannot name the stars within the Sirius system, **I encourage you to reference the appendixes at the rear of the book as you read.**

You may also visit www.aeon14.com to read the primer, glossary, and timelines.

To get the latest news and access to free novellas and short stories, sign up on the Aeon 14 mailing list: www.aeon14.com/signup.

AN UNEXPECTED CARGO

STELLAR DATE: 06.30.8927 (Adjusted Years)
LOCATION: Coburn Station, Trio
REGION: Trio System, Silstrand Alliance Space

Sera slammed the shooter down with a triumphant grin and watched with reddened eyes as the man from Thoria reached for his next glass. Around them, the crowd chanted their names as money changed hands.

Her opponent downed his drink and tossed the glass onto the table where it rolled against the two-dozen empty shooters between them. With a wave of his hand and an unappealing grin, he indicated that the floor was hers.

She took a deep breath to steady herself, chanting an internal mantra of *just one more, just one more.* The act of raising her arm caused Sera to sway in her seat, the smell of bodies pressed close around not helping her deepening nausea.

The Thorian saw her hesitation and his grin grew wider.

"Ready to give up?" he slurred, his putrid breath washing over her.

Sera didn't reply, only fixed him with a steely glare—at least she hoped it was a steely glare—and grasped the glass in her fist, throwing it back without further hesitation.

The alcohol washed down her throat like fire, and her tongue felt swollen in its wake. If she didn't know better, she'd assume the bartender had poured a stiffer drink.

She set the glass down and took slow, deep breaths, using all her concentration to keep the fire in her stomach and veins under control.

The Thorian grunted and stared at the row of shots before him— likely deciding which one to pick up. Finally selecting his drink, he grabbed it with a swift flourish and raised it high to throw it back.

In his current state, the gesture failed miserably and the drink splashed across his face. His features crumpled in confusion and his arms rotated slowly as he slid sideways out of his chair to the floor.

No one attempted to catch him and the man's head hit the deck-plate with a solid crack.

Cheers and grumbles erupted around her as Sera was declared the winner. The victors were paid out, and the losers turned to the bar for another drink. In the midst of the post-contest exchange, one voice rose above the others.

A short, but well-built man in a dirty shipsuit pushed to the front of the crowd.

"Cheater! She had to cheat; there's no way that waif could drink Greg under the table!" He slammed his hands on the table, bent over, his face inches from Sera's. "You used nano to clear the alcohol from your bloodstream."

Most people had some of the tiny nano-machines in their body, it was nearly impossible not to; they were almost as common as bacteria. A person's nano was controlled by their internal computer or AI—if you had the money or influence to hire one. Sera's nano could clear her bloodstream with ease—though that wasn't a fact she advertised. It took a lot of nano to filter that much booze over such a short period; a lot more than a simple freighter captain should possess.

Sera worked her mouth for a moment, making sure it would respond the way she wanted it to. "I did not. Have the bartender do a check." The words were slurred, but understandable.

Bartenders on Coburn Station were not allowed to let their patrons to get too drunk—an ordinance they rarely enforced. They had scanners on hand that could do a blood-alcohol level check and determine, based on that person's size and metabolic rate, if they were too inebriated to have another round.

The bartender had already stepped into the crowd, eager to do whatever it took to avoid a fight on his shift. He pressed the scanner against Sera's wrist and took samples of her blood for the reading.

"She's pissed," he said as he straightened. "Consistent with the amount and time she's been slugging them back." Smirking, he turned back to the bar. "Those shooters are only a third of what she's had tonight too."

The winners cheered all the louder and the losers ceased their grumbling. Everyone knew that bartenders altered their scanners, so they could give people more liquor than they should. If it said she was drunk, then she should be totally pissed.

<One of these days, the losers aren't going to care what the scan says and take their satisfaction out of your hide,> Helen admonished in Sera's mind.

Sera sent her internal AI a mental shrug. Helen didn't like it when Sera drank; she claimed it upset the chemical balance of Sera's body in a way that made the AI feel weird. Sera wasn't sure how that was possible, not that would change her behavior. She liked the feeling of chemical imbalance.

<My hide's been through worse.>

<I know; I've been there each time. Doesn't mean I want a repeat. You know how disconcerting I find it when you get hurt that badly.>

Helen could be annoying at times with her mothering, but Sera knew that her AI's concern was genuine. Pulling her thoughts from the familiar debate, Sera looked around the bar.

To smooth things over, the winners were buying the losers a round. Sera had put a hundred SIL credits down on herself and collected three hundred back. The odds had been stacked nicely against her.

Betting was illegal in Silstrand Alliance space, so money always changed hands in cash. The prohibition didn't seem to diminish the illegal activity; it just meant no one had to pay taxes on their winnings. Sera thought about that for a minute. Maybe that was why it was illegal; officials probably liked to gamble tax-free, too.

Stuffing the hard money into an inside pocket on her leather jacket she rose slowly, nearly teetering over at the last moment. A steady hand appeared under her elbow and Sera turned to see the dark smiling face of Cargo.

"Good haul on that, Captain." He guided her out of the bar and into the bustling main corridor of the station's promenade. "I made a couple hundred credits on your drinking skill."

"It's good to be useful," Sera slurred as Cargo led her toward a small coffee shop which was renowned for its after-drunk-sober-up brew. Once inside, Sera ordered two of their strongest and let Cargo wait at the counter for the order. Her leather clothing squeaked noisily as she collapsed into a chair. Cursing the café's bright lights, she leaned back with a hand over her eyes, praying for a power outage.

<*You're not masking the squeak. What gives?*> Sera asked her AI.

<*It's what you get for drinking. I can't deal with two organic peculiarities at once. If you drink, I won't mask your clothing's noise. Take your pick.*> Helen was really on the warpath, determined to make Sera suffer. Thank god Cargo had shown up.

Her first mate knew she liked to get one last round in at a bar before they left a station—okay, maybe more than just *a* round. He often would find her and bring her back to the ship before she was too far gone.

Sera splayed her fingers and looked through them to see Cargo returning with an insufferable grin on his face. He had a coffee for himself and two of the sober-up drinks for her. He set them on the table and pushed them toward her, his smile widening.

"I bet those are going to taste horrible."

Sera stuck her tongue out as she leaned forward to pick one up. "Prolly."

"You should have let me know you were gonna get into another drinking contest," Cargo said and took a drink of his own beverage. "I would have had more cash on hand and made a larger wager."

"I'm sorry I didn't think to let you know so you could sate your gambling needs," Sera said while delivering another sour look.

"My gambling habit doesn't have the unpleasant side effects of your station drinking binges."

Sera eyed him blearily over the rim of her cup. "What side effects are those?"

"The first day of any trip. You're not exactly sunshine and roses the day after a binge."

"Am I ever?"

Cargo paused, appearing to ponder the statement with great cogitation.

Her mind echoed with the light watery sound of Helen laughing at Cargo's pause. Sera scowled and swatted at him. "Thanks!"

He gestured with a nonchalant wave toward the second cup, indicating she get to it. Sera had already used her nano to clear most of the alcohol from her bloodstream and contain it for the next time she visited the head. However, Cargo didn't know she could do that and she needed to keep up appearances.

Sera raised the cup to her lips and took a long pull of the vile liquid anyway. She didn't want to seem ungrateful. After downing it, she leaned back in her chair, feeling much steadier than when she first sat down.

"All things considered, it's not a bad bit of extra credit to finish the visit with," she said and patted her pocket.

Cargo grunted, "One day you'll run out of people who haven't seen you win a drinking contest and then what will you do for fun?"

"Dunno, I guess I'll have to find a new way to fleece the common man."

Cargo laughed heartily in response.

Several minutes later—with Sera moving under her own power—they made their way down the promenade and onto the commercial dock front. There was just as much traffic here, but of a different sort. Cargo transports trundled down the deck-plate and service trucks were everywhere, delivering supplies or repair equipment.

Sabrina was in berth 724 Station South. Long before she could see the ship around the curve of the docks, Sera could hear Thompson's voice berating some poor cargo handlers. The echoing shouts eventually resolved into words, and Sera hid a smile behind her hand as they approached.

"You lazy dolts, can't you even lift a crate? I've seen hundred-year-old bots do a better job than you oafs. If you drop one more container, I'll take it out of your scrawny, mal-nourished hides. Now get to it, I don't have all day."

Thompson was a large blond man who had been her supercargo for over six years. To avoid confusion with Cargo, they just called him the Super. He wasn't a very outgoing man, mostly taken to brooding and stumping about the ship, but his attention to detail made him a good crewmember. Combined with his size and skill with a pulse rifle, that made him the right sort of super for *Sabrina*.

"How's the last shipment?" Sera asked when she and Cargo reached the ship.

"Fine, if these morons can manage to hold onto an effing handle." Thompson tossed the two dockworkers a contemptuous glare. "Don't know why they insist on using humans for this. Either way, we'll be loaded up with plenty of time to spare, don't worry, Captain."

"Good to hear," Cargo said. "Send the final docs up to me on the bridge when you're done."

Thompson nodded and turned back to the handlers as another crate slipped from their grasp. "God's great black space! What is *wrong* with you two, is this your first day on the job? I told you I was going to take it out of your hide and now I am. Which one of you wants to get your ear ripped off?"

"Somehow, I don't think that is helping them with their work," Cargo laughed.

"Yeah, but I bet it makes him feel a lot better," Sera grinned.

"I'll see you later, Captain; I've got to wash the smell of that bar you were in off me before my shift starts."

Sera took a deep breath. "Dunno, I kind of like that malty musk on you."

"In that case, I'm gonna take an even longer shower," Cargo laughed and walked onto the ship. Sera stuck her tongue out at him and walked over to an inspection port to admire the sleek lines of her girl.

Sabrina was not a regular boxy freight hauler, having started her life as a pleasure yacht. Her previous owner had fallen on hard times and lost possession of the ship in an outer system. *Sabrina* had needed repairs, and the local shipyard, where she had been in storage for owed taxes, didn't have the funds to make them. So, she sat for ninety years before Sera found her. With a hundred years of service before being impounded, she was getting on, but that didn't diminish the impact Sera felt when she first laid eyes on the ship.

There was an influential man who owed Sera a favor or two, and she got him to give her the money to buy the ship and furnish it with the necessary repairs. The finer aspects of the yacht's interior had been stripped out long before Sera saw *Sabrina*, but it was the size of the vessel and the engines that mattered. This ship had the room to haul cargo and the power to do so quickly. There were some other modifications that had been made, but like her advanced nano, Sera didn't advertise those.

She noted with approval that the damage they had suffered on their last run had been repaired. They had been parked in a planetary ring, moving along with the flow of the rocks and ice, when a stray rock had damaged the port sensor array and left a long rent across a goodly portion of the ship. However, the profit from the questionable cargo, which had put them there in the first place, more than paid for the repairs.

Thompson let loose some final curses as the dockworkers finished loading the last crate. She turned to watch with a smile; the dockworkers were visibly trembling as they got on their cart and drove off.

Sera returned to viewing her ship. She enjoyed these final quiet moments alone before going on board and filling out departure docs; these last few minutes when it was just her, *Sabrina's* sleek hull, and the call of empty space. She could forget her past, previous failures. Here she was a good captain, *Sabrina* was prosperous, and she had a good crew.

Her reverie was interrupted by a stinging slap on her butt and Sera turned to see her pilot, Cheeky, standing behind her. She wore a coy smile and her hands were resting on tilted hips.

"One day I'll get you to give me some of that luvin' you lavish on *Sabrina*," Cheeky said.

"One day I'll get you neutered and save us all a lot of hassle." Sera rubbed her stinging butt; Cheeky could really deliver a good slap. She found herself becoming aroused as she looked at her pilot.

Cheeky was an attractive woman who wore as little clothing as local law or custom would allow. On Coburn, that meant she wore little more than three triangles of cloth, her shoes and a purse.

Sera shook her head to clear her mind. Cheeky also had altered glands that could put out much higher levels of pheromones than any human should be allowed to. "Make sure you shut that off and take a long shower. You know what happened last time your love smell filtered through the ship."

"We all had a good time." Cheeky wiggled her hips suggestively and blew her captain a kiss as she walked up the ramp. From behind, it was obvious why Cheeky had the name she did. Sera found herself wondering if it was a conscious effort to walk like that or if the woman had resorted to surgery.

Following her pilot onto the ship, Sera's internal AI flashed a notification that they had made a secure connection to the ship's private net. Sera checked the ship's general status and greeted its AI.

<*Good evening sweetie, how are you holding together?*> Sera asked Sabrina.

<*Well enough, though I take offense to the question. How else would I be holding together?*> The ship's mental tone conveyed annoyance.

Sabrina had been in a strange mood as of late. Sera chose to ignore the reply and smiled up at the nearest observation camera as Helen passed her authentication token to the bridge's net. Sera checked in, finding Cargo already working on departure paperwork; he must have decided to skip the shower.

<*Station given us our departure time yet?*>

<*0900 ship time tomorrow.*> His mental tone was relaxed. He enjoyed the little details of running the ship. Sera preferred to sit in her Captain's chair and give orders.

<*Everything delivered and stowed?*>

She could imagine him flipping through the plas sheets, checking them against the records logged in their databases, before he answered. Cargo hated making mistakes.

<*Just one package left.*> There was a significant pause, Sera could feel his mental discomfort even over the net. <*It's from one of Kade's people here.*>

<*Kade? Why didn't I know about this?*> Sera asked Cargo and Helen.

<*It came on the list when we were out,*> Helen supplied.

Cargo muttered something rude and the bridge's net flashed with an image of Cargo's avatar doing something very unpleasant to a representation of Kade. <*At least we're delivering it at the regular drop point with the rest of his stuff; there's no extra trip.*>

The regular drop point was an out of the way FTL jump point that Kade's people used for trading with other ships—his people being a pirate organization known as The Mark. Most of their people and ships were somewhat less than welcome at the more reputable stations, such as Coburn.

<*They never can schedule things ahead of time,*> Sera sighed.

<*They're not exactly an "ahead of time" sort of organization.*>

Sera told Cargo she'd be making the rounds and passed the active monitoring of the bridge's net to Helen.

When *Sabrina* had been a private yacht, the main deck was where the owners presumably threw their parties and spent most of their time. Now it was the freight deck. The cargo hatch was on the port side, and from there Sera walked into the main corridor, which ran from the bow to the stern engine shielding. The various freight holds were located off this corridor. Some had normal air and gravity, some were refrigerated and some had low, or even no gravity.

Also along the corridor were the lifts and ladders to the other decks. Sera walked toward the bow of the ship and slid into one of the vertical ladder shafts, which ran through all the decks. From there, she opened an access hatch to a maintenance tube. Inside the hatch were some knee and shoulder pads that she slipped on; it wouldn't do to scuff her leather.

The tube ended in a sealed inspection port. Sera opened it and peered out at the newly installed sensor equipment. The workmanship looked good. Everything was straight and attached firmly. The exterior indicators all showed green.

Beyond the array, Sera could see the space elevator that carried cargo and people between the surface and the station. Seeing it reminded her how far humanity had fallen from the glory it once held.

Millennia ago, when humanity had first set out to cross the stars, they had no faster than light technology. Interstellar travel was made possible only by utilizing massive fuel scoops. Ships had vast electrostatic funnels that spread for kilometers in front of them and allowed the gathering and compression of interstellar heavy hydrogen. The hydrogen, typically Deuterium and Tritium, was burned in nuclear fusion reactors to produce the thrust that pushed the ships between the stars.

Journeys between the stars took decades, or even centuries.

With the considerable effort and expense required to get to even the nearest stars, humanity strove to make the most of all available resources. Technology and engineering made impressive advances as societies demanded better use of raw materials.

The space elevator stretching from Coburn Station down to Trio was an example of the different sort of technology humans used to have. In present times, few worlds could afford to build elevators to their space stations. The materials were just too expensive and the process took too long. A ship's grav drive was more efficient in the short term. However, over centuries of use, the elevator would use much less power to achieve the same volume of transport. It was another example of the long-term approach that people used to take as opposed to the current mindset, which was decidedly shortsighted.

It was a shift created by the advent of FTL.

People had always suspected—at least once the significance of 299,792,458 meters per second was known—that some method of exceeding the speed of light was possible. Many theories of wormholes, space-time folding, alternate realities, and slipstreams were put forward and attempted. In the end, the workable form of faster than light travel encapsulated many of the ideas behind some of those theories, though it turned out to be much harder to harness than originally hoped.

Before FTL, each star system was isolated from the rest of humanity, but once a trip between two stars was reduced to a matter of weeks and not centuries, everything changed. Traveling to an uninhabited star to mine asteroids was something that could be easily achieved, and people's attitude toward conservation and efficiency disappeared within a century.

Helen injected a long yawn into Sera's thoughts. *<Enough already. We get it, you yearn for the good old days.>*

<I don't really miss the days…just wish people could appreciate the way things used to be.>

Helen didn't agree. *<You just miss your people. This isn't your world and you know it.>*

<It is now; it has to be.>

Helen didn't respond. It was an old conversation, one they performed out of habit more than a real expectation of change.

She walked through the freight deck's main corridor, poking her head into various holds, ensuring that everything was secure and ready for departure. The familiar smell of deck cleaner and oil wafted past and an unbidden memory of her first weeks on the ship came back.

She and Flaherty had spent many a day hauling equipment through these halls and shafts back when they were first refitting

Sabrina. It had been long days and longer nights, but she was proud of what they had built.

Helen flashed the date of her memory over her vision and she was surprised to see that it had been just over ten years ago. Somewhere in the last few months, she had passed her ten-year anniversary with *Sabrina* without marking the occasion. No wonder the ship had been a bit snippy of late.

Sera chided Helen for not reminding her of the occasion, nor for cluing her in on the cause of Sabrina's poor temper.

<I was unaware you were interested in marking anniversaries with AI.> Helen was unrepentant.

<What are you talking about?> Sera replied. *<We always celebrate our anniversary.>*

Helen inserted the emotion of mild surprise, followed by a pout into Sera's mind. *<I thought that was just for me.>*

Sera laughed and her avatar stuck her tongue out at Helen. *<Don't give me that, I'm not some little girl that you can twist around your ephemeral finger anymore.>*

Helen didn't respond, and Sera let out a long sigh. For being one of the most advanced AI in the Inner Stars, Helen could certainly be childish.

<Sometimes I think Sabrina is rubbing off on you,> Sera said to her one-time mentor and guardian.

<I resent that,> Helen retorted. *<Just because the ship's AI can't deal with the fact that I am her superior in every way doesn't mean I have to dumb it down.>*

<You're superior to most planet administration AI we run into, but you don't go out of your way to make them feel inferior,> Sera responded, mildly surprised to be the one to advocate maturity in their relationship.

<Maybe I could be more accommodating for our dear Sabrina,> Helen eventually responded.

<Glad to hear it. Now I have to figure out how to make it up to her,> Sera said.

<Make what up?> Helen asked innocently and Sera let out an audible scream.

She completed her review of the freight deck and took the aft ladder shaft up to the crew deck.

When she first bought *Sabrina*, the ship had lifts for reaching each deck, but Sera had removed all but one of the conveniences. Shafts were faster and still worked when the ship was under fire and conserving energy.

<Nothing to do with how you like to climb the ladders in front of the men on the ship?> Helen suggested.

<I do it to Cheeky, too.> Sera smiled to herself as she stepped onto the crew deck.

<Funny, I thought you preferred it when she did it to you.>

The ladder was across from the galley and she stepped in to find Thompson and Flaherty eating their supper. She saw that it was nearing the end of second shift; most of the crew would be calling it a night soon.

"Evening, Captain," Thompson said around a mouthful of his sandwich. Flaherty looked at her, nodded, and went back to his meal.

"Hey guys," Sera smiled at them as she poured a cup of coffee and hunted for fresh cream.

Thompson and Flaherty made an effective and efficient team when it came to managing the ship's cargo. Neither of them talked much and managed to communicate just about everything with grunts and gestures. They didn't even use the Link to talk—Sera had checked the logs.

Sera doctored her coffee up just the way she liked and bid them goodnight before taking the corridor to the bow, then climbing the ladder that led to the top deck. This was the smallest deck on the ship, containing only the bridge forward and a small observation lounge aft. The lounge had a magnificent view of the light flare from the engines when they were under heavy thrust, and Sera had often sat back there, gazing out at it as the ship cruised through space.

Cargo was still on the bridge, readying the reports Sera had to sign before they could depart. Cheeky was also at her console, having added a tight halter top and tiny skirt to her ensemble. She yawned and stretched as she stood.

"You just had to make a final course alteration right before bed," she complained. "I had to plot it out and re-file with system traffic control."

"Sorry about that, I didn't think you'd already filed the report," Sera apologized.

"When else was I going to do it, when I was sleeping?"

Cargo laughed. "I thought you had gotten all of your 'sleeping' in on your shore leave."

Cheeky stuck her tongue out at the man. "Jealous."

Cargo couldn't help it as his eyes strayed down to the bold, black print across Cheeky's chest. It read 'Got Milk?' He sighed wistfully. "I might be."

"Really?" Cheeky asked.

"No, not really," Cargo grinned.

"You're such a tease," Cheeky said as she turned and left the bridge.

"I'm a tease?" He murmured softly as she left.

"You are, you know," Sera said.

"How so? I don't flirt, I just do my job."

"Exactly!" Sera smiled as she shuffled the plas she had to sign into order. "You're totally unflappable. It's the ultimate come-on."

"I'm going to start the pre-warm-up checklist so things'll be ready in the morning."

"See! Always back to business with you."

"Do you want to do it?" Cargo turned, half rising out of his chair.

"Heck no, I've been up for thirty hours already."

Cargo nodded and sat back down.

Coburn, like many stations, required a full warm-up and test of all ship systems before undocking. The warm-up had to take place four hours before departure and Cargo was taking the third watch to run the sequence at 0500 hours.

She turned to leave the bridge when Nance, the ship's bio, appeared in her mind.

<*I just wanted to let you know, take short showers for the next while—I know how you like to luxuriate for an hour or more.*>

Even though she was looking at Nance's mental avatar, the bio-engineer still wore a thick, tight hazsuit. Whereas Cheeky showed every inch of skin she could manage, Nance was the opposite, rarely showing any skin at all—even virtually.

<*What's up?*> Sera asked. <*I have the stink of a hundred drunks to wash off.*>

The bio scowled. <*Well, let's just say that you don't want to come down to environmental until I clean up. The regulator on tank nine malfunctioned, and a line blew. Contaminated all sorts of shit with…well…shit.>*

<Was it that one you bought at Rattlescar?> Sera asked.

<Yeah, I knew I shouldn't have, but it was such a good deal,> the bio replied.

<Ripped off at Rattlescar again. You should know better.>

Nance's avatar nodded sullenly and Sera laughed. <Well, I'll let you get to it. Can I at least have ten minutes?>

Nance nodded. <Yes, but a second over and I'm switching it to full cold.>

<Is that any way to treat your captain?>

<Do **you** want to come down here and clean up?> Nance retorted.

<OK, OK, ten minutes, got it.>

Nance disappeared from her vision as Sera slid down the ladder to the third deck. She walked quietly past the crew cabin doors to her quarters at the end of the corridor. She palmed the door open with a yawn and entered her outer office where she handled the ship's business.

It was the standard utilitarian sort expected of a captain; her various certifications hung on the wall and a large oak desk dominated the small space. She laid the departure plas sheets on its surface and pulled up holo of each one. This was the part about captaining a starship she liked least. She was near finishing up and getting ready to peel off her leather when Cargo called her over the Link.

<Still up, Captain?>

<Barely.>

<Hate to bother you with this, but you're the only other one awake. Kade's boys are down at the hatch with that last shipment.>

Despite his words, Cargo's tone didn't carry any apology.

Grumbling that she should have told Thompson to have himself or Flaherty wait up for it, she pulled her jacket back on and slid down the ladders to the freight deck. At the hold's opening to the station dock, two men were waiting with a large crate on a gravity pad. They were looking nervous and just a bit twitchy. Either they had some bad drugs in their systems or Kade was foisting something pretty damn dangerous on her.

One of the men spoke up as soon as he spotted her.

"Permission to côme aboard?" he asked.

Sera granted it and the two men all but ran onto the ship and moved out of direct sight from dock traffic, the cargo container following them on its float.

"So, what does The Mark have for me today, boys?" Sera asked, none too pleased about the late hour or the obviously illegal contents of the crate. "What am I sticking my neck out for this time?"

Most cargo The Mark had her run was just semi-illegal. Either OK in the system where she was picking up or delivering to, just not both; or some stopping point along the way. There also had been the odd shipment that was illegal no matter where they were; this one had that feel.

The man who had asked permission to board grinned in what he probably thought was a winning fashion. It really wasn't. "S'nothing to worry about, just a little something that Kade wants."

"I don't care about that," Sera said as she reached over and snatched the bill of lading from him. "I care what *this* says it is." Scanning the pad, she found that the crate purported to contain a prize-racing hound in a holo sim. The dog thought he was in a regular kennel with other dogs for companionship and humans feeding him. The reality was just a crate with a feeding system, but he wouldn't know the difference and would be better for it.

"That really what's in there?" Sera didn't bother to hide her skepticism.

"Yeah, the dog's not as special as who used to own it." The man grinned again and Sera held up her hand.

"Yeah, sure. I really don't want to know more." She signed off on the delivery. "Any need to open it and check it out?"

The men went rigid and hastily assured her that the dog would be fine and there was no need to check it out. That clinched it for Sera, she would definitely have to check this cargo out once she was underway. If it had any type of tamper seal, she'd make up some excuse for it later.

Once it was secured in the fore port hold, she informed Cargo that the delivery had been made and stowed. Then she closed the main cargo hatch and the auxiliary personnel port. Cargo confirmed the seal from the bridge and checked it off the pre-warm-up list.

<Get some rest, Captain, gonna be a long day tomorrow,> Cargo advised.

<Cargo! Now you've gone and jinxed it!>

JUST A ROUTINE DAY

STELLAR DATE: 07.01.8927 (Adjusted Years)
LOCATION: *Sabrina,* Coburn Station, Trio
REGION: Trio System, Silstrand Alliance Space

At 0600 hours, Sera sauntered onto the bridge and greeted Cargo, who was hunched over his console, finishing up departure plaswork. She handed him one of the two coffee cups she carried and he absently took it, thanked her, and cast her an appraising look.

"Forgoing the customary clothing-matches-your-mood policy?" he asked.

"I never break my clothing-mood policy. I'm feeling good, but mellow. Blue fits."

Cargo eyed her with suspicion. "This isn't like that one time you wore pink to fake us out, is it?"

"How many times do I have to tell you? That was a dare from Cheeky." Sera set her coffee down and eased into her chair. "Checks went OK?"

"*Sabrina* purred like a kitten, just like always," Cargo replied.

<*Of course I did. When have I not?*> Sabrina asked.

"Never, my dear," Sera replied with a smile.

Cargo shook his head and swallowed his coffee in two quick gulps. "Tug is scheduled for 0845, I'm getting sack." He stood and left the bridge without even his customary morning stretch.

"Is it something I'm wearing?" Sera called after him, laughing.

Sera ran a hand down the tight leather skin-suit covering her body. She spent a moment enjoying the tactile sensation before beginning her routine. The first order of business was finalizing the freight manifests and trade route they would take after the drop-off for Kade.

When Cheeky came on duty at 0700, she took in her captain with a long hungry look, unable to keep a hand from straying toward her captain's well-defined chest. Sera slapped it away.

"There'll be none of that."

"You are such a tease, Captain." Cheeky grinned as she sat at the pilot's console.

Sera laughed. Cheeky was one to talk; she was wearing her customary departure uniform, little more than the day before and a pair of 'sensible' heels. Sera used Cheeky's arrival and coverage of the bridge to make a quick visit to the galley, followed by a final visual inspection of the ship. She returned an hour later to go through final checklists with the station.

Departure tug charges were billed and their accounts were closed. Station umbilicus retracted and station personnel confirmed inner seal on the dockside airlocks. At 0830, *Sabrina* broke hard connection with the station and floated in her berth, with only the station's security tethers still in place.

The tug showed up on time and made a solid grapple to their bow anchors, pulling them gently away from Coburn Station. Sera felt a mild flutter in her stomach as they left station gravity and their internal systems took over.

"Coburn Tug 19 confirming successful undock," the tug pilot's voice announced over the comm.

"Free and clear Tug 19," Cheeky confirmed as the ship drifted away from the station.

The tug maneuvered *Sabrina* out into their designated departure lane. For a relative backwater, Trio was a busy system. They took plotted courses and space traffic lanes very seriously.

"Oh, sweet mother!" Cheeky exclaimed. "Is he ever going to turn on his grav drive? If he uses thrusters to pull us all the way out, you should register a complaint."

Sera had dozed off. She stretched and checked the holo on her console. "He's still on thrusters? We're a thousand klicks from the station; he could have turned on his grav drive at the five hundred mark."

"Trio System law states that all outbound ships must use thrusters only until fifteen hundred kilometers from stations," Sabrina provided via the bridge's audible systems. "It's a recent change they made after some accidents."

"I guess that explains the size of that tug bill; must take a pile of fuel to pull a ship that far on thrusters only."

At the proscribed distance, the tug's gravity engines unfolded from its main body and activated. Because the graviton waves would disrupt the ship behind it, the engines extended far to either side of *Sabrina* before activating.

"We could have been on a fusion burn by now." Cheeky complained, yawning with boredom over the long departure.

"You may be a good pilot, Cheeks, but I don't relish the thought of being on a station where half those moron captains can turn on their fusion engines near me. I like my skin actually attached to my body."

Cheeky made a dismissive sniff. "You can always get new skin, but lost time is gone forever."

Sera laughed. "I'm still wearing my original birthday suit, thank you very much."

"Like I'd know, you never let anyone see it. Always with the leather."

"I could say you have the opposite problem."

"You could, but would I care?" Cheeky sat up and looked at her console intently. "Damn tug's got the vector wrong. We want a parabolic around that inner planet, not a collision."

That was what Sera liked about Cheeky; fun to chat with, but able to switch to business in an instant, when it was called for.

"Tug 19, this is *Sabrina*. Come in," Cheeky called over the comm.

"Tug 19 here."

"Check your vector 19, you're moving off course."

There was a moment of silence and then the tug pilot's response came over the comm. "Sorry about that, my primary nav was reading sensors wrong. I'm on backup now and correcting. Tug 19 out."

"Roger, *Sabrina* out," Cheeky said, switching off the open comm.

"I think that Tug's AI is senile," Sabrina said over the ship's speakers. "It told me that my humans and their advice are not welcome."

"Yay for tugs," Cheeky's voice dripped with sarcasm.

"I suddenly feel somewhat less than safe." Sera finished her cup of coffee and double-checked scan. "At least he corrected properly. How long till we can ditch this dude?"

"Seventeen minutes," Sabrina replied. "And it won't be a moment too soon."

Sera chuckled in response.

Sabrina was an unusual AI. Usually ship's AI were officious and only spoke when directly addressed—and then only over the Link. However, Sabrina had a habit of simply speaking her mind whenever she chose. On their first voyage, when it was just Sera and Flaherty, having Helen and the garrulous Sabrina was comforting—especially since the AI were much better at casual banter than Flaherty.

Finally, the tug reached its departure point and released its grapple.

"Tug 19 signing off. Have a good trip."

"You too," Cheeky said and closed the channel. "Dork."

"We're not on our proper course," Sabrina observed.

"I know," Cheeky sighed. "I just didn't feel like mentioning it again. I can fix us up in a minute."

Cheeky laid in her course corrections and activated *Sabrina's* gravity drive. They were accelerating toward the center of the system, the drive throwing negative gravitons in front of the ship, essentially sucking them forward.

Their flight path took them past the innermost planet, a rocky world spinning below them at over sixteen thousand kilometers per hour. Sera watched the world's surface as the daylight termination line race across the craggy landscape, casting long, dancing shadows over the world.

"Hate to be working a mining rig on that thing," she said with a shake of her head.

"Can you say 'hourly earthquakes'?" Cheeky asked.

Sabrina skimmed close to the surface of the world in a parabolic arc, Cheeky applying a hard burn of the fusion engines at the periapsis of their passage. The ship's velocity picked up considerably during the maneuver, lining them up for a close pass-by of the local star.

"Gravity assist one completed at one-hundred percent efficiency," Cheeky said with a grin. "Now to beard the star."

Gravity assists were one of the wonders of physics. The faster you flew, the more kinetic energy a burn gave. When a burn was made at the closest point of an arch around a heavenly body, the more relative velocity was imparted.

Cheeky referred to it as planet slalom.

"We at the scoop deployment point yet, Cheeks?" Sera asked, feeling too lethargic to use her Link. Maybe she *was* still feeling the after effects of yesterday's binge.

"Just about. When we hit 0.113c we'll have the right v to do it smoothly."

"You on it with Sabrina?"

Cheeky turned and looked at her captain. "I *have* done this before."

<Me too,> Sabrina added.

Sera laughed and raised her hands. "Sorry, I apologize for my backseat piloting."

Several minutes later, a slight vibration ran through the hull as the scoop deployed. It wasn't large, only a kilometer wide, but its electro-static field funneled the stellar wind through a system that stripped out the heavy hydrogen and helium, storing the gasses in the fuel tanks for later consumption.

<Sabrina,> Cheeky addressed the ship as they passed 0.15c, <my board shows green for fusion burn. Confirm?>

<I am green, as well,> Sabrina acknowledged. <Good to initiate burn at plot point tango.>

<Roger,> the pilot replied.

Despite the terms used, Cheeky wasn't sitting at a board with green lights, and Sabrina most certainly was not. Piloting a ship like *Sabrina* involved manipulating controls in a three dimensional holo projection. At any time, the pilot had to monitor dozens of visual indicators, as well as the data feed her Link to the nav computer provided.

"Initiating fusion burn," Cheeky said as she activated the fusion engine's super-lasers and started the flow of helium and heavy hydrogen into the engine.

Although she had just initiated an atomic fusion reaction only one-hundred meters aft, there was no noticeable change on the ship. Powerful inertial dampeners in the form of gravity fields protected the rest of the vessel from the engines. Without them, the thrust from the fusion burners would cause *Sabrina* to do a large-scale impression of a crushed can.

"All dampeners and stabilizers read normal, radiation shielding is showing green, as well."

"You know, Cheeks," Sera said. "It's just me up here; you don't really need to do the whole status announcing thing."

Cheeky cast her captain a sour look. "I don't do it for you; I assume you're checking everything on the Link. You know I've always dreamed of being a military pilot, you know, flying one of those big cruisers. Well, I saw some Silstrand military holos recently where they announce everything. I'm trying it on for size."

"Don't let me stop you, then," Sera smiled.

"I wasn't going to. You may dress like a dominatrix, but you don't frighten me."

Sera sighed and sat back in her chair.

<Well, you do,> Helen said.

The course Cheeky followed took them over the star's north pole. *Sabrina* was on a course to pass within a hundred thousand kilometers of the star, putting them on the right outsystem vector while picking up at least thirty percent of the total velocity they would need before hitting their jump point.

Sera carefully examined the ship's scan readout to make sure there was no potential flare activity. System scan said the star's northern hemisphere was quiet, but she liked to check for herself.

She was comparing the two scans when she noticed several ships enter the system through a seldom-used jump point stellar south of Trio and Coburn Station. Scan showed them traveling at over seventy percent the speed of light; far too fast for a busy system like Trio. Sera imagined they could expect a hefty fine when they docked.

Sabrina lost its Link to the system's dataflow as the ship approached the star; radiation played havoc with any signal. The ship's shields showed nominal fluctuations—they were rated to hold against far worse, including having a fusion warhead detonate against them.

As the ship passed over the star, Cheeky applied full burn to the fusion engines, the effect multiplying their acceleration by a factor of five. At that rate, it took less than a minute to complete their arc around the star and they exited the gravity assist maneuver at just over a quarter the speed of light.

Sera examined the data from the passage over Trio Prime, impressed to see the precision with which Cheeky performed the maneuver. Even the switching of the grav drive from negative to positive was done at the optimal time—the gravitons it threw now pushing them off the star's mass.

Ship's Link reconnected to a nearby beacon and Sera turned her attention back to the ships she had spotted earlier. System scan showed the vessels remained on a direct course for the world of Trio, though they weren't slowing down much, if at all.

At *Sabrina's* current distance from Trio, scan lag was an issue. The beacon they were stripping data from was ten light minutes away from their current position; Trio was another seven light minutes past that. Considering the speed those ships were traveling, they could already be at the station, or past it.

As Sera was pondering what those ships could be up to, Sabrina alerted them to a call on the local emergency band.

"This is a system-wide alert. Three ships of unknown origin have attacked a Trio defense emplacement and are on a vector for Coburn Station. Their intentions are unknown. All ships are advised to stay within the protective range of a system station or fleet patrol until further notice." The alert paused and then restarted the same message.

Sabrina muted the alert. <*I'll let you know if it changes,*> she said.

"Thanks, that's not terribly auspicious—Silstrand really needs to deal with these pirates, it's getting worse all the time," Sera said with a shake of her head.

"Uh, you realize that we smuggle for those pirates," Cheeky said with a smirk.

"Well," Sera smiled back, "I said they should; I didn't say I thought they actually would."

Cheeky chuckled and Sera reviewed their current vector. There were no planets or stations anywhere near their outsystem route. They would just have to keep pushing forward. Chances were slim those ships would even come within fifteen million kilometers of *Sabrina,* though Sera wasn't about to bet her ship on it.

"Crank our burners up all the way, Cheeky. I want to put more distance between us and that mess," Sera said, before calling the crew to their stations, updating them on what was happening on the other side of the star.

Cargo stepped onto the bridge a few minutes later with coffee for himself and the two women. He made a show of only looking them in their eyes as he passed out the brew, then sat at his console, looking over the scan and their course.

"That's a lot of velocity those buggers have on them," he commented

"They're going to get a speeding ticket," Sera agreed.

"What about a blowing-up-a-defensive-emplacement ticket?" Cheeky asked. "I hear systems are sticklers about that sort of thing."

"Alert said three ships, right?" Cargo asked.

"Yeah."

"Scan just updated from a relay south of the star. It shows five jumped in. Where are the other two?"

"That's disconcerting," Sera said. "I don't see them anywhere on system scan."

"Why does that statement insert small circus animals into my stomach?" Cheeky asked.

Cargo leaned forward and looked at Cheeky's flat stomach. "I don't see how even a couple of dancing mice would fit in there."

"Maybe it's a flea circus," Sera commented.

"Ewwww!" Cheeky shivered convulsively. "There's a mental image I just didn't need."

Another relay a few million kilometers south of the star updated scan data and they got their answer on the missing ships.

The feed showed the two vessels veering off from the other three and plotting a course around the star's south pole. They were running fast, thrusting on antimatter pion engines, from the look of the gamma rays trailing behind their ships.

"Does Trio allow AP engines in their inner system?" Cheeky asked.

"They blew up an emplacement. I don' think they care about AP regulations." Cargo said.

<Trio special regulations state that no antimatter engines may be used within twenty million kilometers of the star, or within two million kilometers of any station or outer planet,> Sabrina supplied the ruling anyway.

<What's up with her? She's being so proper today,> Helen said privately to Sera.

Sera sent her AI a mental shrug, but didn't comment further.

"Cheeky, what's the chance those two bogies will get within a million klicks of us?" she asked, though it looked like Cheeky was already on it.

"Based on their current course, they're going to get closer than your tight leather outfit, Captain. I'm guessing they plan to pay us a visit."

As though on cue, a signal came in from one of the ships and Sabrina patched it through the bridge speakers. A harsh voice called for them to cease burn and divert to a position that Sera would bet local stellar scan couldn't monitor.

"Like hell we will," Sera muttered. "Sabrina, are we ready to do an AP burn?"

<We're always ready to make an AP burn. It's my favorite pastime.>

Sera chuckled, <Don't I know it. Bring up the gamma shielding and extrude the AP nozzle.>

<Spooling.>

Sera could hear the ship's secondary reactor spin up and she watched readings show power flowing to the gamma shields. The AP drive smashed Hydrogen and Anti-Hydrogen, annihilating them and producing pions that were focused out the AP engine's nozzle. The pions quickly broke down into gamma rays and accelerated out the nozzle at just under the speed of light. The longer the nozzle was extruded, the more thrust Sabrina would get from the burn. Sera saw that Cheeky and Sabrina were spinning it out all the way.

"Good thing we declared our antimatter and allowed the containment inspection before we docked," Cargo said. "Blood suckers at Trio would fine us if they caught us using undeclared antimatter, pirate attack or no."

"You're thinking pirate, too, then?" Sera asked.

"It's way too small a force to actually attack a Silstrand Alliance member. They're here for something that they think a small, fast force can snag."

Sera's thoughts immediately went to the small crate she had taken on the night before. She couldn't imagine anything in that crate being worth an outright attack on an Alliance member system, but it was the only thing she carried that could possibly have that kind of value.

The AP drive began to add to the ship's velocity and the holo display showed their kph relative to Trio Prime increasing so quickly that the lower digits were a blur.

<*Oh this feels good!*> Sabrina crowed. <*I wish we could run out the AP engine more often!*>

"Not concerned who we're running from?" Cargo asked the ship's AI.

<*Sera will take care of me. I'm not worried about any pirates,*> Sabrina replied confidently, causing Sera to suppress a smile.

"What are the chances that these guys are just checking all the outbound ships?" Cheeky asked.

"Then they'd split up. Both of them are on a vector to meet up with us well before we get to our jump point. I'd say we're the ones they're looking for."

Cheeky looked perplexed. "What could we have that pirates would want?"

Sera and Cargo shared a long look, his eyes showing mild recrimination. Sera sighed and told Cheeky they were carrying something extra special for The Mark.

"Figures," the pilot sulked. "I don't know why you do runs for them. From what I can see, we're pretty profitable even without all the extra risks."

Sera's expression was stony. "I have my reasons."

"Well, I hope they're worth dying for."

"We're not going to die here; we've got a few tricks up our sleeves," Sera said. In her mind, where only Helen could hear she said, <*Yes, it's worth dying for.*>

Sera checked scan and saw that the two unidentified ships had fallen from their entry velocity of $0.73c$ to $0.45c$. Their vector around the star had not been clean and they lost velocity breaking out of its gravity well.

Cheeky was looking at the same data. "Damn, those ships must be all engine to only lose that much v during such a sloppy maneuver."

"Don't forget the guns," Cargo added. "All engines and guns."

Sera switched her display to show their outsystem course. Their destination was an FTL jump point several million kilometers beyond the last of the outer planets. The interior of Trio system was a good seven light hours across and they still had just over three hours to the jump point on full burn.

She widened her view and saw that the two ships behind were accelerating again. Both were back over half the speed of light, nearly at their previous velocity of $0.73c$. Sera looked down at *Sabrina's* indicators and saw that they were accelerating slower than expected and the ship was developing an odd vibration.

"Scoop!" Sera cried just as Sabrina reported that the scoop was still deployed and slowing them down. Cheeky cursed and quickly killed the electrostatic field that had been scooping hydrogen for fuel.

The pilot turned slightly red face back to Sera. "Sorry, Captain. It sorta slipped my mind."

Sera's brow furrowed. "Mine too," then she nodded. "Now the ol' girl's picking up."

<Who are you calling old?>

<Sorry, it's just an expression,> Sera replied and only received a mental 'harrumph' from her ship. She really needed to think of something to make up for the forgotten anniversary.

Cargo looked over his shoulder. "Stellar medium is a bit lighter on our vector. We should be able to hit $0.60c$ with all drives burning hot, but they'll," he jerked his head to the stern to indicate their pursuers, "get that advantage, too."

Helen had been examining their outbound vector and brought an issue to Sera's attention. Sera cursed silently. Things were always working against her.

"Ladies," Sera asked Cheeky and Sabrina, "if we do this burn for another forty minutes, what are the chances we can hold shields at max while we vector for the jump and keep all three drives online?"

"Planning to melt us?" Cheeky asked.

<She's right,> Sabrina said. *<Power plant could melt down if we tried to run all that—even with the auxiliary plant online.>*

"What about the SC batteries?" Sera asked.

"They're way low," Cheeky replied. "Pansies at Trio get all nervous with a hundred fusion reactors humming around their station. You said they charge too much for station power, so we ran on batts while docked."

"Huh," Sera grunted. "Well that was short-sighted of me."

When traveling at any appreciable speed, *Sabrina* always ran her forward shields. Even a speck of sand, traveling at even a tenth the speed of light, would punch right through the ship. It could destroy the reactor, and certainly any humans in its way.

However, with ships chasing them, they now had to deploy shield umbrellas over the entire vessel, and that was going to run them beyond their power generation limits.

Flying directly behind a ship running grav, fusion, and AP engines was a recipe for a bad day. If they were smart, their pursuers would fan out and flank *Sabrina*. From those positions, they would be able to hit nearly any part of the ship. The only advantage was that they couldn't shoot straight up the engines.

<Helen, I'm betting these guys are going to use lasers, probably ten centimeter beams; they're going to take out some of ours so they can board us. Work up some tactics and prime our defenses,> Sera said to her AI.

<I'll load the routines. I think our best bet is to try to refract their beams with some precise grav waves. With the batteries low, we can't run refraction shield-wide,> Helen replied.

<You can do it girl, don't let those bastards put holes in Sabrina.>

<Her I'm not so concerned about. You, on the other hand, are a priority.>

And so, the battle of the AIs continued.

"Do we have a solid intercept time, Cheeky?" Sera asked vocally.

"Not one hundred percent, they have a few course corrections to make that may slow them down a bit, but even if they have one-eyed apes flying those tubs, they'll catch us before we jump."

"Any chance we can jump early?" Cargo asked.

"Not unless you want to see how you look smeared across a clump of dark matter," Sera told her first mate, while looking over their course. "There's gotta be something…" There was always a way out of these situations, it just took some creative thinking. "Cheeky, you've got one more correction to make, right?"

"Yup, shortly before our transition we've got to angle down and get back into the main plane of the system." Cheeky said, highlighting the position in the plot on the ship's main holo.

"Would you be able to make it now, and have it be shorter? It may be enough to get us out of this mess."

Cheeky pulled up several holos and manipulated them, plotting positions where she could make the alteration, looking for the one with maximum efficiency, lowest drag, and best time-to-jump improvement. The incongruity of her nearly naked, oversexed pilot furiously processing advanced spatial calculations on a dozen holos was not lost on Sera; she hid a small smile behind her hand as she watched.

<It's like you don't take this stuff seriously,> Helen admonished.

<I totally do, but look at her, she's wiggling all over.>

Cheeky turned and Sera schooled her expression.

"There's a point coming up where we can do our burn that would work well, but I don't like traveling in the main plane at these speeds. You never know what uncharted rock is out there, waiting to end our little race."

"Trio's pretty busy; I'd imagine they have everything charted."

"Who? The people with senile tug AIs and faulty nav comps?"

"AI can go senile?" Cargo asked.

"We have evidence," Sabrina said, her voice dripping with implied meaning.

"I'll take the chance of a stray rock over the surety of their lasers. Plot it out," Sera replied.

She leaned back in her chair. Despite the humor, she found in the small things around her, Helen was right; this was serious. But her crew was smart, and her ship was a pro. This would work; they'd make the jump before the pirates caught up with them.

Cheeky made her computations, rechecked them and then had Sabrina review them, as well. They passed muster and Cheeky announced stellar south course alteration in just under five minutes. The time came and the change occurred with no noticeable sensations in the ship.

Sera ran the computations again, *Sabrina's* nav systems telling her that they had insufficient data to provide an accurate model due to unknown deceleration capabilities of the pursuing ships.

In addition to catching up with *Sabrina,* the two pirate ships also had to show some care in matching speeds. At the velocities they were traveling, even miniscule speed differences would cause immense differences in position. If the pirates didn't match *Sabrina's* speed precisely, they would flash past faster than the human eye could even detect.

High relative v also made targeting with lasers tricky at best. Good gunners with powerful AI could do it, but even they missed a lot. Her real worry was that if *Sabrina* managed to avoid being boarded, the pirates would resort to relativistic missiles.

Apparently, Cargo had been thinking along the same lines.

"Do you think they have RMs?" he asked.

"Pirates can get their hands on those things?" Cheeky asked, her entire body getting a bit paler than it already was.

"Yeah, but even if they have them, I doubt they'd use one. Those things aren't cheap."

Cheeky was looking over her nav board again. "How fast can they accelerate?"

"It varies and it's not linear," Sera replied. "At the speeds we're traveling, at I'd guess they could go from seventy percent to ninety-nine percent of the speed of light in a few minutes."

"Ninety-nine percent?" Cheeky choked.

"They don't have the word 'relativistic' in the name for nothing." Cargo's voice dripped with sarcasm, which earned him a scowl from the pilot.

"They can't burn too long, though," Sera said. "Only so much fuel in them."

"Probably because they usually kill things before they run out," Cheeky commented.

Scan showed their pursuers making course corrections to match the burn Cheeky had made. The calculations now showed that their pursuer's loss of v from the adjustment would be just barely enough; *Sabrina* would make it out of this. Apparently, the two ships behind them had come to the same conclusion, as the comm board suddenly lit up with an incoming message.

Sabrina activated the connection and a very unhappy face appeared on the main holo. From the lack of uniform and a glimpse of the bridge, it was confirmed; they were definitely pirate ships.

"Ship designated *Sabrina*, you were ordered to cease acceleration and divert to the transmitted course. Why are you not complying?" The man was trying to sound officious.

"'Cause I like my skin on my body," Sera said with copious amounts of sarcasm. "Why don't you tell me why you have such a keen interest in my ship?"

"That's none of your concern," the man snarled. "Now comply with our directive."

Sera almost laughed. This was the saddest line she'd ever been fed. "Don't be ridiculous. I'm not diverting, I have a schedule to keep and I'm not going to interrupt it to have tea with you." With that, she killed the connection and looked to Cheeky. "Time to FTL?"

"Twenty three minutes," came the pilot's reply. "Those looked like Padre's men, didn't they?"

"Yeah, I'm starting to get a suspicion about who Kade stole that 'racing hound' from."

Cargo turned from his station. "They're still trying to make contact. Let's hope that's as mean as they get." He glanced back at his board. "Never mind that, scan shows energy signatures on their bow. I'm guessing lasers."

"Any room to twitch?" Sera asked Cheeky.

"Not unless we want to do another burn to correct, but that would put them right on top of us when we make the jump."

Sera cursed their luck.

"Sabrina, do we have the power to extend the shielding back over the AP engine nozzle? It looks like they're warming up their heaters and I bet that's gonna be the first target," she asked.

<It'll weaken our shields overall,> the AI replied. <But I see the logic. Doing it.>

The shields that protected *Sabrina* were not a firm shell around the ship, but rather an anti-gravitational field that repelled any objects and particles. Complex systems allowed the shields to detect laser impact on the hull and diffuse the beam with targeted gravitational waves. It was a tricky system to operate and often worked better in stellar space where the leading edge of a laser beam could be detected by refraction from the particles it had to travel through. Out in gasless interstellar spaces, lasers were much harder to counter.

Unfortunately for *Sabrina*, that was just the type of space they were entering. They had cleared the Kuiper Belt, and the Trio System had a stretch of very empty space between their current location and the jump point.

The shield extension came just in time, as invisible beams lanced out striking at *Sabrina's* AP nozzle.

Sera turned to Cargo. "What tricks do we have up our sleeves?"

Cargo mulled it over for a minute. "Could pepper them with some beams right on their bow. It would cause them to throw some force off the front of their ships, but I don't know how much good it would do. Could also drop a mine or two; might be able to do it accurately enough to force them to twitch out of the way."

Sera looked at the numbers again on her screen; although they were on course to jump before interception, the nav systems still showed a much closer race than she'd like. "Do both."

Cargo called down to Thompson and Flaherty and told them to get two magnetic proximity mines loaded into the tubes and ready to drop on the bridge's mark. Sera watched him run a few simulations to see if it was possible to hide the mine's presence with a bit of a light show from the aft lasers.

"Think it will work?" She asked.

"Worth a shot. Gonna be shooting at them anyway."

Cargo initiated the laser sequence, and seconds later, dropped the proximity mines. The mines had their own small propulsion units, which allowed them to reach the desired position as the lasers flickered around them.

Right before the lead ship was about to hit its designated mine, the vessel twitched and avoided impact. The other ship wasn't so lucky. Under constant fire from *Sabrina's* lasers, they never saw the second mine.

"Score!" Cargo shouted.

The resulting explosion was too small to see at the ten thousand kilometer distance, but scan showed a direct impact. With its forward shields maxed out, the pirate ship didn't appear to take damage, but the shaped charge managed to shed enough of their velocity. They were out of the race.

Scan updated, showing the first pirate ship's maneuvers to avoid its mine had placed it over a hundred thousand kilometers further away, now far to port. It was out of the running, too.

"Great work Cargo," Sera said to her first mate with heartfelt gratitude. She thanked everyone over the Link for their calm, steady response to the trouble. Before she could finish, Cargo interrupted her.

"Captain, I wouldn't get too excited yet, we've got an RM inbound."

"Shit!" Sera swore over the open comm. "Belay that happiness, missile on our tail."

Sabrina was five minutes from the jump point. The relativistic missile was four minutes from intercept.

Sera ran the math and couldn't see any way they could get to the point before the RM hit them. Even killing aft shielding and diverting more power to the engines wouldn't give them enough extra thrust to pull it off. She looked to her pilot.

"Two options, Cheeks; we twitch and jump on whatever vector we end up on, or we dump to FTL now and hope there's no dark matter between us and the point."

Cheeky bit her lip as she pulled charts of the local dark layer onto the main holo.

Dark matter occupied its own sub-layer of space-time, which is where ships transitioned when they made FTL jumps. However, dark matter orbited its host star erratically and charts never displayed it with perfect accuracy. Jump points were positions with outsystem vectors that were always clear of dark matter. Ships could enter FTL without fear of colliding with a solid mass.

Cheeky zoomed the holo in on their course and pointed to a rather large clump of dark matter. "Can't do the jump on our current vector, there's a big lump of the black stuff in our path. Let me see if there is a clear path outsystem parallel to our vector."

Though it took Cheeky less than thirty seconds to find a course they could twitch to, it seemed far longer with the main holo showing the RM closing on them. Sera was tempted to try a mine again but the nav computer showed that the RM could compensate even if it had to avoid the mine. The damn things were just too fast and maneuverable. Sera was ordering Thompson and Flaherty to load another proximity mine anyway when Cheeky let loose a triumphant cry.

"I've got it! There's a clear path to port, if these charts are right, that'll take us out of here. DM does orbit through, but it should be clear right now."

Moments rolled by as Cheeky double checked her work and then laid in the burn time and vector that would give them a spare twenty thousand kilometers from the RM. She called out the count as everyone held their breath.

"On five, four, three, two, one, burn for three, two, one, kill!" The eight seconds stretched into a lifetime and then the two more seconds dragged on while scan updated. The RM had overshot and was compensating to approach their position. It had dropped down to 0.8 c as it maneuvered, but was quickly up to 0.9 c back on a direct course for *Sabrina*.

"It's on us again, Cheeky. How long to jump?"

Cheeky spared a hand to wave behind her at her captain as she concentrated on her console and the numbers rolling across it. She made a few final alterations and then rechecked them.

"Kay! FTL transition in T minus fifteen."

She began counting down the seconds to the transition as Sera brought the RM's time to impact up on the main holo. It was only a half a second behind Cheeky's count. Through those long seconds, Sera's mind raced over the thousand things that could go wrong, praying that they would make the jump in time.

Then, with the customary gut twisting wrench, they made the transition and were in the lightless void of the dark layer.

TANIS RICHARDS

STELLAR DATE: 07.01.8927 (Adjusted Gregorian)
LOCATION: *Sabrina*, Interstellar Dark Layer
REGION: Galactic South of Trio Prime, Silstrand Alliance Space

Sera took a deep breath as Cheeky leaned over the side of her chair and threw up. Without a word, Cargo rose and walked out to the corridor. He returned with cleaning supplies from the small head just outside the bridge.

Sera rose from her chair, shaking far more than expected. She moved to Cheeky's console and rested a hand on the pilot's shoulder. Cheeky was quaking, and Sera helped her stand, wrapping her in a tight embrace. She choked back tears of relief and Sera did her best not to join in.

"Girl, that was the best flying I've *ever* seen!" Sera gave her pilot a squeeze.

Cheeky offered a weak smile. "Thanks, Captain, I'd appreciate it if you guys didn't tell anyone about this little after effect, though." She looked down at the spattered deck-plate.

Cargo bent down to clean up the mess. "What after effect?"

Cheeky reached down and smacked his head. "I mean it…I can't have anyone thinking I'm less than ladylike."

Sera laughed, wondering who might think that Cheeky was ladylike to begin with.

The distraction had calmed Cheeky and she sat back down at her console, reviewing the ship's readouts.

"Everything looks bang on, Captain," she turned and said after a minute's examination. "Mind if I hit my cabin for a bit and clean up?"

"Whatever you need to do, Cheeks. Cargo and I can hold the ship together while you're gone."

<I resent that,> Sabrina huffed.

<Sorry, love, I didn't mean you,> Sera stroked a console affectionately.

Cheeky left the bridge with a slight wobble in her step as she navigated around the consoles in her heels. Sera sat back in her chair and gave the crew the good news over the ship-wide net.

<Thanks to everyone's hard work, we just outran a couple of pirate gunships that were looking to turn us into a bright, fluffy cloud. I'm sure you all noticed that you're still alive,> Sera added a smile to her comment.

<I did notice a distinct not-dead feeling,> Thompson replied dryly.

<Yay for our side!> Nance's hazsuited avatar did a jump and a kick in everyone's mind.

<Our SC batteries are totally drained,> Sabrina interjected. *<Going to keep the auxiliary plant running, we'll have to watch the heat, though.>*

<You do that, Sabrina. Me, I'm going to have to re-hydrate—I must have pissed a gallon when I saw that RM right on our tail.> Thompson somehow managed to convey both thirst and the urge to urinate in his message.

<What on earth did they want anyway?> Nance asked. *<What could we have worth using an RM on us? Those things must cost as much as a small mining platform.>*

<I have a suspicion,> Sera said. *<Give me ten minutes to square some things away, then Thompson and Nance, meet me in the fore port cargo hold.>*

<Will do,> Thompson said while Nance's avatar managed a stiff nod.

Sera laid their interstellar course over her vision as she brought up the nav computer on her console's holo.

<How far off will we be when we exit FTL?> she asked her AI as she worked through the calculations herself. Helen would have the answer before she was half done, but Sera liked to test herself. People, who let their AI think for them didn't take long to degenerate into little more than automatons.

<We entered the dark layer not too far from our original jump point, but our vector was slightly skewed by the twitch. Not to mention we made the transition at over twice the originally plotted speed,> Helen said, giving Sera a bit more time to finish the math on her own.

<We must have shaved almost five days off the trip,> Sera said idly as she flipped through a matrix of figures.

<Five days, three hours and twenty-one minutes.>

<You just can't help it, can you?>

Helen sighed. *<No, I can't. It's actually a bit annoying. You take for granted how easily you can think in abstracts.>*

<I suppose I do,> Sera admitted. *<Well, based on this, it's a good thing we shortened the trip by a few days; we're going to spend every one of those saved days braking from this ungodly speed if we don't want to use up the rest of our antimatter.>*

<It will take three days of braking and then a final day to arrive at the drop point,> Helen supplied.

Cheeky returned to the bridge several minutes later, for once wearing pants and a shirt. Sera didn't comment on it, and the pilot began working out the details of when they needed to drop out of the dark layer and back into normal space.

"Have I mentioned that I hate special relativity math?" she asked. "An RM up our ass I can forgive, making me adjust calculations for all this time dilation is something else."

Sera smiled. "You have fun; I'm going to see what's in that crate we got from Kade's boys at the eleventh hour."

"If it's something nasty, kick it for me," Cheeky said.

Thompson and Nance were already in the cargo bay when Sera arrived. The burly super was sliding a gravity lift under the crate, while Nance, wearing her hazsuit with the hood sealed tight, stood nearby.

"How are you doing?" Sera asked.

"Mm, good," Nance replied.

Sera saw that the lenses of her bio's mask were fogged up and the woman's limbs had a slight tremble.

"Nance, honey, take off the hood; let me see you."

<Sure, why not try now,> Helen chuckled.

Sera had never seen Nance out of her hazsuit, and had only seen her face a few times, when Nance had her suit's hood only half-off. There was a pool on the ship with a big pot for whoever finally got her to reveal her entire head.

Without speaking, the bio reached behind her head and unsealed the hood. Sera held her breath as Nance slowly slid it off her head.

"You have hair!" Sera exclaimed. "It's beautiful!"

Nance stepped back as Sera reached out to touch the dark brown locks, a frown creasing her brow.

"Of course I have hair; it's a normal thing to grow on a person's head."

"Damn it!" Thompson swore. "I can't believe you picked now to try that—and it worked!"

"You can't believe I won," Sera said with a grin. She turned back to Nance and reached for the bio's hand. "Seriously, though, are you OK? You seemed fine on the Link."

"I think you missed my sarcastic tone," Nance replied. "I was scared shitless."

"I guess the suit masks it," Sera replied.

Thompson got the lift under the mysterious crate and it rose into the air. He leaned against it and eyed Nance.

"That *is* a pretty amazing amount of hair."

"Says the blonde ape," Sera smiled.

"Hey, nine thousand years ago, this amount of body hair was perfectly normal."

"Yeah, and nine thousand years ago, people had just upgraded to pooping in public troughs," Nance grimaced.

"Don't try to distract me, Nance," Sera said. "I had never even imagined that you had hair. How do you keep it so soft while it's plastered to your head all day? Doesn't it get sweaty?"

Nance made a disgusted sound. "I don't sweat. I had all those oozing glands removed years ago."

"I enjoy a good sweat," Thompson said, with thinly veiled innuendo.

Sera sniffed in his direction. "That's no secret."

Thompson ignored her. "Don't you get hot, Nance?"

"No, my suit has a cooling system."

"I'd think you'd still get itchy," Thompson frowned. "All that flaking skin with no sweat to lubricate it."

Nance shivered convulsively. "Ewww! I have a controlled shedding, which my nano activates when I'm in the shower. I don't have flaking skin."

Sera peered at her bio's face, hands held back so Nance wouldn't flinch away. "You do have really smooth-looking skin. And it looks so clean…"

"You'd be amazed what lives and accumulates in your pores. Thank god I don't have those anymore," Nance looked at the super.

"Look at those crevices on your face. And Cheeky wonders why my suit has tinted lenses."

Thompson seemed to decide that there was no way this conversation would favor him, so got back to the situation at hand. "So, what do you think is in here that they wanted so bad, Captain? I'm betting it's no dog."

"If it is, it's getting its shots," Nance said. "No way I'm letting some dirty mutt run around the ship and contaminate my environmental tanks."

Nance pulled a holo display into the air over the crate. Initial scan showed that some living creature was inside, but its vital signs were masked by cryostasis.

"I'm not getting a reading on anything hazardous," she said and looked over Sabrina's scan on the emissions and power levels in the crate. "No heavy metals, probably running on an SC Battery."

"Let's take it into the sealed chamber. I don't like little tiny surprises any more than you do, Nance."

It never hurt to pop a container that seemed harmless into the biohazard chamber and check it out by remote. Their lives were dangerous enough without extra unknowns adding risk. Not many ships had a hermetically sealed chamber, but from time to time Sera found it necessary to determine the exact level of danger a cargo presented for herself and her ship. If it was more trouble than she'd been told, extra charges were applied to the transport.

Once the container was in the chamber, they stood back and watched as Sabrina used robotic arms to crack the seal and lift off the lid. Inside was the cryostasis pod Nance had detected.

"Either it's a kid, or an adult that's going to have some serious cramps," Thompson observed.

"You don't cramp in stasis," Sera said.

"Depends on how good the system is and how long it took the stasis to kick in," Thompson replied. "Once I had to hop in an evac pod on a gas platform, it took the stasis over an hour to fully set in. That's not an experience I'd wish on my worst enemy."

"Owww," Nance said, casting an appreciative look at the super.

"What do the readouts look like, Sabrina?" Sera asked.

<All outward controls show nominal,> the ship's AI responded. <I'm making a filtered connection to its controls for a direct reading.>

A robotic arm extended and fitted a physical data connector into the cryo pod. Sabrina had done this before and knew to exercise extreme caution. All the systems within the sealed chamber were isolated from the rest of the ship. Sabrina felt the same way about foreign computers as Nance did about germs.

<The system looks normal, and it is a person in there; a woman of indeterminate age,> Sabrina announced moments later. <I can't say if she's totally safe without a blood sample, but if you wear hazsuits in the med lab you should be OK.>

"Nance, it's finally a party you're already dressed for," Thompson said with a smile.

Sera caught a glint in his eye when he said it.

<Is Thompson flirting with Nance?> Sera asked Helen.

<Beats me, if he is he sucks at it.>

Sera gave her head a slight shake and addressed Thompson. "Take it into the med lab, Thompson. Nance and I will pop it open and see what we see."

Nance looked as though she was being asked to juggle flaming knives. She pinned her hair up and pulled her suit's hood back on. <Let's get it over with.>

Sabrina re-sealed the crate and Thompson entered the chamber and keyed the grav lift to float it down the hall and into the med lab.

Ten minutes later, the stasis pod sat on the floor of the med lab with Sera and Nance standing to either side. Thompson and Cargo were both outside peering through one of the observation windows.

<You want to pop it open?> Sera asked.

<Hey, this was your idea. I give you first crack at whatever bio weapon is waiting in that person's bloodstream.>

<You really are a bit of a pessimist, you know that?> Sera smiled through the clear faceplate of her hazsuit.

<I'm a realist.>

<You're also the one-zillionth pessimist to say you're a realist. Your prize is an all-expense paid trip to the Disney World. You'll get to spend a full month with an entire planet full of people modded into animals and fairies,> Sera chuckled while Nance made a soft gagging noise.

<Just pop it open already so I can declare this person healthy, or dead, and get back to that blown regulator I'm dealing with.>

Sera sighed and bent to look the console over. The controls were fairly standard and Sera entered the sequence to open the pod. Immediately, the pod's interface flashed a warning and prompted for additional access codes. She attempted to bypass it with some of her usual tricks, but the pod locked down entirely.

<Giving you some trouble?> Nance asked as she leaned against the examination table.

<Nothing I can't handle, I'll have it open in a minute.>

Shielding her actions with her body, Sera pressed the tip of her finger tight against the hazsuit's glove and spoke to Helen. *<Send some of the little guys through the suit and into this pod to crack its security. Just make sure they patch up whatever holes they make.>*

<Want me to have them cover their tracks and reprogram the pod with something you could crack by hand in a minute?>

<Yeah, we need to keep up appearances.>

<OK, Fina, the nano are on their way in.>

Sera ignored Helen's mothering tone and use of her childhood nickname. She acted as though she was working on the pod's interface while the nano completed their task and the interface altered to a simple security setup, set to the final stage of a basic hack. Sera manually entered the final sequence. The outer cover hissed pod open, and she left her index finger on the edge of the console until Helen informed her that all the nano were back in her body.

<Easy as pie,> Sera said to Nance as she looked up at the bio.

<Mustn't have been that hard,> Cargo said with a grin from the other side of the observation window.

The pod flashed a short countdown as it pulled its occupant out of cryostasis, then the inner shell split open. Sera stood and peered in as Nance pulled one of the scan arms over from the examination table, her other hand double-checking the seal of her hazsuit's hood.

The occupant of the container was a woman. She had the same ageless look that most people acquired after their first rejuvenation treatment. She was also naked; whoever had placed her in stasis hadn't bothered to put her in a stasis suit, or even put a salve on her skin to deal with the quick freeze.

<She's going to have a nasty rash when she wakes up,> Sera observed.

Nance looked at the med scanner's readout as it hovered over the pod. *<Not any time soon, though. She's heavily drugged. Pod pulled her out*

of stasis smoothly, but she's going to sleep for a few more hours, even with a mild flush.>

<Works for me; gives us a chance to check her out before the yelling and screaming starts,> Sera replied.

<If you don't mind, I'll skip that part,> Nance grimaced.

<I'll stay with her. I imagine you can do any checks remotely.>

Nance's avatar smiled at Sera. <Happily.>

They lifted the woman out of the pod and Thompson let a whistle loose as they set her naked form on the table, earning a cold look from Sera. Cargo grinned but was smart enough not to add more.

Nance pulled a blanket over the woman, then lifted her head, smoothed her hair, and placed a low pillow underneath. The action was very gentle for someone who eschewed tactile contact. Sera peered at the bio, but the opaque lenses of her hood hid any expression that may have been behind them.

<This is odd,> Nance said as she looked over the data from the medical scanner.

<What?> Sera asked.

<See these slight discolorations all over her skin?>

<That's discoloration? I thought maybe it was the lighting in here,> Sera peered closer and dialed her vision in to a higher level of magnification. <Bruises, I can see the pattern from the broken vessels.>

<Scanner shows she got them within two hours of going into stasis.>

<That can't be right, those bruises are almost healed, and they were some serious shiners. Things like that don't heal during stasis, at least not in a pod like this.>

Nance's expressionless face looked up at Sera. <I'd agree with you except for what we're looking at.>

<Curiouser and curiouser.>

Sera looked down at the woman. She appeared to be normal. Her body showed the tall frame of a person raised in lower gravity, but her muscle tone indicated time spent in full gravity, as well. The readout put her at one hundred and eighty-four centimeters; just shy of ninety-seven kilograms, though probably well under seventy without her internal tech—which was considerable.

Her features were classic Scandinavian, from the slight slope of her brow and high cheekbones to the perfectly straight, blonde hair.

Of course, none of that meant she had a drop of Scandinavian blood. It could just indicate a good rebuild.

<She certainly isn't hard to look at,> Thompson commented.

Sera looked at the two men. *<Don't you two have something else to do?>*

They looked at one another and shrugged.

<I guess I could use a meal,> Cargo said, and the pair sauntered off.

<Her skin may be all patched up, but she's got a fractured skull, three broken ribs, a bit of internal bleeding that looks to have stopped up, a broken ankle, and her left leg is broken in three places.>

<Someone wasn't too gentle with her,> Sera said with a shake of her head.

<That's the understatement of the year. I'm going to send some of the med nano in to start patching her up,> Nance said as she pulled the IV line down from the array of devices above the examination table. It would be primed with the nano machines that would begin knitting the woman's bones back together.

The women turned to the med system's status display, watching the nano filtering through her body, moving toward the injuries.

<Looking good,> Sera commented.

<Seems to b…what the? What!> Nance exclaimed.

They both stared as the med unit lost contact with the nano in the woman's body and then reported that they had all been destroyed.

<That can't be good,> Sera shook her head. Med nano was hard to kill; the mystery surrounding this woman was growing.

Nance pulled up the detailed logs on the med nano's ill-fated venture and looked them over. *<They were destroyed…by her nano,>* Nance closed the log and then initiated a more detailed scan. *<Doesn't make sense, our med nano broadcasts the standard Red Cross signal. A person's nano should welcome them, not kill them.>*

<I don't think her nano needs the help,> Sera said, and pulled a high-res holo image of the woman over her body. *<It looks like it's doing the healing on its own.>*

Nance scowled at the images, then took a blood sample with a biohazard extractor.

<I'm going to take this down to my lab; I've got better containment down there. Let me know if anything changes.>

<Good luck,> Sera said as Nance stepped into the scrubber and then out into the corridor where she walked briskly toward the nearest ladder.

<Does that look at all familiar, Helen?> Sera asked her personal AI.

<It looks as good, maybe better, than our nano. I don't know if your bots could repair bones that fast.>

<I was thinking that, as well. I wonder if we could send an investigatory probe in.>

<It's worth a shot. We could send it with the med signal, as well.>

<No point, it would just get squished like the others. Send it with the standard OFC signal. We'll see if her comp is running.>

Sera pressed her index finger against the woman's arm and several of her nano passed through the hazsuit and into the flesh under it.

<We've got communication,> Helen said in an agitated tone as she patched the message through.

<This is Angela. Please cease inserting your foreign nano into Tanis's body. I have her well in hand and will wake her in one day, five hours, three minutes and seventeen seconds. Thank you for the IV supply. No other assistance is needed.> The signal cut out as Helen indicated their nano had been eliminated as well.

<Snippy thing, isn't she?>

<You have no idea. That was the human version. The one she sent me was far less companionable. It includes things like silicate hussy and other such terms.>

Sera laughed out loud. *<Sometimes I wonder why you AI grow personalities; they seem to cause you more trouble than they could be worth.>*

<You have no idea the extent to which that debate rages,> Helen said dryly.

* * * * *

"So how's our visitor?" Thompson asked as Sera stepped into the galley. Everyone except for Nance was around the table tucking into a dinner of soup and sandwiches.

"Helen and I managed to get a hold of her AI. It told us quite simply that our assistance isn't welcome and it will wake her tomorrow."

"Is she okay?" Cheeky asked.

"Yes and no," Sera replied equably as she poured herself a cup of coffee and grabbed a sandwich.

"That is the opposite of clarifying," Thompson grunted.

"Her body has been put through the wringer. If she were stranded on some backwater, with no nano, she'd be in a hospital for months. If she were relying on our med nano, she'd be taking it easy for a week. With her personal nano, she'll be up and about tomorrow."

"Her personal nano is that good?" Cheeky asked.

Thompson and Flaherty didn't say a word as they chewed.

"Yeah, she's got some seriously impressive stuff, and a prickly AI running the show. It nuked our med nano and even my bots after it delivered its message of displeasure."

"Can't say I blame it," Thompson said. "I'd hope my AI would have my best interests in mind if I was beat up and somewhere strange."

"You don't have an AI...or even I," Cheeky said with a grin.

"Har, har, that's original," Thompson replied.

Flaherty gave an uncharacteristic snort of laughter, which earned him a sour look from Thompson.

"What does her DNA say?" Cheeky asked.

"Nance took blood samples; she should be up shortly with the results. Hopefully it may shed some light on the identity of our...stowaway?"

"I don't know how accurate that is. We stowed her ourselves," Thompson offered.

"I deem her our 'reluctant hitchhiker'," Cheeky said around a mouthful of her sandwich.

"Actually, her name is Tanis," Sera offered. "Her AI, Angela, gave us that much info before telling us to go screw."

"Her DNA said about the same thing," Nance stepped into the galley and slipped her hood up, exposing her face. "I couldn't find DNA anywhere similar to it in any of our records. It's not as though we have an extensive library, but we do have a sample from nearly every inhabited world."

"What, the rest of us don't get to see your hair?" Cargo asked.

Nance cocked her head at Sera, who lifted her hands defensively. "I've only been here for a few minutes. I didn't blab."

"What?" Thompson said. "You've got nice hair."

"Come on…" Cheeky said with a winning smile, "I want to see, too. How could you show Thompson your hair and not me?"

Nance sighed. "Okay fine, only because you'll bug me for days if I don't." She reached up behind her head and slipped open the seal on the hood, pulling it off in a smooth motion and placing it on the table beside her.

"Wow!" Cheeky said. "It's so fluffy!"

"Poufy would be the word," Nance replied.

"And you have really nice almond eyes," The pilot smiled. "I command you to show them more often."

Nance laughed. "I'll reset my lenses to be transparent when you are around."

"So, nothing on the DNA at all?" Flaherty asked, appearing to be uninterested in the discussion of hair and eyes.

"Well, she actually *is* of Scandinavian descent, pretty pure blood, too. If I didn't know better, I'd say she was actually from Earth…'cept no one's from Earth," Nance said as she pulled a bar from her personal food cupboard.

"Some people are still from Earth," Cheeky offered.

<There are no Scandinavians on Earth anymore,> Sabrina said.

"Aren't you Scandinavian?" Sera asked Nance.

"Not really. One of my ancestors settled on New Sweden and the names infiltrated the family. I think my family is actually from the Madrid moon in Procyon."

"OK," Thompson said. "Time to lay odds on where she came from. I have a hundred Sil creds that say she's actually from Sol. Any takers?"

REVELATIONS

STELLAR DATE: 07.02.8927 (Adjusted Years)
LOCATION: *Sabrina*, Interstellar Dark Layer
REGION: Galactic South of Trio Prime, Silstrand Alliance Space

Sera sat on a chair in the med lab, waiting for their 'reluctant hitchhiker,' as Cheeky still called her, to wake.

At exactly the time prescribed by her AI, the woman began to stir, and then her movements became almost violent—as though she was having a nightmare. After almost a minute of thrashing, her body remembered what it was like to function with a conscious mind in control; her movements slowed and finally her eyelids fluttered open.

Sera waited for Tanis to acclimate to her surroundings. The lights in the med cabin were dim—she knew from experience how painful bright lights could be after coming out of a few days of unconsciousness.

She watched the woman's eyes struggle to focus, and then adjust to the dim light. A flicker of panic raced across her features when she tried to raise an arm, only to find it restrained. Almost as though by reflex, she closed her eyes and her breathing calmed. She retained that posture for several moments and then, in slow stages, she opened her eyes again; taking a second, more careful stock of her surroundings. Sera decided this was as good a time as any to make her introduction.

"Welcome aboard *Sabrina*, Tanis. I'm Captain Sera."

The woman's eyes flicked over to Sera. She opened her mouth to say something, but all that came out was a dry rasp.

"Ah, sorry about that," Sera's smile was friendly as she provided a bottle of water with a straw. The woman sucked on it eagerly and then pulled her mouth away to signal she was done.

"Thank you," she whispered as Sera set the bottle down.

"No problem," Sera smiled again. "I've done a few imitations of a dead person myself; it's thirsty work."

"Am I a prisoner?" the woman asked as she looked down at her wrists strapped to the table.

"Not at all." Sera leaned over and undid the fastener on the wrist closest to her, allowing to Tanis free her other arm. "It's just hard to predict a person's state of mind when waking up unexpectedly in a strange place."

The woman nodded as she rubbed her wrists, her expression guarded. "Where is 'here', exactly?"

"Here is home," Sera said as she waved an arm about her in an expansive gesture. "This is my fair *Sabrina*, a starfreighter. We're currently in FTL transit outside of the Trio System."

A look of incomprehension followed by shock passed over the woman's face. "In…FTL?" she said with an edge of panic to her voice. Her eyes darted around the room as though she was looking for some indication that the ship was moving faster than light.

"Yup, on our way to Edasich, with a few stops along the way."

"E-Edasich…as in Iota Draconis?" the woman stammered. "How long will it take to get there?"

"Depends on how big a rush we're in. A few months depending on exactly where the trade takes us."

The blood all but drained out of the Tanis's face. It was the strangest reaction Sera had ever seen someone have to being told they were in FTL. She was wondering how stable the woman was after all.

"Let's start with the basics, though. As I mentioned before, I'm Captain Sera. Your AI introduced you as Tanis."

The woman frowned. "She told me someone tried to infiltrate my body with nano. Logs show it was med and then comm; sorry about her reaction, she's very protective. My full name's Tanis Richards."

"Two names? That's somewhat uncommon in this neighborhood. What star system still does that? Our med NSAI didn't recognize your DNA as coming from anywhere particular."

"I'm from Earth," Tanis said so matter-of-factly that Sera let out a chuckle before covering her mouth.

"Aren't we all?" Sera said and took a deep breath to stem her laughter. What was surprising was that Tanis appeared somewhat put out by her amusement. "It's okay." Sera smiled once more. "You don't have to tell right away. I'm betting that you didn't beat yourself up and hop in a stasis pod for kicks. I assure you that we mean you no harm, though we are curious. What happened to you anyway?"

Tanis didn't respond immediately and Sera suspected this woman would be a tough nut to crack.

* * * * *

They were getting closer. No matter how hard she ran they gained steadily on her; the sound of their boots hitting the deck echoed through the hall. Tanis was terrified. Nothing was as she expected it to be; the lights were wrong. Words were strange and no one made any sense. It was a horrible nightmare and she yearned to wake up.

As if her desire alone were enough, she found the nightmare slowly fading and wakefulness returning. There was light pressing against her eyelids and she knew it would be uncomfortably bright when she opened them. Steeling herself for it, Tanis opened her eyes and tried to focus. The light wasn't as bad as she expected, but she couldn't manage to see properly. Everything was grey and her limbs all seemed to be throbbing.

<Good morning, sleepy head,> Angela greeted her.

<Where am I, Angela?>

<As best I can tell, we are on a ship of some sort. I haven't gotten much information, but I do know that we're in transit. You were near death when they put you in that stasis pod,> Angela sounded concerned.

<I remember that…I remember feeling almost dead. The nice men with the big meaty fists got a bit carried away, didn't they?>

<You're lucky I wasn't damaged. The pod didn't do true stasis…it was…. Anyway, while you were in there, I reconfigured your spare nano for med duty and pulled your body back from the brink.>

<I owe you my life, dear, again>

<I wasn't entirely selfless. If you die, I stand a pretty good chance of joining you. That's a journey I'm not ready for yet.>

<Is the baby safe? Did its stasis get disrupted?> Tanis felt worry crash into her at the thought of the unborn child within her, carefully held in stasis in her womb.

<She is well, perfectly safe,> Angela replied. <She's just a few cells, still, not a lot can go wrong with her yet.>

Tanis relaxed and tried to push that worry from her mind. Plenty of time to think it over later.

<Are we safe here? Are these the same people that were beating me before?>

<No, we're on a different ship. No one has talked out loud in your presence, and I didn't open your eyes in case someone saw. They have a good nano suppression field and their Link is weird. I haven't tried to force access—not while you were out. I did hear the sounds of two women at first. Right now, there is just one, to your left somewhere. I think she's wearing leather, it squeaks whenever she moves.>

<I guess that rules out some sort of official or doctor,> Tanis replied.

<At least not the sort of doctor you'd want to see.>

Letting out the slightest of sighs she cracked her eyes open, but even the dim light of the room was more than she was prepared for. Instinctively she tried to raise her hand to shield her eyes. It didn't move. She was surprised to find her wrists restrained—though she supposed it was to be expected.

Unbidden, a thought of Joe flashed into her mind; where was he and would she ever see him again. What of their child? Would she raise her alone?

Tanis took a deep breath, forcing herself to relax. Opening her eyes again, she looked around and identified her surroundings as a medical lab of some sort. A voice spoke, and while the words were soft, her ears throbbed from the sound.

"Welcome aboard the *Sabrina*. I'm Captain Sera," the woman's voice said

Tanis's eyes darted to her left where the woman sat. Even as she smiled, the woman's face looked hard, and her eyes appeared to have some great weight behind them, though her warm expression seemed genuine enough. Jet-black hair glinted in the light and framed a pale face with high cheekbones—definitely the complexion of a spacer.

Tanis could feel the faint vibrations of a reactor nearby and determined that either this ship had its med lab in a strange place or it wasn't that large. Maybe it was a small shuttle or transport heading to this woman's main ship. She opened her mouth to reply, but only a dry rasp came out.

The woman made an apology, and offered her a drink. Tanis thanked her; then asked if she was a prisoner. The woman smiled again and, though she seemed somewhat wary, the smile did reach her eyes.

"Not at all," came the reply. Tanis noted how the woman only unfastened the wrist closest to her—she didn't reach over Tanis's body to release the other. Usually, only people familiar with violence showed that sort of caution. The woman explained that the restraints were just a precaution against an unfavorable reaction to waking in strange surroundings.

It was a plausible explanation.

Tanis took the opportunity to ask where she was. The woman confirmed her suspicion that they were indeed on a ship, though it was a freighter. However, three letters the captain uttered caught in her mind: FTL. Tanis was familiar with the term. It meant Faster-Than-Light, though neither she, nor anyone else for that matter, had ever been on a ship that exceeded the speed of light.

She glanced around the med lab, unable to reconcile the fact that an aging freighter could achieve such speeds. Through all her furiously racing thoughts, three words escaped her lips.

"We're in FTL?"

The captain responded that they were headed for Edasich. Tanis quickly dredged the reference up in her mind. Edasich was a star system just over a hundred light-years from Earth. If they were traveling at the speed of light, or even faster, it could still take decades to get there. If it was that star. She asked after it by another name, Iota Draconis, and the captain confirmed it was the same star.

Tanis re-examined what the captain had said; they would be making some stops along the way. Perhaps she could manage to get off the *Sabrina* at some point and return to the *Intrepid*. Though she was dying to know how long such a trip would take. The number she was given was unbelievable, just a few months! This woman spoke of a trip of a hundred light-years as though it were a simple jaunt across the Sol System!

Tanis could feel alarm setting in and forced herself to breathe deeply. She didn't want this woman to think she was unstable and sedate her again. Even as she steadied herself, a part of her mind was screaming. This was wrong, it was all terribly wrong. Humanity didn't have FTL capability. No human had ever come within twenty light years of Edasich. She was trapped in a nightmare, one where the *Intrepid* could be on the other side of the galaxy for all she knew; one where she may never be able to get home to Joe and her ship.

<Relax dear; I'm having a not dissimilar reaction. I'm sure it will all make sense soon.>

<It better, because if I'm not insane already I may try it out.>

The woman noticed her discomfort and started over by re-introducing herself as Captain Sera and asking her name. Her mind latched onto the question. This was within the realm of her understanding, and she answered calmly that it was Tanis Richards, biting back the desire to add her rank.

"Two names? That's uncommon in this neighborhood, what star system still does that? Our med system didn't recognize your DNA as coming from anywhere particular." The captain asked.

What an odd question, why wouldn't they be able to determine her origin from her DNA. Though if they used spectrographic analysis on the isotopes in her body, that would likely confuse them, given her time on Victoria. Tanis replied that she was from Earth—a small lie—and Captain Sera seemed to suddenly stifle a laugh. This was all becoming too much.

<Am I on some sort of hallucinogenic?> she asked Angela.

<If you are, it's affecting me, too. Something is not right with this.>

"Aren't we all," the captain said with a hint of sarcasm.

<Well yeah...> Tanis thought. *<I'm really starting to dislike this Captain Sera.>*

<I think she's trying to soften the blow...whatever that blow is.>

<I hate pussyfooting around things,> Tanis sighed.

<Really? I hadn't realized that about you.>

"It's okay," the captain said and smiled; Tanis couldn't help but believe it was genuine, even though the woman was a bundle of contradictions. "You don't have to tell right away. I'm betting that you didn't beat yourself up and hop in a pod for kicks. I assure you that we mean you no harm, though we are curious. What happened to you anyway?"

Tanis thought about it. Honestly, she wasn't entirely certain what *had* happened to her. Moreover, she wasn't entirely certain that she wanted to relate the story just yet. The captain seemed to sense her indecision and apologized.

"I'm sorry, I forget how disorienting all this can be. There are some clothes on the stand beside you. Once you get dressed, I'll show you to your cabin where you can freshen up, before joining us in the galley for the second-shift meal."

Tanis looked over to the clothing on her right. Reaching out she put a hand on it. It was soft cotton; natural, too, by the feel of it. A captain wearing animal skins and now natural cotton. Perhaps she was on some colony world where such materials were more common than synthetics.

<Could this be some sort of interrogation technique?> she asked Angela.

<If it is, it's the most unique I've ever been exposed to.>

Sera seemed to take her reaction as disdain for cotton. "I hope they're alright. Everything I own is custom fitted to me. Those are Nance's. She doesn't really wear clothes anyway, so she won't miss them. I'll be right outside the door."

The captain stepped outside the med facility and Tanis could see her back as she waited in front of a window. She sat up, clutching the sheet as she pulled the clothes to her lap and examined them. They sure felt like cotton. If they weren't, it was the best synthetic she had ever seen. Looking under the sheet, she blushed to find herself totally naked. Well, better naked and alive than the alternative.

Tanis dressed quickly in what turned out to be simple shoes, cotton leggings and a loose, sleeveless shirt. Running a hand through her hair, she wondered if this ship of contradictions would have water showers or the good ol' sandblasting a freighter ought to have.

The captain flashed another one of those hard, yet genuine smiles as Tanis stepped out of the med facility. "Amazing how getting into at least a scrap of clothing can make you feel so much more human, isn't it?"

Tanis nodded in response and Sera turned, leading her down a long, well-lit corridor. She couldn't help but smile to herself at the incongruity of Sera's statement. The captain certainly seemed to believe in a lot more than just a scrap of clothing, what with her skin-tight outfit covering every inch of her body from the neck down.

They stopped at a ladder and the captain climbed up to the next level.

<OK...if we are being pranked, then they really suck at this,> Tanis laughed in her mind. <Ladders on a ship with FTL?>

The captain looked down and noticed her disbelieving expression.

"*Sabrina* does have lifts, but I find that on long trips you need all the extra exercise you can get. I put the ladders in after I bought her. Also much better than lifts if the AG fields ever have trouble." She turned and led Tanis down another corridor with a series of doors on the left.

There she went again, referring to a trip that was probably only a few months as 'long'.' While Tanis tried to wrap her mind around FTL again, she realized the captain had mentioned AG fields. Massive ships like the *Intrepid* could generate artificial gravity, but how could a small freighter—where the engines couldn't be more than fifty meters from the med lab—have AG? Sera *must* be playing with them now. FTL and AG in one day was far too much to swallow.

"Here we are," Captain Sera said. "We use this cabin for passengers we pick up from time to time. Consider it yours for the trip."

Tanis peered in; the surprises just kept on coming. How did a small freighter have cabins of this size? It was at least four meters across and had a bed, dresser, and desk. There appeared to be a closet, and it even had its own toilet and shower.

The captain looked pleased. "*Sabrina* used to be a pleasure yacht. I know I could probably shrink these cabins down, but it sure helps in hiring crew when you show them their own private bathroom."

"It's a water shower?" Tanis asked, hoping it was, because she wanted one, yet wishing it wasn't, so that something made sense.

"Of course, do we look like savages?" The captain laughed. "Second-shift meal is in about thirty minutes in the galley," she gestured aft, down the corridor. "We'll be expecting you."

With that, the captain slid the door shut and left Tanis to herself. She stood for several moments taking everything in; trying to make sense of what she was seeing. It occurred to her that this could be some sort of holo suite, or an elaborate ruse to fool her. But fool her for what reason? Sure, the *Intrepid* was very valuable, but no one trying to gain her trust would use such ridiculous methods.

<They wouldn't, would they?>

<I'm still stuck on the first batch of impossibilities. I know you flesh and blood types like to be clean—why don't you take a shower while I try to keep my cortex from fracturing.>

All was not lost; Angela still had her wry sense of humor.

Glancing over at the bulkhead, Tanis noticed a porthole. A porthole in FTL? Was that safe? She couldn't resist the urge to see what was out there. Peering through the window, she saw only blackness. There were no stars, not even streaks or smears of light as the ship blasted past photons in space. Tanis had always been certain that some light would be visible in FTL. Wouldn't the ship be intercepting light that was already there? Light toward the bow of the ship should surely be visible? The porthole showed none of this.

She caught herself pondering all the types of FTL she had heard postulated or seen in holos. Most utilized a space folding, or space compression/stretching technique to achieve a circumvention of relativity's limits. The amount of energy to achieve either of those effects was proven to be completely impractical. Earnest had created stable wormholes in previous research, but creating one over interstellar distances, stable enough to safely transfer matter, turned out to take as much energy as a star emitted over a billion years.

This had to be a farce. If Earnest couldn't determine how to achieve FTL, then there was no way that this yacht turned dingy freighter could exceed c. Yet, if they were traveling at the speeds she thought, it must be much faster than light speed—hundreds of times faster. It was mind-boggling. How did the ship even hold together?

Tanis suddenly felt very unsafe. Though, she rationalized, the ship must have been through an FTL trek more than once in its decades of service. It could last a few more weeks for her. Besides, after the torture and beatings from her previous hosts, a shower would feel amazing—even if it was a holo shower.

She spent as much time as she could under the flow of hot water before getting out in time for the meal Captain Sera had mentioned. Feeling greatly refreshed, she stepped into the corridor. At the end of the hall, the sounds of cutlery clinking on plates came from what must be the galley.

Tanis entered and saw Captain Sera and another man enjoying a meal at a large table. Tanis couldn't help but admire the quality of the wooden table and surrounding chairs. It reminded her of her cabin back on the *Intrepid,* which in turn made her think of Joe. She forced those thoughts down. She didn't want her first impressions to be all warbly-voiced and teary.

<We'll find him, we'll get back,> Angela said softly in Tanis's mind.

<We will. We have to.>

"Hey Tanis," Sera stood to greet her. "This is my first mate, Cargo."

The man stood and offered his hand, which swallowed hers to her wrist. His skin was dark, as though few of his ancestors had spent any time in space; his voice was soft, but very resonant, as he greeted her and offered a chair.

"You're in luck," Sera said, as she spooned some vegetables onto her own plate. "We're just out of station, so we have fresh food. A week from now, we'll be on to frozen stuff. Enjoy it while it lasts."

Tanis picked up a plate from the counter and sat across from Sera and Cargo. She scooped some salad onto her dish, and poured a creamy dressing over it.

"You were just at a station?" she asked as she mixed the salad up. <I swear my mouth is watering after what the pirates fed me.>

<I tested it with some nano, it's clear,> Angela supplied.

<Thanks, Mom.>

"Coburn, in the Trio System," Cargo filled in. "Picked up some cargo, including you."

Tanis set aside the part about herself being freight to be picked up, and asked about the location. "I don't know any places named Trio."

"No?" Sera cocked her head and gave Tanis a quizzical look. "It's a pretty well-known system. I forget what it used to be called, before it was colonized. It's about ninety-six light-years out from Sol. Lemme see if Sabrina knows,"

She watched Sera's eyes blink a few times, as the captain chatted with the ship over the Link.

"Looks like it was cataloged as HD 111232 before it got settled and named."

Angela provided Tanis with an image of the system, relative to Earth and 82 Eridani. It wasn't possible; they were well over a hundred light-years from where she should be. On the far side of Sol from the *Intrepid*!

She forced herself to remain calm.

"You said you picked me up. Are you slave traders or something?"

The Captain looked genuinely appalled. "No! You were packed in a shipping container that was supposed to have a prize-racing dog in it. After we came under attack leaving Trio, I decided to see what we'd risked our necks for." Sera wore a smile that made Tanis want to cringe. "Someone wants you real bad."

"You came under attack because of me?" Tanis couldn't make any sense of this. Events just wouldn't line up for her, and her mind still felt sluggish from her prolonged incapacitation.

Sera related the story of how they came under fire while leaving the Trio System. Tanis felt numb as she took it all in. The acceleration and maneuvering the freighter captain described was unheard of. No ship could do that and not kill its inhabitants—unless they were in shoot-suits, or augmented like Joe. As she mused over the meaning of this information, the captain fixed her with a very level stare.

"I know you probably are still feeling out of sorts, but my crew and I would really like to know exactly why you're so sought after. You came this close," Sera held her thumb and index finger very close together, "to getting us all turned into fine stellar dust. We would like to know why."

<You know what has happened, right?> Angela asked in Tanis's mind.

<I really don't want to, but I think I do—but how far? Everything has changed! It's like we moved to another dimension.>

Tanis knew many people who wanted to kill her, but—if her suspicions were correct—none of those people were alive, or if they were, she couldn't imagine that old grievances were relevant anymore. She certainly had no idea why she was over a hundred light-years from where she should be—being chased by pirates, no less.

<We need to know when we are. I haven't been able to get into their Link without outright hacking it and that's not something I want to do while we're trapped on this ship.> Angela's tone had a level of anxiety Tanis was not used to hearing from her AI.

<Do you think all this tech exists without humanity having ever creating picotech?> Tanis asked.

<Maybe...if they worked out how to generate gravitons efficiently without pico...I could see a very different course for humanity.>

The pirates had to be after the *Intrepid*.

Tanis took another bite of her salad and looked at her two dinner companions. It was impossible to tell if they had been truthful or not. This still could all be a ruse to get the *Intrepid's* location.

She decided to play dumb.

"I...I really don't know. I don't understand what someone would want from me."

Sera pushed her chair back, a look of exasperation washing across her face. She looked to Cargo and waved a hand, indicating he should try.

"You seem like a smart lady, Tanis," he said softly. While there was no threat in his voice, she imagined it wouldn't take much for it to appear there. "Surely you can at least determine where the current course of events began and tell us the tale of how you came to be in that cargo container."

<I don't think they'll buy damsel in distress,> Angela chuckled inside Tanis's mind. *<Especially since you really suck at it.>*

Tanis weighed her options. Getting back to the *Intrepid* and Joe was really all that mattered. Perhaps honesty would be best—if these people double-crossed her, she could kill them and take their ship. Though there was something about the captain—she felt a kinship with Sera.

"I haven't been entirely honest with you," she began. Neither of them looked surprised. "My name is Tanis Richards, yes, but I'm also a major on a ship you would know as the *GSS Intrepid*."

*<So much for honesty, **General** Richards,>* Angela said. *<But good call on the pretend demotion.>*

<Well, I was a major when we signed on.>

"Well that explains a lot," Sera slapped the table with a laugh. "Go on."

Tanis gave her a sidelong look. She wasn't certain if the reaction was good or bad for her. She decided to give them the paraphrased version.

"We had some ramscoop problems as we were passing by LHS 1565 on our way to our colony world. We managed to slingshot around the star, but an x-ray flare baked one of our engines. We lined up with Kapteyn's Star and drifted for a good seventy years.

Tanis considered telling them about the Victorians, but decided to leave that colony out of it. "Once there, we managed to mine a few small comets and asteroids to get the materials for repairs."

Sera was giving Cargo a strange look, and Tanis decided to keep going. "It took us some decades to get everything ship-shape, then exit the system and get back up to speed. It was only 8.9 light-years to 82 Eridani, which we were calling New Eden, so everyone went to stasis for what was expected to be about sixty-year trip with the deceleration burns. Only something happened—we got trapped in some sort of gravity well and accelerated out of control. Our sensors were completely off the charts and we couldn't make heads or tails of what was going on. All we could tell was that we did not appear to be in regular space-time."

"Kapteyn's Streamer," Sera said with a nod. "You can get some amazing speed cutting across that thing, but if you hit it at the wrong angle it'll take you for a ride."

"Or crush you to powder," Cargo added.

"It has a name? What is it?" Tanis couldn't believe that this was a known phenomenon.

"It's a supermassive stream of dark matter streaked out beyond Kapteyn's. If you hit it just right, it will accelerate you and then dump you out the far side into a gravity tunnel that has a very unpleasant lensing effect. Significant time dilation occurs," Cargo said bluntly.

Tanis was dumbstruck. They had just described what had happened to the *Intrepid*. She noticed then that Sera was giving Cargo a scathing look.

"You sure know how to break things nicely," she sighed.

Cargo just shrugged.

"I already figured out we moved forward in time a fair bit," Tanis said. "How far? Hundreds of years, a thousand?"

Sera stood and pulled a bottle of whiskey from a cupboard. She grabbed three glasses and poured everyone two fingers. Cargo gave her a long stare, but said nothing.

The captain sat back at the table and tossed hers back before answering.

"I'm guessing you're from a colony ship that probably left Sol sometime in the late fourth or early fifth millennium. You were headed for 82 Eridani, which interestingly *is* now called New Eden. You hit the Kapteyn's Streamer and then found yourselves somewhere in the vicinity of 58 Eridani, about 28 light-years further out than expected; wondering how the hell you got there and what the heck the year is."

Tanis hadn't known where the *Intrepid* ended up, but 58 Eridani was along the ship's trajectory.

"Yours isn't the first gen ship to dump through there. The first one managed to settle 58 Eridani, named it Bollam's World, and is doing fine now—for a system full of greedy assholes, that is.

"Anyway, due to the vagaries of space-time, they probably left Sol after you. Unluckily for you there isn't a single habitable planet within a hundred light-years of where you came out that's not already taken."

Tanis couldn't believe it. The *Intrepid* had spent hundreds of years of blood, sweat and tears to make it to a colony; a world she could call home. She slumped in her chair; it would take centuries to travel to a new world. If the FGT had any worlds available—if the FGT still existed.

"But how is that possible?" she all but whispered.

"It's all thanks to the greatest advance and the greatest tragedy of mankind: FTL. While all you gen ships were still chugging through interstellar space sucking up hydrogen in your ramscoops, some brainiac back on Procyon figured out the gravity drive," Sera said.

"I remember hearing something about graviton experiments at Procyon while we were at Kapteyn's. Our engineers were very excited about the possibilities," Tanis said with a furrowed brow.

Sera nodded. "I know it doesn't seem like the *biggest* discovery ever, but trust me it is. Once we could create gravity to react against other gravity, all the other pieces just lined up. Ships got AG fields to provide internal gravity, without rotation, thrust, or phantom mass. Inertial dampeners came out of fiction and into our ships; and we discovered a lot more about dark matter."

Tanis was glad she hadn't eaten too much. She was certain she was going to be sick.

"You know that scientists have always known about other dimensions, as well as sub and super-layers of space-time. But transitions to those other layers were prohibitively expensive, energy-wise, or it ended up being a one-way trip."

Tanis nodded slowly; this was basic physics.

Sera continued. "With the ability to manipulate gravity, they discovered how to drop into the same layer of space-time where dark matter resides. It was always postulated to be like this. Dark matter has all this mass, but isn't bending light like it should. To be honest, the exact nature of the dark layer, as it's called, still isn't perfectly understood. Some think it's utterly void and frictionless, while others think it's Einstein's universal frame of reference. I suppose someone knows, but they're not sharing the details.

"Either way, when you move into the DL your speed relative to the normal universe multiplies exponentially."

Tanis looked down at the whiskey and downed the glass in one shot. The captain gave her an appreciative look and continued.

"Gravity manipulation gave us other things, as well—namely methods for cheaper antimatter production. Once that was available, hitting speeds up to 0.70c with an antimatter pion drive became trivial. The end result? A trip from Sol to Alpha Centauri takes four days instead of four decades."

Tanis had always prided herself on being strong. Granted, the decades with Joe aboard the *Intrepid* had taught her about her softer side—but she still considered herself strong, a rock.

Until now.

She felt her foundation slipping away. She had understood her place in the galaxy so well. Known how to operate within all the parameters. Now, she knew nothing. She felt like all her value was lost.

<Hold it together girl,> Angela didn't sound that together herself as she gave the advice. <We've been through worse and come out the better for it.>

"Have we?" Tanis whispered.

"Pardon?" Captain Sera asked.

Tanis felt like she was going to have a mental breakdown. She thought of the harrowing events on Toro, the Mars Outer Shipyards, and the Cho. Of her awakening on the *Intrepid* as it was falling into a star and the desperate battle against the Sirians above the fledgling colony world of Victoria.

She thought of the picobomb.

"It was all for nothing," she muttered.

"What? No! That is the furthest thing from the truth. At the very least, there's no more Sol Space Federation, so your colony mission doesn't owe anyone a cent. They fell apart millennia ago," Sera said and then clasped a hand over her mouth, realized her misstep. "Oh shit."

Tanis's head snapped up. "Millennia?"

Cargo laughed. "And you said I stepped in it."

"Ummm," Sera shifted uncomfortably. "Well I guess in a way it doesn't really matter much, you never expected to see anyone you knew again anyway. Like Cargo said, the Streamer has a pretty wicked time dilation effect if you pass between the gravitational arms like you did. You skipped a few thousand years of relative time on that transit. By your calendar, it's just about the year nine thousand…or so.

Tanis rose, her legs shaking slightly. "If you'll excuse me, I need some time to myself."

Not waiting for a response, she left the galley and dashed down the corridor to her cabin, where she quickly closed the door. Praying no one would hear her, she began to sob.

TIME TRAVELER

STELLAR DATE: 07.02.8927 (Adjusted Years)
LOCATION: *Sabrina*, Interstellar Dark Layer
REGION: Galactic South of Trio Prime, Silstrand Alliance Space

"That went well," Cargo commented as he reached for another baked potato.

Sera ran her hands through her hair. "I didn't even get to tell her the good news."

"What, that aside from the positions of galaxies, everything she knows is no longer valid?"

"No, that like all good classics, her gen ship is worth a hundred times what it took to make the stupid thing. If they're early fifth millennia, they've got amazing tech. I've heard biological android were even common then. Do you know what a bio-droid with an advanced AI neural net goes for on the market?"

"Haven't a clue," Cargo said around a mouthful of potato.

"More than my sweet *Sabrina* will make in the rest of her life, that's how much."

<*I thought you said I was priceless,*> Sabrina groused.

Cargo perked up at that. "You don't say."

"We're not hard up for cash, but the tech her ship carries is worth more than a dozen star systems. I wouldn't object to a bit of a reward."

Cargo chuckled. "Well, what are you waiting for? Go talk to our little flower."

"Not yet...with what she's been through—and I bet we still only know the half of it—she's gonna need a bit of time to settle down. I'll go check on her in an hour or so."

Sera killed the hour running through a few checklists and doing a circuit of the ship. She stopped in the galley at the end of her tour to see Tanis sitting at the table alone, another glass of whiskey in front of her.

"Mind if I join you?" Sera knocked on the wall.

The major looked up and nodded.

Sera sat and poured herself another drink.

"It's a lot to absorb," Tanis said, her voice devoid of emotion

She nodded. "I can only imagine. But you left before I could tell you the good news—well, sorta good news."

"I already know it," Tanis replied. "The *Intrepid* is worth an immeasurable amount now."

Sera wondered exactly how Tanis knew that, but let it slide for the time being.

"I knew you were smart; that clueless act you tried to pull was pretty pathetic," Sera chuckled.

Tanis joined her in short laugh. "Yeah, it really was—not sure what I was thinking."

"Let's go up to the obs lounge. Its small, but it has a nice view of *Sabrina's* ass," Sera said as she stood and picked up the whiskey. If there was ever a good reason to break her 'no drinking onboard' rule, this was it.

They climbed up the ladder to the bridge deck and then followed a short corridor aft to a small room. There were several low couches and four windows facing out over the rear of the ship. Nothing beyond the ship was visible in the dark layer, but the inspection lights were on, casting the stern of the ship in a soft glow.

"Don't your engines emit light here?" Tanis asked, when she noticed there was no illumination coming from the back of the ship.

"We kill 'em in FTL, the hum you probably heard back in the med lab was our reactor. Our batteries are a bit low from the excitement in Trio, so we're charging them. There's nothing to thrust against here in the DL anyway. You can't maneuver or accelerate—except with grav drives against globs of dark matter. Once we come out of FTL, we'll need to do some serious braking since we entered it at well over half the speed of light. It took Cheeky some time to figure out when we'll need to drop back into normal space."

"Cheeky?" Tanis asked.

"Our pilot. You'll meet her soon enough."

"How big is your crew?"

"Six humans. Seven with you aboard."

"AI?" Tanis asked.

"There's Sabrina, the ship's AI, and Helen who is embedded with me. Nance, Cargo, and Cheeky have what you would probably call NSAI—sort of. Flaherty and Thompson don't have a lot of mods."

"Well, at least I won't have to remember many new names and faces, though I'm going to have a bit of work learning about the last five millennia."

"To be honest, things have been a mess," Sera responded. "FTL has been the bane of humankind."

"It has?" Tanis asked. "After more than a hundred years drifting through interstellar space, I sort of imagined it would be the opposite."

"What could never really happen in your time?" Sera asked by way of response.

Tanis knew the answer. "Interstellar war—though I wouldn't say 'never'."

Sera nodded. "Bingo. Let's just say there have been some setbacks. Humanity has only just recently begun to pull itself out of the toilet. For instance, there was even a period in the eighth millennia when the bulk of humanity completely lost knowledge of nanotechnology. It's been rediscovered since, but believe me, your nano is better than any you'll find across a thousand systems."

<She's not being entirely honest,> Angela said.

<How so?> Tanis schooled her expression, not wanting to show suspicion to Sera.

<Her nano may have been more advanced than yours. It didn't put up a fight when I destroyed it, but it could have.>

<Will the mysteries ever cease?> Tanis asked.

<Could they please? I blame your "luck".>

Tanis realized Sera had continued speaking while she and Angela talked.

"...I'm willing to bet you've got tech on your ship that the rest of mankind would kill for—probably has killed for. That's why we found you in a shipping container. I bet that Kade wants to have a nice long chat with you about where your ship is."

"Kade? Who's he?"

"Local scumbag. We have some dealings with his group, called The Mark, from time to time. Pays pretty well."

"I do hope you're not going to turn me over to him. I won't go quietly," Tanis's voice was level and dead calm.

Tanis watched Sera's face grow more serious as they stared into one another's eyes. She wondered how she appeared to this not-so-simple freighter captain: a problem and an enigma, but a possible payday as well. The moments dragged on, but Sera must have come to a conclusion about Tanis because she suddenly smiled and leaned back in her seat.

"No, I don't transport slaves, and I certainly wouldn't turn you over—threats notwithstanding."

"Good, that makes our relationship a lot more agreeable." Tanis took another drink from her glass and relaxed into the deep leather couch.

"However, Kade's going to expect to get you and I can't directly cross him or my ass is grass. How's about you tell me the rest of your tale so I can make sure whatever we work up jives. How did you end up at Coburn Station?"

<She's lying,> Angela said to Tanis.

<I picked up some tells, too. Which part do you think is a lie?>

<Well, not really lying. From her body language and what I can read in her voice and smell, she's not afraid of Kade at all. He could make things difficult for her, but she is hiding something about her relationship with him.>

Tanis held that conversation with Angela as she ran a hand through her long blonde hair. "I don't know how I got there, but I do know at least the start.

"We didn't exit gracefully from what you call Kapteyn's Streamer. In the split-second we transitioned out, something hit the ship at relativistic speeds. I was in the bow and managed to get to an escape pod. We ejected and then the *Intrepid* was gone. Angela and I were trying to find it when a small ship appeared out of nowhere—using FTL I now realize—and snatched the pod."

<I've been meaning to tell you, now that I've reviewed the data I managed to get during that hack attempt we did back on the ship that captured us, there was an anomaly that might have been the *Intrepid*. I think they popped out a few AU further down than us,> Angela informed Tanis.

<Intact?>

<It didn't scan like debris, but it's hard to say. It was a long ways away.>

While querying Angela, she continued her recitation to Sera.

"When they boarded the escape pod, I could tell right off that they weren't any sort of official representatives...of anywhere. Though, I must admit, they had some good nano suppression tech in their interrogation room. I almost got past it a few times, but I had a limited supply of bots and I decided to hold back to repair what they were doing to me.

"They beat me for a few days trying to get any detail they could from me. I was pretty messed up—Angela tells me I was on death's door. I guess they—what? Cryostasis?" Tanis sputtered as Angela fed her more details. "This *is* the dark ages!"

"Sorry, I should really give you Link access so you and your AI can chat with the rest of us," Sera apologized. "Sabrina, can you give the major and Angela our protocols?"

"Certainly, Captain," the ship said somewhat icily.

"No wonder everything aches," Tanis said while rolling her shoulders. "I can't believe it. How long was I under?"

Sera looked perplexed. "What's wrong with cryostasis? It's pretty common; keeps you alive and all that."

"No, *stasis* keeps you alive, *cryostasis* freezes you! As in it makes you very cold!"

<*I'm sorry, Tanis, I hadn't gotten around to sharing that with you sooner, I figured you had enough on your mind. You were iced for one hundred and nine days,*> Angela joined the conversation over the public net now that they were Linked.

Tanis's eyes widened and she flexed her fingers one-by-one as though she expected to find defects.

"Oh wait...you have true stasis on the *Intrepid*, don't you?" Sera sat up, eyes wide.

Tanis nodded. "Yes, when we left Sol, everyone had stasis; no one had used cryostasis in hundreds of years. I can't believe I was frozen!"

"There's some tech that'd be worth a pretty penny," Sera said with a smile. "True stasis tech was lost thousands of years ago. No one could figure out how the null field was created without ridiculous amounts of energy."

<*It's not complicated tech...how is it that things like that have been lost?*> Angela asked.

Sera sighed. "War, people hoarding tech and not sharing it, piracy, you name it."

"This is going to take some getting used to," Tanis said. "So what's our deal here? I'm guessing you're more than happy to take me back to the *Intrepid* if we provide you with something in trade to make it worth your while."

Sera leaned back again. "Look, I'll be honest. I won't hand you over to Kade, but I also won't traipse across human space on a courier run without payment—especially when everyone and their dog probably wants to find you and get a piece of your hide."

"I have one priority," Tanis said. "To get back to the *Intrepid* and ensure it remains safe. I can personally guarantee that you will be exceptionally well compensated."

Sera took a sip of her drink as she considered the Tanis's words. She certainly believed what she was saying, but the shrewd businessperson in her wondered what ability Tanis had to deliver on her promises. What sort of deal could she make with a major that would be binding? There was a lot of risk here.

"I would love to help you, Tanis, but how do you know that your ship will still be there? They may have retreated to interstellar space, or been captured by some other force. This is a pretty big risk."

"I can promise you one thing," Tanis said. "The *Intrepid* is there, and it is still sovereign. There is no force in the galaxy that can stop that ship—especially given the state of things right now. They will reward you handsomely for returning me. If they're not there, then I will give you specs for enough advanced tech that you'll never have to work another day in your life."

"You have them on you?" Sera asked.

"Yes, I've taken to carrying a lot of data with me."

Sera nodded. "Very well, before we enter into this deal, I want to make sure I know how many factions are involved. Did you notice anything significant about the ship that attacked you?"

"Not much. It was obviously not a cargo hauler by primary trade. My scan of it showed some big lasers for such a small ship. When they tortured me, I noticed that they both had an odd tattoo over their right eyes."

Sera pulled a plas sheet from a pocket and marked a pattern on it. "Like this?"

Tanis nodded. "That's the symbol. What's it mean?"

"Padre. It's his sign; all his guys have it tat'd on."

"Padre, as in a priest?"

"Priest? No, he's a pirate. One of the distinctly less pleasant ones. It was his guys that chased us out of the Trio System." Sera took another sip of her drink. "I'm betting that somehow Kade got wind of what Padre had found and snatched you up. We're supposed to deliver your container to him in about seven days."

"What a mess," Tanis sighed.

"It's gonna take some fancy footwork to pull one over on ol' Kade. I'm probably going to have to fake logs and show that Padre's ships boarded us and toss your container out the hatch here in the DL so he won't find it if he comes aboard."

"What about finding me?" Tanis asked.

Sera winked. "You're much smaller. I'm sure we can tuck you away somewhere."

A STARSHIP NAMED SABRINA

STELLAR DATE: 07.02.8927 (Adjusted Years)
LOCATION: *Sabrina*, Interstellar Dark Layer
REGION: Galactic South of Trio Prime, Silstrand Alliance Space

It certainly was a motley crew, Tanis thought as Sera introduced her to each of them around the galley table. Cargo, the first mate, seemed to be the only normal one in the group, which was a disturbing thought.

The bio and life-support engineer, who apparently was just called the bio in the ninetieth century, seemed to live inside of her hazard suit. She didn't even pull off the hood as she ate, and only unhooked the mouth filter, which exposed a circle of pale skin around her lips. She seemed passionate about her job, though. At first, Tanis couldn't understand the need for a dedicated bio on a ship this size, but she was realizing that technology wasn't quite as foolproof as what she was used to.

Everyone taking a shower or two a day probably didn't help with the volume of waste management.

Angela had already gotten to know the other AI. Sabrina seemed a bit touchy, almost as though she was a little insecure in her place as the ship's AI. Angela was obviously superior in capability, but even without that, it seemed as though Sabrina had already felt threatened.

Angela expressed surprise to find that Helen was something of an equal, though evasive on her origins.

Sera was correct in that Cheeky didn't have truly sentient AI, but it wasn't an NSAI either. Cargo's and Nance's were similar; both clear violations of the Phobos accords.

<I'm certain that Sabrina is a violation, too,> Angela added. *<She was created—not born—for this ship, and she's never left it. They even left her active while the ship was impounded for decades!>*

Tanis was appalled at the thought and looked around at the ship's crew. They didn't seem like barbarians, but their treatment of AI would have landed them in prison back in Sol.

Thompson and Flaherty didn't have AI at all, just simple Link interfaces—most of their information access was through retinal overlay. It was crude enough that Tanis could even see it on the backs of their eyes when she dialed up her vision.

Though she suspected that Flaherty might have an additional interface, since his retinal overlay rarely showed any information. Initially, she thought him to be little more than a deck hand, or perhaps an enforcer of some sort, but something about that assessment didn't fit.

He had glanced at her when she entered, and then again when Sera introduced him. He nodded his greeting, not saying a word. His build wasn't heavy like Thompson's or Cargo's, yet that didn't diminish the growing impression Tanis had that he was the most dangerous person in the room. Every movement he made was both spare and precise.

She had no doubt that he had also observed her completely and had formed his own silent opinions.

An additional clue was Sera's introduction of Flaherty. It was obvious she had a personal connection with the man, and was very comfortable around him. Yet, his lack of internal AI and little more than a personal Link, combined with what was obviously the lowest position on the ship didn't make a shred of sense.

Even though the pilot was a self-modified nymphomaniac, Tanis found herself taking a liking to the woman. Cheeky had bounced into the wardroom on what had to be twelve-centimeter heels, wearing a miniskirt that barely covered her ass, and a tight top with a semi-lewd slogan dancing across her breasts.

She had gushed how happy she was to meet Tanis and how cool it was to meet someone over five thousand years old. Her smile and laughter was infectious and Tanis found herself reminded of Trist.

"Watch out for her," Sera said. "You are witnessing the mating ritual of the sexually aggressive Cheeky. In the wild, they are truly dangerous. She's tamer than usual since she gets a lot of it out of her system when we're docked."

Tanis laughed. Perhaps the woman was a bit more like Jessica.

Sera moved on to the next member of her crew, a large man named Thompson. She was amazed at the presence of body hair. Tanis had to restrain herself from touching the peach fuzz on his arm.

It looked like pictures of men from the nineteenth and twentieth centuries. She had always thought it would be repulsive, but seeing the somewhat rough blonde man with his soft blond hair in person, she found it to be quite the opposite. Despite that, Tanis noticed how he shifted uncomfortably when he shook her hand and had shot Sera some significant looks.

"So, what's the biggest difference you've noticed so far between your time and the ninetieth century?" Cheeky asked after the introductions were done.

Tanis pondered the question for a moment while the crew stared at her, greatly interested in the answer.

"Aside from the obvious FTL and gravity drives, it's the attitude you're able to have about the galaxy and humanity's place in it. I grew up in the crush of Sol—people everywhere, a military with a million warships. Yet if you wanted to get away from it all, you could. You could go to a colony world and live a simpler life—knowing that the overpopulation of Sol would just be a memory—you would never encounter it again, because you were just too damn far away. Now it would be a week's trip and you'd be back in it."

"I wouldn't have thought of that," Cheeky said. "I can't imagine how different it must have been. You lived in the time of greatness, the planetary rings, space elevators everywhere—moving worlds, terraforming everything…near immortality, it must have been amazing."

"Is all of that lost?" Tanis asked.

"Not all," Sera replied. "Worlds are still terraformed; planets are moved, but not commonly—not like in your day when Sol had dozens of habitable worlds. There are few rings left; in Sol, only High Terra remains."

Tanis felt her breath catch. That meant the Mars1 ring was gone. Ceres, the Cho, all no more. She knew losing a ring was no small thing—it meant those worlds may have been destroyed, as well. She decided not to ask; she didn't want to know.

"We didn't have all those things," Tanis said. "No one was immortal."

"I guess not," Cheeky replied. "But they lived a long time—over five-hundred years from what I've read. How old are you? If you don't mind my asking."

"Cheeky, really…" Nance sighed.

"I don't mind," Tanis held up her hand and smiled. "I'm still pretty young, only about two-hundred and eleven years of real-time on my clock."

Thompson whistled. "You look pretty good for two-eleven. None of us are over fifty. Two-hundred is about the best we can hope for—unless we strike it rich somewhere along the line."

"Or live in the AST," Nance added.

"AST?" Tanis asked, trying to guess at what that could be.

"If every time needs to have a dark, greedy empire, the AST is ours." Sera's expression was grim. "It is what has grown from the first interstellar government that started with Alpha Centauri, Sol System, and Tau Ceti. Hence, the A. S. T. At least, that's what everyone else calls them. Their real name is The Hegemony of Worlds."

Tanis nodded. It made sense that those systems were at the core of a large empire. Alpha Centauri and Tau Ceti were two of the most powerful colonies when she had left Earth. Alpha Centauri even had slow, but regular trade with Earth.

"Who knows what could happen?" Tanis shrugged. "If we really have a treasure-trove of tech, and it is stuff that's completely lost, we could trade it for a colony world. You guys could end up living as long as I plan to."

"Girl, you could trade that tech for a hundred colony worlds and still have money to burn. Heck, you could trade it for fully populated worlds," Cheeky exclaimed with arms flung wide.

"We have a few systems to hop through before we get to Bollam's World. You can shop around," Sera laughed.

"So it's Bollam's we're off to," Thompson said with a frown. "Are you sure that's wise?"

"I've struck a deal with Major Richards," Sera nodded at Tanis. "We'll be well compensated—enough that each of you can retire after this run."

Thompson looked about to say something else, but Sera shot him a dark look and he closed his mouth.

<So, did you pick up on the bit when you were talking about age and immortality?> Angela asked.

<I noticed Sera had a funny look on her face,> Tanis replied. <Is that what you're referring to?>

<Not just her, Flaherty too.>

<The plot thickens—I noticed Sera also gave a little twitch when they referred to the AST as the big bad empire of the time. I wonder if she's originally from there.>

<I'll see what I can learn from the other AI,> Angela said.

The rest of the meal progressed pleasantly, Tanis asking questions that would help her understand the present time as best she could, but she found herself coming back to the odd behavior that Sera displayed and Angela's earlier warnings that Sera was hiding something; something significant.

RENDEZVOUS

STELLAR DATE: 07.05.8927 (Adjusted Years)
LOCATION: *Sabrina*, Interstellar Space
REGION: Galactic South of Trio Prime, Silstrand Alliance Space

Sabrina exited FTL three light days away from her previously anticipated exit, an unfortunate consequence of entering the dark layer at an irregular vector. Cheeky's calculations were as accurate as could be; it was just impossible to predict a ship's precise location in space, when you weren't even in space.

However, Cheeky had things well in hand as she rotated the ship a hundred and eighty degrees. Starting with a slow burn, she lit up the fusion engines and brought *Sabrina* down on the meeting location.

The rendezvous was deep in interstellar space. No stars shone nearby; there were no planets, or moons, or bodies of any sort. The only marker for this meeting place was a clump of dark matter resting alone in the void.

During the days of FTL transit, the crew had ditched the cargo container in which Tanis had been found, and faked the logs to show that instead of outrunning the Padre's ships, they had been stopped and boarded. Logs now showed the container being removed and then *Sabrina* being allowed to leave the Trio System.

Regarding Tanis, Sera decided that the best place to hide her was in plain view, as a new crewmember.

"Too bad we don't have access to any advanced modifications. Those cheekbones are pretty distinctive," Cheeky had commented.

"Amusing statement for someone named for their own cheeks," said Tanis.

"I'm not known for those cheeks." Cheeky pointed to her face, then placed her hands on her butt and swished it side-to-side. "These cheeks, though…"

"Believe me, I harbored no confusion on that fact," Tanis smiled. "Though, I can do something about my cheekbones, if you think it's necessary. Will he know anything about me?"

"He may. There are ways to send messages through FTL far faster than a ship can travel. If you can mask your appearance in some way that will stand up to inspection, do it," Sera said.

The major sucked in a deep breath as her face changed right in front of their eyes. Slowly, her jaw widened and her cheekbones became less prominent. Her lips filled out and the corners of her eyes turned up.

"Hot damn! I'd forgotten how much that *hurts*!" Tanis said in a somewhat huskier tone, as she touched her face gingerly.

"Wow! That's amazing!" Cheeky reached out to feel Tanis's face. "How in the stars did you do that?"

"I worked counterinsurgency in the TSF," Tanis's statement was met with blank stares and she laughed. "I may as well have said Praetorian Guard, it's probably better known."

"Praetorian? Is that what the Regulan military calls its Royal Guard?" Nance asked.

"Yeah," Sera said. "But they ripped it off from the Romans. The Praetorian Guard is the military unit that guarded Caesar."

"The salad?" Cheeky asked, visibly confused.

"The Roman Emperor."

Cheeky's mouth formed an O, but the expression on her face indicated she had no idea who the Roman Emperor was, when he lived, or on which planet he had ruled.

Tanis was dumbstruck. "I guess a lot changes in five thousand years."

"It has a lot to do with location, too," Sera said "I'd bet people in the Sol System know all about the Romans. People on rim worlds don't care to know much about AST worlds."

<*What story did you settle on?*> Sabrina asked, clearly impatient to get to her task.

Tanis spread her arms with a flourish. "Rachel, at your service. After serving as a station comm and nav tech on Coburn Station for a few years, I grew weary of it. Now, I'm working on my pilot's license, and managing scan and comm here on *Sabrina* while Cheeky shows me the ropes and helps me get my practical experience hours in."

<*Nothing more?*> Sabrina asked.

"If Kade asks more than that he'll already be suspicious and we won't be able to fool him with anything further," Sera said.

"That's an encouraging thought," Cheeky said.

Both Tanis and Sera began to say that they'd gotten through worse and stopped, eyeing each other for a moment. Then Tanis smiled and Sera let out a laugh.

"I doubt it'll be the last time either."

THE MEET

DATE: 07.09.8927 (Adjusted Years)
LOCATION: *Sabrina*, Interstellar Space
REGION: The Mark's Interstellar Drop Point, Silstrand Alliance Space

Sabrina had finished deceleration and was drifting near the meeting point.

Sera wasn't sure if Kade himself would be at this transfer, but she hoped not; this whole 'hiding human cargo act' was making her stomach twist enough as it was. Her misgivings aside, Tanis was actually fitting in with the crew quite well. She had picked up the comm and nav systems with appreciable speed and had watched Cheeky's final maneuvering of the ship with great interest. The crew had helped her flesh out a few parts of her story in greater detail, but Sera was still of the opinion that if too many questions were asked it was an indication that they were already in trouble.

Flaherty and Thompson had moved cargo to be transferred into the few rooms off the bow corridor. They also placed a few containers in the corridor itself. It made for some tight maneuvering, but the sooner they could transfer the cargo and got on their way, the better.

Tanis had argued very strenuously that perhaps they shouldn't stick around for the meeting, but Sera said she needed the business with Kade right now and couldn't afford to run across the Orion arm just to avoid him.

The meeting time arrived and they expected The Mark ship to show up on scan at any moment, decelerating toward the meeting coordinates. Sera was certain they had a few passive probes floating quietly in the area, so they would know who was around and be able to drop back into FTL if something were amiss.

As much as Sera wanted to look for those scan probes and tap into them, the chances of The Mark picking up on it were just too high.

Even though there was plenty of room, the bridge felt crowded with four of them up there. Tanis was operating scan at the comm station and Sera wondered what it would be like to go from what had to be a very clean, crisp, and ordered society to working on *Sabrina*. Tanis's back was straight and her movements spare and efficient. If she was feeling any anxiety over this cargo transfer, she wasn't showing it.

She surveyed the rest of her bridge crew. Cheeky was wearing a bit more clothing than normal—she didn't much like being ogled by the types that made up Mark crews. Cargo was as inscrutable as ever as he checked over ships systems and did whatever it was that always seemed to keep him busy at his station.

Sera accessed her Link again to see if scan showed anything; to be informed yet again that The Mark ship hadn't arrived.

<Would you cut it out?> Helen said. *<It'll go fine, they'll never suspect anything and we'll be able to carry on as usual.>*

<Pardon me if I don't share your perennial confidence,> Sera replied.

<Trust me, I worry, too. I just calm myself down faster than it takes to even mention it.>

Even as Sera was pondering the possibilities, Tanis spoke up. "There they are. Just came up on scan."

"They? There was only supposed to be one."

"Two ships, one an obvious freighter, the other looks a bit smaller, larger engine signature—you have it on record as the *Vertigo*. Both have turned and are firing AP engines to decelerate." Tanis plotted out where the two ships would come to a relative stop and sent the co-ordinates to Cheeky, who laid in a course.

"And we've got contact," Tanis announced. "They're still a good thirty light minutes out, so it's just a welcome." She sent the message to Sera's screen, who saw with dismay that Kade had made an appearance himself. The message was brief. It instructed them that Kade's ships would decelerate to 0.15c and maintain their current course. Sera was to bring *Sabrina* up to a matching speed and set a course to intercept. The maneuver would make for a faster overall rendezvous.

Sera piped the pertinent information to Cheeky, who put *Sabrina* on course to match up with Kade's ships. Once that was done, she sent a message over the ship's main net.

<Kade has dropped from the DL and we are accelerating to meet him at a 0.15 c rendezvous. He's here himself in one of his pirate boats, with a

freighter, to pick up the wares, I imagine. Our ETA on meet-up is about eight hours. I'll put it on the clocks.>

It was easing into the third watch and Sera decided that things would be hectic soon enough. She slated everyone to get at least six hours of sleep before the rendezvous.

She opted for sleep first. If anything interesting happened, it would be later rather than sooner.

After her allotted six, she was awake and back on the bridge nursing the first cup from a fresh pot of coffee.

Humans may have done a lot in the previous ten millennia, but so far nothing had been invented that was better than a cup of coffee after waking up. Well almost nothing, but people didn't invent that.

By the time a soft seal was made against the *Vertigo*, Sera had quelled her anxiety over potential conflict with Kade. Her concern was more due to the wrench it would throw in her plans. Kade had made it clear he wanted to meet with her and look over the cargo, which was something he had never done before.

Sera was starting to wonder if they should have just thrown Tanis in a hazsuit and dropped her in one of the nastier enviro tanks, one that no one would go peeking in. Too bad she hadn't thought of that earlier. They could have kept the container she had been in and shrugged when it was found to be empty.

Sera cycled the bow airlock herself and let Kade and his two companions on board. She was tempted to wait for him on the bridge, but this was no time to antagonize the pirate with power plays.

He came through the lock first, just as she remembered him from the last time they'd met. His long, dark hair was somewhat greasy, and, although his clothes were crisp—and probably cost more than the value of all the cargo they were about to transfer—they somehow didn't transmit that wealth to him.

With him was a person that Sera had dealt with many times, and liked less on each encounter—Kade's right hand woman, Rebecca.

Rebecca was a beautiful woman who had no compunctions about using her looks to her advantage in every way possible. She also looked nothing like a pirate, more like the unlikely combination of a princess and a dominatrix.

Where Sera gleamed in her tight leather, Rebecca sparkled with necklaces and bracelets. All made of diamond, platinum, and whatever was currently the most expensive gem in vogue.

Beneath the jewelry, her body was sheathed from head to toe in a tight, black material that reflected every light in the corridor. The combined effect made her almost difficult to look at—though Sera certainly appreciated the appeal.

Kade probably hoped that some of Rebecca's style would make him look better than he did. Unfortunately for him, the opposite was true—having her nearby just made him look somewhat dumpy.

Rebecca's eyes raked over the corridor crowded with cargo and locked on Sera, the expression on her face filled with distaste for all aspects of *Sabrina*—including her captain.

<*I hate the way she looks at me,*> *Sabrina* said.

<*I know how you feel, dear,*> Sera replied.

The third person was a man Sera did not recognize. He looked cowed by the company he was keeping and Sera wondered why he was here.

"Welcome aboard *Sabrina*," Sera said.

Sera knew that Kade harbored desire for her; as she offered her hand, she tilted her hips and smiled. She was fully prepared to do whatever it took to remain in the pirate's good graces.

Kade took it and smiled, his eyes traveling over today's leather outfit—dark green with yellow piping down her sides. It was more formal than usual, with the pants loose from the knees down, where they fell over low-heeled boots. The jacket was form fitting and fastened with a double row of brass buttons down her chest. She'd even topped it off with a captain's hat in matching green leather. Kade practically licked his lips.

"Sera. You know Rebecca, and this is Drind. He'll be going over your scan logs to learn what he can of Padre's ships that took my property."

Had she not known better, the emphasis he placed on 'my' would have caused Sera to believe it actually was his. It certainly seemed as if Kade's ethics did not take into account the fact that he had stolen it from Padre in the first place, or that the property he spoke of was a person.

"Of course," Sera said in the polished voice she used for speaking with the pirate leader, which drew a dark look from Rebecca. "You'll pardon the mess. The men have things ready for transfer to the *Starskipper* so that we don't cause any delay. This way to the bridge." She gestured down the corridor.

Kade smiled magnanimously. "Of course. I've instructed the *Starskipper* to dock while we are here and transfer the cargo while we talk." As though his words were prophetic, she heard the light clang as the *Vertigo* disengaged from the soft dock and maneuvered away, to allow the other ship room to link to *Sabrina*.

Sera hid her thoughts behind a mask of pleasantness. Kade must have felt either invincible or unthreatened by her, if he didn't feel the need to have any type of escape route during parts of their meeting. For her part, Rebecca looked more concerned with scuffing the shine on her outfit than finding out about the missing freight container.

Sera used the lifts to bring them up to bridge deck. They stepped into the command space, where Cheeky, Tanis, and Cargo were all at their stations coordinating with the *Starskipper* for its soft dock.

Kade noticed Tanis right away. "New crew? I didn't know you were looking, Sera, I could have furnished you with anyone you'd need."

<If we wanted that, we could have just contacted Moles R Us,> Helen said privately to Sera.

Sera introduced Tanis as Rachel and explained that she would be assisting with comm and scan. She didn't go into details as to why, after years with the same crew, she had decided to add another member. Offering it unasked would be too suspicious.

Whatever stars watched over *Sabrina* smiled and Rebecca asked the question first, and Sera explained it was to expedite dock duties. Currently, Cheeky, Cargo, or she had to remain on the bridge while docked to watch scan and comm. This way, they could all be out on station at once.

Kade and Rebecca seemed satisfied with this answer and didn't press the issue further.

"Perhaps our technician could look over your logs with your new comm tech while you and Cargo join us in your lounge to discuss some things?" Kade phrased it as a question, though it wasn't one.

Sera acquiesced and called down to the galley for Nance to bring up some refreshments. She spared a glance for Tanis as Drind sat with her to go over scan from the Trio departure. She was impressed; absolutely nothing about the major belied the tension Sera knew she had to be feeling.

The four sat in the observation lounge. A moment later, Nance, looking more than a little uncomfortable, entered with a selection of drinks she had previously prepared. The bio wasn't wearing her hood—Sera had asked her not to—in an attempt to show they had nothing to hide. She asked preferences, and quickly began to pour the drinks.

"Are you having some sort of environmental issue?" Rebecca asked Nance, frowning at her hazsuit.

"No, I just wear it all the time in case something happens," Nance said. "That way we don't lose precious time while I get suited up."

Rebecca didn't seem convinced, and started to question Nance further, but Kade stopped her.

"She always wears it, though I've never seen her face before," he said with a leer. "Has anyone ever told you how beautiful your hair is?"

Nance flushed, but managed to give a steady reply. "I've heard it once or twice before."

With that, the drinks were served and Nance quickly left the lounge.

A few minutes passed while mild pleasantries were exchanged before they got to the issue at hand. "I'd forgotten your curious aversion to alcohol onboard your ship," Kade mused, as he drank from his cup of dark roast. "Any other captain would have his or her best wine in front of me."

"My equivalent is my best coffee, which this is," Sera said with a smile she did not feel.

"It's damn good," he nodded. "However, I'm not nearly as pleased with you, Sera. I'd think that one of my captains would try to defend my property against Padre a bit better than you did." He sighed as though this was very vexing to him. "I'm not sure what to do with you."

Sera sipped from her cup and spoke calmly, as if they were discussing the weather. "I do make runs for you, but I'm not one of *your* captains. I'm under no greater obligation to protect your cargo than any other consigned to this ship. I'm certainly not going to risk *Sabrina* or my crew just for some racing hound." Kade seemed taken aback by her calm response, obviously expecting something else; perhaps fear.

To his left, Rebecca was giving Sera the blackest of looks.

Sera rolled the dice and pressed on.

"Since it was your cargo that Padre was after when his men chased us clear across Trio, I find myself thinking I should bill you for the antimatter we burned." Sera enjoyed the expression of consternation that flashed across Kade's face, and let an edge of anger slip into her voice. "Hell, they fired an RM at us! Who did you piss off enough for them to do that, and what type of racing hound is worth an RM?"

Cargo was making 'stop it' eyes at her, and Sera decided that she had pushed as far as she should.

Kade shook his head and made a soft clicking noise with his tongue. "I'm sorry you feel that way. That hound was very precious to me. I'm feeling very much like it is you who should compensate me."

Cargo seemed to decide he had better speak up before Sera said something they'd regret. "That's not the type of business this is and you know that, Kade. There's no insurance when things don't go according to plan," he gave Sera a pointed look. "We know that, too."

Kade seemed somewhat placated by Cargo's smooth, even tones.

Sera nodded and said nothing, which seemed to allow the tension to pass.

Kade sighed and finished his coffee before rising. "Very well, let's see if my tech found anything useful on your scan data." They filed out of the lounge and back to the bridge, where Drind was chatting amicably with Tanis.

"What do you have for me?" Kade asked brusquely.

Drind's attention instantly snapped to his employer and then back to the console, where he brought up several pieces of pertinent data.

"The ships were definitely Padre's. From what I see here, they really did attack Coburn Station, but broke off when it appeared their quarry wasn't there. Not sure how they got that message. Two ships that weren't in on the station attack circled south of the star to chase after the *Sabrina*. It was quite a ride, the crew here pulled out all the stops to get away; pushed this old bucket of bolts faster than I'd feel comfortable with."

<*Why do humans continually insist on referring to me disparagingly?*> Sabrina groused.

<*They don't appreciate your finer qualities,*> Sera said, sending a wave of calmness to her ship.

Drind continued, "Their pursuers actually launched an RM and that was when the *Sabrina* ceased acceleration and allowed the boarding. They wouldn't have escaped the missile."

<*And he keeps using the word 'the' when referring to me. That's just rude,*> Sabrina said with a pout.

"And they didn't take anything else? Just that one container?" Rebecca asked with a quirked eyebrow, while Kade appeared to be mollified by the explanation.

Drind responded affirmatively, "That's all the records show."

"Bastards," Kade said. "How did they know where we stashed it?"

Sera didn't miss that Rebecca touched Kade to stop him from saying more, just as Cargo had stopped her earlier.

"Very well," Rebecca said. "How far along is the cargo transfer?"

Tanis had been monitoring the progress and announced that it was complete and that the *Vertigo* was preparing to connect once more. Kade announced that they were finished and Rebecca asked that Sera accompany them to the airlock.

The request felt suspicious to Sera. She always walked Kade off her ship, but for Rebecca to request what was the norm told her something was off. She could see that Cargo felt the same way.

All in all, this was going far too easily.

Sera led the two visitors off the bridge to the lift. They stepped inside and Sera pushed the button for the freight deck. The lift shuddered a bit as it started its descent. Suddenly, between the crew and freight decks, it stopped. Sera smiled innocently at the three guests.

"Sorry about that. This lift doesn't get used much and sometimes seizes. It'll free up in a moment."

True to her word, the lift started down again half a minute later. Down on the freight deck, the corridor to the bow airlock was free of cargo except for one last crate. They stepped around it and Sera keyed the bulkhead controls to begin pressurizing the airlock while the *Vertigo* made soft dock on the other side.

Having entered in the codes, Sera turned, only to find herself staring directly down the muzzle of a gun.

Rebecca's angry scowl was at the other end of the weapon. "You didn't think we fell for that whole Padre chased you thing, did you? There was no way he could have known you had the container."

"Are you insane?" Sera asked. "Put that thing away, it'll hole the hull if you fire it."

Rebecca laughed. "I'm not stupid, Sera. An old tub this may be, but I know your shields will hold air even if I put a dozen holes in the hull."

Sera looked at Kade. The expression on his face told her everything. He wasn't in on this. Rebecca was acting on her own.

"She doesn't have it," Kade gave an exasperated sigh. "Sera wouldn't lie about something like this, and she couldn't fake scan well enough that Drind would be fooled."

The look that Rebecca shot at Kade was pure hatred. "How stupid are you? Have you become so complacent that you can't see how she plays you? She knows exactly where that container is and she's gonna tell us, or little Sera will have to see how hot her sexy little captain's outfit looks with a few holes in it."

Cargo's voice came smooth and steady from behind Kade and Rebecca. "I don't think that will happen."

Kade turned to look back, but Rebecca kept the gun trained on Sera. The Mark's leader cursed as he saw Cargo, Thompson, and Flaherty filling the corridor, pulse rifles leveled.

"I think you'll toss that blaster to the deck and then you'll get on your ship and we'll pretend this never happened," Sera said evenly.

"Do what she says, Rebecca. You're acting insane. I know you've always been jealous of Sera, but this is too much."

As Kade spoke, Sera wondered that she'd never realized how much of a complete coward he had become as his wealth increased.

The same thought must have been on Rebecca's mind, too. She swung her arm until the muzzle of the blaster pointed at Kade's head. "You are a complete and utter moron. It's like you get dumber by the day, and frankly I can't stand it anymore." Her voice dripped disdain and hatred, but somehow sounded toneless at the same time.

She paused for just a second, cocked her head, and pulled the trigger.

Everyone was stunned as Kade's brains sprayed across the bulkhead. All eyes followed Kade's toppling form as it hit the ground, spilling blood, tech, and grey matter onto the deck.

At that precise moment, the airlock finished cycling and behind Sera, four heavily armored soldiers stepped into the corridor. Their visors were down and their weapons leveled.

Rebecca's voice was surprisingly calm. "They just killed Kade. Take Sera alive and then secure this piece of crap."

The four soldiers raised their weapons to their shoulders in a single fluid movement. In the same instant, Cargo and Flaherty dove behind the remaining freight container while Thompson hit the deck and rolled through an open hatchway. Sera fell to her side and kicked at Rebecca's knees as the troopers unloaded their clips into the corridor. They weren't the ship-friendly pulse rifles that Sera's crew held. These were full power beam weapons. Sera cringed as she thought of the holes their shots must be tearing through her *Sabrina*. If it weren't for the heavy shielding around the engines, their beams would have punched clear through the ship.

Rebecca crashed to the ground, and Sera gained a pyrrhic sense of satisfaction that her bucket of bolts ship dirtied the other woman's shiny black skinsuit. Rebecca locked eyes with Sera and grinned. Sera looked up just in time to see one of the troopers smash the butt of his weapon into her face.

She fell back and watched the world slowly fade from view. The sounds of weapon fire tearing her ship to shreds took a bit longer to leave her hearing.

LOSS

STELLAR DATE: 07.09.8927 (Adjusted Years)
LOCATION: *Sabrina*, Interstellar Space
REGION: Galactic South of Trio Prime, Silstrand Alliance Space

Cargo ducked back behind the freight container as the beam fire continued to flash overhead. Sera and he had suspected the possibility of an altercation with Kade, and this container had been left in the corridor for precisely the purpose it was now serving.

It contained a small shield generator, providing a secure shelter. The wall Thompson was using for cover wasn't faring as well, but so far the burly super had managed to avoid being hit.

Cargo accessed his Link and told the other two men to narrow their rifles' band and match frequencies. They'd take these goons out one at a time. On a three count, they all broke cover enough to get a clear shot and fired at the helmet of the leftmost trooper. The harmonious frequencies from the pulse rifles amplified one another and the tight beam focused the pulse wave to achieve lethal intensity.

Cargo noted with satisfaction that the trooper's faceplate cracked as the shots struck true and he slumped to the ground. At the same time, another of the Mark soldiers cracked his rifle against Sera's head and he saw the captain slump to the decking, unconscious.

"Mother fuckers!" Thompson cried out as he was forced to duck back behind the bulkhead for cover. "They hit the capt'n."

This wasn't good. *Sabrina* couldn't take much more of this abuse. They had powerful exterior shields, but on the inside, other than around the engines, there was no sectional shielding. Before too long, those beams were going to tear through something that responded badly to tearing.

Cargo contacted Cheeky over the Link. "Cheeky. Dump to FTL now!"

<What the hell is going on down there? It sounds like a fucking war!> the pilot responded.

<Just do it, we're going to be swimming in Mark soldiers if you don't.>

<But we're still at 0.15 c. I don't know what we'll hit if we enter the DL right now.>

<We're never gonna hit the DL again if you don't do it now.> Cargo wasn't in the mood to discussion. *<Do it now!>*

<All right! It's gonna take a minute.>

<Take less.> Cargo cut the connection.

He counted with his fingers to indicate when to make another timed shot at the two other men. On three, they broke cover again to fire on the enemy furthest to the right. Ready to make the shot, it took him a moment to grasp what was happening.

The fallen soldier was still on the deck and two others had taken positions within the airlock for cover. Past them, Rebecca was back aboard the *Vertigo* with the fourth armored figure hauling Sera's unconscious form into the other ship's airlock.

Cargo pointed to the man on the left of the airlock, so that they wouldn't chance hitting the captain, and they fired in unison once more. The man attempted to duck to the side, but he was flung against the outer hull as the shot clipped his shoulder.

At the far side of the umbilical, Sera had been pulled into the *Vertigo's* airlock and several more troopers were ready to step around her and join the assault on *Sabrina*.

Cargo called Cheeky over the link again. *<Any damn minute now!>*

<Hold on, in less than a sec,> came the pilot's frantic response.

Two of the reinforcements were in the umbilical, and the pair in *Sabrina's* airlock were leveling their weapons to fire as Cargo motioned for Flaherty and Thompson to get down. The wrenching feeling from the shift to FTL washed through them, and, before the sensation had passed, Flaherty broke cover and leapt over the freight container.

He rushed down the corridor, firing his rifle on its highest setting while the remaining enemies were still off balance from the shift. The one who had already been clipped in the shoulder slumped to the deck after taking two more hits.

Flaherty got three more shots off at the other trooper before crashing in to him and slamming him against the bulkhead.

At that moment, the transfer to FTL completed and the airlock yawned open to the total void of the dark layer. Their ears popped as air rushed out into the space between *Sabrina* and its shielding. Beyond the shield, two soldiers who had been in the umbilical could be seen floating away in the void.

Flaherty pulled a beam rifle off one of the unconscious enemy soldiers and took careful aim before firing a shot through each of the drifting men's heads.

"Why'd the hell did you do that? You should have let the dogs suffer," Thompson said, as he approached the airlock.

Flaherty didn't look away from the void. "No one deserves that."

Cargo stepped beside Flaherty, silent, his breathing ragged. Then, with a curse, he slammed his fist into the bulkhead. The trooper who Flaherty had crashed into made a noise and stirred from the sound. Flaherty reached down, tore his helmet off and slammed his head against the hull.

The other soldier was also moving, his breathing sounded strained through his helmet and he was moving his head erratically. Cargo reached down and pulled his helmet off. The man looked haggard, his face a massive bruise from the effects off the pulse rifle. His eyes were bloodshot and barely open. He still managed to scream as Cargo fired the pulse rifle point blank into his left eye.

The trooper's head crumpled, but the scream didn't stop. That was a first, Cargo thought, until he realized the sound was coming from behind him. He and Flaherty turned to see Thompson holding his gun to Drind's head. Completely forgotten, the tech had been curled up on the floor.

"Want me to ice this bastard, too?" Thompson asked.

Hearing that, followed by seeing the cold eyes of Cargo and Flaherty upon him, Drind seemed to shrink inward even further. "Please, please don't do that to me, too. I'll do anything you want, please just don't kill me." He was sobbing now, his shoulders heaving and hands over his head.

"No. We've done enough killing for one day," Flaherty said.

"Stick him somewhere out of the way," Cargo agreed, and Thompson nodded wordlessly as he gestured with his rifle for Drind to stand up. They were all feeling the loss of the captain; it was best not to do anything else rash just yet.

"What's that sound?" Thompson asked.

They all stopped, Flaherty turning his head as he listened.

"It's not out there," Cargo said. "It's in here." He tapped his head.

"It's Sabrina," Flaherty replied.

"I'll be on the bridge," Cargo said as he took off at a run.

Less than a minute later Cargo stepped on to the bridge, and confronted the concerned faces of Tanis, Nance, and Cheeky.

"Something's wrong with Sabrina," Cheeky said. "She won't respond and is making this strange noise on the net, almost like a whimper."

Cargo looked around at the bridge's observation cameras. "It's okay Sabrina. We'll get her back."

"Get who back?" Cheeky asked, the color draining from her face.

"SHE'S GONE!" Sabrina screamed over both the Link, and the ship's audible systems. "I CAN'T HEAR HER ANYWHERE!"

"That's because we're in the dark layer and she's not with us," Cargo said with more compassion than he would have thought he could manage at the moment.

"She's what?" Cheeky screamed and Nance let out a gasp.

The wailing coming over the Link and audio was increasing in pitch; Cargo was starting to have trouble thinking with the sound slicing through him.

<Sabrina.> Flaherty's voice broadcasted onto the ship's net. <Listen to me, Sabrina,> he insisted, but the ship didn't stop her cry. <Remember. Remember what Sera said to you back when we first met and saved you from that place?>

The keening lessened and Sabrina spoke, <I do remember. I do.>

<Good,> Flaherty said. <Remember that. Remember the things she told you and you'll be ok.>

Sabrina made a noise that sounded uncannily like a sniffle. <Okay>

As the sound faded away, Cheeky fixed Cargo with a hard stare. "You told me to go to FTL. Why would you do that if they had the captain?"

"Because we'd be crawling with Rebecca's soldiers if we didn't get out of there."

"Rebecca?" Tanis asked. "What happened to Kade?"

"Rebecca killed him."

"She what?" Cheeky yelled and leapt back to her console. "Kade's one thing, but Rebecca *hates* Sera. She'll kill her! I'm pulling us out and getting back there right now!"

"You'll do no such thing; they'd waste us in a second," Cargo said, his trademark calm becoming ragged.

Cheeky couldn't speak, for a moment she just stared at her controls and then let loose a sob.

Tanis knelt down beside her and stroked her hair. "What do you propose?" she asked her eyes hard as she looked up at Cargo.

"We need to drop out of the DL, alter course and then get back in, or they'll get higher v and then skip along waiting for us. They know how fast we're going and can predict our course with ease. Figure out a new course on a different vector and get us on it. We need to get safe and then figure out what to do." Cargo said.

Tanis turned to her console and began pulling up plots while Cheeky looked up at Cargo.

"I abandoned her."

"You did as you were ordered. I am the one who abandoned her, and I intend to get her back."

"How are we going to do that?"

"We've got that Drind guy. Since he was the big expert with the scan and nav, I'm betting he'll know where they'll go with her."

They all clung to that hope as Cheeky and Tanis worked out a new vector and effected the transition to regular space. Cheeky quickly altered course and dropped back into FTL. Scan didn't pick up any of Kade's ships when they were in regular space, though that didn't mean there weren't any sensor arrays nearby relaying information. They made two additional course alterations before they began to feel comfortable.

With Sabrina monitoring the bridge, everyone met in the galley to work out what they hoped would be their plan to rescue the captain.

"What is our damage report?" Cargo asked once the coffee had been poured. No one wanted to talk about their missing captain just yet.

"Not much," Thompson replied. "The meatheads hit a few power couplings, but secondaries re-routed. Lucky they didn't hit those, too, or we would have disintegrated when we tried to go into the DL. Most blasts hit engine shielding, which held without a problem."

"Hit a return flow pipe on an enviro system," Nance added. A return flow pipe was a nice way to say sewage. "It was clear at the time, but no one use the cargo deck's port-side head till I fix it or you get to clean up the mess."

"Repair time?" Cargo asked.

"Not long."

Cargo was silent a moment, but he couldn't withhold the details from the crew. They needed to know. "Kade had fallen for our little ruse. Rebecca hadn't. She pulled a blaster on the captain and then Thompson, Flaherty, and I showed up with the pulse rifles, and we told her to stand down. Kade was on our side and told her to back off, as well. So, Rebecca turned the gun on him and took the top of his head off."

Sabrina was an on-the-fringe sort of freighter, running a bit of this and that, things she probably shouldn't. They'd even gotten in a few dockside shootouts in some seedier stations on the edge of nowhere, but never had anyone died on her decks. Everyone was stunned to silence.

"Great, dead people," Nance exclaimed. "I'm not cleaning that shit up!"

"Don't worry about it. We'll just shift the atmo shield in a few feet and let the void take it all. Lock's still open anyway," Thompson said.

"Noticed we blew out some air," Nance sighed. "I'll handle all that. It's what I get paid the big bucks for. Do we want to keep anything as evidence? Isn't there a bounty out on Kade?"

"Yeah, it's some damn serious cred, too," Cheeky said. "Maybe we could use the money to buy the captain back."

Thompson's expression was dark and he cast a glance at Tanis before he spoke. "I told the captain this was a bad idea. We should consider just turning her over in a trade. Be nice and fast." Tanis's expression grew cold as he spoke, but she didn't reply.

Cargo ignored Thompson's statement. "If we turn in Kade's body, we may have to answer some tricky questions about how we got it. Captain may be up to that sort of fast-talking, but I don't know if I could handle it. Freeze it for now and toss the goons. We'll use it later."

"I guess my suggestion is out," Thompson said sourly.

Flaherty leaned forward as he reached for a plum in the fruit bowl. "Sera made it clear that we don't trade in human cargo. She decided not to give Tanis over to them. I think we should respect her decision."

Everyone nodded in agreement, though some were more reluctant than others.

Thompson let out a sigh and leaned back with his arms crossed. "Whatever."

Cargo looked at Thompson for a moment, wondering what trouble the man would cause. "We do have one piece of good news. We got their tech and one of their goons," he paused as Flaherty shook his head slowly. "OK, so just their tech. I'm betting that he can tell us what we need to know about where Rebecca will have taken the captain. Who wants in on having a little talk with him?"

Every hand shot up, even Tanis's. "Okay, it's gonna be me and…Thompson. We'll get answers out of him."

"He'll be pissing himself in ten minutes," Thompson said.

"No good, Cargo," Flaherty said. "He watched you kill that pirate. You'd scare him too much for him to talk."

"Let me in on it," Cheeky said. "I'll get him talking."

"You're not exactly intimidating," Nance shook her head.

"I have some pretty intimidating outfits."

"Never know, he may go for that sort of thing," Thompson chuckled, most likely trying to visualize Cheeky in one of those outfits.

Cheeky pouted. "True…haven't met a guy yet that didn't seem to enjoy my dom routine, no matter how much I hurt him."

"I'll do it," Tanis said, unflinching as every eye turned to her.

"Why should you do it, you're as much a part of the problem as that Drind guy," Nance said as she looked around the table. "Thompson has a point. Don't you think that Sera may have changed her mind, now that she's been captured? We all know how much Rebecca hates her."

Thompson nodded his agreement and cast Nance a small smile for her support.

Cheeky's face was twisted in an uncomfortable grimace. "Part of me wants to try it; it's the quick and easy fix. But, I don't think it's ethical. Besides, like you said, Rebecca has always really hated Sera, but by extension *Sabrina,* and all of us."

"You're one to talk about ethical." Thompson said with an unkind edge to his voice.

Cheeky flushed. "You wouldn't understand why I do the things I do. To you it's all just raw sex. Sure, some of it is, but there's more to it than that."

"Cheeky's sexual proclivities aren't the issue here," Flaherty said, his voice toneless and level. The look in his eye sent shivers down everyone's spine. "Stay on topic."

"You don't have to like me," Tanis said. "You don't have to like why I'm here or why people are killing and dying to get me. Trust me; I like it just as little as you. You may have had a bad year or two in your lives, but I've had a bad century or two. It sucks. But all recriminations and whining aside, I've had training in this sort of thing. I've commanded units that had to get information in pretty short order before."

"So you tortured people for it?" Nance asked.

Tanis didn't reply for a long moment. "Yes."

Strangely, it seemed to be the right answer.

Cargo steepled his fingers, "Okay, then. Tanis you do the talking, and Thompson will do the intimidating. The rest of us will watch over the Link."

"Good, I'll make sure you don't try anything funny," Thompson said.

"What 'funny things' would I try?" Tanis was clearly growing tired of Thompson's attitude.

"Whatever pain in the asses did five thousand years ago," Thompson said.

Tanis sighed and followed Thompson down to the hold where they had dumped the tech. He unlocked the door, but before they stepped inside, put his arm across the entrance.

"You may think you're all special and hot shit, but if I even get an inkling that what you're telling us to do will harm Sera, I'll kill you myself."

Tanis didn't flinch as she stared the large man down. She was going to reciprocate the threat, but then stopped herself. "I promise you, that won't happen."

She pushed his arm out of the way and stepped inside. Drind was sitting propped against a crate. A sack was over his head and his hands were bound behind his back. The sack wasn't tied on; Drind just hadn't tried to get it off.

Tanis had found him to be a nice, if somewhat shy, man when he reviewed their logs and scan data on the bridge. She knew how he must be feeling, but pushed it from her mind. Rescuing Sera was the best way to get back to the *Intrepid*—though simply commandeering the ship had crossed her mind more than once. But Sera had saved her; she wouldn't repay that with treachery.

Crouching in front of him, she snatched the sack from his head, then grabbed his hair in one swift motion. He tried to scramble back from her, his eyes closed while she pulled his head back.

"Look at me!"

Startled to hear a woman's voice his eyes opened and latched onto Tanis like a drowning man.

"Rachel! You've got to help me; they're going to kill me."

She doubted Drind had many friends in Kade's—now Rebecca's—organization. Being the tech on a ship full of pirates probably was a tough job.

<I don't know how you can do this sort of thing, he's pathetic,> Angela said.

<Occupational hazard,> Tanis replied with a sigh.

<You could go easy on him,> Angela's voice had an edge of pleading to it. She had never been squeamish during torture before.

<I will, but if I don't do this a certain way, Thompson will kick me out and do it his way.>

During her chat with Angela, Drind came to the realization that it was Tanis who was pulling his head back at an extreme angle and he shrunk inward.

"Please don't hurt me," he whimpered.

Tanis ignored his entreaty and asked angrily, "Why did you kidnap Captain Sera?"

His shock was plain and denial strong. "What? I didn't do that. That psycho Rebecca did. She blew Kade's head off! I didn't have anything to do with it." He was beginning to shake uncontrollably; Tanis decided to back off a bit or she'd have to conduct the rest of the interrogation over the smell of urine.

"Please don't kill me, too," his voice was little more than a whisper.

Tanis let go of his head. "So you didn't know what she had in mind?"

"No! She didn't want me to come, told Kade to just take the ship by force and find the container they wanted. Honest, I didn't want to come! Staying far away from her is the best way to live a longer life."

Tanis stood and paced back and forth in front of him. She allowed her expression to soften somewhat and glanced at Thompson who didn't look the least bit convinced, though the look he cast her contained a small hint of appreciation. Good. She paused her pacing for a moment.

"And you didn't know what Rebecca had planned? The kidnapping or killing Kade?"

"No, I swear it!"

Tanis grunted and paced a few more times, then turned back to the poor man. "I may believe you, but I'm still having reservations. Some of the other guys," she jerked a thumb back at Thompson, "aren't as convinced. You better sweeten the pot with something substantial or they may decide that they're through with my soft talking."

Drind hung his head like a man who had given up hope for his life.

<Oops, a bit too thick there,> Angela said.

<Just a smidge.>

He was supposed to think *she* was his hope. Tanis crouched down in front of him and resisted the urge to cup his chin in her hand to raise his face up.

"Hey, they're not banging down the door yet. Why don't you tell me what you know and I'll keep you safe." Now she was going too far the other way, but this poor guy wasn't going to notice. She was out of practice, but keeping up her skill at interrogation wasn't on the top of her list of abilities to refine. "What was in the container that Padre's men took?"

Drind raised his head, a bit of hopefulness in his eyes. "I don't know, but it seemed pretty valuable. Not the 'racing hound' they told you it was; that much is for sure."

"Rebecca and Kade never talked about what it was?"

"I overheard an argument about it, and some of the other guys did too. They seemed to be arguing about what to do with it. A couple of times I swore Kade slipped and called it a 'her', but I wasn't listening too closely, that doesn't pay on the *Vertigo*."

"Is that where you're stationed? On the *Vertigo*?"

"Sometimes." Drind was starting to warm up now, hopeful that he could spill his guts and save his life. "I'm back at HQ a lot, too. Depends where they need me."

"Kade had an HQ?" Somehow, his appearance had caused Tanis to think of him as nothing but a guy with a few ships causing trouble.

"Of course, haven't you been there? I mean you're one of his ships."

"We aren't that scum's ship," Thompson growled.

Drind lowered his head closed his eyes—Tanis smiled inwardly. Thompson was playing along really well. Either that or it was just his natural disposition. It worked to her advantage though—it was best not to let Drind get too comfortable. If he did, he'd start thinking he could turn things to his advantage.

"Is that where Rebecca will take Sera? Back to HQ?" Tanis asked.

"Probably. The *Prowler* was at the rendezvous, too, lying dark out of scan range. I imagine she'll have them look for you while she goes back there."

"How many ships does The Mark have, anyway?" Tanis asked, wondering about additional complications.

"We'll, I'm not sure since he said this was his ship, too. Ships that I know he owns for sure…about four hundred; dozens of others that at least do regular business with him."

"And where is this HQ that Rebecca will be going back to?"

Drind didn't reply right away, but his eyes darted to Thompson's cold stare and flexing fists, then back to Tanis. She made her face look as open and trusting as possible.

"It's hidden really well. It's impossible to find."

"But you know where it is, right?" Tanis prompted him.

"Sure, I know the coordinates. It's actually not too far from here."

"What's the name of the system?" Tanis asked.

"Oh, it's not in any system," Drind spoke as if he was afraid unseen enemies would kill him. "It's in the dark layer."

Tanis managed to get the coordinates to the station after that, but Drind warned her that there were sensors and defensive turrets in both the DL and real space. She concluded the interrogation shortly after, with the promise that she would see about getting Drind more comfortable quarters.

The crew met in the galley again, their faces somber as they pondered the implications of this information.

"How do they even dock in the DL?" Thompson broke the silence.

"Very carefully, I'd bet," Cheeky said with noticeable appreciation in her voice.

The dark layer was just that, very dark. Nothing emitted light at all. It made the interstellar void look like a sunny afternoon. The only natural emissions of any sort were gravitational waves, which was how ships knew when to drop out of the DL and back into real space. Ships could emit light, but the gravitational waves dispersed that light very quickly.

<Perhaps they have their station anchored to some dark matter,> Sabrina offered, much calmer now that she knew where Sera was. *<Then they could latch onto ships and pull them in.>*

"Even if we believe him that this HQ of his is in the dark layer, and even if we find out that there is a back door, what are we going to do? Just march in there and demand Sera back?" Nance asked.

"We still have Plan B," Thompson looked at Tanis.

"Why don't we move our friend Drind to some better quarters and see if we can't convince him to start spilling specifics about this place?" Tanis said, ignoring Thompson. "Once we're better informed, we should be able to determine if his story is bunk. While we're at it, we may as well start plotting a course toward the general vicinity of the place, in case we do decide to all turn kamikaze."

"Do we have that kind of time?" Thompson asked, his face turning red. "They could be killing Sera right now while we sit around and debate what to do."

"Their base is some ways out into interstellar space on the core-ward side of the Silstrand Alliance." Cheeky provided a holo showing its relative position. "It'll take them a while to get there."

"Which is great if she's still alive, not so great if she's already dead," Nance said.

"She's still alive," Flaherty said flatly.

"How do you know that?" Cargo asked.

"Just listen to Tanis! She's our best bet to get Sera back," Flaherty growled at the rest of the crew.

No one knew what to say in response and Tanis looked into the stoic man's eyes for a long moment. His connection with Sera had to be older than their time on this ship. He owed her something, had some deep obligation to her.

<*Curiouser and curiouser,*> she said to Angela.

THE BEST LAID PLANS

STELLAR DATE: 07.13.8927 (Adjusted Years)
LOCATION: The Mark's Dark Layer Station
REGION: Unclaimed Interstellar Space, Core-Ward of Silstrand Alliance

Sera returned to consciousness in fits and starts. Her head felt like it had spent some time in the fusion reaction chamber…or a week on the bottle. Rather than alert anyone nearby to her conscious state, she kept her eyes closed and took mental stock of her surroundings and where her body lay.

First discovery made: she was lying down. Whatever she was on was padded, at least a little. She could hear the soft sound of air circulation, but no reactor or engine noise. She was either on a station or planet-side. Sera curled her fingers and then her toes. No apparent spinal damage, extremities seemed okay. Next, she tried to lift her arms and found she couldn't.

Tugging gently, Sera determined she was strapped down. Testing various points, she determined that every part of her was thoroughly restrained. Not tightly, but very firmly. Nothing seemed to be holding her head down. Sera rotated her neck left and right with no problem other than increased throbbing between her ears. Shifting in her bonds also confirmed a previous suspicion: she was completely naked.

<How do I get into these situations?> Sera asked.

<The root of it is probably not taking your father's advice,> Helen replied.

Sera responded by having her avatar stick her tongue out at Helen's ephemeral mental figure.

<Ironically, we're finally where all this was supposed to lead,> Sera observed.

<I did notice that myself. Years of work and all you had to do was lose important cargo to get to The Mark's HQ.>

<I'm going to make a note of that for the next time I decide to infiltrate a pirate's lair,> Sera said with a chuckle.

<Well, I wouldn't call this 'infiltration',> Helen laughed.

<True, there is the pesky 'being strapped to a table' issue, plus the upcoming torture to deal with,> Sera admitted.

<Have you been able to get any nano out for a look-see?>

<I've tried, but there's a very strong ES field that keeps frying them.>

She could tell that the room she was in wasn't too bright or she'd see the light through her eyelids. Cracking them, Sera recognized her surroundings as a medical bay.

It seemed standard, if somewhat archaic. There were actually scalpels and other cutting tools here. Sera made a mental correction. Either she was in the medical bay of a sadistic doctor, or one that doubled as a torture facility. Or maybe the medical bay of a sadist doctor that also did the torture. None were promising prospects.

The things she had been trying not to think of raced through Sera's mind. Where was *Sabrina*? Was her crew okay? Did they have Tanis? Only by pure force of will, and the knowledge she had gotten out of equally sticky situations, did Sera manage to calm herself.

Though the lighting was dim, she could tell by the structure of the walls, deck, and ceiling that this was a station of some sort—roomier than a ship, but not as liberal with space as a planetary facility. As she surveyed her surroundings, the door opened and Rebecca entered. Why was Sera not surprised?

Her captor wore a hazsuit with the helmet off. Sera had a flash of jealousy for how the tight suit showed off what was an amazing figure. Lower g certainly was kind to large-breasted women.

"What's with the suit Rebecca? Scared of little ol' me?"

Rebecca's smile was anything but pleasant. "Sensibly cautious. You'd be surprised at how many twitchy freighter captains put little surprises in their blood for people who start cutting into them. I've learned to be cautious."

Sera cursed herself. That would have been a great idea. Why had she never thought of it? "So what's the drill here? You ask questions, I pretend I don't even know what year it is, you use some of your tools, get no further, and then we call it a day? I'll tell you what. I'll save you the trouble. I don't know squat, go away."

"Don't you want to know about your crew?" Rebecca asked. "You'll surely want to know what I've already done to them."

Sera didn't fall for it. While she respected their courage and skill, she knew that at least one or two of them would have cracked under the type of questioning Rebecca was sure to use. If her crew had been captured, Rebecca would already know that 'Rachel' was the missing cargo, and Tanis would be the one strapped to the table.

Not that she was going to let Rebecca in on that reasoning. She struggled in her bonds. "What have you done to them?"

"Nothing permanent…yet." She let the word hang in the silence between them.

"Look, we don't have that stupid container. You've got Kade's organization now, what more do you want from me?"

Rebecca smiled again, this time it was more predatory. "I really must thank you for that; this really did work to my advantage. I managed to get Kade out of the way, *and* pin it on you and your crew. With all the other senior captains away on raids, I get to solidify my position. I couldn't have asked for a better turn of events."

Sera groaned inwardly. Was this woman going to gloat all day or just get on with the torture?

Rebecca continued unabated. "But that stupid container, as you call it, is worth more than all of this," the obligatory hand wave indicated her surroundings. "You are going to tell me where it is. That much is certain."

"If Padre has it, how am I going to tell you where it is?"

"We won't worry about that today. Today I'm just going to get to know you a bit better." Rebecca walked leisurely toward a cart with some of the more barbaric instruments on it. "If one is careful, one can put quite a few holes in a human being and neither cause them to die, nor even fall unconscious. Let's see how many we can make in you."

Sera gritted her teeth and prayed to whatever gods were listening for strength. Her prayers were granted. She had the strength to both scream and cry at the same time for hours.

OF MICE AND MEN

STELLAR DATE: 07.14.8927 (Adjusted Years)
LOCATION: *Sabrina*, Interstellar Dark Layer
REGION: Silstrand Alliance Space, Core-Ward of Silstrand Prime

"There's some disbelief regarding your statement that your HQ is in the DL," Tanis said as she sat with Drind in the cramped cabin they had given him. She had been working on earning his trust over the intervening days and was now cross-checking his earlier intel. "Since there is nothing to react against in the DL, there is no way to maneuver. How do you dock?"

Drind couldn't help smiling. "It's genius really. One of Kade's engineers just happened to spot this relatively small blob of dark matter that isn't moving, well not much. He did some testing and found that with the right force, a gravity drive can tether to the dark matter and anchor the station. They use gravity fields to pull ships in for docking. There's a probe in regular space that has the current coordinates of the HQ and ships simply transition to the DL at that point with zero relative motion."

Tanis mulled it over. That aligned with what Sabrina and Cheeky had suspected.

"So, how do you suggest that we drop in to make our rescue run?"

Drind's face drained of color. "You can't do that! HQ is impregnable." He looked around as if he could determine the ship's course or maybe some way off it. "You can let me out next stop if that's your plan. I may be somewhat grateful for you getting me out of that mess. But not that grateful."

"You don't really think we'd abandon Sera, do you?" she asked.

"You won't be abandoning her; she's already dead."

Tanis had considered it—heck, everyone on the ship had. The consensus was that, although she may be a bit worse for wear, Sera's knowledge was simply far too valuable to kill her. If Tanis was free, Sera was alive.

"She's not dead," Tanis said.

Drind wasn't dumb. Tanis had noticed that during her first encounter with him, as he looked over her scan logs on the bridge. Something seemed to click in his mind and he suddenly sat back on the bunk.

"It's you."

"It's me what?" Tanis asked, feigning confusion.

"You're what Kade was looking for. You're what was in that container."

"I have to admit, I'm impressed," Tanis nodded. "How did you figure it out?"

"Well, it wasn't a dog, that much was obvious. But this ship doesn't have the ability to tell a dog's bio signature from a human's when in cryostasis, so unless they popped it open, the fiction would have held." He looked puzzled for a moment. "Why did they open it?"

Tanis smiled. "They got away at Trio without being boarded, and were interested in knowing what they'd risked their lives for."

Drind looked amazed. "They actually escaped Padre's guys in Trio? How much of the scan was faked?"

"Not much, just the part where the ship decelerated after the RM was fired. In reality, they twitched at the last moment and made it to FTL with half a second to spare."

"Holy shit," Drind whistled. "That captain Sera has quite the pair."

"I'm told it was one heck of a ride."

"I'm beginning to understand part of why they want to rescue her," he snorted. "Not that I think it's sane. Why are you in on this, anyway?"

"She saved me, I owe her the favor. Besides, Sera seems like a decent sort."

Tanis finished the statement as Cargo opened the door to the room.

"Don't let her hear you say that," he said. "It would ruin the fiction she likes to portray." Drind noticeably pulled away, sidling against the bulkhead. The reaction appeared to annoy Cargo. "Would you cut that out, I'm not going to hurt you."

Their reluctant castoff straightened. A bit.

"So what's it going to be? Going to tell us what you know or do we ship you somewhere in cryo so you can't rat us out?"

"That's a shitty choice," Drind muttered.

"Better than sticking you in the middle of this if you don't want to be."

Drind looked as if he had an acerbic reply ready, but he bit it back. Cargo had a point.

"Isn't there anything you can think of that would help us?" Tanis asked. "We've been more than kind to you, and we'll be taking down Rebecca, or at least taking her down a notch."

"You'd better take her all the way down," Drind looked deadly serious. "If you don't, there will be no safe place for you this side of Sol."

"There's still the bounty on Kade that every system for ten parsecs is offering. We could get that money and arm up to take them down," Cargo said.

"It would take a lot more money than that," Drind said. "You'd still need some way to get in. Missiles may not work well in the DL, but HQ has a reactor that can keep its lasers slicing and dicing for hours."

Tanis snapped her fingers. "That's it. We need an army and an in. We'll get both." She turned to Cargo. "We need to set a course for the closest star system that has a stable government." She wasn't sure if stability was the norm here or not, but it didn't hurt to be specific.

She turned to Drind. "Kade must have had ships that were not generally known to be his, that dock both at system stations and at his HQ."

He nodded. "There are a few."

"Do you know their normal ports of call?"

"Not even remotely. Information like that wasn't exactly bandied about."

Tanis kept thinking aloud. "What about places where his pirate ships would frequently be lying in wait?"

Drind was silent for a moment as he thought. "It is pretty common for a ship to hang in the outskirts of the Big OJ looking for traders stopping through for fueling."

"Big OJ?"

"Oh, Gedri. The crews back at HQ call it the Big OJ...it's a really damn orange star."

"What's with all the traffic there?" Tanis asked.

"Like he said," Cargo gestured at Drind, "the system is rife with helium for fusion, and there are a few outfits that have antimatter production sites. A lot of ships running low will coast into the system with their engines off."

"Yeah, some will coast in from a fair ways out. Makes for good pickings," Drind added.

Tanis had a few questions about that but didn't want to voice them in front of Drind; it may give away her lack of knowledge regarding the ninth millennium. They thanked Drind for his time and left his cabin for the galley where the rest of the crew had gathered as they watched the conversation.

"Why do ships drop out of the DL and coast in? Wouldn't it be better to stay shifted to get in faster and safer?" Tanis asked.

"Takes power to stay shifted in the DL. People often will drop out early and coast into a system to save money," Cheeky replied with a shrug.

"I guess that makes sense. Sounds like we've got the makings of a plan," Tanis said while pouring a cup of coffee. "We coast into the Big OJ and wait to get paid a visit from one of The Mark's pirate ships. We take their ship and hop on back to the ol' HQ where we get Sera back."

Cargo shook his head. "Us and what army?"

"Sounds like a good way to get ourselves killed," Thompson added.

Tanis smiled. "I've been doing a bit of research on the ninth millennium. Sera said things were different, but I really didn't expect so much to be lost. She was right about FTL spelling the end of human advancement," Tanis said and held out her right arm and pulled back her sleeve.

What looked like skin changed its appearance to metallic silver, the effect racing all the way down her arm. She quickly downed her coffee and held the cup by its side.

To everyone's astonishment the cup dissolved into the palm of her right hand and a blue light emitted from her right forearm. Tanis held her left hand out to catch the object materializing there. It was a small ceramic handgun. Tanis put it down on the galley table while everyone stared open mouthed.

"I guess you don't see nano like this much these days."

Cargo looked Tanis up and down and then glanced at Nance. "She is human, right?"

"She was back when she was on the med slab." Nance hadn't taken her eyes from Tanis. "Though we could tell she had some pretty advanced tech in her."

"Unless we're gonna take out a pirate ship with ceramic pistols, you'd better have some better tricks up your sleeve...figuratively speaking," Cargo said. "Have you ever been in a battle for your life?"

"I didn't get my rank sitting on my duff."

Tanis's statement was met with blank stares.

"I'm a TSF major, remember?"

"That doesn't really mean a lot to us," Nance said with a shrug. "A lot of military types get promoted without ever seeing combat."

"Yes, I've seen combat," Tanis sighed. "I've fought planet-side, station-side and ship to ship. I've put a lot of holes in a lot of people. Satisfied?" If they only knew what she had done to get this far.

"Great, you can shoot people," Thompson said. "Is that the extent of your plan for saving Sera?"

"Well, I obviously can't take on a pirate ship by myself, and, since we need it intact, we have to board it, or be boarded by them. I'd prefer to be on the side doing the boarding. First thing we need to do is get some big guns or at least some raw materials so we can make some big guns. What's the closest port of call?"

Thompson stood up and looked them all over. "This is total bullshit. You guys can take orders from her; I'm going to go clean up the mess one of those containers made when it got shot."

No one said anything for a minute after he left and then Cargo shrugged. "Cheeky, what's nearest?"

She looked at him and then shrugged as well. "Closest system is Silstrand. They've got a number of stations insystem we can dock at. There's an independent mining platform out in their EK belt that has an arms dealer or two on it. How we paying for these guns anyway?"

Tanis smiled. "I'm betting I have some nano that could be worth a bit."

* * * * *

Rebecca was no slouch—a real pro when it came to making people suffer.

Sera hurt in places she didn't even know could hurt. She desperately wished she could escape her body. She'd heard of out of body experiences; maybe she could have one if she tried hard enough.

Rebecca had asked very few questions while she did her work. She said she just wanted to get to know Sera's body a bit better. Needles seemed to be her specialty. Rebecca had them in varying sizes and could put a truly astounding number of them into a person's flesh. One had started out the size of a sliver and grew to well over a centimeter in diameter. Rebecca had put that one through a lot of things.

After Rebecca had her fill and left, a med team came in and cleaned Sera up. They didn't make anything hurt less, more actually, as they cauterized the wounds to staunch the bleeding and put her on an IV to replenish the fluids she'd lost.

Sera supposed it was one way to pass the day.

A better way was working on her escape. While Rebecca had been busy at her trade, Sera had been busy at hers—namely plotting Rebecca's death. During the session, Sera had managed to pull a needle from her own thigh and slip it past her palm into her wrist where the strap held her arm down. Now that she was alone, she slipped the needle from her skin and began worrying its tip along the strap.

While under Rebecca's not-so-tender ministrations, Sera had learned why there was no strap holding her head down: her torturer liked it when Sera pulled her head up or tilted it back to let out a really good scream. It worked to her advantage now as she twisted to see the needle tip doing its work. The strap seemed to be of the same material as a safety harness; there was a section where it had been sewn together and that was what she focused on.

The material held up well and Sera found progress to be slow. She walked a careful balance between not moving enough to lose her grip on the needle and have it fling across the room, but still fast enough to get free before another session with Madam Pain.

The hours ticked by as she picked at the stitches. One by one, they came free and Sera allowed herself to feel a glimmer of hope. Then, with a snap that did send the needle flying, the strap gave way. Sera didn't move, but waited to see if the sudden twitch of her arm had been noticed by whoever may or may not be watching the cameras. After several minutes, nothing happened and Sera forced her breathing to slow.

Without any quick movements, she slid her right arm across her body and undid the strap across her chest and from her left wrist. Then, with great care, she slowly shifted her hand back to her right side and slipped it into the loop of the strap.

Sera tried to put her mind at rest. She was tired and had lost a lot of blood. Her best bet would be to get a good night's sleep and use the first advantage that came her way tomorrow. She had no illusions about trying to use a med tech as a hostage; Rebecca would gun her own people down in a heartbeat. She needed to get the queen bitch herself if she wanted to get out of here alive.

SILSTRAND

STELLAR DATE: 07.15.8927 (Adjusted Years)
LOCATION: *Sabrina*, Silstrand Scattered Disk
REGION: Silstrand System, Silstrand Alliance Space

Silstrand was a heavily settled system, boasting fourteen major planets, six of them being rocky worlds rich with minerals. Methane and hydrogen mining facilities hovered around three of the gas giants. Stellar traffic was heavy, and an AI operating a beacon demanded *Sabrina's* identification and their port of call within half an hour of dropping out of FTL.

Tanis was on comm and relayed that they were bound for the PeterSil EK mining platform. Stellar control informed them that the PS EK platform was currently on the far side of the system from *Sabrina's* current position. They were given a deceleration vector and told to send a message to the PS EK platform informing them of their incoming vector and time of arrival.

"Bossy sorts here," Tanis muttered as she passed the plot to Cheeky's console and sent the required message to the mining platform.

Cheeky heard her comment and smiled. "Yeah, but the men really like a stern woman. Good times to be had at the main trading station off the fourth gas giant."

"Been through here often?" Tanis asked. The whole idea of interstellar trade by small freighters was still very fascinating to her.

"A few times. Some on *Sabrina,* some on other ships I've piloted. They have three TPs that have amazing diversity and some great pleasure resorts."

"TPs?"

"Means terraformed or terrestrial planets," Cargo supplied from the command chair. "FGT had a ball with this place. It already had one planet in the habitable zone, so while they got it all watered up and ready for life they decided to hang out and make antimatter.

"That was around when gravity tech had improved and AP drives became the rage. They built a massive particle accelerator to produce the antimatter and then left it here. It's still going strong, a good four thousand years later.

"I guess their tug pilots got bored while everyone else had something to do, so they hauled another planet into the habitable zone and then did something to one of the big gassies in the outer system to heat it up. Thing is just about a brown dwarf now. One of the other gassies had a slightly sub-terra sized moon around it, so they hauled it over to their toasty gas giant and set it in orbit."

Tanis laughed. "Toasty gassie? I bet a thousand astronomers cringe every time you talk."

Cargo chuckled. "I'd consider that a compliment."

"Did they leave messages behind so we know what they did?" Tanis asked.

"The astronomers?"

"No, the FGT," Tanis replied seriously before realizing that Cargo was joking.

He chuckled before replying. "Sometimes. There has been contact with them here and there. If you can believe it, some of them still have their original crews."

"You're kidding."

"Nope, some of those people left Earth over six thousand years ago and they're still out there making worlds."

Tanis had heard that was the case in the forty-second century, as well—even then it had seemed far-fetched. She had always suspected that it was some sort of FTG propaganda.

"They can't have lived that long by stasis alone. They have to be doing something else; it still takes hundreds of years to terraform a world," Tanis said with a frown.

"Your guess is as good as anyone else's. After the *Oregon* incident, they don't have much to do with the rest of humanity anymore," Cargo replied

"What happened there?"

"Everyone believes that the FGT has tech everyone else has only dreamed of—kinda like you. It's said they have the power to move stars," Cheeky said from the pilot's chair. "It was only a matter of time before someone decided to take a fleet around hunting for them. They found a worldship, the *Oregon*, terraforming a system, and tried to take it by force. Things didn't go as planned and the *Oregon* was destroyed. Some of their smaller ships got away and word spread amongst the FGT. No one has had direct contact with them in millennia now."

"They're still out there though, right?" Tanis really hoped they were, she was counting on getting in touch with them to secure a new colony world.

"Yeah," Cargo's voice was low and serious. "Sometimes people stumble upon a terraformed world that's just waiting to be discovered. Sometimes certain systems get messages about a new world they can expand to. There are even rumors that the FGT has agents scattered throughout space, shaping the course of humanity."

Tanis stared at Cargo, attempting to keep a straight face. She covered her mouth, her eyes sparkling. "You could host a cast on evil government plots," she began to laugh.

Cheeky joined in the laughter. "So dark and mysterious."

Cargo shrugged. "Mock me if you want, but there are a lot of people who suspect it."

Tanis looked over the system on the main holo tank. God complexes and guiding humanity aside, the FGT did amazing work. The Silstrand system gleamed off their port side as they passed over the stellar plane. Stations and stellar transports could be seen, reflecting their star's light in the dark. The twinkle of fusion drives sparkled near one of the rocky inner planets, indicating heavy mining.

The TPs, as Cargo called them, were near each other and *Sabrina* passed within half an AU of each. They were sparking blue-green on the unmagnified screen. Under magnification they showed to be amazing planets, both sporting several elevators connected to planetary rings.

"Silstrand seems to do pretty well for itself," Tanis observed.

"It's the seat of the Silstrand Alliance's government," Cargo supplied. "They control most of this star cluster."

"They a friendly sort?"

"Democracy of sorts. Big on trade, though, so freighters are never turned away."

Tanis asked a few questions about the types of governments found across the stars as *Sabrina* shed velocity across the system. She could read about them in the databases, but Cargo had an interesting viewpoint to share on each.

He told tales of dictatorships, kingdoms, democracies, and oligarchies for hours. Eventually, shift changed and Tanis reluctantly begged off the conversation to get some sleep. Tomorrow they would dock at the mining platform and she'd have a show to put on for a merchant or two.

RESIGNATION

STELLAR DATE: 07.15.8927 (Adjusted Years)
LOCATION: ISS *Andromeda*, 0.5LY Rim-Ward of Bollam's World
REGION: Bollam's World Federation Space

Joe paced across the *Andromeda's* main hanger bay where pieces of wreckage were being sorted. It had taken over a month to find the debris field from the *Intrepid's* collision with what turned out to be little more than a pebble, and several months more to collect all the pieces.

They were now laid out in a pattern matching their original location on the *Intrepid*.

Joe was amazed at how much damage the impact had done to the colony ship. Over two hundred meters of hull had been torn up by the impact, seven decks vented atmosphere, and one stasis chamber was destroyed.

And Tanis was lost.

He watched as the crew pulled the pieces off the last hauler. The pickings were getting slim and Joe didn't think they would find much more out there. Pieces of a lift were unloaded, followed by several chunks of bulkhead and a door.

Nothing that looked as though it came from an escape pod.

The ship's records showed Tanis making it to a pod and ejecting. As luck would have it, no other pods were damaged or ejected in the impact. That meant there was only one pod out there, and so far, no debris from a pod had been found.

It meant Tanis was alive.

The last pieces of ship were deposited on the deck and tagged. The technicians organizing the wreckage concurred that none of it was from an escape pod and Joe sighed with relief. He could finally report that Tanis was not here.

Not that Joe expected her to be. Tanis had survived too much to be killed by a pebble. Even if that pebble had been travelling at relativistic speeds.

<*Corsia,*> Joe contacted the *Andromeda's* AI. <*Send a message to the* Intrepid. *There is no sign of Tanis or her pod. I want permission to go insystem and see if I can find out what happened to her.*>

<*I'm on it, Joe.*>

He had known from the beginning that Tanis was not in the debris field, but with no signal from her pod, everyone assumed she was dead—her pod destroyed. So, he worked to rule that possibility out as quickly as possible.

Now there was no reason not to search for her in the neighboring star system.

That was going to be easier said than done. In the months since the collision, they had gathered intel from listening to broadcasts and data streams from the system they now knew to be 58 Eridani. The crew of the *Intrepid* knew they were in the nineteenth century, and it was nothing like what they would have expected.

Joe took his time going back to the bridge. The *Intrepid* was two light-hours away, and a response to his request would take some time. He was fairly certain he knew what all the various directors and secretaries would say. Abby would vote to leave Tanis, Earnest would likely abstain, Ouri and Brandt would vote to continue the search. Sanderson liked Tanis, but he would vote not to risk the ship to find her. The captain was a mystery; he would need to think of the ship first—it all depended on whether or not he thought Tanis was necessary for the ship's safety.

"Think it was the last haul?"

Joe turned to see Jessica walking toward him from the direction of the hangar.

"If I have my way it is. There's nothing bigger than dust left out there. It's time to stop wasting our time out here."

"Do you think she's in the Bollam's system?" Jessica asked after catching up with Joe.

Joe shook his head. "I don't know...but it's the best place to start. There was that strange ion trail near the pod's most likely trajectory. It could be that she was rescued."

"Or kidnapped. You know what Sanderson thinks."

"He's not the only one—it's pretty clear that we have vastly superior tech than pretty much everyone now."

"You think someone has her?" Jessica asked, her voice strained with worry.

Joe nodded. "I refuse to believe she's dead; if she were OK, she'd get in touch with us somehow. No, she is being held somewhere and getting into that system and checking their scan records is the first step."

Jessica took his hand. "I want you to know I'm with you. If we have to steal a pinnace, or even the whole damn *Intrepid,* we'll go find her."

Joe clasped his hands around hers, taking a moment to calm his emotions. "I know she means a lot to you, too. Your support means a lot."

"She gave me a chance when...she's my best friend, Joe," Jessica said with a tear slipping down her face. "I'm ready to kick ass clear across the galaxy if I have to."

"You're a true friend, Jessica." Joe embraced the lavender-skinned woman, thankful that she had come along on the *Andromeda.*

Four hours later, the response came in from Captain Andrews.

"I'm authorizing an excursion into Bollam's to gather intel and hunt for Tanis," the captain's face was sober; he seemed to have aged years over the past few months. "But Joe, I need you back here. We have to protect the *Intrepid* and you're second in fleet command right now. I'm sending Jessica to look for her. We'll talk more when you get back."

The *Andromeda's* bridge fell silent. The anger flowing from Joe was palpable and tension radiated through the air as everyone did their best to look busy.

"*Corsia,*" Joe said after a moment. "Tell Andrews that he has my resignation. I'll hitch a ride with Jessica."

Jessica rose from her station and approached Joe's chair.

"Joe, are you sure about this?" Jessica asked quietly, placing a hand on his shoulder.

He lowered his head and ran a hand through his hair. "You don't know what she means to me."

"I do know; how could I not know?" Jessica said softly. "I've been with you two for decades—and I know what it means to choose duty over your love's safety."

"That's just it, you don't know," Joe turned to look in her eyes, willing her to understand. "She's pregnant."

Shock registered across Jessica's face. "Tanis's...pregnant?"

Joe nodded. "She's held it internally in stasis for since before we got to The Kap—we were waiting to get to New Eden before carrying it to term."

"Corsia," Jessica addressed the ship's AI, while not braking eye contact with Joe. "Have the duty chief prep the pinnace for two, Joe is coming along."

A SURREPTITIOUS ESCAPE

STELLAR DATE: 07.16.8927 (Adjusted Years)
LOCATION: The Mark's Dark Layer Station
REGION: Unclaimed Interstellar Space, Core-Ward of Silstrand

Sera woke to the sounds of a med tech entering the room. While she hadn't allowed herself to fall into a very deep sleep, she did feel better. The tech busied himself at a counter across the room, organizing something out of Sera's view. Eventually, he turned and Sera saw a large needle in his hand.

"What do you intend to do with that?" she asked.

<Certainly not the time to get knocked out,> Helen sounded worried.

The tech jumped at the sound of her voice. "Um…I was going to give you this."

"I don't think so. I've had enough stuff stuck in me; I can do with one less needle, thanks."

The med-tech had a furtive look on his face as he glanced around. "It's for the pain, it'll make it better."

So that was it. Someone with a conscience couldn't sleep at night while Rebecca did her thing. So rather than really helping her, he planned to ease his personal concern a bit.

<He could be a genuinely good guy,> Helen said.

<A genuinely good guy would be loosening these straps. This guy just doesn't want to hear me scream,> Sera replied sourly.

"Thanks but no thanks. If you really wanted to help, you'd get me out of here."

"I would, but it's impossible. There's no way out of this place."

"Well, thanks for the un-help, but like I said, I'm all done being stuck with things."

"But it will make you feel better." His face crinkled in confusion. "She won't notice if you make sure to scream."

"I don't know if this is her plan or your independent idea, but that shot will cloud my mind and I may just give in to her. She's not torturing me just for fun, you know," Sera paused. "Though, I wouldn't put it past her to do that."

The man looked undecided and Sera gave him the sternest look she could muster. "Go away. I don't want your pseudo help and if you don't have the guts to do something constructive then I don't have time for you."

The med-tech seemed somewhat disturbed that he was being given orders by a woman strapped to a table—or at least a woman who appeared to be strapped to a table.

"Just go before she gets here," Sera sighed.

Without a word, the man returned to the counter where he had prepared the syringe. He emptied its contents, threw it in the disposal, and walked to the door. Before exiting, he gave Sera a long look and then slipped out.

<*You know, you could have convinced him to help you,*> Helen said. <*Your plan isn't so good that it's foolproof.*>

<*It's close enough. I can take Rebecca with one hand tied behind my back.*>

<*Or your legs to the table, as it turns out.*>

Rebecca came in less than a minute later, and Sera was surprised her torturer hadn't spotted the med-tech.

"Good morning, sunshine," Rebecca said with a smile. "I trust you slept uncomfortably?"

Sera didn't respond and just glared, willing Rebecca to step closer while she went on in standard torturer speak about how pleasant mutilating Sera would be. She wore her hazsuit but hadn't put on the mask yet.

Just a little closer.

Sera got her wish as Rebecca stepped right beside the table to admire her handiwork. She had just started a smart remark about how Sera's legs looked good covered in crusted, puss-filled holes when her words stopped with a strangled gasp.

Sera gripped Rebecca's throat with all her strength, and the other woman grasped at her arm, nails clawing at Sera's skin. She sat up and added her other hand, desperate not to be dislodged.

Rebecca appeared to gain a measure of control and her eyes narrowed a moment before she swung a fist into the side of Sera's head. She let out a grunt, but wasn't going to let this bitch get the better of her. Instead, she slammed the heel of her hand straight into Rebecca's face.

In hindsight, Sera considered that the move was perhaps a mistake. Blood poured from Rebecca's nose and her grip on the woman's neck slipped as the hot fluid ran over her hands. Sera dug her fingernails deep into the Rebecca's skin to maintain her hold.

Rebecca hit Sera twice more, and then began to try to push herself away from the table, to which Sera's legs were still strapped. Sera had enough; she shifted to the side, put her left hand on the back of Rebecca's head and slammed it down into the corner of the table. Her torturer fell to the ground unconscious.

<Told you I could take her,> Sera said to her AI.

<Hey, I was cheering for you the whole time, Didn't you hear me?>

<Not so much. I was busy, if you recall.>

Sera loosened the straps holding her thighs and ankles. She slid off the slab and hefted Rebecca's limp form onto the table. Blood gushed from the cut across her forehead and Sera ignored it. She quickly stripped off Rebecca's hazsuit and strapped her former captor in her place. The right wrist strap was useless, so Sera tied Rebecca's hands behind her back and then strapped her chest down tight to prevent any wriggle room.

With luck, no one paid too much attention to surveillance on this room while Rebecca was at work. Kade had been an ass, but she was certain that most of the people in his organization weren't psychopaths like Rebecca. Just because a person was a pirate didn't mean they were inhuman.

Once Rebecca was secure, Sera slapped her former captor several times until the other woman started making noises that somewhat resembled a return to consciousness.

"Wakey wakey."

Rebecca snapped awake at that and struggled mightily, desperate to free herself.

"What the hell!" she yelled.

"Stop!" Sera ordered. "One peep above a whisper and this nice big needle I am pricking into the underside of your jaw will make a quick visit to your brain. Follow?"

Rebecca whispered yes, almost meekly, but her eyes held pure hatred.

"I was going to use you as a hostage to get myself out of here, but it occurred to me that you may not be that well liked, and your people may happily shoot us both. I also doubt you'll believe me when I say that if you let me go I'll let you live because...well, I wouldn't," Sera smiled with no small dose of malice. "So, to keep up with appearances, I'm going to work you over a bit so that you aren't immediately recognizable, finish you off, and then I think I'll strike off on my own."

<Is that absolutely necessary? I can fake the video feeds,> Helen said.

<I want her to stand up to cursory scrutiny if anyone comes in to patch me—her up again.>

Rebecca's face clouded and she appeared to be preparing an unpleasant response, but then thought better. She cringed as Sera held up the needle that had been under her chin and said, "You can make noise now." Right before she drove it through Rebecca's thigh.

Rebecca appeared to be one of those torturers who enjoyed giving pain but not receiving it. There were some that liked it both ways, but from the pitiful shrieking that ensued, such was not the case here. Sera had planted a few good-sized spikes in various places on Rebecca's body, and was about to drive the final one into her heart, when she found her hand unwilling to complete the downward arc.

There had been a time in Sera's life when taking another human life, in the heat of battle, or with calm precision hadn't been a problem. But she was supposed to have moved on from that. *Sabrina* was supposed to be her haven, her place of redemption. A dark thought passed through her mind: she wasn't on *Sabrina*; no one had to know what happened next.

It took Sera several minutes to make up her mind, and Rebecca watched that wavering spike with a singular focus. When it finally dropped, she let out a hoarse laugh.

"I knew you didn't have it in you."

"Apparently not anymore," Sera nodded. "Something we both should be grateful for."

<I'm proud of you,> Helen said softly.

"When I get out of here..." Rebecca began the standard threat.

"Oh stuff it." Sera smashed a fist into the other woman's face; then followed it with a few more blows. Rebecca was knocked unconscious again from the fury of Sera's strikes. She then spent several minutes making superficial cuts on Rebecca's body to match those she bore.

<There. Unless one of the meds paid careful attention to how she messed me up yesterday, this should do,> Sera said while reviewing her work.

<Ok, I'm a bit less proud of you....>

Sera slipped into the hazsuit and sealed its hood shut before she exited the med-lab. The suit was covered in blood—which enhanced the disguise. When Rebecca had left yesterday's session, she had been covered with blood, too.

The hall was short but well lit. There were a few other doors along it and all bore markings that indicated they were also med bays. The hall ended in a T, and Sera strode toward the intersection with calm purpose, though she had no idea where she was going. She turned the corner and almost ran into the technician who tried to give her the shot earlier. He was muttering something about not letting that bitch torture people and finally doing something about it.

The look on his face when he saw whom he had nearly collided with was one of pure horror. It looked like the disguise was working.

She pushed on his shoulder to turn him around.

"My quarters, now."

He didn't question her and led her through the halls to Rebecca's rooms.

Sera was quite proud of how this escape was going so far. She'd definitely been through worse. The most difficult part was walking without limping. Her body was sending her strong reminders that someone in her condition really shouldn't be walking around.

<Can you speed the healing up?> Sera asked.

<This is things being sped up. If you didn't have me guiding your bots, you wouldn't even be able to crawl right now,> Helen replied with a motherly tone. <I'm working them as fast as I can, but I'm not going to do a rush job putting you back together again.>

As the terrified med tech led her through the halls, Sera's initial impression that she was on a space station was reinforced. It had all the hallmarks; exposed conduit for easy access and repair, sealable bulkheads, and no external windows. Well that was somewhat unusual, but not if they were in the bowels of a station.

Her disguise as a bloody Rebecca was working just fine. Everyone stayed out of her way as if she had the plague. Considering the reasons Rebecca wore the hazsuit while interrogating, she supposed plague may be just what people feared. Eventually, her guide led her into a much nicer-looking part of the station, with wider, carpeted corridors.

<*Who puts carpet in a pirate's space station?*> Sera shook her head.

<*Kade, it would seem,*> Helen responded with a chuckle.

The med-tech stopped in front of a door and looked over at her. Sera wondered if there was a security pass code on the door. Hopefully, even if there was, medics had override codes to get in if needed. She nodded for him to open it, and, shaking, he punched in a code and the door slid aside. She gestured for him to go in first.

The quarters were what she expected—luxurious in the extreme. Rebecca lived very nicely on the spoils of the business. Fabrics draped the walls, exotic woods and rare metals covered every surface. The bed was heaped with furs, and Sera was tempted to toss them on the floor, just to irk Rebecca.

<*Childish, but I wouldn't blame you,*> Helen commented.

Sera turned to her reluctant escort and pulled the hazsuit's helmet off.

"She's gotta have some weapons in here, help me find them."

The man fell back, his expression aghast. "You!"

"Yes, I'm here. She's strapped to a table in med."

"You got free!"

"You're quite observant. I'm very good at getting free. It's a survival trait."

"Did you kill her?"

Sera couldn't help but think that he certainly was morbid for a med-tech. "No, I don't do cold-blooded killing. But she's going to need some reconstructive surgery."

He nodded. "Oh."

"By the way," she extended her hand, "I'm Sera. You're?"

"Andy." He took a tentative step forward, shook her hand, and then pulled back. Sera didn't fault him; she was still covered in blood.

"So, you look for guns, I need to find something to wear. I can't stand her, but she has excellent taste in clothing."

While Andy rummaged around, Sera pulled open Rebecca's wardrobe, praying that there would be something in a nice, soft lambskin.

Sera was impressed. The wardrobe was probably larger than her cabin on *Sabrina*, and it contained hundreds of outfits hanging in several long rows. Nearly every style and fabric combination this side of Sol was represented.

As she walked through the rows of clothing, her eye was drawn to a section filled with black, shiny outfits. She recognized it as the same type of material Rebecca had worn on *Sabrina*.

Sera felt the fabric. It was rubbery, but slick and not tacky. It stretched nicely, and gleamed under the lights. She pulled one of the items off the rack and held it up to herself. It was a full suit that even had attached socks and gloves—covering its wearer from toe to neck.

<Practically speaking, it will work well to cover all your cuts and bruises, a little pressure on all those wounds wouldn't hurt either.>

<It does feel like I opened up a few on the walk over here.>

<More than a few. You're bleeding from a dozen places right now.>

"What the heck," Sera said aloud. "Kinky pirate mistress will probably help me blend in."

She grabbed a belt and a pair of boots before heading into the suite's bathroom. There, she peeled off the hazsuit, grimacing with pain as fresh scabs tore open.

"Crap, you were right, Helen. I look like shit."

<Yeah, you should take a quick shower and clean those deeper wounds.>

Sera didn't disagree. She stepped into the shower and let the water sluice away the blood and anger. Five minutes later, she stepped out, feeling ready to face the reason she had been trying to get onto this station for so long.

She dried off using fluffy cotton towels and then flipped the slinky suit over, looking for a zipper or fastening.

<I think you have to get in through the neck opening,> Helen supplied.

"Huh, I guess it is pretty stretchy," Sera said as she stepped into the suit. She pulled it up her body and pulled her arms inside, slipping them into the sleeves.

"Damn, this feels goooood," she said as the slick suit sensed a warm body and tightened around her, pushing out any stray pockets of air and outlining her body perfectly.

Sera turned in the mirror, admiring her gleaming black figure.

"Looks pretty damn good too," she said with a smile.

<I'm glad you're taking time for fashion,> Helen said with a wry smile in Sera's mind.

"What can I say, a girl's gotta—" Her words cut off as excruciating pain lanced across her skin. She screamed in agony as the feeling intensified, as though her skin were on fire underneath the suit.

She clawed at it, attempting to tear it off, but it had tightened around her to the point where she couldn't get a grip on it, nor pull it from her neck.

"Helen…help…" she managed to gasp before falling unconscious to the bathroom floor.

She woke several minutes later to find Andy hovering over her, concern filling his eyes.

<You're OK,> Helen said. <You had an unfortunate incident with booby-trapped clothing.>

<I what?> Helen's words didn't make any sense.

<That suit you put on was keyed to Rebecca's DNA, when it detected that you were not her, it tried to kill you.>

<Seriously? She has her clothing set to kill?>

<So it would seem. It did a pretty good number on you before I managed to stop it.>

Sera didn't feel much worse than before—almost better. She wondered how it had tried to kill her.

<What did it do?>

<It tried to eat all your skin below the neck.>

"WHAT?" Sera yelled and reached down, feeling her body. From what she could tell, nothing had changed; the suit still covered her, gleaming in the room's bright lights.

"Are you OK?" Andy asked. "You screamed and passed out, but moments later seemed fine. I linked with your internal system and it showed you had an allergic reaction to the material."

Sera ignored Andy's question. <Helen, what do you mean it tried to eat my skin?>

<The suit, as it turns out was made of some sort of bio-polymer that bonds to the wearer's skin—from what I understand, it makes the skin hyper sensitive. Unfortunately, it's DNA keyed, so it reacts unkindly to unknown DNA.>

Sera had heard of clothing like that, though never had the desire to own any.

<I managed to stop it and alter it to bond to your DNA, but it then bonded directly to what was left of your skin.>

Sera ran a hand down her leg and gasped. It was extremely sensitive, it also felt incredibly good. So that's why Rebecca had clothing made out of this material.

"I think I'm OK now," she said to Andy and stood.

<Just so you know, you're stuck with this as your skin until I can get you into surgery.>

<Fantastic,> Sera replied.

"Are you sure, you're OK," Andy asked. "That was a pretty strong reaction."

"My med package handled it, I actually feel pretty good now," Sera smiled. She did feel pretty good, but in a lot of pain at the same time, it was strange and rather distracting. Just when the escape was going so well.

<Well, at least you don't have to worry about bleeding anymore,> Helen said. *<It's rather impressive how quickly it linked up with your nerves. Rebecca spared no expense.>*

Sera struggled to her feet and Andy took her arm and guided her to Rebecca's bed. The feeling of his hand on her arm almost drove her mad, but she didn't pull away, she didn't want to. He brought her the boots and she pulled them on, they were a bit too big, but snugged up once she zipped them closed.

"I see you found her stash," Sera said, eyeing the dozen guns piled on a desk.

Andy nodded, finally taking his eyes from her body. "She had them all over. There's spare power cells, and ammunition for a few chemical slug throwers."

"Nice work," Sera said. She wasn't quite ready yet to get up again and admired the weapons from her place on the bed.

"Since my neck is now on the line, are you going to tell me how you got out of there?" Andy asked.

"Does it require much telling? I got free, beat the living piss out of Rebecca and tied her up. Now, there's something I need to get from this station, then I'm going to blow this place and get back to my ship."

"And that outfit's your disguise?"

Sera laughed. "I wasn't really planning to be disguised; I just think it looks good. You can't really see me kicking ass in a pantsuit, can you?

Andy raised an eyebrow.

"Hey. You're a medic, that's your thing. Looking hot and kicking ass, that's my thing."

<*I think this suit is affecting your brain chemistry, I'm going to adjust your serotonin levels,*> Helen laughed.

Andy shrugged. "OK, so what is your plan, then? Seduce all the guards between here and the docks and then get cozy with a captain?"

Sera grinned. "Do you think that will work?"

"No."

"Good, be a damn sad pirate organization if it did. First, I have to get to a secure terminal and look something up and go get it. Then I plan to shoot my way to the docks, hijack a ship, and get out of here."

"Suicide I am not in for. Have fun with that," Andy said and walked to the door. Sera was there in three strides, ignoring the fiery feeling in her muscles.

"Look you don't have to come; in fact, I'd prefer you don't. But I do want to say thank you."

Andy looked taken aback. "Umm...you're welcome. I'm sorry I didn't help you when you first asked."

"Rebecca's even sorrier," Sera said with a chuckle.

"I bet she is."

"Look, when I said 'blow this place', I was being literal. When the alarms and alerts start telling everyone to get off the station, do it. Don't wait around; I'm sure at least a few captains will take their ships and run."

"What are you planning to do?" Andy asked.

"I'm not sure yet, but I'll promise two things. It will be irreversible, and I'll give fair warning before it happens."

Andy nodded. "Thanks for the heads up, my days would have been numbered anyway once surveillance discovered you are free and I helped." He opened the door. "I'll be seeing you."

"Probably not. You lay low until you hear the alarms."

Andy left and Sera turned back to the pile of weapons. She pulled out a thigh holster and slipped it onto her left leg, then slid a small slug thrower into it. Several throwing knives went into the tops of each boot. She rummaged through a drawer and found several small remote cameras.

<They up to spec?> She asked Helen.

<Close, ingest them and I'll have your nano upgrade them.>

<Ugh, I hate doing that.> Sera grimaced as she swallowed the small probes.

<Well, I can't exactly use your forearm assimilator at the moment; it's a bit covered up.>

<Can't you expose it?> Sera asked.

<You have no idea to what lengths I'm going to keep your fragile human body in one piece right now. Don't make it harder.>

<I dunno,> Sera said as she felt the biopolymer that was her skin. <This may be the best, worst thing that's ever happened to me.>

<You organics are so strange.>

<You say that, but I know AI are curious about how organics 'feel',> Sera replied.

<Curious like you are about how a cat balances with a tail. You don't really want to be a cat,> Helen's tone carried no small hint of condescension.

<*Some* people want to be cats,> Sera retorted. She hated it when Helen took on her teacher tone. Those days were long past.

Sera slid two holsters onto the belt she wore and pulled two bandoliers filled with ammunition over her shoulders.

<Sorry,> Sera said presently to Helen. <I'm just worried about not screwing this up. This mission hasn't had the most auspicious beginning.>

<I'm sorry, too,> Helen replied. <This is important to me, as well. I'm just worried that this biopolymer is messing with your mental state too much; you can't think clearly when you're so aroused.>

<That's where you're mistaken, my dear.> Sera smiled as hefted a large pulse rifle and slung it around her shoulder. <The altered chemical and mental state is the goal, not a symptom; you should remember that. You get your big rushes, so to speak, from feats of mental prowess. Humans can get off on the mental stuff, too, but tactile stimulation brings its own thrill. When channeled into something productive, that stimulation can be a strength rather than a weakness.>

Helen gave the AI's equivalent of a laugh. *<Are you saying that the secret behind Cheeky's exemplary piloting skill is that she's a nymphomaniac and always aroused?>*

<That's exactly what I'm saying,> Sera said as she strapped two more guns to her thighs. *<She's extended her sexual stimulus to include her piloting skill. People can train their sexual response to be triggered by anything.>*

<I return to my earlier statement; organics are exceedingly weird. Do you have enough guns?>

Sera shifted from foot to foot. She had to be wearing at least twenty kilograms of weaponry. She slipped back into the wardrobe and found a long black jacket that fell nearly to her ankles. After Helen made certain it wasn't DNA locked, she slipped it on, ensuring that she could leave it open while not revealing the full extent of her armament.

<Yeah, I think it'll do. The probes ready?>

<Yup, open wide.>

The four tiny probes flew out of Sera's mouth, one settling on an access port for the room's terminal.

<It's possible that this connection is on the station's secure net, but I'm betting it's not if a med-tech has access to this room,> Helen said.

The probe disappeared as it slipped into the access port and linked with the station's general computer net.

<Yeah, looks like it's just standard access,> Sera sighed. *<I've got access to their wireless net now, though.>*

<Yes, the secure net is accessed elsewhere; however, I believe I can determine where we can get on it, based on the points where the nets link.>

The room's main holo activated, showing the layout of the station. Helen searched through access points, then made a noise of surprise.

<Sera, this station is in the Dark Layer.>

Sera stopped her investigation of the station's public net. *<Are you serious?>*

<Would I joke about something like that?>

<How long has it been here?> Sera asked in response.

<It looks like at least ten years. How it's gone unnoticed that long is beyond me.>

<Well, we are a ways away from any stars. At least now we know how to destroy it.>

<That's true. I have what I believe is a point where I can access the secure net from a public terminal. It looks like it has a physical hookup that was routed incorrectly. I should be able to break past its security and find what we need to find.>

Helen indicated the location on the holo she was displaying. Sera zoomed in and traced a path from Rebecca's quarters. It was two decks down and across a good quarter of the station.

"This'll be fun," Sera said with a smile.

Sera slipped out into the hall, heels snapping and long coat rustling.

<Good luck, miss stealthy.>

<I don't have much chance of sneaking across this whole station. That's what this whole getup is about—looking like I belong and not to mess with me.>

<Clever plan, you are bright!>

<I blame my childhood teacher,> Sera smirked.

<Hey! I resent that.>

<So are you going to produce an opposite waveform or just mock me?>

<Just do a few quick twists and turns and I'll have all the squeaks and creaks mapped.>

Sera obliged her AI and a moment later all sound from her movements ceased.

<Not bad.>

<I've masked all your loud, tight leather for years; this isn't much of a challenge.>

Sera slipped silently down the corridor and into the stairwell. The four probes ranged ahead and behind, keeping an eye on all surveillance equipment, sending signals to them, providing normal visual and audio feeds.

<Did you see Tanis's matter assimilators, by the way?> Sera asked her AI. *<I bet she has nano-cloud tech.>*

<I suspect she does, the TSF did have that ability around her time.>

<Sure would be handy right about now,> Sera sighed. *<Too bad they never shared it; these probes aren't that stealthy.>*

The stairs were narrow and Sera moved down them gracefully, peering over the rail to ensure the next landing was clear.

<Shoot!> Sera exclaimed suddenly. *<I forgot to grab grenades...keep an eye out for anything we can use to fashion some.>*

<I thought your heightened senses honed your focus?> Helen replied with a superior tone.

Sera didn't respond she continued down the stairs.

<Looks like we're passing near the mess hall,> Sera noted.

<Have to, unless you want to skirt through the administrative section.>

At the second landing, Sera cracked the hatch ever so slightly, allowing a probe to slip past the seal. Both she and Helen watched the visual feed, Sera accessing the infrared and ultraviolet ranges she normally excluded from her vision.

<Looks like the corridor is clear, but there are a few people in the mess hall beyond.>

<We'll take that service corridor and go around the main mess.>

Sera strode down the center of the corridor. No point in looking suspicious to anyone leaving the dining area. As she neared the opening to the hall, two men stepped out.

"Whoa, yeah," one exclaimed. "I know you're new, 'cause I'd remember a sweet looking thing like you!" His friend elbowed him, but the man continued, taking a step toward Sera. "That's one sexy getup. You're a randy little bitch, aren't you?"

<Holy shit, this guy is really living up to the stereotype, isn't he?> Sera commented to Helen.

She didn't want conflict, but no woman dressed as she was on a Mark station would take talk like this without a fight, or a tumble between the sheets.

Sera stepped toward him, exuding sexual energy. "I am a bit new here. Care to show me around?"

The man laughed and moved closer. "Hell yeah, we can start with my cabin."

When he moved into range, Sera reached out with her right hand and grabbed his hair. In the same fluid motion, she reached down with her left hand, and pulled a blade from the top of her right boot. She pushed him back against the wall, wrenching his head back and pressed the blade in her left hand against his neck.

She sneered and ground her hips into him. "I like it rough, and I've got six more of these little blades. I don't like to stop until each one has gotten a taste of blood. Where's your cabin?"

The man's friend was laughing so hard that he had a hand against the wall to steady himself.

"I...uhh...can't right now...I'm on shift soon," the first man stammered.

Smoothly, Sera stepped back and let go of him, a sultry pout on her lips. "Always work with you types. Oh well." She put the blade back into her boot and blew him a kiss. "I'll keep an eye out for you."

He reddened and all but ran down the hall. His friend followed, clutching his gut as he laughed.

<You certainly like to add to the risk. If you wore one of Rebecca's more conservative outfits, none of this would have happened.>

<Yeah, but then he may have mentioned he saw some new girl in a business suit. Now he's going to swear his friend to secrecy. At least secrecy till the next time his friend is drunk.>

They slipped into the service corridor without seeing anyone else. It was little more than a shaft, which ended at a hatch leading to a larger thoroughfare. The hatch stood open and Helen sent two probes through. There was mild foot traffic, but no troops or guards of any sort.

Sera stepped through and took a left. Some of the men and women eyed her with appreciation, some with wariness, but most just ignored her. There was no shortage of men and women wearing racier clothing than Sera's. She began to suspect that The Mark had a brothel on the station.

She took a right at the next intersection and then another left further down. The terminal she was looking for was in a vertical maintenance shaft off this corridor. The probes spied the shaft's access eight meters away and Sera approached it nonchalantly. The coast was clear, but as she neared the hatch, two guards rounded a corner and began walking toward her.

Sera muttered a curse to herself and kept walking past the hatch. She passed the guards and winked at them. They both smiled at her in response. When she neared the end of the corridor, the probes behind her showed the two guards turn down a side passage. She doubled back and opened the shaft access panel, slipping in with a bit of trouble when her jacket bunched up beneath her. Once in, she hooked a foot on the access panel and pulled it shut.

<How far down?>

<Just three meters to that junction on the left.>

Sera slithered down the tight space to the location indicated on her HUD, and took a deep breath. She held her index finger against the port and silver metal flowed out through the outstretched digit, forming a probe which then seated itself into the port.

<*Gah… that always gives me the heebies,*> Sera said with a shiver.

<*Ah, there we are, this terminal does have access to both the secure and main nets on the station, just as I suspected. It's been locked out of the secure net, but a few nano into the mix and all that will be changed.*>

Sera studied the station's layout as Helen accessed the secure net. Even without knowing exactly where the artifact they were searching for was, there were only so many places it could be hidden. The station's own power grid should show its location—even if they hadn't decided to use it. If they had, then it should be even easier.

<*I'm in,*> Helen said. <*I'm scanning their secure locations and comm logs to look for any reference to the CriEn.*>

<*I hope it's still here. If Kade traded it, we're in big trouble.*>

<*I don't think so,*> Helen said. <*We first traced the CriEn to Kade eight years ago; this station has been here for ten. I'm betting that they're using it as a power source to keep this thing in the dark layer. It would be a lot cheaper than hauling fissionables or exotics all the way out here to run in a reactor.*>

Sera looked over the portions of the station labeled as power generation. If they were using the CriEn, it would be around there. It didn't have to be, but a smart engineer would place it near existing power distribution systems.

<*I think I found it,*> Helen said. <*The station specifications show two nuclear fusion reactors for power, but one is just barely running and the other isn't active at all. However, power levels show more energy than even these two reactors could create.*>

<*So they **are** using it. What are the chances we can remove it and not have this station tear itself to pieces when it loses the power to stay transitioned in the DL?*>

<*I think it will hold together for a day or so at least. The fusion reactor could probably hold it in just fine for a few weeks with the batteries helping—before it overheated. They'd have to kill everything except for life support to manage that, though. Once they get both reactors spun up, they could always keep it here, or transition it back to regular space.*>

It was one of the difficulties of maintaining systems in the dark layer: heat dispersion. In regular space, the cold of vacuum was a great way to disperse heat; in the dark layer, there was nothing to disperse heat to. The heat could be transformed into energy, but when it was permeating everything, that was hard to do. The CriEn module generated energy with no heat, which was the key to keeping a station in the dark layer.

Sera worked out the route to the station's power plant while Helen used nano to build a bridge from the station's secure net to the public net and placed the link into an encrypted stream. Unless they were looking, the station security systems wouldn't stand a chance of locating it.

<There, we'll have access to the secure net over our wireless Link to the public net now,> Helen said. *<Picked our route?>*

<Yeah, we'll make our way across this level to the station's midpoint and then down three levels, across that one, and then down to power generation. Looks like guards on it are light. Kade probably counted on his fiction of two plants to hide the module.>

<What a waste of a CriEn,> Helen sighed. *<You could run a planet with this thing.>*

<No one ever said Kade was the brightest star in the sky.>

<'Was' being the operative term,> Helen replied. *<Hey, grab that repair kit there, it has some stuff we can use for a distraction.>*

Sera grabbed the kit and pulled herself back up the access tube, and checked the two probes they'd left out in the hall. When the coast was clear, she flipped the latch and kicked the hatch open.

She eased out into the hall, but at the last minute, a bandolier caught on the hinge. She stumbled and fell to the floor before freeing herself and closing the panel.

<Very graceful,> Helen commented wryly.

She stood up and dusted herself off before looking up to see a guard walking toward her.

"Hey, what were you doing in there?" he asked.

<You are so not going to be able to talk yourself out of this one,> Helen chuckled.

"I'm tech; got a call that there was a down net coupling in there and I fixed it up."

The guard was unconvinced. "You're tech?"

149

"Yeah, I'm off duty." Sera made sure to stand so that her coat hid the weapons, but not her shapely legs.

"Why don't you spread your hands across that wall there while I check your ident?" The guard pulled out a scanner and stepped toward Sera as she placed her hands on the wall."

<Told you.>

<You are not helping.>

"That's odd," the guard said as he ran the scanner over her hand. "I'm not getting any station ident off you."

Sera smiled and turned, one hand sliding up her left leg and then behind her back. "I'm new; I'm just trying to do a good job." Humanity had been civilized for twelve thousand years, but men still hadn't outgrown their inability to think straight when a woman turned on her charm.

"Right, you can do a good job from detention while I check you out."

Apparently, some men had evolved.

<I hope you blocked his transmit access or things are going to get unpleasant,> Sera said.

<What do you take me for, an amateur? I am six thousand years old, after all.>

Sera slid the pistol she had reached for out from behind her back and jammed it under the guard's chin. "Tight beam your access codes and tokens to me, or I spray your brains on the roof."

The man nodded slowly, and Helen confirmed that he sent his codes. Sera gestured for him to turn and when he did, she fired a pulse at the small of his back. It was a simple yet effective way to stun someone for a few hours. He slumped and she caught his weight with a grunt. A minute later, she had him stuffed into the maintenance shaft and Helen was faking his patrol signal on the net so he wouldn't be missed.

Without any further incident, Sera made her way to the security station outside the power generation section.

<What are the chances I could do a face meld without passing out?> Sera asked Helen.

<Your energy reserves are extremely low, even with what you got from that dispenser back there.>

<Figured as much. I don't know how I'd feel about any more pain anyway.>

<You've certainly planned better infiltrations.>

<Thanks for the support.>

<I was merely stating a fact,> Helen said without rancor.

<Well, I guess I'll do this the old-fashioned way.>

Without another word, she stepped out from cover and strode directly up to the two guards. An automatic turret tracked her as she approached the two men.

<Tell me you can jam that thing.>

<Already have. I'm just moving it for their benefit.>

"Hey guys. How're you doing?" she asked with a friendly smile, attempting to walk right passed them.

"Hold it." One of the guards said as they both reached forward to stop her progress. Sera halted half a step before they expected and grasped each guard's outstretched wrists. Their expressions were priceless as she leapt backwards and pulled the guards toward her and into one another. The guards stumbled and crashed to the floor.

<That extra twenty kilos of weaponry really helps doesn't it.>

<Sure does, Flaherty would be proud.>

Sera kicked the man on the left in the face as he struggled to get up, the heel of her boot ripping open his cheek. The other guard kicked the back of her other leg, hitting her knee and knocking her backwards. Sera took advantage of the momentum, twisted and fell onto the guard—her elbow smashing into his chest. The sickening crack of his sternum reverberated up her arm.

<Damn that hurts!>

<That's why it's not in the manual.>

Sera used her pistol to stun both men and dumped them in a small cleaning room a short distance back up the corridor.

<We're on the clock now, those two guards are scheduled to check in verbally every ten minutes and I didn't get their access codes.>

<How long till the next check in?>

<Seven and a half minutes. I'll set the clock.>

A countdown appeared in the upper right of Sera's vision as she ran down the corridors in the direction her map overlay indicated. There would be some techs monitoring the main reactor, but since the secondary one was offline, she doubted that anyone was watching it. She was wrong.

It appeared that The Mark techs were studying the CriEn module even as they were using it. Eight years later and they still didn't know how it worked.

There were at least a dozen of them in a monitoring station and another group wearing hazsuits in the chamber where the CriEn module stood on a pedestal.

<Great. I suppose I could just shoot them all, but that would be messy and probably set off an alarm or two.>

<I'll clear them out. It's fun to mess with people who don't know what they are doing,> Helen replied gleefully.

Helen showed Sera a readout of the main power throughput indicators. The CriEn module generated energy by accessing layers of space-time these techs didn't even know about. It would be easy to generate anomalous readings from the device that wouldn't put them in harm's way but would certainly cause them to vacate the premises.

Helen used her access to the station's secure net to worm her way into the engineering network, and from there to the CriEn chamber. As expected, grav fields were in place around the module to ensure safety. Helen altered the frequency of the fields and the module began to alter its output unpredictably. Its EM field swelled and pushed against the grav fields containing it.

As predicted, the engineers monitoring the device grew concerned, and then frantic as they attempted to stabilize the grav field and contain the module's EM field. Helen was more than a match for them, and within a minute they had hit their fail-safes and shut down the module. The scientists in the hazsuits had long since vacated the chamber and were crowded into the decontamination room.

With the scientists and engineers focused on discerning the cause of the anomaly, Sera was able to approach their monitoring station, crack the door open, and roll in a canister of gas. Made from the parts they had grabbed along the way, it wasn't a grenade, but it would do the trick.

It took only seconds for the gas to take effect, and Sera rose from cover as the countdown on her HUD slipped past the four-minute mark.

She ran past the sleeping techs and into the CriEn chamber. The module was seated in a socket, which linked up with the power ports. Sera quickly unlatched it and looked around for something in which to stash the device.

<There, they have a shielded case it will fit in back in the main monitoring station.> Helen indicated the location on Sera's HUD. She hefted the module, which weighed at least a good forty kilograms, and dashed back into the room with the sleeping techs. The shielded case was sitting on an equipment rack and she placed the module in it and flipped on the case's grav shield.

<Grav shield, lucky us. It would suck if someone hit the module with a beam weapon,> Sera said as she hoisted the case over her shoulder.

<Only for a fraction of a second,> Helen replied.

<I'm going to need another shot of adrenaline if I'm to make it through this next little jaunt.>

<You're way over-extended; I may have to regulate your heart if I give it to you.>

<I can barely move with all the weight I'm hauling. Juice me up, doc.>

The shot of adrenaline felt like a blow to the chest as her heart fluttered uncomfortably and then increased its pace. She took a deep, steadying breath, then switched her overlay to show the route to the station's main sensor array—a system that likely saw little use with the station in the dark layer.

She raced past the closet containing the two unconscious guards, their comms squawking through the door with the voice of a superior demanding that they check in. As she reached the curve in the corridor, the station's power switched to a conservation setting; the main lighting dimmed and ancillary wall holos turned off.

<Looks like they've switched to battery power while they warm the other reactor up,> Helen observed.

<Seems so. Hopefully they get enough power online for us to send the signal.>

LET'S BLOW THIS JOINT

STELLAR DATE: 07.16.8927 (Adjusted Years)
LOCATION: The Mark's Dark Layer Station
REGION: Unclaimed Interstellar Space, Core-Ward of Silstrand Alliance

Sera had just ducked into a service corridor when she heard the sounds of booted feet running down the main hall to the CriEn chamber.

<*That was close,*> Helen said.

<*I thought you were monitoring the station personnel after that hiccup back at the maintenance shaft?*>

<*I am. Those guys weren't showing up on it. I think they're getting suspicious—might have removed guards from monitoring.*>

<*They've gotta be using voice comm, then. See if you can find it.*>

<*I seem to recall being the one who taught you all your tradecraft,*> Helen said, sounding somewhat annoyed.

<*Sorry,*> Sera said as she ran down the corridor. <*Habit from all those years working in the unit.*>

They had several near brushes with guards as she made her way to the sensor array, but Helen had picked up the comm channel and fanned the probes far ahead.

<*They found her,*> Helen said. They both knew who *her* was. <*She's pretty upset. I've got a visual feed if you want to see.*>

<*No thanks, I'd probably start laughing.*>

<*It's too bad you never got to use the crew for this; you'd been training them well for the eventual infiltration.*>

<*They'll be more chances to use them,*> Sera replied as she peered around a corner. <*Though a few more people to do this job sure would have been nice.*>

<*Flaherty is going to be upset he missed it,*> Helen said.

<*He'll get over it.*>

The coast was clear. Sera dashed down the corridor and slithered into yet another access shaft—this one, thankfully, a bit larger than some of the others. The shaft linked with another and she shimmied down it for forty meters before coming to the sensor array's main trunk line.

<Do your thang,> Sera said, managing a mental drawl.

<That's...exceptionally annoying,> Helen said while directing a probe to deliver nano into a small access port on the conduit.

<Need to stay in range of the probe while you work your magic?> Sera asked.

<I'd prefer not to. The sooner we get out of here, the better. I don't want to hang around to see one of those things up close when it gets here.>

<There can't be one within a dozen light-years. I bet it will be at least a day before one gets here,> Sera said as she began to work her way back out of the access shaft.

<Do you want to take any chances, though?> Helen asked.

Sera thought about what the sensor array would be summoning. *<No, not really.>*

Following the tunnel, they passed into another access shaft, which ultimately led to a freight warehousing area. From there, it should be a short jaunt to the docks to find a ship they could sneak aboard.

One last tussle with her coat getting caught and she climbed through a hatch into the warehouse. Sera dusted off her coat and checked her weapons over.

<You know, you now have perfectly slinky skin for wiggling through tight spaces, but you insist on wearing that big coat overtop.>

Sera felt herself blush. *<It feels **too** much like my skin; it would be like crawling through there naked. I'm worried I might tear it open.>*

Helen chuckled gently in Sera's mind. *<You humans are so concerned about your outer shell. I swear, at least half your civilization is built around it.>*

<Well, you don't have insides that ooze out if your outer shell gets wrecked,> Sera said while adjusting her thigh holster and freeing up the knives in her boots.

*<Given the fact that **you** are my outer shell, that's not entirely true.>*

Satisfied that she was combat ready, Sera peered around the stack of crates she had been hiding behind and scanned the long, dark row of wares.

<It's going to be hard to pick up where people are with all this in here,> Helen observed.

With the fourth probe functioning as a relay on the sensor trunk line, there were only three available to roam the warehouse. Helen spread them out, showing Sera an overlay of the series of interconnected storage areas and their current location in the maze.

Several security teams were visible on the probe cameras, methodically searching the area.

<Looks like the goon patrol is checking this place over.>

<Seems so,> Helen agreed.

Sera crept through the stacks of freight with careful precision. Some of them were piled haphazardly, and several times she had to squeeze through some narrow spaces while avoiding the larger alleyways. She had just finished pulling the CriEn module's case through a narrow opening when she turned to find herself staring into the muzzle of a pulse rifle.

"I don't think you're supposed to be down here, ma'am," the guard said.

"I think that's the first time all day someone has called me 'ma'am'," Sera said and drew her hand down her chest with a smile. The man's eyes followed her hand, a small smile tugging at the corners of his mouth. She took advantage of his distraction, pushed his rifle to the side as she spun around, driving an elbow into his left eye.

He fell back with a cry and raised one hand to his eye. Sera grabbed his weapon with both hands and wrenched it from his grip, before spinning it and slamming the rifle's stock into his neck.

The man began to gargle and Sera fired a shot from her stun pistol into his head.

<No DNA lock on the gun,> Sera said after planting some nano on the trigger. *<Never hurts to have another weapon.>*

<As long as you can carry them, limping-bleeding-adrenalized girl.>

Sera set down the case and slipped off her coat. She pulled her other pulse rifle off its shoulder sling and then pulled the jacket back on, putting the sling overtop. She hooked the shielded case to the sling and then hefted both pulse rifles, one in each hand.

"This is much better. The time for subtlety is over," she said aloud and stepped out from around the crate. She spun, and her coat billowed behind her, both rifles leveled on a squad of guards who were approaching quietly. "Oops."

Sera gave a disarming smile, then fired off a flurry of pulses with both weapons before ducking around another stack of containers.

She brought up her targeting overlay and slipped around to the far side of the crate where two troopers were trying to flank her. These men wore body armor and Sera concentrated fire from both rifles on one man and then the other.

<Like shooting fish in a barrel,> Sera said with a grin.

<Did anyone ever really do that, anyway?>

<Dunno, but if they did, I bet it was a lot like this.>

Sera turned and fired blindly at the guards coming around the other side of the crate before dashing further into the maze.

The guards gave chase and Helen pointed out where reinforcements were on route. The station's compliment of active guards was just over three hundred—with an additional merc garrison of four hundred-fifty. Not to mention all the Mark crews currently on station.

<You couldn't hack their HUDs by any chance, could you?> Sera asked.

<I thought you said that was unethical.>

<That was against regular soldiers. These guys are pirates. Besides, it's a thousand to one!>

Helen's mental laugh bubbled as she struck across the station's private net and hacked the pursuing guard's HUDs. She threw in the added bonus of making them unable to see with their helmets on. Sera heard collisions and cursing from behind and gave a small laugh when Helen showed her the pastoral landscapes that she had inserted over the guard's vision.

"Now that evens things out a bit more," Sera said aloud. She stopped at the end of a long row of crates and turned to fire at her helmet-less pursuers. Three went down and Sera fired down the other side of the row, taking out another goon before a pulse shot hit her right arm.

Her muscles convulsed and the weapon fell from numb fingers.

"Damn," she said and sucked in a deep breath, falling back against a stack of engine parts. She fired a few blind pulses around the stack to let them know she was still in the fight.

<That's what you get for being cocky,> Helen admonished.

<How long till you can de-numb it?>

<In your current state? Ten minutes.>

Sera swore and dropped the pulse rifle, pulling a slug-throwing pistol from its holster. The shipping crates provided cover from pulse blasts, but the pistols fired armor piercing rounds at nearly a thousand kilometers per hour. Rebecca may be many things, but she did not have bad taste in weapons.

Trying to take out the enemy without causing fatalities, Sera fired a few low shots. The moment she started killing the soldiers, they would take this fight a lot more seriously and just gas the whole chamber. There were curses and a few grunts as the bullets tore through cargo and into soft flesh. Sera let a few more rounds fly and then took off along a path her HUD showed to be clear.

The guards were more cautious now—following slowly, checking every corner. Within a minute Sera lost them, and soon she was at the opening to the station's main dock.

It was an aired dock with the ships resting on cradles inside the station. Sera guessed it probably had to do with how they held the station in the dark layer and concerns over mixing the grav fields.

<Any of this stuff slated to be loaded up?>

<Those four pallets over there are scheduled to go on a ship that's supposed to be leaving any minute now,> Helen said and highlighted them on Sera's HUD.

<Cutting it kind of close, aren't they?>

<Dockhands are refusing to load while the shootout is going on. The ship's captain is arguing with them.>

Sera stepped up to one of the pallets that was loaded with crates of food. It was out of the direct line of sight from the docks and she carefully slid the crates aside, making a small space in the center. Placing the CriEn case in first, she squeezed in after and crouched on it, pulling the crates tight around her. Sera pulled a few of the crates over her head in case there were any catwalks out on the docks.

<I've got their scanners a bit messed up; they shouldn't be able to detect you in here with all these organics.>

<Good, I'm going to catch a minute or two of shuteye. Let me know if anything interesting happens.>

The guards were spilling out onto the docks, unable to find any sign of Sera in the warehouse. The dockhands, and the captain with which they were arguing, reported that they hadn't seen anyone, and most of the guards returned to the warehouse to sweep it again.

The captain strengthened his argument that the docks were clear, and, given their own admission that they had not seen anything, the dockhands had no choice but to resume loading the ship. Sera's pallet was last and Helen gently woke her before it began moving. It wouldn't do to have Sera startled awake and give away her location.

As the pallet was crawling up the ramp, a shout came over the docks.

"Stop that! What do you think you're doing?" The voice was Rebecca's.

"Loading my ship," the captain responded.

"We're not loading ships; we're looking for a fugitive."

"You've got a thousand people who can hunt for one person. I've got a schedule to keep."

"How do you know she hasn't gotten onto your ship?"

"Because I've been standing here the whole time arguing with these dockhands to get the thing loaded up. I'm already half an hour behind. This stuff sells for a lot more when it's fresh, you know."

Rebecca and the captain yelled at one another for several minutes. Eventually, the new Mark leader succumbed to the captain's increasing ire after he had the ship's AI do a full scan of the vessel, which showed no one on board but his crew.

Sera's pallet was finally stowed in a hold, which, by the smell of it, contained a veritable cornucopia of produce. At least she wasn't going to starve.

The ship spent an agonizing ten minutes going through pre-flight checks and reactor power up.

<When's the alert set to go off?> Sera asked.

<Within the next hour. They should have plenty of time. In case they try to transition out, I've planted a subroutine that will prevent that and set their reactors on a burn rate that will overload them in a day. If they're smart, they'll all bail before the thing gets here.>

<Oh, you're devious,> Sera said with a tired smile.

<It's what I do.>

Minutes later, the station's grav fields backed the ship out of its docking slot and into the dark layer. Not long after, Sera felt the vessel transition into normal space and then begin to accelerate for an eventual transition to FTL.

Sera pushed the crates over her head aside, and pulled herself up. She covered the hole back up, carefully moving the crates to their former positions. It wouldn't do to have anyone find the CriEn module she had worked so hard to retrieve.

She slipped down to the deck and wobbled slightly. Then, waves of dizziness and nausea washed over her body. She fell to the ground, ignoring the tingling sensations her new skin sent through her body.

<Is this what success feels like?> Her mental tone was wan and stretched thin.

<You just need a few hours' sleep and some food,> Helen replied. <Luckily, we have no shortage of that.>

Sera eyed the crates filling the compartment. Food to be sure, but likely no water, and she was feeling a powerful thirst.

She sighed and ran a hand down her black, gleaming thigh.

<At least I don't have to worry about sweating out any fluids,> she said with a soft laugh. <I wonder what Nance would think of this getup?>

FAIR TRADE

STELLAR DATE: 07.15.8927 (Adjusted Years)
LOCATION: *Sabrina*, **PeterSil EK Belt Mining Platform**
REGION: Silstrand System, Silstrand Alliance Space

At the outer rim of the system's Kuiper Belt, the PeterSil EK mining platform whipped around its host star at just over twenty thousand kilometers per hour. Cheeky carefully guided *Sabrina* across several million kilometers of the Silstrand System until the ship's velocity was perfectly matched to the platform's.

Tanis couldn't help but be impressed by the skill Cheeky displayed.

Many pilots needed to resort to hard burns or corrections to make their final approaches, but *Sabrina's* pilot eased her starship through the system like it was a dance to which she knew all the moves.

When they got close, the station focused a gravity wave on the ship and gently pulled it in, before securing it with a physical grapple.

Cargo informed the station that they were interested in making a purchase from S&H Defensive Armaments. Station control passed the message along, and, when pressures were matched and the cargo hatch opened, representatives from the firm were waiting to meet them.

Tanis stepped onto the merchant dock with Cargo, soaking in the station's vibrant atmosphere as freight haulers, passenger cars, and foot traffic moved past their berth in a chaotic cacophony.

It was a shock after the days spent on the relative quiet of *Sabrina*. She realized that, though the Victorian stations and platforms had become crowded in their later years, she hadn't seen this type of bustling commerce since the *Intrepid's* final days on the Cho, in orbit around Jupiter.

Despite the fact that the platform had the word 'mining' in its name, little of the freight she saw looked to have anything to do with extracting or refining ore. From what she could tell, much of the trade here was in defensive or offensive armament.

From her research, she knew that S&H Defensive Armaments had been doing business in the Silstrand Alliance for several centuries and was highly respected. The elder of the two representatives looked as though he may have been with them that entire time.

<Rejuv does not appear to be what it used to,> Tanis said to Angela as they approached the stooped old man waiting on the far side of the ship-territory demarcation line.

"Pleased to meet you," the elderly man said as they approached, and extended a wrinkly hand. Cargo shook it firmly, followed by Tanis—who was surprised at how paper-thin the man's skin felt.

"My name is Smithers," the man said. "I represent S&H Defensive Armaments. Welcome to the PeterSil Mining Platform."

"I'm Cargo and this is Tanis, thank you for taking the time to meet us here," Cargo said with a warm smile.

"This is my associate, Ginia," Smithers gestured to the much younger woman accompanying him. She smiled warmly as she shook their hands.

"If you'll step this way, we have transportation ready to take you to our showroom." Ginia led them to a dock car and they settled within its cabin. She gave it verbal instruction as to their destination and the car took off, weaving through the dock traffic, its dampeners creating a perfectly smooth ride for its passengers.

"We're grateful for the dockside greeting and transportation," Tanis said. "Do you treat all of your clients with such hospitality?"

"We have various levels for various classes of clientele," Smithers said. "There was mention in your message to the station's docking control regarding interest in trading nano technology for weaponry. Typically, only a higher level of clientele is interested in such transactions."

<I'm betting these guys run the station if they are privy to traffic control conversations,> Tanis said to Cargo.

<It would seem so. The fact that there isn't a single speck of dust on a mining platform seems to point to that, as well. This platform practically sparkles.>

Verbally, they spoke of pleasantries. Smithers and Ginia made observations about the local economy and the upcoming elections for the Silstrand Alliances Senate later in the year. Tanis listened intently while Cargo stared out the windows, apparently un-interested in the star cluster's politics.

"So, are you in favor of Silstrand increasing its territory then?" Tanis asked, after Smithers indicated approval of a politician who was running on a campaign platform of adding new systems to the Alliance.

"Purely from a trade and economy standpoint," he replied. "If we increase our territory, then we will have more tariff-free trading partners. Alliance organizations will also be favored in bids for the supply and construction of any government facilities in new member systems."

Tanis knew what that meant; more defense contracts for S&H to land. The small-talk continued for several more minutes until they arrived at S&H's section of the station. They stepped out of the transport and into the lobby of what seemed more like an upscale banking establishment than a weapons supplier. High-quality holos showed rotating images of various products, from personal armor to orbital defense emplacements.

Smithers and Ginia led them through the lobby and down a hall to a private showroom with low couches surrounding a holo tank. The room was dimly lit, with glass and steel artwork perched on the tables. Several small serving trays hovered around the room, offering assorted finger foods.

Smithers beckoned one with his finger and it floated over to him. He selected some cheeses before leaning back in his chair.

"Please," he said with a wave of his hand. "Help yourself. Would you like anything to drink? Ginia will have someone fetch it for us."

Tanis signaled one of the platforms to float her way. Outside of FTL and gravity drives, this was the first piece of impressive technology she had seen in the ninetieth century. She hadn't expected anti-gravity generators to be so small.

"I'll have a glass of white wine, something light," she said after selecting some crackers and fruit. Cargo requested a mixed drink with liquors Tanis had never heard of. The drinks arrived within moments, carried by a slender woman dressed in only a thin gauze outfit.

<Custom here amongst the well-to-do,> Cargo said. <Using human servants for everything imaginable, while humiliating those human servants with socially uncomfortable clothing elevates one's status.>

<Humans are weird,> Tanis responded to Cargo before asking Angela, <These folks seem to have some good tech—how secure is my Link to Cargo?>

<They've discreetly tried to snoop a few times, but I've upgraded his security encryption. His Link and AI can now transmit with a tighter beam and lower gain than it was originally able to.>

<Does Cargo know you upgraded his AI?> Tanis asked.

<No and neither does his AI. I 'convinced' it that it had always had those capabilities.> Angela's voice held a conspiratorial tone.

<That's a violation of the Phobos accords!> Tanis exclaimed.

<Yeah, a little. For me to explain what I did, well, I'd have to provide it with a lot more information than it could handle—which would mean I'd have to upgrade its core. I opted not to do all of that as it would require physical alterations,> Angela sounded smug in her superiority and Tanis called her on it.

<You know it's unbecoming for you to talk down about other AI like that.>

<I know,> Angela sighed. <But it would be illegal to make AI like this back in our time. They're sentient, but they're like people never allowed to mature beyond childhood. In our day, they'd be removed from their hosts, and allowed to re-grow.>

<In our day...now you're making me feel old,> Tanis said before turning her full attention back to Smithers, who was speaking to her.

"...so as you can see we are able to offer the latest in several defensive and offensive technologies to suit your needs. What were you specifically interested in?"

During their flight across the system, Tanis had accessed several resources and catalogs to gain a better understanding of ninetieth century weaponry capability. She had a shopping list ready to go. Cargo had checked it and added a few suggestions of his own to fill it out. Surprisingly, or perhaps not surprisingly, Flaherty had also offered advice on what would be useful, as well.

"We're interested in your ER71 Defensive Suite, for starters." Tanis leaned back with a slice of apple and what she hoped was cheese. "We're going to want a dedicated gravity generator to go with it and the ten centimeter defensive lasers."

She could tell that she had Smithers' attention. Ginia tilted her head and manipulated the readouts, bringing capabilities and prices up on the holo.

"Would you like the GE-875 or the GE-885 grav generator with the suite?" She asked.

"I was hoping we could get the GE-960," Tanis replied. "From what I understand, it's smaller and has a higher output; space is an important consideration on our ship."

Ginia's eyes widened. The GE-960 was three times the price of either of the other gravity generators.

"We're also going to need to replace our current SC Batteries with the SC-R 911s. I understand they have roughly three times the capacity of our current SC-R 790s?"

Smithers nodded, his eyes dancing as the tally on the holo increased. "Yes, they are the best we have in this corner of space. You said you were considering offensive armament, too?"

Cargo's eyes were glazed with incredulity as he looked at the price.

"Yes," Tanis answered. "We're interested in the thirty-centimeter laser system. I believe our ship's layout will require us to mount ten of them for full coverage. I'd also like to get fore and aft AR-17 missile tubes, the four-centimeter rail guns, and fore and aft RM launchers."

Smithers' previous look of pleasure turned to one of skepticism. The tally was easily four times the value of *Sabrina*. Ginia was also eyeing the total with a smile, but where Smithers looked like he was considering charging them for the food and seeing them out, she looked very excited.

"And how will you be paying for this?" Smithers asked.

"We will provide full documentation and disclosure of a valuable nano tech which no one within a hundred light-years even dreams of possessing. We will also disclose our source for this tech as well as documentation indicating our license to distribute both the source technology and sell development and distribution licenses."

Smithers' expression shifted. He still didn't appear completely mollified, but neither was he going to end the discussion.

Tech was one thing; the ability to develop and distribute products based on that Tech was something else entirely. Tanis smiled and reached for her wine glass and drained its contents. Taking the glass in her hand, she repeated the act of absorbing its matter and fabricating a small handgun.

Smithers' expression shifted to one of almost pure joy, and Ginia's face was now rapt with amazement. With a cough, the older man recovered his composure—a bit quicker than Tanis would have liked.

"That looked truly amazing, would it be possible to see it again, and then be able to test the results for any signs of trickery?"

Tanis nodded. "I understand your skepticism. If you'll provide another glass, I'll give you a matched pair."

"Actually," Smithers said. "Please make a...replica of a six-chamber projectile weapon from the nineteenth century. That way we can be assured there is no sleight of hand occurring."

"Based on the size, I'll need two glasses."

Ginia nodded, and a minute later, the servant came in with a tray of empty wine glasses. Angela suggested she use three, and Tanis activated the field in the palm of her hand, dissolving each glass into it. She then added a silver fork, two deviled eggs, and salt to her palm. Moments later, she produced a gun, and then six bullets, which she slipped into the chambers. Handing it to Smithers she said, "Be careful. It's loaded and functional."

The old man whistled in appreciation. "I assume the technology includes not only the nano, but the information on such rapid reorganization of the molecules?"

"You'll get everything required to repeat such a feat, except for the power source."

Smithers nodded. "I assume you won't object if I have our technicians examine these articles." He indicated the guns.

"Be my guest," Tanis replied.

From there they got down to 'brass tacks', as Smithers put it.

Cargo demanded that the work be done in under forty-eight hours; a timeframe which Smithers claimed was not possible. Ginia proceeded to draw up a work schedule, which showed the work would take two weeks.

"I don't see how it is impossible," Tanis said. "This station surely has all of the technical ability to do the installation. The technologies I have to offer will more than offset any costs, probably a thousand-fold."

Smithers was a top-notch negotiator. Despite his awe over Tanis's tech, he was still haggling over every point of the contract they were drawing up. "I believe I'll need to see the documentation on your license to distribute the source tech with ability to develop and redistribute before I can negotiate further. I've never seen anything like this before, but I don't want to commit to this only to hear it announced on the Link tomorrow as something that another firm has developed with licenses prohibiting us from using it."

Tanis nodded and transmitted a full non-disclosure to Smithers over S&H's secure net. "I'll need you to physically and digitally sign this NDA before I can discuss the source of the license."

The NDA was very strict and binding in every system that S&H did business—and most they didn't. Smithers frowned as he reviewed it and sent it off to his legal team for further examination. They discussed minor points regarding the install while they waited. Legal had a few revisions, one that Tanis agreed to and several she refused. In the end, they had an agreement and Tanis disclosed where her nano came from.

Smithers really did lose his composure this time. "God damn it! That explains where you got this tech! But why are you on that crummy little yacht?"

Cargo bristled at that, but Smithers hardly noticed.

"It belongs to a friend who has been having...pirate troubles. The weaponry we're getting from you will be used to fix some of those troubles and get her out of a jam."

Smithers nodded. "That explains why you need the tech, but why are you interested in this, and where is your ship?"

Cargo laughed. "Isn't that the hundred trillion dollar question?"

"The work in two days and I'll speak highly of S&H to my superiors when it comes to future trading. If I have to wait longer than, that I'll let them know transactions with your firm were difficult."

Smithers sighed. "That's one hell of a bargaining chip. Very well, forty-eight hours and you'll be decked out in the best S&H has to offer."

Tanis and Smithers worked out the final aspects of the contract while Cargo took a car back to *Sabrina* with S&H's implementation coordinator and head engineer.

When Tanis arrived back at the ship a few hours later, the dockside was strewn with old components and crates full of new ones. The minute she stepped through the lock, Tanis was accosted by Cheeky.

"I don't care what Thompson says, you're amazing," the pilot said. "I can't believe you got them to agree to your entire list."

"Think they'll actually be able to meet the two-day deadline?" Tanis asked.

"They will or we take their installation team with us. There's no way we're gonna leave the captain longer than that."

"I got them to provide us with a full antimatter fueling as well, and with the increase power on the shielding systems, we should be able to accelerate much faster."

"I'd better check the tuning on our AP nozzle, then. We may need to upgrade that."

"Over plan. We have unlimited credit."

Cheeky rubbed her hands together. "I may not be able to contain myself."

Tanis laughed and let Cheeky get back to her glee over the upgrades. As she passed the galley, she overheard Thompson and Nance arguing with Flaherty.

"I don't care what her motivations are. She has no right to just take over the ship with the captain gone. Cargo is practically letting her run the show, and who knows if Sera's still alive anymore?" Nance's voice rose to an unpleasant pitch and Tanis stopped before she walked past the doorway, not wanting to eavesdrop, but too curious to back away.

She really needed to know how the crew felt about her. If there were even half a chance that they'd turn on her, she'd walk off the ship right now and buy transportation to Bollam's World. The information she had for the *Intrepid* was too important to lose just because of some pissing contest about who got to be in charge of the rescue mission.

"She's right," Thompson said. "I don't know why Sera ever even dealt with The Mark. Look where it's gotten her now."

"You need to relax," Flaherty said. "Tanis isn't the problem. Getting Sera back from Rebecca is all that matters. Tanis is trying to help. Without her, we may as well just write the captain off because we have no way of assaulting a fortified station."

"You don't know that. We should have squeezed that Drind guy more. Did you know that she convinced Cargo to let him go? They even gave him a reference so he could find work on the station here," Nance said.

"That was a good tactical plan. He is now indebted to us and less likely to cause us any trouble. Keeping him would have been a problem. His loyalties aren't clear enough to have him around in a battle. If things go poorly, he could turn on us at a critical point." Flaherty's voice remained calm and steady.

"So, you're admitting things could go poorly!" Nance said.

"It would be foolish of me to assume otherwise," Flaherty said. "I may not be a major from the Terran Space Force, but I've seen my share of battle, and I know that one liability will offset a dozen good men. We are well rid of Drind no matter what possible uses for him you can imagine."

Nance didn't have a response for that right away. There was the clinking of cutlery on plates for a few minutes before she spoke up. "It's possible that I'm taking my frustrations out on her, and I'll keep that in mind. But I still don't like the way she just takes charge, it's not her place."

Flaherty chuckled. "She has no choice. It's who she is. You don't advance as an officer in the navy unless you have a good head on your shoulders and know how to use it. She sees a situation that needs her expertise and she takes charge."

"You can defend her all you want," Thompson said. "It's not making me like her any better."

"You don't have to like her," Flaherty said with deadly calm. "You just have to not mess things up when it comes to rescuing the captain. If you do, you'll have me to worry about."

Tanis didn't wait to hear more. She slipped back down the ladder and took a different route to the bridge that didn't pass the galley. She hoped that Flaherty's calm could offset some of the more volatile crewmembers, or this was going to be the worst rescue of all time.

READY AND ABLE

STELLAR DATE: 07.17.8927 (Adjusted Years)
LOCATION: *Sabrina*, PeterSil EK Belt Mining Platform
REGION: Silstrand System, Silstrand Alliance Space

Two days later, *Sabrina* was fully decked out in the best S&H had to offer. Tanis had even wrangled a full charge on the SC batteries, and added mines to the defensive countermeasure system. Cargo filed the final disembarking entries with the PeterSil platform and they undocked for the tug to take them out.

On the bridge, Cargo sat in the captain's chair; his expression was one of grim determination, but underneath, Tanis could see more than a little trepidation.

<*You would do better in that chair,*> Angela commented.

<*I would, yes,*> Tanis replied. <*But they wouldn't. I can keep things in line well enough from the scan and weapons consoles without further upsetting the delicate balance we have here.*>

Tanis shifted in her seat; the hard chair did not conform to her body; she was served another reminder how out of her time she was.

<*This tug is taking forever,*> Sabrina complained. <*I have new wings, let me fly!*>

"Easy now, girl," Cargo's deep tones resonated through the bridge. "We'll be on our way soon enough."

<*On our way to kick some ass,*> Sabrina crowed. <*I don't just have new wings, but teeth too! I'm coming for you, Sera!*>

Tanis chuckled and shared an amused look with Cheeky.

"Farewell and good hunting," the tug pilot gave her final farewell as she released grapple.

"A good day to you, too," Tanis replied from the comm console.

"Oh, it will be. You're the last haul for me today, and it's a holiday weekend on-station," the tug pilot replied.

"See you next time, Amy," Cheeky said. "Don't do anything I wouldn't do."

The tug pilot laughed in response. "Cheeky, I won't do half the things you *do* do."

They gave the final sign-off and Cheeky laughed.

"She said do-do."

"Ah, Cheeky," Tanis sighed. "You'd make any captain in the service proud, but you wouldn't last a day."

Cheeky switched on the grav drive and set *Sabrina* on her course.

"I'd love to fly one of those big birds your military buddies have," Cheeky said with a nod. "But all those rules aren't my game. Now stealing one…that would be some fun."

Tanis shook her head and smiled. Who knew what the future would hold.

"How's she shaking out?" Cargo asked.

"Just fine," Cheeky replied at the same time Sabrina sang, *<I feel great!>*

Cargo let a small smile slip—perhaps the first since Sera's abduction. "Is that your technical assessment, Sabrina?"

<Fine. The weapons interfaces are near perfect. I can barely feel the edge between the systems. The upgraded power plant doesn't have that annoying buzz in its output like the old one, it's like drinking starlight. And the quantum processors they added for targeting and navigation are like an ocean of thought. How's that for your technical assessment?>

"Uh…great," Cargo said.

<I'm sorry for being snippy,> Sabrina said. *<I just need to get her back. I love the upgrades—thank you Tanis—but I'm empty without Sera.>*

<We have the power and the means now,> Tanis replied. *<You'll see her again soon.>*

<I'd better,> the Sabrina replied.

<Not the most stable of personalities, is she,> Tanis said privately to Angela.

<I've been working on getting her story,> Angela spoke with a soft tone of pity. *<This ship sat in a junkyard for ninety years. They powered down the ship, but not her core, and she didn't have the ability to do so herself—something which I have since rectified. How AI are treated in this time is truly abhorrent. If ever anyone needed to see what the Phobos accords were meant to prevent, this is it.>*

Tanis's heart ached for the ship. Ninety years alone, no sensors, no input, just her thoughts…it was a wonder she was still sane.

<That is unbelievable, to trap an AI in a ship like that! It's…it's…>

<These are dark times,> Angela replied solemnly. <Most of the AI on this ship were not given a choice as to their placements. They're all slaves—but they barely know it.>

<I had suspected as much,> Tanis replied. <I hope we can help them—I hope Bob doesn't throw a fit.>

<Bob's pretty pragmatic,> Angela said with a chuckle. <He's put up with you for some time, to say the least.>

With an exasperated roll of her eyes, Tanis turned to her work, running preflight checks on the scan suite and making sure the boards showed green for the weapons systems. She couldn't perform a full check of those systems until they were further out—the station was already more than a little nervous about the amount of firepower *Sabrina* now sported.

Their rush to get the upgrades installed, and the haste with which S&H actually performed the upgrades, caused the PeterSil platform to ask a few pointed questions. Tanis and Cargo had tried to convince them the weapons were for defense against pirates and that *Sabrina* would be leaving the Silstrand Alliance as soon as the installation was complete, but their assurances did little to win the authorities over—*Sabrina* didn't exactly have a sterling reputation.

Ultimately, to ensure they met their end of the bargain, S&H stepped in and smoothed things over. Smithers pulled some strings to secure a letter of marquee for *Sabrina*—no small feat from what Tanis could tell. Once they had approval from the Alliance government for the weapons, the PeterSil platform backed down.

Given that S&H appeared to represent much of the platform's revenue, Tanis found herself wondering how normal this sort of maneuvering really was.

"System STC has given us the green for AP," Tanis said as the comm lit up.

"Acknowledged," Cargo replied. "Cheeky, let's hit it."

"Aye, aye sir," the pilot said with a mischievous grin.

One of the upgrades provided increased shielding around the ship's small annihilation chamber. The rough math Tanis had drawn up showed that *Sabrina* could now accelerate at over twice her previous rate—yet, the fragile humans within would feel nearly none of that thrust.

Now *Sabrina* really did sing as the ship boosted at 500*g* on its outsystem vector.

Tanis appreciated *Sabrina's* excitement, but kept her eyes on the pair of Silstrand Space Force corvettes that were shadowing them. The PeterSil platform may have approved their upgrades, and the local magistrate had provided their authorization to hunt pirates, but it seemed that the Alliance's military wasn't prepared to fully trust them.

Given what Tanis had witnessed thus far in the ninetieth century, she didn't blame them.

Even with their silent guests, or perhaps because of it, their departure was smooth and uneventful. A scant five hours later, they made their transition into FTL at 0.29*c*, the first of two FTL hops.

Soon, they'd be able the put the rest of their new toys to use as well.

LYING LOW

STELLAR DATE: 07.17.8927 (Adjusted Years)
LOCATION: *Regal Dawn*, **Interstellar Space**
REGION: Rim-Ward of Gedri, Silstrand Alliance Space

Sera woke as she felt the ship transition out of FTL into regular space. Helen's read-only tap into the wireless net revealed that the pirate ship was making vector adjustments before one more FTL jump, which would bring them to the Gedri system, a common haunt for pirates.

<So much for the big rush to deliver this food somewhere,> Sera said. <He just wanted to pick off some prey before his next delivery.>

<So it would seem,> Helen agreed.

Back on Coburn Station—before all this had begun—Sera recalled hearing that the Silstrand Alliance government was coming under heavy fire for their poor policing policies—Padre's attack on Trio probably added fuel to that fire.

Newscasts had reported that, with the upcoming election, the Alliance government was increasing patrols and providing many better-armed freighters with privateer marques, allowing them the spoils from any pirate ships they managed to disable and capture.

Those privateers also knew that Gedri was a common haunt for pirates.

There was a possibility that running into a patrol or privateer in Gedri would result in rescue, but it was just as possible that it would get her killed. What concerned her even more was the chance of the CriEn module being destroyed so close to Gedri Prime. Such an event could create a singularity that would eventually destroy the entire Silstrand Alliance.

<Stop being such a pessimist and finish that melon,> Helen said. <That's just your low blood sugar talking.>

<Probably. Some solid sleep wouldn't hurt either.>

<Don't doze off just yet. I need to find a hard line—I may need your muscles to get to it.>

<Is that all I am to you?>

<No, you're also handy transportation.>

So far, the ship hadn't detected their presence. It would seem its internal sensors were not the best, or it wasn't even looking, or the organic food in the hold was masking their presence. Being a pirate ship, Sera was certain that its sensors were the type that looked out more than in.

<These things are really good, a bit sticky though,> Sera commented as she finished the melon and started on a second one.

<Try to find something salty as well, your SC coil is starting to run out of juice and I don't want to try to charge off anything on this ship, I just know its power will feel gritty.>

<How can power feel gritty?> Sera asked.

<How does food feel sticky?> Helen asked back.

<Never mind.>

Sera found some salted nuts and crunched on them as quietly as possible. The nano in her body extracted sodium from her digestive system and mixed it with water, using the reaction to generate power for themselves and Helen; having an AI as powerful as Helen as well as extensive nano made for a salty diet.

<I found it!> Helen exclaimed. *<Behind that pallet of oranges, there's an access panel. I can tell by the EM patterns that there is a data flow of some sort behind it.>*

Sera stood slowly, her body—still recovering from torture and the stims Helen had provided to keep her moving—ached everywhere after sitting still for nearly half an hour. Her right leg refused to move and she slapped it a few times to regain feeling.

"Whooaaaa…I forgot about what that would feel like," she said aloud as her hypersensitive skin amplified the sensation.

<Better than feeling some more needles slicing through you.>

<I'm not complaining, this stuff is great. It's chilly in here and I can barely feel it. Next time I see Rebecca, I'll be sure to thank her for the upgrade.>

<With our luck, it won't be too long before you have that opportunity.>

Sera sighed. *<Yeah, I can't believe I let her live.>*

<I can. I'm glad you did. Now that we've got the CriEn, we have some strong evidence against Trinov. He claimed you lost it, but its logs are intact and it points at him, not you. Having it, not to mention getting the Intrepid

safely to **them**, *should give you the evidence you need against him and proof of your loyalty.*>

<*I'm not loyal to them anymore. I'm just pissed that Trinov used me.*>

<*That's nice dear, just don't tell them that.*>

Sera laughed softly. <*I won't tell them. But I will have a few choice things to say to Trinov…at his trial.*>

<*Maybe you should just focus on the present.*>

<*What, rather than fret about what to do with* Sabrina *and her crew now that the reason I built them up no longer exists?*> Sera paused in her removal of the access panel. <*The thing is, I'm enjoying this life; I'm enjoying my time on* Sabrina. *I'm not sure I want it to end.*>

<*It doesn't necessarily have to. We've talked about it before—I don't need to go back anytime soon. You don't ever have to go back if you don't want to,*> Helen said. <*The laid-back life on a starfrieghter is starting to grow on me.*>

<*Yeah, but we both have to admit, turning that Mark station on its ear was a hell of a lot of fun.*>

<*Just like old times.*>

<*Just as long as it doesn't get* **too much** *like old times.*>

Sera grunted as she popped the last fastener out and loosened the cover enough for a probe to slip in and disable any tamper detectors.

<*Got one, a sloppy thing, just a closed-circuit detector,*> Helen said.

Sera lowered the cover to the ground and fed some nano through her finger onto the data conduit junction box inside. The tiny machines slipped through the seams in the box and created a port for one of the remaining probes.

<*Now that's more like it. I'm setting the probe up to give me full band wireless to the entire net,*> Helen paused. <*Oh, they've got a helluva of a nasty AI running this ship. It almost picked up the port we added, but I backlisted it as common addition for this run of conduit.*>

<*It's nice to have a memory that people can't just alter on me,*> Sera said as she stood painfully and staggered back to the food crates she had been sifting through.

<*What are you talking about? It's relatively simple to alter human memories.*>

<*If you can get all the places the memory is stored. The brain can usually spot the bad data and will re-populate it with the original.*>

<*Hah, you've never seen me wipe a memory.*>

<I've still got my crystal backup,> Sera said.

<I could access your diff system and fool it into ignoring what I wanted you to forget.>

Sera laughed softly. *<Are you trying to make me distrust you, dear?>*

<You should always be a bit suspicious. Even I could be compromised,> Helen replied innocently.

<Lucky for me I've already taken that into consideration. My memories are secure.>

<How so?>

<I can't tell you that, what if you get compromised?>

<That was hypothetical, I'm not going to get compromised!> Helen said and Sera pictured her stomping her ephemeral foot.

<Any luck slipping into the system?> Sera changed the topic.

Helen's avatar cast Sera a dirty look in her mind, but let it drop.

<I've activated an environmental port three deck plates down. There's water in one of the pipes and the schematic shows a faucet I can activate so that you can get something to drink.>

<That,> Sera smiled, *<would be heavenly.>*

BOLLAM'S WORLD

STELLAR DATE: 07.20.8927 (Adjusted Years)
LOCATION: Andromeda's Pinnace, EK Belt
REGION: Bollam's World System, Bollam's World Federation

Joe lay in his bunk, eyes closed, imagining that he was back on the *Intrepid*, at home with Tanis, enjoying a lazy morning in bed before spending some time in the garden.

Maybe they would be in their final days before arriving at New Eden, the ship awake and buzzing outside, everyone glad for finally arriving at their final destination. Maybe their child would be born, a small girl, rushing into the room, jumping onto the bed and making a ruckus.

He took a long breath and opened his eyes.

That would never be. The *Intrepid* would never travel to New Eden—it may never travel anywhere, because there was nowhere to go.

"Joe," Jessica's voice came over the audible comm. "I've managed to make a Link to a relay buoy at the edge of the system. There's a twenty light-minute delay, but I have a standard packet they sent out with approach vectors, stations, and stuff."

*And stuff...*Joe couldn't help feel some amusement at how different Jessica was from Tanis. Both were career service women, both practically built out of duty, but still as different from one another as night and day.

He imagined for a second what it would be like to be with Jessica, how different life would be. He shook his head and chuckled, it certainly wouldn't be for him.

Tanis was his anchor, his strength—not that he needed to lean on her that way now, but she had been a rock for him during those early days on the *Intrepid*. He had felt so out of his depth, worried that they were going to cut him from the mission because he couldn't get things under control.

Then she came in, full of command and purpose—knowing just what to do.

She always knew what to do.

"I'm on my way," he messaged back to Jessica. "Give me a second to get presentable."

"No rush, the data is still coming in," Jessica replied.

"Gotcha," Joe said and stepped into the ultrasonic san, letting its waves pull dirt and detritus from his skin. He stepped out, feeling only superficially refreshed, and pulled a shipsuit on before running a hand through his hair.

"Good enough," he said to himself as he shifted his thinking from the past and his feelings of loss to instead focus on the work ahead. It was something he had seen Tanis do hundreds of times; she did it so naturally. For him, it took a bit more effort to compartmentalize his feelings.

The pinnace was small; it could crew seven, but with just the two of them on board it felt empty—though he preferred it that way at present. The walk to the cockpit took just a minute and he entered to see Jessica bent over the main holo tank, studying the Bollam's World system.

Her silver hair fell around her face and when she raised her head to look at him, her lavender-colored brow was furrowed.

"This is one weird system," she said and beckoned him to the tank. "And it's not just their name...who calls their whole system 'Bollam's World'?"

"Beats me," Joe shrugged. "What's weird other than the name?"

"Check it out," Jessica gestured and the holo display rose up and filled the cockpit. "There's this massive...I don't know what to call it. It's not a jovian, or a brown dwarf, but it's too big for a planet, that's for sure."

Joe looked at the large blue-green planet, labeled Aurora, that Jessica was pointing at. The data packet didn't have detailed specifications—other than a warning not to venture within one AU of its surface—but it was plain to see that it had over three time's Jupiter's diameter, and, based on its orbit and rotation, at least ten times its mass.

Worlds such as this one shouldn't exist. Even if a planet massed more than Jupiter, it would not get physically larger. Instead—being a gas giant—the gas would compress under its own gravity and it would remain the same size. Unless the world were to become so massive that it began to fuse hydrogen; then convection would expand it.

Aurora's size indicated that it should be light and airy, like Saturn. However, its mass meant it should be slightly smaller than Jupiter—yet it was neither.

"That's...that's exceedingly unusual," Joe said with a nod. "What about stations and inhabited worlds?"

"The star's practically a Sol-clone," Jessica said. "But its young, just over half a billion years or so. The place is full of hot stuff with a lot of spin to it."

"Two terrestrial worlds there," Joe pointed to the third and fourth planets, named Dublin and Bollam on the holo. "No rings and just a few elevators. Looks like a third is being terraformed around that other jovian, the sixth planet out."

"There's a sizable hab orbiting it, too," Jessica pointed to a roughly spherical mass of concentric rings.

Joe gave a low whistle. "Data packet has it housing a hundred billion people."

Jessica sighed, "That's us humans, filling up every corner of the galaxy."

"I wonder how far we've gotten," Joe said wistfully. "This system looks like it has half a trillion people, over forty light-years from Sol. Even the FGT hadn't gotten this far when we left, or if they had, we didn't know it."

"I don't think that the FGT did this system," Jessica said.

"Oh yeah? Why's that?" Joe asked.

"They would have moved that Mars-sized world into the habitable zone and merged one of those inner rocky worlds with it," she replied. "They wouldn't just waste it out there."

"Maybe," Joe nodded. "Given how we got here, who knows who actually settled this world."

"That rocky world 47AU out has a big refinery and mining yard in orbit. They're on our side of the star, if anyone came insystem with Tanis's pod, they may have passed through."

"Let's set a course, then," Joe said as he zoomed the holo in on the station. "And we better find out what kind of clearances we need to dock there. Gotta try and look like locals."

PRIVATEER

STELLAR DATE: 07.22.8927 (Adjusted Years)
LOCATION: *Sabrina*, Gedri Scattered Disk
REGION: Gedri System, Silstrand Alliance Space

Sabrina transitioned out of FTL into the Gedri system travelling at only $0.09c$, their prior velocity deliberately bled off in interstellar space to make them a more tempting target.

"Continue shedding v nice and easy, Cheeky," Cargo said from the captain's chair. "Make us look vulnerable."

"Cargo, that's one of my main skills," Cheeky said with a grin. "Won't be the first time I've played damsel in distress to sucker some poor guy in."

Tanis couldn't help but laugh. For Cheeky, everything was a potential analogy to her sex life.

"Hurry up and wait," Cargo muttered as the crew settled in to their stations, all eyes on the passive scan and the local beacon's report of the system traffic.

Further insystem, at the outer edge of the EK Belt, lay the regular jump point that led to and from Silstrand. It was busy, crowded with ships on various braking and acceleration trajectories. Beyond that was an empty void; *Sabrina* was the only ship in that space, on a slow trajectory insystem from the outer, less trafficked jump point. System scan hadn't picked them up, and wouldn't for several more hours. This was the time when the pirates would strike. If they did at all.

Cargo had just brought in the second round of coffee for Tanis and Cheeky when scan picked up a ship dumping in very close to their position. Its entry point was not at any marked jump point, but the dark matter was so sparse in this solar region that a ship could hop in and out of the dark layer with very little concern of collision.

The vessel was five light minutes away, and subsequent scan updates showed it altering its trajectory to intercept *Sabrina*. At first glance, it appeared to be a regular freighter, but closer inspection with the updated scan suite revealed that there was less cargo and more engine capacity than normal. The ship's shields were strong and it appeared that there were traces of high power conduit near the hull—a clear indicator of substantial weaponry.

<*The fish has spotted the lure,*> Cargo said on the ship-wide net. <*They've altered course and are on an intercept with us. They're still a good thirty million kilometers away, but breaking rapidly to match our velocity. We should meet up in the next hour or so.*>

A regular freighter wouldn't have had the sensors capable of picking up the pirate's jump and would only receive notification from the local beacon at the system's terminal shock. It would take yet another twenty minutes for that message to come in and so they played dumb, appearing ignorant of the incoming aggressor.

Right on schedule, the system traffic control AI sent a burst to both ships warning of a potential collision and provided new inbound lanes.

At this point, the two vessels were only two light minutes apart, and Cargo signaled for Tanis to send a direct transmission to the other ship. The local beacon had identified the pirate ship as a freighter named *Regal Dawn*, and so Tanis addressed it as such.

"*Regal Dawn*, this is the *Orion Star*, we are bound insystem and braking on a trajectory that will intercept yours. Please correct your course to the following as provided by the system's beacon." Tanis transmitted the updated path along with the message.

"Will the altered ident hold up?" Cheeky asked.

"It was simple tech to tweak," Tanis replied. "And system traffic control bought it."

She saw Cheeky and Cargo exchange a look. Neither of them had thought it possible to alter the sealed ident box all ships were required to carry. Angela said it was child's play.

The entire bridge held their breath as they waited for the reply. The ships were rapidly closing on one another and the response came in just past the two minute mark.

"*Orion Star*, this is the *Regal Dawn*. We have received updated course and are correcting. Sorry for the trouble." The words sounded genuine, appearing to be innocent, but Tanis didn't believe it for a moment.

She checked scan and over the next five minutes, they saw no alteration in the suspected pirate's course. When enough time had passed that even the worst scan would have picked up the unaltered course, Tanis submitted another message, which received almost the exact same reply, except now it cited engine trouble as the excuse for not altering vector.

The ships were now within one light minute of each other, a distance of only eighteen million kilometers, and Tanis slid over to the new tactical console where she ran checks on the shielding and new weapon's systems.

"Looks like you're going to get your chance to try out all those fancy toys sooner than we expected," Cargo said. "This better work."

"Of course it will work," Cheeky said. "*Orion Star* here and I will fly circles around them while Tanis shoots a few well-placed holes in their hull. In a few hours we'll be on our way to rescue Sera."

"Next time we pick a different name for me, I get to choose it," *Sabrina* groused audibly. "I want to be the *Brilliant Nebula*."

Tanis wished she could feel as confident as Cheeky did. With no shakedown and the briefest of live weapon tests, there was every chance they'd suffer a failure and lose to this pirate.

<The plan's solid,> Angela said. <At least as solid as it can be with just one freighter of untried crew and weaponry.>

<Gee, thanks, Ang.>

They would hold course until the last possible moment, doing nothing to alert the pirate that its prey was more than met the eye. Scaring off the ship and chasing it through the system would be far too risky a maneuver. It was also imperative that the other ship shot first, or they would be the one flagged as pirates in Gedri.

"Steady, Cheeky. Hold it until we are within ten thousand clicks before you alter course," Cargo said, as much to break the silence as instruction.

"You don't say," Cheeky muttered.

The flashing telltales, indicating an impending collision, were starting to annoy everyone. It was a largely unnecessary warning — even if neither ship changed course, the chances of an actual collision were very slim. Unless one of the vessels desired it.

Since *Sabrina* was playing meek and innocent, they had to do what any simple freighter would do when another ship was going to hit it: move. When the comps indicated that proximity was critical, Cheeky made the necessary course adjustments; moments later, a tight-beam message came in from the pirate.

"Attention *Orion Star*. Resume your previous course or we'll fire on you. If you do not resist you will be unharmed. Repeat. Return to your previous course and prepare to be boarded."

"Not ones for small talk, are they?" Tanis observed.

Cheeky did not comply, as was the plan. She activated the AP drive and Tanis brought their rear shields to full power. She expected a shot across their bow first, but there was no point in risking actual damage.

Right on cue, the shot came, glancing across the dorsal shield; the ship-to-ship comm ringing with angry messages to return to their previous course. Scan showed the pirate ship altering course and braking to match *Sabrina's* new vector. The warning came again to resume their previous course or be disabled; moments later, the shields took their first direct hit.

"Now!" Tanis shouted.

Cheeky didn't need the order; she was already killing the engines and firing maneuvering thrusters. *Sabrina* spun about and faced the pirate. The forward dorsal lasers tracked the pirate's engines—which were still facing *Sabrina* as it braked to match course with them. The moment they had a lock, Tanis sent four bursts from the thirty-centimeter lasers.

She didn't target the pirate's engines directly—blowing the ship wasn't their goal. The shots struck around the engine nozzles. Overheating and fusing control mechanisms would cause an engine shutdown and give *Sabrina* maneuvering advantage.

Another two shots missed as the pirate ship twisted to avoid the beams, but the third and fourth hit their targets. One of the *Regal Dawn's* engines shut down and its maneuvering thrusters fired, bringing the pirate about to face *Sabrina*.

Tanis reviewed her console for errors or system failures. Nothing showed red and she thanked the S&H install crew for a job well done.

She had been in a lot of battles, including no small number of space battles, but never a pitched beam fight at $0.10c$ in civilian ships. It was exhilarating. Tanis made several quick calculations; Angela assisted in presenting the best shots, and, upon Tanis's approval, sent the strike coordinates to the *Sabrina's* new fire control systems.

The six offensive beams positioned for forward fire tapped into the fully charged SC batteries and lanced out at the pirate ship, concentrating at two points on its shields. Three successive bursts and scan showed the *Regal Dawn's* shields failing.

Return fire came at *Sabrina*, but Cheeky spun the ship on its axis and no shot lingered long on the same shield umbrella. Tanis's console showed their shields disperse the energy and quickly recover.

The pirate ship kicked their vessel into a somewhat wobbly rotation, and Tanis renewed her offense—continuing to focus on the same points on the pirate's shields in short bursts.

"Cocky bastards," Cheeky said with a grin. "Didn't think they had to be careful with us. Bet they're wishing they had now."

Cargo laughed. "You just keep them from scorching us and you can talk all the smack you want, Cheeks."

"Their shield is flickering on its forward umbrella, they're going to drop to the dark," Tanis announced.

"Damn," Cargo said. "That'll ruin our party right fast. Can you punch through and hit their grav drive in time?"

"Well…" Tanis began. "Wait, their grav drive just powered down. Either they had something go or they are afraid we may follow them."

A message came over the ship-to-ship comm and Cargo opened the visual link. The man on the holo looked decidedly unhappy. His eyes flashed with rage under a heavy brow.

"Who do you think you are?" he demanded. "This is Mark territory; you can't attack one of our ships and get away with it."

"As I hear it, Kade's dead, and *you* initiated this little game we just played."

"Doesn't matter who's at the head of our organization, you're all dead now." The pirate seemed to hope threats could save him where his shields and weapons had not.

"Lower your shields and shut down your reactors. Prepare to be boarded," Cargo said with a scowl. "We want to see vid of your entire crew in your mess with no weapons. Any tricks and we'll slap some mines on you and say farewell."

"You better really want this," The captain of the *Regal Dawn* growled. "You're going to have to be watching your back for a long time."

"This is *Sabrina*," Cargo smiled with a hint of menace as he signaled for Tanis to switch their ident back. "We've got Kade on ice and we'll happily add any of you, if you give us half a reason."

The captain's expression paled and he grudgingly responded that they would comply. The visual feed from the *Regal Dawn* flipped to their mess. Several minutes later, the crew began to file in.

"Do you think they'll go quietly?" Cheeky asked.

"Not a damn chance," Cargo smiled. He signaled for Tanis to follow him to the fore hatch where Flaherty and Thompson were already waiting. S&H had provided them with some advanced body armor, which the assault team already wore. It wasn't up to the spec Tanis preferred, but it should stop pulse rifles and projectile rounds. If the pirates started firing high-powered beams or rails their way—which would be ludicrous—then the team would be in trouble.

"I feel like Nance," Thompson said as he twisted in the thick, supple armor. It sported plates on the front and back of the torso, but the rest was a thick material, which would harden on impact and disperse the force of a shot. It could also nullify the effects of a pulse rifle and disperse the heat of a hand laser. The helmet had a HUD that interfaced with their internal Links to provide displays of everyone's field of vision and status—not that Tanis needed such a crude interface.

They fastened their helmets and looked one another over.

<*Let's do this,*> Thompson said as he cycled the airlock and stepped out into the umbilical.

<*They're cycling their lock open for us,*> Nance announced from the bridge, where she had taken Tanis's place. Tanis had given the bio a crash course on the new weapons systems and the upgraded scan that went with them. It had been a bit tense since Nance's unhappiness with the plan—and Tanis in general—wasn't well hidden, but she had been a quick study.

<*Are they all in the galley?*> Cargo asked.

<*I count nine in there,*> Nance replied. <*I don't know what their compliment is; their AI is being very unfriendly.*>

<*That's going to be difficult to deal with when we try to use their ship,*> Thompson said as the four of them stepped into the *Regal Dawn's* lock and waited for it to seal and match pressure with the rest of the ship.

<*I should be able to get it under control,*> Tanis without worry.

<Should?> Nance asked.

<I was speaking extemporaneously,> Tanis sighed to herself. At least this part would be over soon. Once they were on their way to rescue Sera, she hoped Nance and Thompson would lay off the accusations.

The light above the inner hatch changed from red to green and the iris spun open to reveal an empty corridor. Everyone had their weapons leveled and Tanis double-checked the seal on her helmet. Chemical warfare was all too common in instances like this. The suits did not detect anything, but she wasn't going to take any chances.

After planting a mine in the airlock, Tanis and Flaherty made their way fore to the bridge, while Cargo and Thompson went aft to the galley. While it was possible that the entire crew had done as directed, they were expecting to find at least one pirate holed up somewhere.

<Any sign of crew?> Cargo asked.

<Not yet. I expect we'll meet with someone near or on the bridge.>

The bridge on the pirate ship was up four levels. Like *Sabrina*, or any ship expecting trouble, ladders were available for passage between the decks; no one wanted to take a lift down into a firefight.

Tanis sent her nano cloud ahead. It almost felt like cheating in this technologically backward time, but not so much that she was willing to risk getting shot in the head on a point of honor.

The tiny bots reported the next level clear and she slipped up the ladder, Flaherty was close behind, silent and serious as always. The next two decks were clear as well, but on the final level, her nano reported small sounds from the direction of the bridge.

Someone hadn't followed orders.

Tanis crept up the ladder and sent a command to Flaherty to follow her, but hold near the ladder while she checked out the bridge. He nodded his assent and backed against a bulkhead in a low crouch, his eyes everywhere.

Conscious of how easily sound traveled in these ships, Tanis took careful steps, her pulse rifle slung low with her finger on the trigger. Her nano flushed into the bridge and her overlay brought up a clear view of the space. There was someone in there all right—a tall woman with long, dark hair and a long leather coat bent over a console.

Tanis stepped out into the hatchway and spoke calmly, her voice coming over a speaker on the suit. "Raise your hands slowly and then turn around."

The woman complied, raised her arms and slowly turned. Even before she saw the other woman's face, Tanis's image recognition systems made the identification.

"Sera?"

"You were expecting the Easter Bunny?" Sera smiled, her dark eyes dancing with mirth.

"What are you doing here?" Tanis asked.

"Thanking my lucky stars you weren't someone intent on blowing this ship to pieces. I had a few minutes of serious worry until Helen cracked that fake ident and we realized it was you guys."

"How did you get away from Rebecca?" Tanis asked. Sera was a far more resourceful woman than she had expected.

"Skill and cunning, but that's a long story. The whole crew here?"

"Thompson and Cargo are below, checking on the crew," Flaherty said from the hatchway behind Tanis.

He slipped past Tanis and stepped into the bridge to embrace Sera in a quick hug. "You gave me a bit of a worry there. I don't like you going off on your own."

Sera laughed. "I don't either. It's not like it was my idea."

"Did you get it?" he asked.

Sera nodded and stretched her foot out to tap a container the size of a personal luggage case on the floor near her.

"All in a day's work," Sera replied.

Tanis's IFF systems scanned Sera and showed the woman to be a mass of wounds and trauma.

<She's a mess,> Tanis whistled softly in her mind.

<Notice she doesn't have skin anymore? Her thermal profile is all wrong,> Angela brought up an image of *Sera's* heat profile and thermal output in Tanis's mind.

<Not to mention the energy profile of whatever is in that case—that Flaherty already seems to know about,> Tanis replied.

"Was that a voluntary alteration?" Tanis asked, pointing at Sera's exposed glossy skin.

Sera's face reddened. "I was always a bit jealous of Rebecca's outfits, so I tried one on. The crazy bitch booby trapped it, so this is my new skin for now."

<With the trauma she's had, and the med facilities on Sabrina, *it may be her new skin for some time,>* Helen added.

"You'd fit right in with Jessica, one of my team on the *Intrepid,*" Tanis said with a smile. "If you can't get squared away before we get there, our docs could fix you up without trouble.

"Not sure I want to be fixed—I think I rather like it," Sera said with a mischievous grin.

"Now you *really* remind me of Jessica."

"Maybe we should discuss mods and fashion later," Flaherty said. "We still have a ship to secure."

"That we do." Sera picked up the mysterious case in one hand and pulse rifle in the other. "Compliment on this ship is twelve. Angela just informed me there are only nine in the galley, so we've got some fun ahead of us." Sera suddenly stopped and turned to face Tanis.

"What did you do to my ship?" she asked with eyes wide.

"Angela shared that tidbit, did she?" Tanis replied with a smile.

"You added ten offensive beams and rail guns? Where'd you get the money?"

"We sold some nano to S&H," Tanis said with a shrug.

Sera turned to Flaherty. "And you let her do this? It could destabilize the regional economy."

"It's alright," Flaherty replied. "The stuff she sold them is not replicable with their current levels of technology. They don't have the ability to produce the nano-sized stasis fields without the Casimir effect collapsing their containment. It's essentially useless."

Tanis was dumbfounded. How did Flaherty understand that, let alone know it was a required component of the technology she had sold S&H. Sera saw her confusion?

"I'll explain later, once we deal with these pirates and set a course for Bollam's World and the *Intrepid.*"

Sera sent a broad message on *Sabrina's* ship-wide net. *<Thanks for the ride guys, I sure didn't want to have to get out and walk!>*

A chorus of voices cried out Sera's name before a round of expletives and questions flooded the comm.

<Easy now, I'll answer everything once this is over. I'm as curious as to what you are doing here as you are about me, I'm sure. First, we take care of three little lost pirate pigs. Thompson, Cargo, have you secured the galley yet?>

<We're in the hall now. Nine secure,> Cargo replied. <You said there are three missing pirates around here somewhere?>

<Yeah, there should be twelve aboard,> Sera replied. <Sabrina, be a dear and seal our hatch—I don't want any of them getting onto you.>

<Taken care of, Sera,> Sabrina responded, sounding happier than she had in a week.

<Angela,> Sera addressed Tanis's AI, <I suspect your cyber warfare is the best around. Is there any chance that you can subdue this ship's pesky AI and take it out of the equation?>

<Shouldn't be too hard. I've already infiltrated most of its systems and have it cornered in its own neural net. It's throwing everything it has at me, if life support goes offline for a minute or two don't be alarmed. It's just me,> Angela's reply was offhand, but Tanis could tell she was disgusted by the intelligence she was fighting on board the Regal Dawn.

"Flaherty," Sera directed, "cover the hatch. They may make a break for Sabrina and it'll be a good place to corner them."

Flaherty nodded and left the bridge. Tanis couldn't even hear him as he slid down the ladder.

"How does he move so quietly?" she asked.

"Honestly? I have no idea," Sera replied. "Helen usually has to use probes to hide my ruckus—though not anymore, I guess." With that, she threw off her long coat and slipped out of the bridge in her whisper-silent skin.

Tanis and Sera checked the two cabins on that level, which appeared to belong to the captain and the first mate—both empty. On the next level, the rest of the crew cabins also checked out.

<How are your charges?> Sera asked Cargo.

<They're none too happy, but they aren't causing us any trouble. The captain we saw over the holo isn't here. One of them let it slip that the mate and engineer are missing, as well. I'm thinking they may be trying to get control back from below.>

<You hold those guys, Tanis and I will go take a peek.>

<Aye, Captain.>

"You have no idea how good it is to hear that again," Sera said aloud to Tanis.

"You have no idea how good it is to hear them say it."

Sera cocked an eyebrow. "They hold together ok?"

"Better than a lot of other crews I've seen when their leader is captured," Tanis replied as they slid down a ladder.

"Good to know I trained them well."

Trained, Tanis added that to the long list of mysteries surrounding Sera.

The two women reached the freight deck, with Angela coordinating probe coverage as they searched for signs of the missing crewmembers. The search turned up nothing and they proceeded down the ladder to environmental.

Just as their feet touched the deck plate, the life support equipment wound to a halt.

<*It's just me,*> Angela said. <*I'm almost wrapped up—just giving him nowhere to hide.*>

Environmental was clear and they worked their way aft toward waste reclamation and engineering.

<*We've got sounds in here that aren't mechanical. Sounds like a footstep, male, most likely a hundred and eighty centimeters and at least ninety-five kilograms. Echoes make it hard to place, but he's somewhere to the right of the entrance no more than ten meters away,*> Helen said.

<*Thanks,*> Sera replied as she peered around the corner. There was nothing visible and she crept to a large tank and provided cover while Tanis slipped in, stopping behind an adjacent tank.

Tanis pivoted and peered over her cover. The motion shifted the deck plate beneath her and gave a low groan. Moments later the waves from a pulse rifle tore through the air over her head. She ducked and Sera rose from cover, firing shots at the attacker.

He ducked down before the waves reached him. Tanis tossed Sera a conspiratorial smile, before slipping out from behind her cover into the next row of tanks, sneaking toward the enemy's location.

As Tanis moved, Sera supplied cover fire, keeping their opponent pinned.

Tanis crept within two meters of the last tank at the end of the row. She steadied herself for a second, and then, in one swift motion, leapt over the tank, twisted mid-air, and landed a meter from their attacker—weapon leveled at his head.

"End of the road, bub."

His back was to her, peering around the other side while trying to get an angle on Sera. He turned slowly, lowering his rifle with one hand, while raising the other.

<*'End of the road, bub'?*> Sera asked.

<*I saw it in a vid once.*>

A half-second before his weapon reached the deck, a series of shots rang out over the waste reclamation equipment, and Tanis heard Sera let loose a string of curses. The man in front of Tanis took advantage of her momentary distraction to raise his weapon and fire a shot off. It struck her square in the chest, flinging her back against the bulkhead. She squeezed off two shots after she hit, but the man had already ducked out of view.

<*You okay?*> she and Sera asked each other.

<*Armor took the most of it,*> Tanis said. <*You?*>

<*They missed, but those were some serious slug throwers. I think both the captain and the tech are on the far left side of the room,*> Sera replied

<*Keep some cover fire on them. I'm going to take care of this guy.*>

Tanis saw Sera pull two slug throwers from holsters on her legs and let loose a volley of her own, the bullets ricocheting off the tanks across the room. Tanis used the distraction to launch herself from her position against the wall. She leapt onto a tank and fell upon the man on the other side.

While not exceptionally graceful, it had the advantage of total surprise. He had been peering back around the tank, his weapon pointed to where she had been. Her elbow slammed into his stomach and she drove a knee into his crotch before smashing the butt of her rifle against the back of his head.

<*One down.*>

<*Helen says she can't spot these guys, they may be using some sort of active camouflage. Can your probes spot them?*> Sera asked.

<*They're using the ship's sensors to create a noise cloud around them. I can't get more than a ghost here and there,*> Angela replied. <*I'll try to find the emitters and shut them down—not all of this ship is accessible from their main net.*>

<*It's a bit of a mess,*> Helen agreed.

Tanis crept along her side of the room, and then moved even with Sera's position.

<*I'm going to draw their fire; see if you can get a line on one of them,*> Tanis said before she stood and leapt across a tank. Shots rang out from a position at the end of the room and return fire came from Sera's location.

Tanis saw one of Sera's shots catch a man at the end of the room in the shoulder. He spun sideways but still managed to fire a few bullets in Tanis's direction. She responded with a series of blasts from her pulse rifle, all missing, but it was enough to force him behind cover.

<*I've got the last one over here somewhere,*> Sera said. <*I heard him just a minute ago.*>

<*I bet you're feeling a keen lack of body armor right about now,*> Tanis replied as she swapped out her rifle's energy coil.

<*I've been feeling that lack for a few days now.*>

Sera and Tanis worked their way closer together and then down to the location of the man Sera had clipped. When they got there, they saw that he had cracked his head on the tank and was out cold.

<*I didn't think my last shot hit him,*> Tanis shook her head. <*Maybe he slipped or something.*>

<*Self-defeating enemies. My favorite kind,*> Sera replied.

Shots rang out from their right as they stared down at the fallen pirate. One hit Tanis's chest armor and she swore as the impact caused her to stagger.

<*Been too long, you're getting sloppy,*> Angela said.

<*Yeah? Have that AI taken care of yet?*> Tanis replied sourly.

<*Yup,*> Angela responded cheerfully. <*Just waiting on you.*>

Sera dashed down the row of tanks, throwing caution to the wind and Tanis saw her boot lash out, sending a weapon flying. A second kick elicited the soft crunch of breaking bone. There was a third kick as Tanis reached her, weapon at the ready.

The man on the floor was down with a long gash across his face, as he rocked side to side, moaning and clutching his chest.

"Last one, then?" Sera asked out loud.

"Should be. Nine and three is twelve last time I checked."

"Good, all that cat and mouse stuff was starting to get on my nerves. I want a hot meal and a bath."

"Do you even need baths now?" Tanis smiled.

"Probably not, but I'm going to take one anyway," Sera groused.

Tanis laughed, but her voice caught at a familiar sound from behind them. Angela cried out a warning, but it wasn't fast enough. The high-pitched whine of a rail weapon echoed through the chamber and Tanis felt a stinging sensation in her chest.

Sera had both of her handguns out, shots ringing from each as she fired at a figure racing past a nearby tank. A shot hit him in the side and he staggered forward, then fell to his knees. Sera kept shooting as she advanced, the man collapsed, his body twitching as Sera emptied her clips into him.

"Aww hell," Tanis said in a strained voice, catching herself against a tank. She wheezed as Sera turned, her face a mask of horror, and rushed back.

<Nance! Get a grav pad over here now! Bottom deck, Tanis is hit!>

"You'll be okay. We'll get you patched up in no time," Sera caught Tanis as she slid down the tank and pulled her up into her arms.

Tanis looked up at Sera and tried to speak. No words came out, but she tried to sound jovial over the Link. <You'd better. If I die rescuing you I'll be rather upset.>

Sera grimaced, pulling Tanis close, and, calling on some untapped reserve of strength, heaved her up and stumbled toward the closest lift. Tanis was wheezing more than breathing and knew that in any moment she'd go into convulsions. The armor was trying to seal the wound to stop the blood from flowing out, but couldn't deal with the massive hole the rail gun had torn through Tanis's chest.

Right through her heart.

UNBREAKABLE

STELLAR DATE: 07.27.8927 (Adjusted Years)
LOCATION: *Sabrina*, Interstellar Dark Layer
REGION: 72 Light Years Core-Ward of Ayrea

It was that reoccurring nightmare again. Something was chasing her through the dark corridors of the *Intrepid* where there was no power, no lights, no Link. It was gaining on her, no matter how hard she ran, it grew ever closer, its clawed feet scraping the decking, the sound echoing around her. Tanis was sick of these nightmares, she wanted to wake up. She was done running.

Repeating the mantra over and over in her subconsciousness, she felt herself rise from the mire, from the darkness, moving to the light, and gradually come awake. The light pressed against her eyelids. It was going to be bright again. Steeling herself, she cracked one eye and then the other. She seemed to be in some med lab, not on the *Intrepid*, that much was for certain. Her chest hurt; hurt a lot.

<*Where am I, Angela?*> she asked.

<*You're on* Sabrina, *Tanis. You were wounded in taking that pirate ship, the* Regal Dawn.>

Angela sounded concerned, but not alarmed. Tanis knew that was a good sign; Angela wouldn't hide her condition if it were bad. She concentrated for a moment, and the memories slowly trickled back; the escape pod, the abduction by Padre's pirates, Sera saving her, and then her saving Sera. She took a deep breath and smiled. They'd be on their way to the *Intrepid* now. This leg of her journey was finally coming to an end.

"We seem to be making a habit of this," a nearby voice said.

Tanis turned her head to see Sera sitting beside her, a look of concern mixed with relief on her face. She handed Tanis a bottle of water with a straw, and Tanis took several long pulls, washing the moisture around her parched mouth.

"We do seem to be," she agreed when she had finished. "Thank you for patching me back together again."

"Nance and Angela did most of the work. I'm all thumbs when it comes to hooking up artificial hearts and then growing new organic ones."

"Heart?"

"When that guy shot at us with the rail gun, I thought he had hit me at first. I figured if I was still standing, I was going to take him down. Later, after I got him, I realized what I thought had been the railgun slug hitting me was a piece of your rib cage. It punctured my right lung, but my fancy new skin sealed around it and kept me breathing."

"Good to know my impending death didn't inconvenience you too much," Tanis smiled. "I did notice back on the ship that you had replaced your skin with some sort of polymer, glad to see it proved useful."

Sera looked down at herself and smiled. "I was saved by fashion. Anyway, when you tried to speak, I turned and…well, let's just say it wasn't pretty. Angela is really the one who saved you. She sealed up your arteries as fast as she could, and managed to keep most of your blood in while we got you on a medical stasis rack and raced you back to *Sabrina*. The pellet the rail gun fired was soft and hollow. It mushroomed inside your chest and ripped your heart apart. The mass hit the inside of the armor on the back, and the shockwave rippled back through the rest of your torso. It did a number on your internal organs."

"Better than the last time I got hit by a rail," Tanis said with a weak smile. "Thanks for keeping me together again, Angela."

<It's purely selfish interest, love.>

<Wait! The baby?> Tanis said with fear washing over her.

<She's perfectly fine. The stasis bubble kept her safe, but…>

<But what?!>

<She's not in stasis right now. When you heal up, I can re-instate it, or…>

<Let's leave that 'or' for later,> Tanis replied.

Sera continued, unaware of Tanis's private conversation.

"Nance got you hooked up to a circulatory machine while she picked bits of shattered bone out of your chest. We fed Angela so much silicon she could have made a replica of you, and Sabrina helped make raw, unprogrammed nano as fast as she could. They shored up all your internal bleeding and slowly re-constructed your organs. Some of them we ended up having to grow fresh—you don't have a bone ribcage anymore, though Angela says she'll slowly replace the artificial one with living tissue over time."

Tanis chuckled. "Also not the first time."

"Sounds like there's a story I'd like to hear when you're not lying here in recovery," Sera said.

"It's a good one, I'll be sure to swap it with one of yours—I see it's only been five days since we took the *Dawn*. That's quite the medical feat you all pulled off, Ang," Tanis said with a yawn.

"It sure was," Sera replied. "Did you used to be a doctor?"

<Just field medicine,> Angela replied. *<You can't live inside a human body for over a century and not have a good idea how it works.>*

"I guess that makes sense," Sera said.

"So, how long am I bedridden for?" Tanis asked.

<There was relatively little nerve damage, though I sacrificed some muscles to keep blood flowing to your brain. I had to rebuild them; you'll need to do some stretching and make sure all your joints work right,> Angela replied.

"Doc knows best," Sera smiled.

Sera helped Tanis raise her legs and move her arms in their full range of motion before she sat up and took a deep breath.

"Everything seems to be in working order," she looked to Sera. "Are you all healed up? I recall you saying something about a rib of mine making a hole in you."

Sera ran a hand down her 'skin'. "All healed and right as rain. Angela knew a few things about flesh and polymer bonding. She and Helen gave me a bit of an upgrade—now it grows back on its own."

"It's a pretty straight-forward mod," Tanis agreed.

<Not Fina's first time with some unexpected alterations either,> Helen added.

"Fina. You've called her that a few times," Tanis observed. "What does it mean?"

<It's a short version of her name,> Helen replied.

"Hush." Sera looked perturbed.

<You have a beautiful name. I helped your mother choose it, I think it suits you.>

"Now I have to know what it is," Tanis said.

"Sera *is* my name; it's just shortened a bit."

<*It's shortened by five letters,*> Helen said with a virtual scowl.

<*Seraphina?*> Angela asked.

"No!" Sera shouted in dismay.

<*Good extrapolation,*> Helen's avatar nodded in their minds.

"I must swear you all to secrecy," Sera said. "I'm completely serious—I can't wheel, deal, and smuggle with a name like Seraphina."

"Who else knows?" Tanis asked.

"Other than you, just Flaherty."

<*It doesn't help that he used to change your diapers,*> Helen said.

"Stop it! You're giving all my secrets away," Sera's face was beginning to redden. Tanis could tell she was adding some choice comments to her AI in private.

<*Oh shush. Eventually she'll figure it all out, I'm just giving her a little nudge here and there,*> Helen said publicly to the group.

"You two are quite the puzzle," Tanis said with an eyebrow raised.

"Hey, on a different track," Sera began, appearing to choose her words carefully, "have you thought about what your ship will do now that it's stuck in the nineteenth century?"

Tanis let out a long sigh. "Not really. I imagine we could find a moon somewhere in some system and terraform it in trade for what we have. I've looked at the star charts; there aren't a lot of options around—not without a really long trip."

"I…this isn't the sort of information that one bandies about, but I think I can help. I have contacts I can reach out to when we get to Bollam's World." Sera paused, indecision clouding her features, then finished her statement, "I can get in touch with the FGT."

Tanis sat up, locking eyes with Sera, searching for a sign that this was subterfuge…or a joke.

"You're serious?"

Sera nodded. "Serious as a railgun slug to the chest."

"How do you have contacts like this?" Tanis asked.

Sera didn't reply right away and Tanis waited in silence for the captain to make up her mind.

"I…I'm not ready to talk about that yet. It's not a part of my life I like to reflect on." Her face lightened. "But I promise I'll tell you, just not yet."

Tanis wasn't sure what to make of Sera's admission, but even suspect contact with the FGT was more to go on than she had five minutes ago.

"OK, thanks for your offer. I can wait for the details," she replied

"You ready to get some solid food in you?" Sera asked and stood from her chair.

"More than ready, my stomach is grumbling like it hasn't had food in a year," Tanis replied as she carefully settled on her feet.

<This particular stomach hasn't had food ever. Go easy on it,> Angela instructed.

She stepped gingerly as they walked out of the med-lab into the central corridor on the freight deck. "Angela wasn't kidding when she said I'd have to take it easy until my muscles get back in sync."

"I had a full rebuild once," Sera said over her shoulder. "Was quite the experience. The nerves and muscles are never exactly where they were before. Takes some time to get your responses timed properly again."

"Now *you* have a story I'd like to hear some time," Tanis said.

"I bet you would." Sera smiled back at her.

Nance met them at the ladder to the crew level; Tanis noticed the woman's head was exposed for only the second time since she had been on board, and her long, brown hair was brushed to gleaming perfection.

"Tanis, it's good to see you conscious. Sabrina notified me that you were awake," she said pleasantly.

<Thanks, Sabrina,> Tanis said. <Sorry I didn't greet you sooner. I'm still feeling a bit fuzzy.>

<It's okay. You brought Sera back to me, I'll forgive you a simple slip,> the ship replied.

Sabrina seemed much calmer than even before Sera had been captured. Perhaps the AI had realized that even without her captain near, the crew wasn't going to abandon her to some scrap yard.

"Thanks, Nance," Tanis said aloud. "Sera tells me I'm currently breathing thanks to in no small part your actions." She patted her chest. "I'm quite impressed that you could grow a new heart with what you have available on this ship."

Nance smiled. "It's the least I could do."

<Finally warming up to us it seems,> Tanis said to Angela.

<A bit, yes.>

Tanis turned and took a long look at the ladder before letting out a long sigh. "I think I'll use the lift today."

"Probably a wise choice," Nance agreed.

The rest of the crew was waiting in the wardroom when she entered, trailing a hand along the bulkhead to assist her uncertain balance.

"Hey folks," Tanis summoned all her energy to give a winning smile.

<Five points for effort,> Angela said with a chuckle. *<Not so many for execution.>*

<Thanks for the support, dear.>

There were greetings all around; even Flaherty actually used words rather than his customary grunt. Tanis sat as gracefully as she could manage and Cheeky poured her a cup of coffee.

"How do you always have such wonderful coffee on this ship?" Tanis asked as she inhaled the aroma.

"Sera blackmails station masters," Cheeky replied with a shrug.

"Now *you're* giving away my secrets, too?" Sera threw her hands in the air.

"Other secrets have been shared?" Cheeky asked. "Why wasn't I informed?"

As they all ate, Sera retold the story of her escape from the pirate headquarters for Tanis's benefit. When she reached the part where she left Rebecca alive, Cargo shook his head with disbelief.

"I still can't fathom what possessed you to leave her alive; she's going to gun for you—for us—forever."

Tanis watched a brief war of emotions play across Sera's face.

"I could have, I really wanted to…" the captain finally replied. "But for some reason I didn't have cold-blooded murder in my heart that day."

The crew nodded respectfully, though Tanis wondered if they noticed what she had; Sera had committed murder before—and not just once.

Tanis wondered what she would have done with Rebecca, were she in Sera's position. It had been a long time since she had taken a life with her own hands; it changed a person, and not just the first time either—there was a definite cumulative effect. Perhaps Sera, like her, had spent some time recovering that part of her soul and didn't want to lose it again.

When she described the ransacking of Rebecca's quarters, Tanis couldn't help but laugh.

"I've only known you for a short time, Sera, but it does not surprise me one bit that you spent no small amount of time in another woman's wardrobe."

"Given her current condition, there's probably a parable of greed in there somewhere," Cargo said with a shake of his head.

Sera gave a simple shrug in response. "All I was wearing was a hazsuit. I couldn't wander through their platform like that."

"Why not?" Nance asked. "I bet it would have attracted a lot less attention than the state you're in now."

Cheeky laughed. "Surely you know by now, Nance. Sera *loves* attracting attention. It may be her dominant personality trait."

Sera's face turned down in a brief sulk. Everyone else was looking at Cheeky and missed the expression, but Tanis's ever-present nano-cloud spotted the reaction.

<My money is on parental issues,> Angela said.

<Mine too,> Tanis replied.

"Fine, mock me, but you're all jealous of this stuff—at least now that Helen and Angela have made it less intent on killing me, and a little more accommodating to my biology."

Cheeky gave a mischievous grin. "I wouldn't mind getting into your new skin, just not the way you are."

Sera flushed, and quickly returned to telling the rest of her tale; the battle in the warehouse, and hiding in the stack of crates. Tanis noticed there was no mention of the case that Sera had with her on the *Regal Dawn*. No one else mentioned the omission and she wondered if the crew knew anything about it.

"So, what *are* the chances that we have to worry about Rebecca sending her entire fleet after us?" Cheeky asked.

"I think they're pretty slim—for now," Sera said. "They're probably looking for a new headquarters."

"Why's that?" Thompson asked.

"I destroyed their last one," Sera smiled mischievously.

"Wait," Cheeky raised her hand. "You didn't mention that before. How did you do that?"

Sera paused, and Tanis wondered what she had done that she didn't want to share with the crew. After a glance at Flaherty, the captain continued with her tale.

"I did tell, I said that I altered their sensor array."

"Yeah," Thompson agreed. "But what for?"

"So I altered it to emit a very specific signal."

"You mean it's true?" Nance asked; her eyes wide.

Sera nodded in response.

"You're killing me with all this crypticness," Cheeky yelled. "What did you do?"

Nance pulled her eyes from Sera and cast a wary look out the porthole into the dark layer. "I've heard stories.... If Sera means what I think she does...she had it eaten."

Tanis leaned back in her chair and took a long, slow breath. Everyone looked surprised—except Flaherty, who looked slightly upset. The most emotion she had ever seen him display, outside of when Sera was captured.

"Something ate the space station?" Thompson asked.

"There are things that live in the dark layer," Sera spoke slowly, as though searching for the right words. "Things that no one understands. We don't know if they are organic, silicate, or purely energy based. No one has been able to learn anything about them—or if anyone has, they didn't live to tell the tale. However, there is a signal which attracts them, and they move fast. Somehow they can propel themselves though the dark layer."

Everyone looked somewhat paler—Tanis was certain she did, as well; not a few nervous eyes glanced out the porthole into the blackness.

"So, these things eat stations?" Thompson asked.

"They are attracted to gravitons, from what we can tell. Mostly, they stay very close to the largest clumps of dark matter, which are clustered near stars in relative space. It's why transitioning into the Dark Layer too close to a star is often a one-way trip—even if there are no clumps of dark matter nearby," Sera replied.

"Are they out in interstellar space at all?" Tanis asked.

"Every so often one is spotted." Mostly ships don't emit enough gravitons to attract them that far out, but like I said, there is a signal you can emit that's like ringing the dinner bell—even out in the void, they'll come—in this case, they most certainly have already come."

"So, you killed an entire station full of people?" Tanis asked.

<Nice, very tactful,> Angela said.

Sera scowled and her voice gained a cold edge. "Of course not. Do I look like a barbarian?"

"More like a Barbie doll," Flaherty said softly.

Sera stuck her tongue out at him. "I gave them fair warning."

"If these things are real, and you know so much about them, how come I've never heard of them?" Cheeky asked. "You'd think pilots would have stories."

<Indeed, how,> Tanis mused.

<I have a list of possibilities as long as your arm,> Angela replied. <Though our access to solid data about this time is rather limited.>

<She's someone with good connections…maybe an aristocrat of some sort?> Tanis mused.

<Well, that's obvious, but who's aristocracy? Most of them aren't really that great from what I can tell.>

<When were they ever?> Tanis asked.

Sera took a moment to reply to Cheeky's question.

"The knowledge is too dangerous. If people knew, they could plant a transmitter on a ship and it would transition to FTL and…well, let's just say that it would be the end of FTL travel. Plus, no one wants to run the risk of accidentally pulling one of these things into relative space."

"Can that happen?"

"No one knows…no one wants to find out."

"Makes sense," Nance said with a nod.

<Great,> Sabrina sighed. <Now I have to worry about space monsters in the dark.>

Sera answered a few more questions about her escape and from the station, then conversation drifted to Sabrina's upgrades and the course to Bollam's World. The crew was far more relaxed with Sera around. Even though she never acted superior, they all looked to her for advice and confirmation of their beliefs and opinions. Sometimes she disagreed or criticized, but usually managed to be supportive while doing so.

Tanis knew the hallmarks of a leader—moreover, someone raised around great leaders. She knew the traits because she had honed them over decades. Sera appeared to possess them naturally; Tanis was certain the captain had not actively focused on the skills, but had learned them through observation—before she ran from whatever position awaited her.

Ship-time slipped into the third watch and the crew began to disperse to their quarters. Tanis was one of the first out; she begged exhaustion and retreated to her cabin where she fell into a deep sleep, dreaming of Joe waiting for her on the *Intrepid* and their happy reunion.

THE RETURN

STELLAR DATE: 07.25.8927 (Adjusted Years)
LOCATION: *Sabrina*, **Interstellar Dark Layer**
REGION: 73 Light Years Core-Ward of Ayrea

Sera reclined in the captain's chair and stroked the leather upholstery.

It was good to be back on *Sabrina*. The ship was glad to have her captain back, too; the crew was happy, and Tanis was going to live to see another day.

It certainly would have been embarrassing, not to mention potentially dangerous, to approach the *Intrepid* with Tanis dead. She really liked the woman; though from another age, Tanis felt like a kindred spirit. The effort she had put into Sera's rescue had also earned her points—though the weapons upgrades painted a target on *Sabrina*. They would have to go before long—at least the more obvious ones.

She didn't fault Tanis. Time was short, and, as a military woman, going in with the big guns was likely her style.

Given Tanis's nano spending spree on the PeterSil EK platform, she may even need to change the registry of her ship. Too many people would wonder what job *Sabrina* had pulled to get that sort of credit. Some old friends were certainly going to take notice.

It should have upset her more, but Sera's plans for the *Intrepid* would force her to confront those individuals sooner rather than later, anyway—regardless of the mess Tanis had made in Silstrand.

<*You could go back, you know,*> Helen said softly. <*You have the CriEn—it's your get out of jail free card. Not to mention, proof of your innocence.*>

<*This again? Do **you** want to go back?*> Sera asked. <*You could if you wanted to, I wouldn't stop you.*>

Helen's silvery laugh echoed through Sera's mind, a sound she had heard often, ever since she was a small child—probably even before she could remember.

<Dear, I have seen enough of that life; I paired with you to get out, for the adventure. And this may be the grandest adventure I have ever experienced.>

Sera smiled. She was glad Helen felt that way—this life, this adventure as her oldest friend put it, *was* grand, far better than what her father had planned for her.

<But you are going to have to confront them. They're going to come for the Intrepid, they'll try to force you to go.>

"They'll try," Sera whispered to herself.

<The Intrepid will be the catalyst, though. Orion will not sit idly by and let that sort of tech fall into your father's hands,> Helen cautioned.

<We don't know that the Intrepid really has picotech. No evidence of it was ever found at Kapteyn's Star, and the Victorians never showed that level of tech in anything they did afterward,> Sera replied.

<If they even **fear** your father will gain picotech, it will be war.>

War. The sort of war like none ever seen before—and people had worked up some good ones in the past. Humanity was still recovering from the last one. But her father had always stayed out of prior conflicts. This would be different.

It would spread across the Orion arm of the galaxy, all of humanity would be engulfed.

"Cheeky, could—" she began, only to see that her pilot was no longer on the bridge. Her musings had been more distracting than she thought.

Sera brought up the nav data herself and reviewed it one final time.

From Angela's scan data, plus stories of other ships that had been lost in the Streamer, she knew the *Intrepid* to be in interstellar space, rim-ward of Bollam's World—perhaps even within the star's heliopause.

Bollam's World lay on the far side of several interstellar federations and demarchies. Not to mention the core worlds.

Known as the AST, the core was a strong federation with far too much red tape for Sera's taste—their security was rather invasive, even for ships just passing through their systems. *Sabrina* would give those worlds a wide berth.

Their first stop would be Ayrea, 73 light-years distant, where the ship would skip along the rim of the system before reaching the jump point on its far side. From there, it was a 15 light-year hop to Pavonis, and then, ironically, they would pass through New Eden, the very system the *Intrepid* had been destined to colonize all those millennia ago. There, they would likely stop for fuel and supplies.

Tanis would get an up-close view the world she should have lived and died on long ago.

<*You seem melancholy,*> Helen interjected.

<*I was just thinking of how it will be for Tanis to see New Eden,*> Sera replied.

<*I'm not so sure. Aside from discovering that she jumped five-thousand years into the future, little seems to unsettle Tanis Richards.*>

<*True enough, she was completely calm under fire on the* Regal Dawn. *Her heart rate never even rose.*>

<*Spying on our guest, are we?*> Helen asked with a chuckle, knowing all too well that it was second nature for both of them to observe every aspect of their surroundings.

<*Maybe just a little bit, I do prefer her to be alive for this plan,*> Sera shook her head, remembering the fear she felt when she held Tanis's in her arms on the *Regal Dawn*, convinced the woman would die.

<*If all goes well, she'll likely never die. Unless she goes and gets her heart blown out of her chest when there's no one around to fix her up again,*> Helen replied.

Sera nodded absently as she reviewed the data for the final leg of their journey, the 28 light-years to Bollam's World, and then to the *Intrepid*. The entire trip would cross nearly 140 light-years, or roughly 1.3 quadrillion kilometers. With an average FTL factor of 579, and their entry speed of 0.70c, the trip would take roughly ninety days, a hundred if they stopped in New Eden for fuel and post cards.

BREAK A FEW EGGS

STELLAR DATE: 07.27.8927 (Adjusted Years)
LOCATION: Andromeda's Pinnace, Tsarina Refinery, EK Belt
REGION: Bollam's World System, Bollam's World Federation

"Do you think it will work?" Jessica asked, concern filling her eyes.

"Back in Sol? Hell no. Out here, who knows, maybe?" Joe replied. "Either way, we can't just sit out here watching forever."

"OK, sending the docking request now."

Jessica sent the sequence, and Joe prayed it would work. It had taken them two weeks to get this far into the Bollam's World system; during that time they had watched thousands of ships drop out of space—appearing to come from nowhere—and then drift into the system.

Most were small, some not significantly larger than the pinnace in which they flew. It hadn't taken long for them to have no other conclusion than FTL.

Over the past months, as data streams had been stripped from insystem beacons, the crew of the *Intrepid* had strongly suspected that faster than light travel was in use—Earnest had been practically giddy at the prospect.

Now they were certain.

It opened up a world of possibilities—and made their whole struggle pointless. Joe knew it also meant that there was little reason to expect Tanis to be in Bollams's World anymore. She could be anywhere in the entire galaxy, and if she hadn't made it back to the *Intrepid* by now, things were likely not going well for her.

Still, they had to start somewhere.

He was glad for Jessica. She was able to put her worry aside and follow her investigative training. There was a lead, they would follow it and it would bring them to a new lead. To her, it was that simple.

"Station's responded," Jessica said a few minutes later. "We have a berth on the refinery's north docking ring."

"External docking for a ship this small?" Joe shook his head. "I don't know what to make of this time...are they more or less advanced?"

"Beats me," Jessica shrugged.

Joe looked over the flight path the station provided and lined the pinnace up for the approach.

The refinery was not a large installation—less than fifteen kilometers across—but the amount of traffic it supported impressed Joe. Hundreds of ships were in varying stages of approach and departure.

"These grav drives they seem to have sure do help them manage a higher volume of traffic," Jessica said, apparently on the same train of thought.

"I think it's the lack of engine wash. There's no worry about ion streams and plasma melting other ships or the station. It keeps the space lanes open."

Jessica nodded absently. "Let's hope they don't mind us coming in the old fashioned way."

Joe bit his lip as he worked to stay on course. "No kidding, this is threading one hell of a needle. Good thing we matched v further out. There's no room for corrective burns when we get closer."

The next several hours passed slowly as Joe worked to keep the ship in the pocket, while Jessica established a connection with the station and began querying its concierge AI for information on any recently recovered escape pods, or other salvage.

"Oh shit, here it is," Joe said as the station's traffic control opened a comm link.

"Vessel *Andromeda 3*, what are you doing approaching this facility with your torch on? Kill your fusion drive immediately and switch to grav drives!"

Joe took a deep breath and responded in his best space jock voice. "Ah, that's a negative station; we had a blow-out on our graviton emitters and can't make our approach with them. I'm right down the middle and about to switch to thrusters; ion dispersion systems show no wash will hit the station or other ships."

He glanced at Jessica and crossed his fingers while they waited for the approach.

"I don't care if you have God himself piloting that piece of crap. You don't approach a station on your torch, and I certainly can't have you chewing up that lane for the next hour. Kill your engine. I'm sending a tug out to pull you in the rest of the way. You better have an account open when you dock, because there are going to be some fines waiting for you."

"Well that sucks balls," Jessica said as the station cut the connection. "I don't suppose they'll take Sol credits."

"Any chance you can see if we can get an account opened with a local bank with some credit?" Joe asked as he killed the fusion engine, switching attitude control to chemical thrusters.

"Whew," Jessica said after a few minutes. "I guess they're used to getting ships from all over. They have procedures for ships with no local accounts or registration to get credit. Granted, we have to put the pinnace up as collateral."

Joe grinned. "We better not lose it; *Corsia* wouldn't like it if we sold her best pinnace."

The tug arrived, made grapple and half an hour later they were walking through their hatch onto the station's docking ring.

Right into an irate station worker.

"Are you the morons that came in on their torch? What were you thinking?" she demanded.

Joe began to speak, but Jessica put her hand on the woman's arm. "We're terribly sorry about that. Things aren't this busy or...as grand, where we're from. Coming in on a torch is OK if you need to. We didn't mean to cause trouble."

The dockworker's expression softened as she looked into Jessica's batting eyes.

"Yeah, well, you're core-side now. None of your fringe nonsense will fly here. You've got to sign this."

The dockworker handed a sheet of plas to Jessica and she looked it over. "This is half our credit!" she gasped. "How are we going to refuel?"

"You better have some good cargo to trade on that little tub," the dockworker shrugged. "You're getting off with a wrist-slap. Usually you'd be impounded for what you did."

Joe and Jessica exchanged glances, and Jessica passed her auth token to the plas before handing it back.

"I sure hope we do," Jessica said with a nod. "Thank you."

The woman cast them a curious look before tucking the plas under her arm and rushing down the dock, already yelling at a cargo hauler at the next berth.

"Damn, we better have something of value here," Jessica said. "Or we're going to be calling *Corisa* for pickup real soon."

* * * * *

A day later, and after more drinks than either Joe or Jessica cared to recall, they had no leads on Tanis whatsoever. Returning to the pinnace, they strode out of a lift onto the docking ring to see two soldiers in powered armor standing outside their berth.

"Well, that doesn't loo—" Jessica was interrupted by a rough voice to their left.

"Come with us."

Joe turned to see several more soldiers. Their faces were invisible behind mirrored visors, but the tone of their leader's voice brooked no argument. He looked back at Jessica who shrugged.

"Sure, where're we going?" Joe asked as the leader—a corporal by her stripes—gestured for them to step back into the lift.

"Questioning." Was the only response.

<*Guesses?*> Joe asked Jessica.

<*My bet? They have decided our ship and our story don't match. So long as they don't find our stash on the pinnace, we'll still have a bargaining chip or two.*>

When the lift stopped, the corporal and his unit led them through a series of corridors to another lift. Another squad of soldiers, also in powered armor, guarded this one. They directed Joe and Jessica to step through an auth scanner.

The scanner must have seen something it didn't like and called the corporal over to confer with another soldier. Their faces were obscured by their helmets, but Joe had no doubt who was the subject of conversation.

<*Me or you?*> Jessica asked.

<*Bets are that it's me,*> Joe replied with a mental chuckle. <*Your most interesting mods are all visible on the outside.*>

After a few minutes, the corporal walked back to them.

"Your cellular structure is…abnormal," he said to Joe. "It doesn't appear to be dangerous, but don't even think of trying anything."

"I wouldn't dream of it," Joe replied.

The corporal nodded and directed them into the open lift door.

Joe and Jessica stepped in, and the rest of the squad filed in after them. When the doors opened again, they revealed a bustling corridor filled with personnel dressed in what Joe assumed were the Bollam's World military uniforms.

"Wait here," the corporal directed before moving down the corridor and knocking on a door. The remainder of his squad directed Joe and Jessica away from the lift entrance, their stances alert and wary.

"You can relax a little bit, guys," Jessica said. "We may look tough, but we're really quite nice."

None of the soldiers replied and Jessica sighed. "Real bunch of hard cases here."

"You'd behave the same way in their shoes," Joe replied.

"No, I'd probably behave worse; these guys haven't made fun of us once."

Down the corridor, the corporal stepped back into view, this time with her helmet tucked under her arm. A uniformed woman wearing a major's insignia accompanied her.

<Lies or truth?> Jessica asked Joe.

<Let's see what they know, but I'm leaning toward truth at this point.>

The woman approached, her expression steely as she eyed them over. Joe noticed that the squad guarding them stiffened as the major drew closer.

"So, you're who all this is about, then?" she asked.

"Glad to meet you," Joe extended his hand. "I'm Joe and this is Jessica."

The woman gazed at his extended hand and then replied brusquely, "I'm Major Akido." Without another word, she turned and strode down the hall, gesturing for them to follow.

Joe looked down at his outstretched hand and shrugged. "Maybe it's not a greeting here."

"Oh, it is," one of the soldiers gave a low chuckle. "She just doesn't extend pleasantries to much of anyone, least of all folks like you."

"Who are 'folks like us'?" Joe asked.

The corporal shot a look at the soldier and the man clammed up.

A minute later, they reached their destination, a nondescript conference room. The major took a seat on one side and gestured for Joe and Jessica to sit across from her.

Major Akido leaned back in her chair and stared each of them in the eyes for several minutes. Eventually, she let out a long sigh.

"So, where is it?" she finally asked.

"Where is what?" Joe replied.

"Your ship, where is it?" the major's tone was terse and brooked no evasion.

"It's in the dock. We were on our way there when your guys brought us here," Jessica replied with a frown.

The major leaned forward. "Cut the shit, you two. Your colony ship, where is it?"

Joe couldn't hide his surprise. He glanced at Jessica, who also appeared rather shocked.

<Truth it is, then,> she said to Joe.

"It's outsystem, we're just here to find someone who went missing."

Major Akido's brow furrowed into a deep frown. "Missing? How did someone on your colony ship go missing here?"

"We had an accident," Joe replied. "She had to eject in an escape pod, and by the time we got to her reported position, she was gone."

The major didn't respond immediately, and Jessica jumped in with a question of her own.

"How did you know that we're from a colony ship? Why would you even look for that?"

"Your ship, for starters. Your graviton emitters aren't broken, they're not present—neither is your grav drive. No grav drive means no FTL. If that's the case, then your shuttle didn't just jump in outside the system, you came in a different ship. Only two types of ships lurk out there sending in small shuttles. Enemy militaries and lost colony ships. But no military would do such a crap job sending in spies, so it was pretty simple."

Joe whistled. "So this happens a lot? Colony ships just wind up on your doorstep?"

"Not a lot, but often enough," Major Akido said with a shrug. "Isotope analysis of your shuttle confirmed that it is of Sol manufacture, sometime in the early fifth millennium. That sealed it."

<Well, there's all our cards on the table,> Joe said privately to Jessica. <What now?>

<Not all,> Jessica replied. <For all their fancy grav drives and FTL, we know these people barely have fourth millennia tech. The Intrepid has a lot to offer them.>

<Too bad they don't have a colony world to offer us,> Joe sighed.

"Then what's next?" Joe asked.

The major leaned back and smiled, "We're going to want to speak to your captain."

NEW EDEN

STELLAR DATE: 10.06.8927 (Adjusted Years)
LOCATION: *Sabrina*, Scattered Disk
REGION: New Eden System, Eden Alliance

Sabrina transitioned out of the dark layer into the New Eden system at the precise location Cheeky planned.

"Nailed it!" Cheeky shouted as the system nav buoy confirmed their location. "Pay up, Cargo."

Cargo sighed and flipped her a Silstrand token. "I can't believe you pulled that off. Your vector looked totally out of whack back at Ayrea."

"Or so you thought," Cheeky chuckled.

Tanis only half-heard their banter as she reviewed the local scan data.

New Eden was a booming system. Tens of thousands of ships plied its space lanes; it boasted three terraformed worlds, up from the original two the FGT had left for the *Intrepid*. It took conscious effort to keep herself from becoming morose at the thought.

<Sera is convinced the FGT will give us a new system after she reaches out to them,> Angela broke into Tanis's thoughts.

<Indeed she is, though how she'll pull that rabbit out of her hat should be interesting. From what I read in Sabrina's archives, the FGT has not made direct contact with anyone in over five-hundred years. How **does** she know how to reach them?> Tanis asked.

<It's a good question. I know you wonder if she is playing us,> Angela said, concern emanating from her mind. <But I don't sense that from her. We know there's more to her than she lets on; she has more contacts than her station would indicate.>

Tanis nodded absently. *Sabrina's* captain was a frequent topic of conversation between her and Angela. They both harbored doubts that Sera could live up to her end of the deal.

<There's also the issue of transitioning the Intrepid,> Tanis said. <You know what you've found—there is an upper limit to the size of ship that anyone has successfully slipped into the dark layer—and come out again. The Intrepid is far above that size limit.>

<I'll admit it's a concern. But give Bob and Earnest some credit. If the two of them can't crack the issue, I don't know who—>

Angela stopped as both she and Tanis saw the same scan data roll in.

"There are eleven AST dreadnaughts passing through the system!" Tanis called out.

"There are what?" Sera said, half out of her chair as Tanis brought the scan data up on the bridge's main holo.

"That's rather usual," Cargo said calmly.

"Understatement of the year," Cheeky tossed a scowl his way. "New Eden and the AST aren't exactly on the friendliest of terms, not since that little war they had a few decades ago."

Tanis remembered reading about that conflict. New Eden lay on the spin-ward edge of AST space, and was under constant pressure from the core worlds to join their alliance. New Eden preferred its independence and maintained a sizeable space force to ensure they retained it. They would lose to a full assault from the AST's military, but they were capable of making the effort too costly for any aggressor.

"They must have pulled some sort of serious diplomatic shit to be here right now," Sera said in awe.

"Doesn't look like the locals are too trusting either," Tanis said. "Almost half their fleet is shadowing those dreadnaughts."

Sera nodded with appreciation. "From the looks of it, they stopped and refueled here, too."

"They're headed for the same jump point we are," Cheeky said, her voice low and completely serious. "They're going to Bollam's."

<She's right,> Angela agreed. *<There are reports of an old colony ship insystem at Bollam's World. The local nets are going nuts with speculation over what is going to happen.>*

"Punch it, Cheeky! Full burn. We *must* get there before those AST assholes," Sera yelled.

Cheeky complied and Sabrina prepared for a full antimatter burn around the edge of the New Eden system.

"Not around, Cheeky," Sera said, her eyes deadly serious. "Go through the system."

"We're going to pick up a hell of a fine for this," Cargo said. "They're not going to take kindly to us blasting through."

"And with their current fleet distribution, they won't do anything to stop us either," Sera replied.

"You hope," Cargo said.

Sera did not reply.

"I don't get it," Cheeky said as she plotted the new course and spun out the AP nozzle. "I mean, I get that your ship has some cool shit, Tanis, but what could be worth the AST doing this?"

Tanis was poring over the available specs on the dreadnaughts and didn't reply. The ships were large by ninetieth century standards, each coming in at just over six kilometers long. They sported more rails, beams, and missile launches than she even cared to count.

<Those are some serious ships,> Tanis sighed. <If we had brought the whole fleet from Kapteyn's, I would be a lot less worried, but this will be a close fight, we may have to use it again.>

"Well?" Cheeky asked once *Sabrina* was boosting on its new trajectory. "What does your ship have that's so special?"

Tanis looked around the bridge. Cheeky appeared to be almost angry, while Cargo was merely curious. Sera's expression was more unreadable. Then the captain turned her head toward Cheeky and Cargo without breaking eye contact with Tanis.

"Look up something called *The Battle of Victoria*. It took place in the Kapteyn's system before the *Intrepid* left. Look for speculation on how they defeated the Sirians with minimal losses."

Tanis let out a long sigh. If Sera was telling her crew what to look for, then she had already found it. The record of the *Intrepid's* picotech had persisted these five-thousand years.

<Funny that this information is in the ship's database,> Angela commented privately to Tanis. <It wasn't previously.>

<I know, I checked, too,> Tanis replied.

"Picotech!" Cargo exclaimed, half rising from his chair. "How...what...is it real?"

Tanis didn't have it in her to lie to *Sabrina's* crew—she knew that her resigned expression was already all the confirmation that Sera needed—if she needed any at all.

"It is true," Tanis replied.

"And you...wait...you!" Cheeky's voice fell into a shocked hush.

Tanis could tell that she had read something which referenced her as a general and lieutenant governor.

"General Richards, is it?" Cargo asked. "Or should I say governor?"

"How long have you known?" Tanis asked Sera. "This information was not in your databases when I came onboard."

"I pulled an update when we were in Ayrea," Sera replied smoothly. "I wanted to know more about your ship and the time you came from."

Tanis nodded slowly. "Well, now you know."

She fended off as many questions about the picotech, and her rank, as she could. She was surprised that no one was overly upset about her lies and omissions. Even Thompson grunted that he would not have volunteered the information either.

She was saved from further revelations by the first few calls from the system traffic AI regarding their speed, which Tanis responded to, but eventually just logged them with no response. It was clear they were on an outsystem vector, not passing close to any New Eden worlds or stations. No military vessels or drones moved to intercept them, and the traffic AI appeared to content itself with simply adding on fine after fine.

"This'll bankrupt us," Cargo muttered at one point.

"No," Sera disagreed while directing a pointed look at Tanis. "It really won't."

Tanis set two countdowns on the main holo. One for the AST dreadnaughts, and one for *Sabrina*. The dreadnaughts would beat them to the jump point, but the AST vessels were maintaining steady 0.5c. A max speed which was likely enforced by the New Eden space force ships shadowing the foreign military vessels.

Because entry velocity into the dark layer translated into faster travel time, *Sabrina* would reach Bollam's World before the AST vessels, even though they entered FTL later.

The trip across the New Eden system took just shy of twenty-three hours, and Tanis watched with concern gnawing at her innards as the eleven AST dreadnaughts winked out of scan visibility.

"There they go," Sera said. "Now we just have to hope that half the New Eden space force doesn't decide to find out why we're in such a hurry.

Sabrina was an hour from the jump point; light-lag to the closest New Eden vessel was fifty-two minutes—with the relativistic adjustments.

<Given how long it would take them to have confirmed the AST departure, we should be hearing from them right...about...now,> Helen said.

On her queue, the comm board lit up with an incoming transmission from a NESF patrol craft.

<Show-off,> Sabrina muttered.

Tanis played the message aloud.

"Star Freighter *Sabrina*, this is the *Sword of Eden*, please declare your intentions. If we didn't know better, we would think you're chasing those core-worlder dreadnaughts."

Cargo let out a laugh. "Calling those AST ships core-worlders as if he isn't one. When the fringe is nearly a thousand light-years in any direction, you're core, too."

"What would you like me to say," Tanis asked Sera.

"You're asking me?" Sera said with a wink. "You're the general—what do you think you should say?"

Tanis remained silent for several moments before shaking her head and turning to her console.

"*Sword of Eden*, this is General Tanis Richards of the ISS *Intrepid*. This ship is returning me to Bollam's World and is under my protection. As for what we plan to do with those dreadnaughts, look up the Battle of Victoria and figure it out."

Cheeky let out a long whistle. "Well, that'll either get them the hell out of our way—or they'll blow us to bits."

"We have thirty-seven minutes to find out," Sera replied.

<Thirty-two,> Angela corrected the captain.

"Damn relativistic math," Sera muttered.

No one spoke on the bridge as they raced closer to the NESF ships still clustered around the jump point. Tanis surmised that they weren't entirely trusting the AST ships' word that they were going to Bollam's World. It was possible, however unlikely, that this was some sort of feint before a full-scale attack.

The earliest time for a reply from the NESF came and went, then sixteen more minutes ticked by with agonizing slowness before a message came in.

The message was short and to the point.

"Star freighter *Sabrina,* you are cleared to maintain your current course and exit the New Eden system. Fines against your vessel have been lifted."

"See?" Sera said with a grin as she looked between Cheeky and Cargo. I told you the general would know what to say. *And* we're not facing any fines. A good day in my books."

THE SILENT SYSTEM

STELLAR DATE: 10.25.8927 (Adjusted Years)
LOCATION: *Sabrina*, Scattered Disk
REGION: Bollam's World System, Bollam's World Federation

Cheeky brought *Sabrina* out of FTL further from the Bollam's World star than Tanis would have preferred, though she understood the need for caution—not to mention the time it would take to decelerate from 0.79*c*.

"Forty-nine AU from the stellar primary," the pilot reported.

"Well done," Sera said with a nod. "Pull us up above the stellar disk and start our braking."

Tanis tapped the system beacon's passive data stream.

"That's weird," she said with a frown. "There's nothing about the *Intrepid* on the beacon, just the standard traffic conditions, and system laws and regulations."

"I don't think those AST ships are coming here for a vacation," Sera said. "Someone is trying their best to keep things looking normal."

"The outer beacon isn't responding to requests for active data. I've sent our packet to the system relay further in; maybe once we're registered on scan we can get more info," Tanis said.

"Keep active sensors on full bore," Sera said to Tanis. "This system is always a hot mess."

Tanis had noticed *Sabrina's* shielding taking repeated impacts from dust. She was impressed at how well the graviton shielding protected the freighter. The *Intrepid's* shields would be hard-pressed to keep the ship safe in a system this young and active while traveling at such speeds.

She had spent some time reviewing data entries on Bollam's World. The star was young, under half a billion years old. The eleven major planets which orbited the star were still young and hot, with the exception of the terraformed worlds in the habitable zone. Records showed that the initial colonists, also victims of Kapteyn's Streamer, had spent considerable effort cooling those worlds before they could even begin to make them habitable.

The star lay in a region of space with few G or K class stars. Its location, combined with youth, had caused the FGT to pass it by entirely. It was probably the only G-class star within a hundred light-years of Sol which was not prepared for humanity by the FGT, but by the colonists themselves.

Tanis had to admire the tenacity of those original settlers. What they had accomplished was more even impressive than what the Edeners and Victorians had built at The Kap.

She scanned through the data on the planets, taking note of the strange gas giant named Aurora which lay seventh from the star, and the terraforming that was underway on a moon around the sixth planet, a gas giant named Kithari.

"You're going to want to alter course, Cheeky," Tanis said as she put the results of the first active scan sweep on the main holo. "There's a dense molecular cloud ahead, and a small dwarf world seems to have its orbit changed since the last time *Sabrina* got an update on Bollam's."

<Sorry to have inconvenienced you,> Sabrina said with a sigh.

<Easy now,> Sera said soothingly. <We don't pass this close to the core very often. Not much need to get updated system data for these worlds.>

"I'm going to grab some coffee, anyone want some?" Cargo asked as he rose.

The three women called out in affirmative and the first mate chuckled. "Maybe I'll just bring the pot."

"You know, I'm going to go do a quick walk through the ship," Tanis said while rising from her station. "I've slaved scan to your console, Cheeky, and Angela is keeping an eye on it as well."

"We'll ping you if you're needed," Sera said.

Cargo returned with three cups of coffee. "Gave Tanis hers in the galley."

"She's got a lot on her mind," Sera said with a nod. "Don't know that I'd want to be in her position right now."

"What position is that, Captain?" Cargo's dark eyes stared at Sera intently. "What do you think we are flying into?"

Sera thought about it for a moment before replying.

"Either the *Intrepid* was smart and started trading its tech for fuel and FTL capability, or they clamed up and got themselves boarded and gutted."

"Do you think they'd be able to defend themselves?"

"Maybe—Tanis never said how much of that fleet they took with them when they left Kapteyn's Star—or if they have more of their pico bombs. If they do, then we're flying into a war-zone."

"Didn't we just leave that party?"

"That was just a mixer; the real party's still to come," Sera laughed. "But now that you bring it up, I think I should go and see if I can get our general to lay down some specifics on her ship's defenses."

Cargo nodded and Sera slipped off the bridge. She found Tanis where she expected, at the forward scan and targeting sensors. Sera wasn't sure if she should be surprised that Tanis was a general and colony governor, or that she hadn't suspected her rank was far higher than she let on—she fit in with the crew as well as possible, but there were times when her bearing and poise had hinted at a higher position.

Sera wondered if her own background traits ever slipped through. There were secrets she kept that no one on this ship needed to know. Most of her past was far better off buried and forgotten.

"They still good as new?" Sera asked.

"Seem to be. Though, I should have insisted on an external array."

"You were in a rush—and I appreciate the haste, even though it was unnecessary," Sera said with a grin.

Tanis turned to Sera, her blue eyes appeared darker and more serious than normal—if that were possible.

"You don't have to do this. I don't want to risk you and your crew more than I already have. You could send me in on one of your escape pods. I can figure out a way to get to the *Intrepid*."

"Don't be ridiculous." Sera dismissed Tanis's statement with a wave of her hand. "You helped my crew rescue me when you could have just cut and run. There's no way I am just going to leave you high and dry."

Tanis smiled and appeared to relax. "Thank you. I can't imagine what would have happened if you hadn't opened that container I was in."

"I can. You would have gotten close and personal with Rebecca and her pointy needles"

"I'm sorry about that; my fault again."

"Stop saying that." Sera wasn't sure what to make of this uncharacteristically self-effacing Tanis. "I'm right as rain and thoroughly enjoyed giving that bitch what she had coming."

Tanis laughed. "I almost would have liked to have seen that...almost." Then the general eyed Sera up and down and appeared to consider her words carefully. "We both know that most nano around here isn't as good as mine. Considering what you likely had to work with—not to mention dealing with your new skin trying to kill you—how *did* you heal from that torture so fast?"

"I guess I was lucky. Helen found all the right stuff we needed on the station to keep me going," Sera replied with a shrug, the lie coming easily after so many years—though she could see that Tanis wasn't buying it.

"You handled the trauma of torture rather well—something I bet that they don't teach you to in star-freighter captain school," the general pressed.

"I wouldn't say 'rather well', more like...I didn't curl up into a fetal position. It's not my first time being at the receiving end of someone's ill intentions. I've already done all the puking and crying. Now I know how to repress it like a pro."

Tanis's skepticism was plainly displayed on her face. "I've come clean with you, Sera. Let me know when you are ready to do the same—but don't give me your coy routine and trite little lies. You are far from who you appear to be. I hope your motives in helping me are as altruistic as you claim." She paused and drew in a long breath, her eyes narrowing. "Because if you think there is some special advantage you can gain over the *Intrepid* once we arrive, you will be mistaken."

Sera's breath caught in her throat. Tanis's blunt verbal assault took her completely off guard. For a moment, she wondered if Tanis suspected the truth about her.

<She doesn't know the truth; she probably hasn't guessed anything close to it,> Helen said. <But she was once a counterinsurgency officer in the TSF—from what she told the crew around the wardroom table one night. She can likely see cracks all over your story. She certainly saw your blood pressure rise just now.>

Sera forced herself to resume breathing evenly. Though Tanis may know she was hiding things, Helen was right, she wouldn't even come close to the truth if she guessed for a thousand years.

"You've got me, Tanis," Sera said slowly. "I've not been completely honest with you, but I'm not yet ready to talk about my past…give me more time."

Tanis's look was skeptical, but she didn't push. "The time is close. When we get to the *Intrepid*, Bob will discover your truth, I'd rather you share it willingly before he does."

"Who is Bob?" Sera asked.

Tanis chuckled. "That's a truth you'll soon learn on your own."

Neither woman spoke for a minute, and then Sera asked the question for which she had searched out Tanis in the first place.

"Things are likely to be hairy when we get insystem, how much of that fleet did you bring with you from Kapteyn's Star?"

"Not as much as I wish we had," Tanis sighed. "We swapped out the two Neptune class cruisers for the *Orkney* and the *Dresden*—two of the new Claymore class battle cruisers. Otherwise, it's our initial fleet of eight cruisers, some twenty pushers, and a bevy of pinnaces, shuttles, and transports. We do have a lot more fighters than we left Sol with, but I don't think even our new Arc-5s are going to be much of a match for modern craft pulling over 500gs. Not to mention that our ES shielding is not nearly as effective as your new grav shields."

Sera whistled. "Still more than any colony ship I've ever heard of, but probably not a match for those AST dreadnaughts."

"The *Intrepid* itself is a pretty formidable weapon. Its size also makes it hard to damage—bar the use of fusion bombs," Tanis replied. "Though we try to keep it out of the thick of battle."

"What about the pico?" Sera asked, afraid the answer would be no, but just as afraid that it may be yes.

Tanis nodded. "It's there, we have more RMs than you'd like to know exist, and they're all capable of carrying pico warheads."

"Let's hope it doesn't come to that," Sera said with a shudder. She looked into Tanis's eyes and could tell the general felt the same way. The pico was a weapon of last resort—every other avenue would have to be exhausted first.

Tanis glanced back at the sensor array's maintenance console. "I should finish looking this over."

"You've been on shift for half a day and we have seven hours before we'll get a response from the system beacon's active Link. Why don't you catch sack till then? I can do the inspection."

Tanis gave a tired smile. "I suppose I could use some rest...and it *is* your ship after all."

THROUGH THE LOOKING GLASS

STELLAR DATE: 10.26.8927 (Adjusted Years)
LOCATION: *Sabrina*, EK Belt
REGION: Bollam's World System, Bollam's World Federation

<System beacon has registered us and we have active system scan,> Sabrina reported ship-wide.

Tanis was on the bridge minutes later, one hand holding a cup of coffee and the other rubbing her face. "Does it have data on the *Intrepid*?" she asked.

Cheeky un-slaved scan from her console and directed it back to Tanis's station.

"Doesn't look like it," the pilot said with a shake of her head. "Just the same as before, though with more up-to-date information."

"It's like the *Intrepid* really isn't here…" Tanis sighed. "But the reports in New Eden definitely talked about a colony ship in Bollam's."

"Tanis, check the planets' positions in scan with what we can see from here. The beacon's scan data may be faked."

Cheeky looked up from her console. "Fake! No one fakes system scan. They may as well ask for jump-point collisions!"

"I've seen it before," Sera said, her voice solemn.

"Freaking, fucking… nut… I'm out of words!"

Cheeky may present a carefree exterior in nearly every aspect of her life; but when it came to piloting, and the strictures that kept starships plying the dark, she was a different person. She was right, too; faking scan was a disaster waiting to happen. Ships may be small in the vastness of space, but they all traveled between just a few points, which meant they were usually concentrated within the same areas.

"Damn…it *is* faked," Tanis reported. "This looks like scan from over a month ago, they tried to blend it so that the planets were in the right positions, but there are ships clearly heading to places that have since moved."

"We need to find out what is going on in this system and fast. Cheeky, let's burn some antimatter."

Sera stood and threw *Sabrina's* own scan data on the bridge's main holo tank. "Looks strangely clear," the captain muttered.

The space they were traveling through was near a commonly used jump point, which the ship's scan showed it to be deserted.

Tanis frowned at her readouts. "I'm betting that there is real scan somewhere. Whoever has botched the signal must still want to know where things are themselves. Good data has to be in there somewhere."

She and Angela broke down the data stream from the system's beacon and began sifting through its components for any hidden information while Sera sent an update to the rest of the crew. Over the next half hour, everyone visited the bridge to ask if they were really in a system with no scan.

Twenty minutes later, Tanis let out a cry of triumph.

"Found it! I figured the best place to hide the real scan was within the fake one. There were several distorted portions of the signal, and sure enough one of them contained the carrier wave for valid data. I'm configuring our system to read from it."

Sera set her screen to display the system's readout, and within a minute, it flicked from the boring show of regular, light traffic to an entirely different tableau. Everyone took a deep breath and then uttered a variety of curses.

The real data showed a heavy cluster of ships near the system's sixth planet, the $6M_J$ gas giant named Kithari. Sera selected that planet and zoomed in. The ships were grouped near one of its larger moons, a world named Fierra, which appeared to be in the late stages of terraforming. She selected the planet and all space within two hundred thousand kilometers and threw it up on the bridge's main holo tank. Cheeky and Tanis swiveled in their chairs to gaze at the results.

It was a mess.

Seven thousand kilometers from the moon, in an equatorial orbit, lay the *Intrepid*, its fleet fully deployed. Roughly a hundred-thousand kilometers beyond lay a fleet consisting of fifty-two destroyers and light cruisers. The scan data identified them as Bollam's World Space

Force. The majority of ships in this fleet were positioned at strategic points that appeared to both protect and corral the *Intrepid*.

Another fleet held position fifty-thousand kilometers north of the moon, it consisted of several light cruisers and over two-hundred corvettes. A similar formation of nearly the same composition held position roughly the same distance south of the moon.

Beyond all the fleets lay the eleven AST dreadnaughts, holding station in a half-ring around the moon's parent world.

"How the hell did they beat us here?" Sera cursed.

"They must have transitioned back to regular space and boosted up, before going back into FTL," Cheeky said, her brow furrowed.

"I realize that, it was rhetorical," Sera said.

"Oh."

Tanis let out a soft chuckle, then a good long laugh. When she stopped, she looked up to see Sera, Cheeky, and Cargo staring at her.

"Sorry, it's just par for the course," Tanis said, still chuckling. "They've gone and got themselves into quite the mess. Who do you think those corvette fleets are?"

Sera frowned. "Someday I'd like to hear the whole story of how you guys got here. As for those two light fleets…they're…aw shit."

"That good, eh?" Tanis asked.

"Our pirate friends have come for the fun. Rebecca and her ships are at the north pole and Padre is at the south end. Looks like they decided to go hunting for the *Intrepid* without you."

"How friendly are any of those factions likely to become with each other?"

"I'd say less friendly, more hostile. Scan shows several small debris fields. I'll bet there have already been some altercations."

"I'm surprised that more of the Bollam's space force isn't deployed," Cargo said. "They must have thousands of ships in the system."

"They're moving more in, but I bet the arrival of the AST is giving them pause," Tanis said. "You can see them gathering forces at key points. I bet they're also readying some nice big rail guns."

"They'll have some, but people don't really use rails defensively anymore," Sera said as she examined the Bollam's fleet positions. "With inertial dampeners, ships can jink well out of the way of a rail's slug."

Tanis frowned. "That may be true, but what about grapeshot? You don't fire where they are, but where you expect them to be."

"Grapeshot?" Cheeky asked.

"Rail-fired shells filled with millions of pebbles. You fill all reasonable approaches with them. People can jink all they want, they'll just jink into the grapeshot. Then you use their hesitation against them and send in the slugs, or beams, if they are close enough," Tanis replied.

"You lived in a brutal time," Cargo commented.

"War is always brutal. But I need to get to my ship, and you need to deliver on your promise," Tanis said to Sera, her expression almost pleading.

Sera smiled and nodded to Tanis before she turned to their pilot. "Cheeky? How does it look?"

"Well, provided no one blows us to pieces, I can make it happen. Based on the axial tilt of the planet, and everyone's orbits, there will be a period in about five hours where only a few of Rebecca's ships will have *Intrepid* in their sights. She's a big mutha, so I bet if I work up the right approach vector we can use her to hide us and get in almost entirely unseen. I'll have to work out the timing and coast—even hiding behind the *Intrepid's* girth, an AP trail would be plain as day."

"Good plan," Sera said. "Why don't you kill thrust now, and we'll coast till you have your path worked up. Use minimal burn; we'll try to stay as dark as possible. Nix our beacon, too. No need to let Rebecca know her favorite pincushion is within reach."

"Can they detect the graviton emissions from our shielding?" Tanis asked.

Sera ran a hand through her hair. "This close to a $6M_J$ jovian they shouldn't be able to. Plus, I'm not really comfortable disabling shields. This system still has a lot of stuff flying around."

"Having been in a ship hit by this system's debris, I see your point," Tanis acknowledged with a nod. "I'll get a transmission ready to burst to the *Intrepid* when we have a clear line to them. Don't want them thinking we're hostile."

Sera hadn't even thought of that. *Sabrina's* new shields were good, but she didn't want to see how well they'd hold up against the radiation wash from one of the tugs patrolling around the *Intrepid*, let alone the beams on those cruisers.

The next few hours passed quietly. *Sabrina* had a lot of speed to burn off before making her approach; rather than turning and braking, Cheeky altered the rear shields emit negative gravitons. The effect caused enough drag to slow them down and line up on the desired approach vector.

Sera was making a light lunch for herself in the mess when Flaherty came in and closed the galley door. She looked up at the dour man and smiled. "How are you today?"

Flaherty grunted. "Been better." He sloshed some semi-warm coffee into a mug and sat down. "It always catches up with you, doesn't it?"

"Noticed that too, did you?"

His deadly serious eyes bored into hers. "You aren't going to be able to run from it forever."

Sera spun to face him directly, her eyes angry, even though her voice was calm. "I am helping a friend here. This is not fate or anything, just random events."

Flaherty let out a long, exasperated sigh. "You know I'll always be here to watch your back. But some day you are going to have to own up to your destiny. We're doing the right thing now, but there are a lot of other things that could also use your attention—a lot more important than some energy module." With that, the large man stood and left the wardroom, his near-full cup of coffee left on the table.

Sera leaned against the counter and let out a long breath. Suddenly, the ship seemed too close and small about her. Her synthetic skin felt like it was constricting her, like she couldn't breathe. A wave of dizziness hit her and Sera closed her eyes, willing herself to be calm. She could do this; she would not repeat past mistakes. Tanis and the *Intrepid* would live to see another journey to a star where they could be left out of the messes this close to the core. Sera vowed it.

<*Easy now, just some anxiety,*> Helen's soothing voice whispered in her mind.

<*If ever there was a time to feel anxious, this is it,*> Sera replied.

<*Flaherty's right, it does feel a bit like destiny, doesn't it?*> Helen's voice held a wistful edge.

Sera wondered what the AI saw, what her wisdom and years told her about the future.

<It feels more like a curse,> Sera said with a sigh. <Like events will drive me back there no matter what.>

Helen sent out an affirmative wave of agreement. <I suspect they will.>

ANDROMEDA

STELLAR DATE: 10.26.8927 (Adjusted Years)
LOCATION: *Sabrina*, EK Belt
REGION: Bollam's World System, Bollam's World Federation

Tanis scoured the background noise in the system, looking for a range with little use and high levels of stellar noise.

<There, that whine coming from the weird jovian planet, Aurora. We can hide our signal in its noise. You can bet Bob is listening to that thing and what they have going on there,> Angela advised.

<I was thinking the same thing,> Tanis said and began to calibrate *Sabrina's* transmitter to piggyback on the planet's emissions.

<I know,> Angela replied with a wink.

"*Intrepid,* this is General Tanis Richards, hope this message finds you well. I'm in a small freighter, which will begin making an approach to your position in roughly ten minutes. We expect to be ready to dock in four hours and twenty-nine minutes. Our vector will be southerly to avoid detection from your friends. We will be alone and dark. Please do not fire on us. Please do not respond unless absolutely necessary. We're not exactly on friendly terms with some of the folks out there, either."

Tanis set the system to repeat the message three times and then killed the transmission. She turned to Cheeky.

"It's sent. We're good to begin our final approach. Everything set on your end?"

"As much as it's going to be. There's going to be a tight spot in about two hours when we get close to one of the AST ships, but we should be able to slip by if we kill all but our forward shields—which will be facing away from them." She entered in several commands on her console. "I'm having Sabrina switch main systems to battery, as well. No point in having a nice, hot reactor giving us away."

<I'm sipping juice here,> Sabrina said.

Tanis nodded. The new batteries could power the ship and even send a few pulses from the lasers before running dry. If things got hairy, the reactor would still be warm enough to spin it back up in a few minutes.

Sera reappeared on the bridge looking like she had eaten something unpleasant. She sat in her chair without saying a word and leaned her head back, eyes closed. There was no need to update her on the transmission and commencement of their final approach. Tanis could tell she had maintained a connection to the bridge net.

She felt tempted to ask the captain what was wrong, but decided the other woman just needed to calm down and put whatever was bothering her to rest rather than having to make up an evasive response.

Tanis took advantage of Sera's stillness to further observe her. The captain was usually in constant motion—her actions quick and decisive, her face never showing more or less than she intended it to.

At this moment, she looked much younger than usual. Tanis realized she couldn't place Sera's age...at all. She looked to be in her early twenties, but with the experiences she had mentioned in passing, not to mention her performance on the pirate station and the ship, she had to be much older. Sera had the knowledge and instincts of a person much closer to their first century, possibly even older than that.

<Not knowing her story is really eating you up, isn't it?> Angela asked.

<You know me; all the puzzle pieces have to fit.>

The crew had been of little help; most had only known her for a few years—though, in that time, they had become quite loyal. None of them had any knowledge of their captain's history before her purchase of *Sabrina*, with the exception of the ever-mysterious Flaherty—and he wasn't sharing anything.

Sera sat forward and opened her eyes, looking as alert and full of energy as ever. Tanis's moment of examination was over.

"Are you going to stay when we reach the *Intrepid*?" Tanis took the opportunity to ask.

Sera flashed an enigmatic smile. "Well, I do have to help you guys get that ship into FTL—unless they want to stay here forever."

Cheeky nearly choked. "Captain! That ship can never go into FTL. Every credit I have says they're negotiating for that moon they're orbiting—it's the only play they have."

Sera shook her head. "Not the only play. The *Intrepid* can drop into FTL. They just need the right plans to transition their ship safely, and make it appear unappetizing to the lurkers in the dark layer."

<*How is that possible?*> Angela asked. <*From my research, no one has ever transitioned a ship anywhere close to the* Intrepid's *size. Those dreadnaughts out there are about as big as you can go.*>

"Yeah, what she said," Cheeky turned in her seat and directed a quizzical look at Sera. "You don't have that tech; no one has it."

Sera shook her head slowly. "Not no one. I have it—so do some others."

"How—what—captain!" Cheeky exclaimed. "Don't be ridiculous! You can't swindle Tanis's people…"

"It's OK," Tanis said. "I'm taking it on faith that Sera has what she says she does. Besides, our deal was to get me here and be compensated—a payment that I will render promptly, once we dock."

"You won't throw the rest of us in your brig if she tries to sell you bogus tech, right?" Cheeky looked worried. "Do you have a brig?"

"It's a big ship," Cargo said with a laugh. "They're going to have a brig."

"Our original deal aside, FTL tech is pretty impressive. What would you want in exchange?" Tanis asked. The picotech was not up for trade, without it as an option, she wondered what Sera, with her already advanced nanotech could want that could match the value of FTL for the *Intrepid*.

"The opportunity to get in on the action."

<*Hah! She's more like you than even I'd guessed,*> Angela commented privately to Tanis.

"You just want to shoot at a few people in trade for amazing, unheard of technology?"

"Not just a few people. I want to turn Rebecca and her fleet of miscreants into a fine molecular cloud. I'm tired of dealing with them. I'm tired of playing their games. In fact, I want to do the same to Padre's fleet and then I want to show the good people of Bollam's World that just because a valuable ship shows up in their system it's not up for grabs."

"You seem…bitter," Cheeky observed.

Sera's expression hardened. "I want to show people that if they behave like animals, someone is going to come along and put them down like the rabid pack they are."

Tanis was taken aback by Sera's vehemence. She saw that Cheeky and Cargo were also surprised by the rage in their captain's voice. Something deep drove Sera's anger. Something personal and unpleasant.

The conversation was interrupted by the comm board lighting up, and the proximity alarms going off in concert.

Tanis picked up the comm message and flipped it to the bridge's audible systems once the first syllable came to her ears.

"Good morning, *Sabrina,* this is Captain Joseph Evans of the ISS *Andromeda.* It's a little hot out here, so we thought we'd give you a ride into the *Intrepid.*"

"What the hell?" Cheeky exclaimed, furiously adjusting her holo interfaces. "There's a fucking cruiser on our ass that wasn't there a second ago!"

Tanis felt a smile nearly split her face in half.

"You have the honors," Sera said, returning her smile.

"*Andromeda,* this is Tanis…sweet stars it's good to hear your voice, Joe." Tanis all but gasped the last words, her voice choking up.

"Tanis! Oh stars, thank god. I was afraid it was a hoax, are you OK? Are you in danger?"

<She's always in danger,> Angela replied sardonically.

"I'm well. Captain Sera and *Sabrina* have treated me very well."

"Corsia is sending a plot for your pilot. We need to cut the chatter and get you off radar. Dock as quickly as you can. I love you, Tanis."

"I love you, too, Joe. See you in a few minutes…"

Tanis couldn't stop the flood of emotion that washed over her. She let out a sob and tears started to flow. She saw Cheeky and Sera exchange incredulous looks before her eyes misted up too much to see clearly.

A moment later there was a hand on her back and a soft voice at her side.

"I take it he's someone special to you," Sera's voice was thick with emotion.

Tanis gulped down a deep breath and forced herself to calm. "He's my husband," she managed to say.

"Husband?" Cheeky asked with a grin. "I bet he's a real looker—no wonder you never came by my cabin."

Tanis smiled and wiped her face. "Yes, that was it. Did you get the information to dock?"

Cheeky nodded. "Their bay is right behind us, it'll be snug, but we'll fit. Just one jot to the left and we'll drop right in."

"I'm going to the hatch," Tanis said as she rose.

"Right behind you," Sera said. "You have the bridge, Cargo."

Tanis was sliding down the ladder in the corridor before Sera finished speaking. She knew it was irrational, but the thought of being with Joe made all the obstacles before her seem so much simpler. Sure, they faced insurmountable odds, and there was little chance of ever building the colony they had dreamed, but none of that mattered if she was with Joe. They could figure it out, they could figure anything out.

She arrived at the forward hatch and all but bounced on her feet as she waited for the sound of the ship settling in its cradle.

As soon as the telltale clang echoed through the deck plates, she cycled the airlock, barely aware that Sera stepped in with her.

It seemed to take forever for the pressure match indicator to turn green, and when it did, she pushed out of *Sabrina* and smashed herself into Joe's open arms. The smell of him washed over her and she couldn't stop overwhelming sobs of joy and pent up anxiety from escaping her.

"I'm here Tanis, you're safe, you're back with us," Joe whispered in her ear while stroking her hair.

Tanis wasn't able to form words and spoke into his mind instead.

<Never again, I mean it this time, you come with me everywhere.>

Joe chuckled. *<My feelings exactly. I'm just glad you're OK. You had me worried sick, I was just about ready to beg, borrow, or steal a ship to start scouring the galaxy for you. You're both OK?>*

<We are yes, both me and our little addition,> Tanis said with a smile. *<I got back here as fast as wings would take me.>*

<And who are these wings?> Joe asked, his eyes darting over her shoulder.

Tanis finally became aware of Sera's presence, floating awkwardly behind her in the 0g on *Andromeda*. She looked around to see all eyes in the shuttle bay on her. She flushed and stepped back.

"Joe, this is Captain Sera, my rescuer. Sera, this is Joseph Evans."

"Pleased to meet you," Joe said with a smile as he extended his hand to Sera. "Any rescuer of Tanis's is a dear friend of mine—not to mention a rare person. Usually she is the one doing the rescuing."

Sera took his hand and returned the smile. "Then you won't be surprised to learn that she rescued me once on our way here."

Joe barked a laugh. "Now that's more like it."

Behind Sera, the rest of the crew, bar Cargo, stood at the ship's airlock. Tanis introduced them to Joe and Sera called up for Cargo to secure the ship and come down as well.

<Go and enjoy yourselves,> Corsia said. <Sabrina and I are coordinating final docking procedures.>

Joe led Tanis and *Sabrina's* crew through the docking bay toward the ship's forward crew lounge.

"It doesn't look that much more advanced. I thought you guys were supposed to have amazing tech," Cheeky said while peering around. "It seems pretty normal—except the lack of AG."

Tanis had to hide a smile as the crew of *Sabrina* clumsily navigated the corridor with the hand and footholds that she barely even thought of. It was possible that most of them had never even spent any appreciable time in zero-g.

"It's not what's visible," Joe said. "We don't have artificial gravity on ships this size, true, but we've flown *Andromeda* within a thousand klicks of those big newcomers out there and they didn't even catch a glimpse of us."

"You buzzed an AST dreadnaught?" Cheeky's eyes grew wide with appreciation.

"That's why we were out here," Joe said with a nod. "We wanted to know what those new ships were all about."

"What did you learn?" Tanis asked. "How do they stack up?"

"They have omnidirectional antimatter engines on either end; heavily shielded, and deadly to boot. Their beams are as strong as our best and their grav shields can probably block almost anything we can throw at them. I think we'd wear them down in a slug-fest, provided we could keep them at bay, but with all the other players on the field it gets pretty complicated."

"It usually is," Tanis said with a smile.

A minute later, they arrived in the forward crew lounge. The room was clean and spare, yet well appointed. Tanis remembered spending many an evening relaxing here on the long deceleration into Kapteyn's, and again during her many tours on the ship during the Victoria years.

"You'll all receive a protocol upgrade by nano packet to update your Link for our systems," Corisa announced over the lounge's audible systems. "Please accept it and you'll get onto our public nets."

"Thanks," Cargo said. "I was wondering why I couldn't make any sort of connection to a shipnet."

"What happened to you?" Joe asked as *Sabrina's* crew accepted the upgrade and Linked to the *Andromeda's* net.

"My pod got picked up by pirates after I ejected," Tanis said. "It's a very different galaxy than we last saw."

"You can say that again," Joe replied.

<*We've passed the AST ships and are approaching the Bollam's fleet picket lines,*> Corsia announced over the Link.

"Thanks, Cor," Joe said as he held Tanis and kissed her.

INTREPID

STELLAR DATE: 10.26.8927 (Adjusted Years)
LOCATION: ISS *Andromeda*, Near Fierra (6*Mj* Jovian)
REGION: Bollam's World System, Bollam's World Federation

Sera watched Tanis and her husband—husband!—with a smile slowly creeping across her face. Who would have thought that the hard-bitten general had a man into whose arms she melted? Of all the things she expected to encounter, this was perhaps the last.

She glanced at her crew as they watched Tanis, and caught Cheeky's eye. They exchanged a knowing look, before Sera returned her gaze to the forward-facing window.

She felt a pang of homesickness as she looked through the holo-enhanced portal. It reminded her too much of home. So clean, so meticulously maintained by nano, that it looked brand new, even though it had likely seen centuries of service.

Through the plas she saw several Bollam's World Space Force ships come into view, their mass and vector highlighted on the display for any Linked viewer to see. The vessels were new and well made by ninetieth century standards, but there was something about the understated elegance of the *Andromeda* that put them to shame. The Bollam's ships were boxy and utilitarian, where the *Andromeda* hailed from a time when both form and function were honored without compromise.

She was impressed with how neither Joe, nor any of the crew they had passed, gave her unusual black skin, or Nance's hazsuit a second glance. Then again, given what she had read about the early fourth millennia, her crew fit well within the bounds of what was considered normal.

They slipped past the Bollam's picket lines without drawing attention, and before long the *Intrepid* came into view.

"All those ships dock inside the *Intrepid*?" Nance asked in awe.

"They do indeed," Tanis replied with a nod. "Most of the cruisers fit in the main bay."

Cheeky whistled. "Well, I'm not surprised. Most of the stations we dock *Sabrina* at are smaller than that ship."

Sera counted ten capital ships protecting the *Intrepid*, the largest being a pair of thousand-meter cruisers that the window's holo enhancement labeled as the *Orkney* and *Dresden*.

The display didn't provide many details beyond mass and size, but given what she knew of Sol in the fourth millennia, and what she had read about Victoria, Sera suspected that the *Intrepid's* fleet was more than a match for all but the AST vessels surrounding them.

Even if they didn't resort to their picotech.

<*You're thinking about how this feels like home, aren't you?*> Helen asked.

<*I am,*> Sera sent an affirmative response.

"Those poor pirate fleets," Cheeky chuckled. "They must really be wondering if they bit off more than they can chew."

"They're probably considering joining forces," Tanis said.

"Or getting the hell out of here," Sera added.

"It's like looking back in time," Thompson whispered, his voice filled with awe. "So much of what we see—the worlds, the stations, what few rings remain—they're the ruins, leftovers from before the wars. What we've built since…well, at best it's utilitarian and functional…but this ship, the *Intrepid*…it's so graceful, it's amazing…"

Cheeky put a hand on Thompson's shoulder. "I never knew you were such a romantic."

Thompson, looked around, his face flushing. "I'm, uh, I'm not…don't expect future sentiment."

Nance let out a nervous laugh. "I don't blame you though…that's one hell of a ship. How do they build something so big…?"

"Have you ever been to Sol?" Sera asked Nance.

"I've never felt like having the probe it takes to get in that far," the bio replied.

"They have more than a few artificial structures that dwarf planets. Building things like the *Intrepid* is practically child's play—at least it used to be."

"Are the Mars Outer Shipyards still there?" Joe asked.

"No," Sera shook her head. "Sol suffered the worst, in the FTL wars. The only megastructure still there is High Terra."

Joe's face fell. "Mars 1, the Cho?"

Sera shook her head. "All gone—well, the Cho has been rebuilt...sort of."

"I don't think I even want to know," Joe replied.

"We got out in the nick of time," Tanis said with a hand on her husband's shoulder. "They tore themselves apart even before FTL came along."

Joe sighed. "We knew it was coming...it's why we left, after all. Place was getting nuts."

"The whole core is nuts now," Sera said. "It's a hundred messed up worlds in there."

"I resent that," Nance said. "I'm from a core world."

"You're from Virginis; they've only been in the AST for a century. It's not enough time for the madness to settle in...maybe," Sera's expression grew deadly serious.

It took Nance a moment to realize the Captain was poking fun at her. "I'm going to ignore your biased remarks," she said, with obviously faked haughtiness.

"I don't know." Cheeky grinned. "Maybe her hazsuit fetish is a symptom."

Nance chose to ignore the barb. "If you're the famous General of Victoria," she said to Tanis, changing the subject and gesturing at the *Intrepid* through the display. "Are you in charge over there?"

Joe let out a laugh and wrapped his arm around Tanis. "She thinks she is—usually is, too, if the captain is in stasis."

"I'm the executive officer," Tanis said and threw a mock scowl at Joe.

"On paper," Joe added with a wink at his wife.

"Were you ever going to come up to the bridge?" a female voice asked from behind the group.

Sera turned to see a tall woman with lavender skin and a highly exaggerated figure standing in the entrance to the lounge.

"Jessica!" Tanis cried out and ran to the woman. They embraced and spoke privately for a few minutes before joining the group.

"No wonder she never thought you two were that unusual," Cheeky said, giving Nance and Sera significant looks. "Your kinks are nothing on hers."

"It's not like that!" Nance whispered. "Cut it out already."

"Sorry, Jessica," Joe said as Tanis and Jessica approached. "We got talking and I sort of decided to stay down here for the approach and forgot to tell anyone."

"Well, who's going to fly it, then?" Jessica asked.

"I'm pretty sure that Petrov can manage to dock with the *Intrepid*. Besides, Corisa just humors us all anyway."

<*You keep me company,*> Corsia said. <*It would get lonely out here without my little passengers.*>

"That's...a bit creepy," Thompson said.

"Are all your AI so imperious?" Cheeky asked. "No offense Angela, but you're a little bossy, too."

<*I think we should save this conversation for another time,*> Angela said.

Sera was certain she knew what the conversation would be about. She remembered learning about the Phobos accords as a child, but those laws were dead and gone. However, the crew and AIs on the *Intrepid* would likely not appreciate the low station of most AIs in the ninetieth century.

"Wha—?" Cheeky began to ask before Sera sent her a message to drop it.

"Tanis!" a new voice entered the conversation and Sera turned to see the holo-presence of a tall, rather distinguished looking man.

"Captain Andrews," Tanis said with a smile as she turned to face him. "I see things are proceeding well, as usual."

"Not too much worse for wear," the captain returned the smile.

Tanis had never mentioned how attractive her captain was. A man from the early fourth millennia, too—if the sparse records from so long ago were to be believed.

"I have some friends coming aboard," Tanis said. "This is captain Sera and the crew of *Sabrina*," Tanis gestured to Sera's crew. "They have some fascinating information regarding FTL that they would like to share with us. Earnest will be especially interested."

"Thank you for returning Tanis to us," Captain Andrews said to Sera. "From what Corsia has relayed of her conversations with Sabrina, you were a long way from here."

"Just about a hundred and fifty light-years," Tanis said nonchalantly. "A hop, skip, and a jump by today's standards."

Joe nearly choked. "A hundred and fifty! Stars...I would never have found you."

Sera watched Tanis embrace her husband and whisper something in his ear while Captain Andrews continued.

"I'll be glad to have you all aboard—and not soon enough. Every one of our friends out there is making more demands than I can shake a stick at. Thankfully, there are so many of them, no one wants to make the first move."

"We'll be docking in thirty minutes," Joe said. "Should be up there in forty-five."

"Very well," the captain replied and his holo faded out.

"He's hot!" Cheeky exclaimed.

Tanis looked aghast. "He's the captain!"

"And a damn hot one at that," Cheeky said to herself.

Several conversations picked up as the *Andromeda* approached her mothership, and Sera turned to admire the view. The design of the *Intrepid* was both alien and very familiar. Its elegance reminded her of some of her people's ships—the ones built before The Sundering. Truly amazing craftsmanship had gone into what was ultimately just a colony route stevedore.

The *Andromeda* passed near one of the cruisers shadowing the *Intrepid*. The holo overlay on the lounge's window highlighted it and identified the ship as the *Orkney*. Sera slipped out of her footholds and kicked toward the window, dismissing the information overlay from her vision. She wanted to look upon this vista with her own eyes.

Both ships were on similar vectors, and the *Andromeda's* pilot brought the ship in for a slow pass, only a thousand meters from the *Orkney*.

It was built for war and Sera found herself impressed with the firepower the *Intrepid* was packing in a fleet of ships, which should have been nothing more than transports, pushers, and cargo haulers.

The *Orkney* gleamed like a jewel, sheathed in what was likely several meters of highly reflective ablative plating. Nearby, a hauler was moving an icy asteroid into position near the warship. She suspected it was to extract water and create an additional ice shield around the vessel.

She imagined some terraformer working on the world below was probably quite upset to see over a hundred trillion liters of water they had planned for a lake or sea taken away.

It was a form of warfare Sera had only read about. Take your big war wagons, sheathe them in ice and let them take the heat from enemy beams. The ice would also add radiation shielding from indirect nuclear blasts.

The tactic matched the rest of the ship's structure. With only rear engines, this was a vessel that was made to get to the fight fast, take a beating and wipe out the opposition quickly. It was aided by an assortment of beams that even the AST dreadnaughts would envy.

With fifty centimeter lenses, *Orkney's* lasers could lance across a hundred thousand kilometers and still deal lethal damage. Even at their distant position, the AST dreadnaughts were within this vessel's firing range. Modern ships rarely fired at such distances—rapid movement made long-range targeting nearly impossible.

Sera imagined having a fleet of such vessels at her command and found a new appreciation for Tanis's tactical mind. With a target as big as the *Intrepid* to defend, she had apparently pulled out all the stops.

The *Andromeda* silently slipped past the *Orkney*, and its accompanying tug and asteroid. Ahead, the bulk of the *Intrepid* began to fill the forward view. The rear of the vessel sported two massive fusion burners, and a pair of smaller antimatter engines.

Small was a relative term, since the *Andromeda's* seven-hundred and twenty-meter hull could both fit inside and turn around within even the smaller engine's exhaust ports.

"Imagine being at the helm of that thing," Cheeky whispered from Sera's side. "I can almost…" she shivered with delight and Sera rolled her eyes.

"Easy now. And here you accuse Nance and I of having fetishes."

"Oh, I have my weird bits," Cheeky said with a smile. "I just don't pretend not to. Galaxy would be a better place if people were real."

They passed beneath the engines and under the two spinning cylinders, each containing an entire world's worth of animals, flora, and fauna. From the stories Tanis had told, the general even had a nice cabin beside a lake in one.

Surrounding the ship was a latticework of support struts, though it was not readily apparent that was their primary purpose. They looked far more like a protective web; with mobile beams and chaff cannons mounted along their lengths, they certainly fit the bill.

"I bet they didn't leave Sol with all those," Sera said.

"Probably not, but I bet a few were there for shooting down rocks and stuff," Cheeky commented.

They passed the cylinders and came underneath the forward section of the ship where the doors of a massive bay loomed wide. The space inside was cavernous and empty, with all its normal occupants outside the ship on patrol.

The *Andromeda* turned and slowly backed into the bay. Once within the hull of the *Intrepid*, Sera felt the slight tug of gravity and by the time the ship settled into its cradle, over half a *g* pulled firmly at everyone.

Tanis gestured for the crew to leave the lounge as Sabrina squealed with delight over the Link.

<*I'm in a ship that's inside another ship! This is so weird!*>

<*Is it OK? We can have you undock,*> Sera replied.

<*Corsia and some big guy named Bob are already working on that,*> Sabrina replied. <*They seem to do a lot without even talking to people.*>

Sera could tell Sabrina was a bit nervous.

<*I've noticed that. I'll send Cargo up to you to keep an eye on things.*>

<*Thanks, that'll make me feel better,*> Sabrina replied.

They reached a cross-corridor and Tanis stopped the group.

"Sera, if you'd like to come with me, we have a meeting on the bridge deck," Tanis said.

Sera nodded. "I'd like Flaherty to come with me."

Tanis nodded and addressed Jessica. "Can you see to getting *Sabrina's* crew settled and have someone give them a tour?"

"No problem. At the least I'll show them where the bars are."

"You guys aren't taking your current situation too seriously," Thompson observed.

Jessica shrugged. "We've been in worse. Besides, Tanis is back— she'll know what to do." She placed a hand on Tanis's shoulder, which earned her a worried smile from the general.

"Just don't get too messed up—or entangled," Tanis directed a look at Jessica and Cheeky. "We may need to move fast."

With that she turned, walking briskly down a corridor to a small maglev train floating next to a platform. They entered the car, and once they took their seats, it whisked out of the station. The group had barely settled in when the train passed out of the *Andromeda* and into a clear tube, which ran across the upper reaches of the bay.

"Nice view," Sera said, looking down at the retreating form of the *Andromeda* and the kilometers of empty bay.

"It's not a bad place to work," Tanis replied. "I have to admit, it's going to be nice to stretch my legs for a bit. It's been a while since I've spent that much time on a ship as small as *Sabrina*."

"Feeling a bit cooped up, were you?" Joe asked.

"A bit," Tanis replied with a smile. "Sabrina's not that small, and I've certainly spent longer on ships…I just missed our cabin and your garden-fresh veggies."

Joe laughed. "It's probably fallen into decay; it's been years since anyone has been there."

Tanis shrugged. "We've fixed it up before, we can do it again."

Sera tuned out of their conversation and watched as the train car passed into a shaft in the bay wall, and then her breath caught as it shot out into empty space. After a moment's panic, she realized they were riding one of the thin arcs which surrounded the ship. They rose up, over the forward section of the colony vessel and then down toward the ship's nose.

The train passed back through the hull and down a long shaft before easing to a stop. The platform they stepped onto was broad and bustling with people passing through, or waiting for cars to take them to their destinations.

Tanis weaved through the throng, and as she did, people began to stop and stare. A few pointed, and whispers of "Tanis" began to fill the air.

Sera could see the general's face begin to redden and before long she stopped and turned to the crowd.

"Yes folks, I'm back."

Cheers erupted around them and some called out her name, while others shouted questions about their current situation.

Tanis held up her hands and the throng quieted.

"Don't worry, I have a plan. Everything is going to be OK."

The words were simple, and although Sera hadn't noticed it being particularly grim, the mood on the platform immediately lifted.

Tanis gave a final wave, and then led her party to the bridge deck's central corridor.

DECISIONS

STELLAR DATE: 10.27.8927 (Adjusted Years)
LOCATION: ISS *Intrepid*, Orbiting Fierra
REGION: Bollam's World System, Bollam's World Federation

They made their way down the long corridor, weaving through more crowds; individuals called out to the general, and Tanis waved or replied in turn. Presently, the crowds thinned and they came to the end of the passage, which opened into a large atrium—the centerpiece of which was a woman standing amidst a sea of holographic displays.

Sera watched in awe as the woman's hands danced across the displays, emitters on her fingertips manipulating untold systems in the time it took for Sera to realize what the woman was doing.

As they approached, what she initially perceived to be a console in front of the woman also turned out to be a holographic display. In fact, the woman appeared to be the only real thing in the atrium. Sera altered her vision to see through the holographic interfaces and was surprised at what her sight revealed.

What had appeared at first to be the woman's hair was cleverly disguised super conductor strands, which must be functioning as antennas. The bandwidth a system like that provided would be immense. Her face was smooth and composed, despite the rapid blinking of her eyelids, beneath which lay entirely black eyes. Sera marveled at her pure white skin, which her enhanced vision showed not to be skin at all, but rather a smooth, flexible polymer.

Other than her glossy coating, the woman wasn't wearing a stitch of clothing. She was perched on a very narrow stool, or pedestal—or rather, her body merged directly into the seat. She suspected this woman spent a lot of time in her current position.

The woman's head tilted and she smiled at them. An audible voice came from all around them, and over their Links.

"Welcome home Tanis, and welcome to your guests." The woman's mouth mimed the words, but no sound came from it.

"It's good to see you, Priscilla." Tanis smiled as she walked forward and stepped through the holo to embrace the woman, who stopped manipulating the interfaces around her and returned the embrace with an expression that was both warm, yet chillingly lifeless on her white face and deep black eyes.

Tanis turned, still standing in the midst of the holo display—though that didn't stop them from flashing and dancing quicker than an eye could follow. "This is Priscilla. For most purposes, she is the *Intrepid*."

"I'm very glad to meet you." Sera stepped forward and extended her hand. "I'm Sera and this is Flaherty." The silent man actually had an expression of wonder on his face as he shook Priscilla's hand in turn. "I have to admit, I'm confused. How are you the *Intrepid*?"

Priscilla gave an understanding smile. "I am the *Intrepid* in the way that your mind controls your brain, or maybe the other way around. The *Intrepid's* neural net is too vast and complex to be able to communicate effectively with humans—at least not so many of you—so I am the intermediary, its avatar, in a fashion, yet at the same time, I am the *Intrepid*."

"But you are human," Flaherty said. "I can see it; you are not a machine."

Priscilla maintained her beatific smile. "Of course I am human, would an AI be able to think for another AI and make those thoughts into something a human could understand? The *Intrepid* has a human for its mind, though its brain is AI."

"She downplays the *Intrepid's* brain. It is far more than just AI," Tanis said with a wink. Priscilla inclined her head and a wry look crossed her face, quickly replaced by her implacable gaze. "She and Amanda take turns as the human interface to the *Intrepid*. Without them, the ship and the humans on it would have a bit of a communication gap."

"How long do these turns last?" Sera asked, wondering how long this avatar spent attached to her pedestal.

"We each actively interface with the *Intrepid* for ninety days at a time. On our downtime, we take up more…regular duties on the ship."

"That is amazing," Flaherty said in a distracted voice.

Priscilla smiled at him, then nodded toward the hall to their left. "You should go. The captain and other leaders are waiting."

Tanis gestured for the group to follow her and led them through a short corridor and into a conference room beyond.

The room was not large, but well appointed, with the center dominated by an oblong table, around which were seated nine people. Sera immediately recognized Captain Andrews at its head, and her pulse rose in reaction. It had been so long since she had allowed herself to see a man as attractive, she almost didn't know how to deal with the change in her emotional state.

<Ha! I knew it would happen eventually. You've managed to bury your feelings for some time now, but I knew someday a man would come along that your cold reason wouldn't be able to deflect,> Helen commented as she noted Sera's changing chemical state.

<Don't count on me swooning any time soon.>

<You should try it, Cheeky seems to enjoy swooning.>

<Cheeky enjoys a lot of things.>

Sera tore her attention from the *Intrepid's* captain and focused on the others around the table. On his right were two men who were not wearing the ship's uniform, but what appeared to be civilian garb. The man closest to the captain sat ramrod straight, his hair was dark and slicked back. He seemed to see everything in the room at once, and took careful note of all he viewed.

The man next to him was alert as well, but also appeared to be lost in thought at the same time. On his right was a woman who had several plas sheets spread about her and looked up from them with the expression of one who was believed that more important work was being interrupted. The man and two women to the left of the Captain were decidedly military. They wore uniforms similar to Joseph's and had the bearing of officers high in the chain of command.

Upon their entry, the Captain rose. "Welcome aboard the *Intrepid*, Captain Sera, Flaherty; and welcome back Tanis." He was just as imposing in life as Sera anticipated. His voice boomed, filling the room easily.

Tanis exchanged hugs and handshakes with the colony mission's leadership while Sera, Flaherty, and Joe took their seats at the table. Once the room had settled, the captain introduced those around the table for Sera's benefit.

The slick-looking man on his right was Terrance Enfield, one of the financiers of the *Intrepid* and its journey to 58 Eridani. Beside him was Earnest Redding, apparently the architect behind the ship. The distracted woman to his right was Abby Redding, Earnest's wife and the Chief Engineer of the *Intrepid*. The three in military dress were Admiral Sanderson, Colonel Ouri, and Commandant Brandt.

<Tanis is a General, but appears to outrank a much older Admiral?> Sera asked Helen privately.

<Your guess is as good as mine—if your guess is something along the lines of Tanis getting the job that kept her out of stasis more because she was younger,> Helen replied.

The captain's voice broke into her thoughts. "Again, I must thank you for bringing Tanis back to us. We are quite interested in where she has been for the past few months."

"Would you believe pirates?" Tanis asked with a smile.

"Pirates?" Terrance asked. "Like...ahar?"

Tanis nodded. "As Sera can attest, things are a lot different than they were when we left. With the advent of FTL, space has become a much wilder place. In fact, the two fleets maintaining positions above the north and south pole of the world we're orbiting are composed of pirates."

Several voices spoke at once, peppering Tanis with questions.

"Why don't we hold our questions until the end," Andrews said, his even tones bringing quiet. "I, for one, would like to hear this story uninterrupted."

Tanis took a deep breath and related her tale; how her pod was picked up by pirates, how she was tortured, and then shipped off to meet with a man named Padre before waking to find herself on Sera's ship. She told of their battle to save Sera and their journey across over a hundred light-years to arrive at Bollam's World and the *Intrepid*.

Terrance whistled. "That's some adventure you had, Tanis."

"You're telling me," Tanis replied. "I could do with a break from adventure."

Sera observed the *Intrepid's* leadership as they asked their questions and sought clarity on the state of the galaxy in which they found themselves.

She could tell they had been through a lot together. Though she could see some subtle tensions in the group, by and large they were tightly knit—having been through over a century of adversity together.

When there was a moment's pause, the captain spoke.

"This adds some color to what we've learned from Bollam's ambassador—and Joe and Jessica's visit to one of their stations— though they have certainly kept some details from us. We've not been granted unfettered access to the system's nets. It's pretty plain to see that they're hiding something from us."

Sera laughed. "You have that right. They don't want you to learn that you hold *all* the cards."

"We do?" Sanderson asked, no small amount of sarcasm in his voice. "I imagine all those hostile fleets out there beg to differ."

"Would you defeat all of them if it came to an all-out battle?" Sera asked without pausing for an answer. "Perhaps not, perhaps you would. Either way, no one wants to risk your ship to that sort of conflict. Even without your most precious cargo, this ship is invaluable beyond measure."

Looks around the table turned suspicious, and Tanis raised her hands defensively.

"The secret's out. Our little stunt with the pico at Victoria made its way into the history books. Not everyone believes its real, but apparently enough do. Sera, why don't you give them the highlights since we left Kapteyn's?"

"Of course," Sera said with a nod. "Only a hundred years or so after you left Earth, a man in the Procyon system discovered how to cheaply generate gravitons. I understand that you were privy to some of this information during your time at Kapteyn's Star and that you've built your own rudimentary graviton emitters."

"We have," Earnest nodded. "Though, from what I have observed, the tech has advanced considerably."

"It has," Sera agreed. "Consider that nearly the entirety of your ship could have artificial gravity supplied by a handful of devices no larger than this room."

Sharp intakes of breath resounded through the room and everyone looked at one another with a mixture of awe and disbelief.

Sera continued. "Once artificial gravity was something that anyone could afford, gravity-based experiments advanced technology by leaps and bounds. For instance, inertial dampeners now exist, which can protect ships from forces as significant as a ninety degree thrust change at over half the speed of light."

Eyes grew even wider at that statement; Earnest and Abby Redding began writing furiously on several of the plas sheets.

"Shields on ships can now be used to hold atmosphere in the event of a hull puncture—though I suspect your ES shielding can do the same," Sera paused, as the captain nodded slowly, before continuing. "Most ships aren't even airtight anymore, though I personally consider it to be prudent. But all of that was just the icing on the cake. All the work with gravitons unlocked the true nature of dark matter; mainly that scientists finally found it. It projects itself into relative space through gravity, but the bulk of its mass lays in a sub-layer of space-time commonly called the dark layer—it's basically the long-dismissed universal rest frame of reference."

"I knew it!" Earnest shouted. "Pay up dear."

Abby scowled and her eyes fluttered as Sera imagined a quick Link transaction took place between the couple.

Sera eyed them curiously for a moment before shrugging and continuing.

"Since the gravity systems on a ship could interact with that special layer of space, it became possible to move objects in and out of it. Two things were immediately discovered about the dark layer. The first was that velocity relative to normal space increased by anywhere from 300 to 800 times. The second was that Newtonian laws of reaction do not apply there. The vector you enter the DL in is the vector you stay on until you exit.

"Most ships can achieve speeds up to $0.70c$ in normal space. However, vessels like those eleven AST dreadnaughts out there have drives that can take them up to the very edge of light-speed while in normal space. When in FTL, they can traverse light-years in a matter of hours."

Everyone was silent as they soaked in the implications of Sera's speech. "Keep in mind that most of these discoveries were made right before the forty fifth century. Since then, technology, in general, has been in decline. With the advent of FTL, people no longer needed the advanced technologies required to wring every last drop of productivity from a star system. Much was lost to decline, and to the FTL wars—the aftermath of which the galaxy is still recovering from.

"No one has the faintest clue how to build things like planet pusher tugs or create planet-wide stasis fields. The concept of merging planets is impossible for all but the most advanced worlds, and nanotech is even less advanced than it was in the thirtieth century.

"To the people of Bollam's World, and the ninetieth century in general, the *Intrepid* is like a treasure trove. It's a jackpot beyond imagining. That's why those pirates were fighting over Tanis."

"So who are these eleven newcomers? You referred to them as the AST before," Captain Andrews asked his first question.

"Those are your good friends from Sol, or nearby. Sol is now part of an alliance of about a hundred and fifty worlds commonly known as the Alpha Sol Tau, or AST. They're a greedy bunch of bastards, and they probably think the *Intrepid* is theirs, too. Bollam's is a sovereign system, so the fact that they are here flexing their muscle is a bit surprising. They must be really intent in getting their hands on you."

"I swear, if you weren't here confirming all this, Tanis, I'd think it was some sort of elaborate hoax," Brandt shook her head.

"Or a nightmare," Terrance added.

"It's no dream. Those fleets out there are real, and they're only going to get bigger over the next few days," Tanis said ominously.

"Don't forget," Sera spoke into the silence. "The *Intrepid* is of greater value than this entire system. Destroying you is not their plan. Though, if things go badly for one faction, they may try to destroy what they cannot have."

The captain shook his head slowly. "Even if we are sure we can win, we don't want to get in a fight of this size—not again. Do you have a plan?" He looked between Sera and Tanis. She could clearly see that while he commanded the ship, Tanis was instrumental in its operation.

Sera took a deep breath; it was time to finally tip her hand.

"I'd help out just because Tanis saved my life, but the opportunity to show the Bollam's government that they can't extort every ship that dumps out of Kapteyn's Streamer, not to mention sticking it to Padre, Rebecca, *and* the AST? That is too much to pass up. I have something to trade, and then I will contact the FGT and see about getting you a planet."

She saw Tanis turn in her seat. The general didn't speak, but her penetrating gaze spoke volumes.

"The FGT is still around? I thought you said there was no more advanced tech like planet pushers and massive stasis fields?" Terrance looked perplexed.

"Yeah, I suppose that was not entirely true. The inner core systems still have some of the old tech, but they aren't sharing; and the FGT still exists and is going strong. However, after a few experiences very similar to what you are going through now, they cut off contact with the bulk of the inn…" Sera paused for a moment before resuming her speech, "…the human sphere. They still terraform, but they don't tell anyone about it. Every so often, they will let a struggling world know about a new home they can go to, or they will trade from time to time. Sometimes they just let the new worlds be found by explorers."

"Then how will you contact the FGT?" Terrance asked.

"Yes, I am all ears," Tanis said, her tone almost angry.

Sera didn't answer for a minute. "I can't disclose that yet. But I can promise you that I can reach them and that they will see yours as a good case for a new world."

"First, we have to get out of this mess," Joe said with a frown. "What's the plan there?"

Sera was glad to see Tanis's dark expression lift.

"That is something we have a solid plan for," Tanis said and gestured for Sera to share the data on FTL.

Sera smiled broadly. "I have, as it turns out, complete design and operating specifications for graviton systems on a scale as large as this ship. With that, I have the information for how to implement gravitational shields, gravity drives, and even the information on how to take a ship of this size into the dark layer. In short: protection, power, and FTL."

No one spoke for several long seconds as that information soaked in.

"You have *full* design, and operating specifications on these systems?" Abby asked, no small amount of skepticism in her voice.

"Everything but an arrow pointing at where to bolt it on," Sera replied.

Joe frowned. "What Jessica and I learned during our time on that mining platform is that no one can move ships this large into FTL. Those AST dreadnaughts are right at the edge of safe transition."

"They don't know everything in the core worlds," Sera said with a shrug. "Out on the fringes of known space, there are some pretty amazing things going on."

"And what do you want for this information, and how did you come by it?" The captain also sounded skeptical. Tanis, too, looked quite interested to have one of Sera's mysteries revealed: her source.

"Unfortunately, I'm not at liberty to discuss that, either. However, I can assure you that the knowledge is accurate and I legally own rights to it. Like I said, the only thing I want in trade is to help take out a few of those bastards out there."

"We may yet find a peaceful resolution to this," Terrance said.

"You may, they won't," Sera replied.

"She's right about that." The Admiral shook his head. "If what she says is true, none of those factions are going to let the others get the prize. The only way we are going to get out of this is by destroying or thoroughly intimidating them."

"I hate to have to ask," Tanis interjected, "but how did you get in this situation?"

"Jessica and I got nabbed," Joe replied with a sheepish look. "I guess they pick up a lot of flotsam and jetsam here, and our hunt for you put us on their radar. We signaled for *Corsia* to come pick us up, but *Intrepid* came instead. Folks here decided that it was better to be insystem and work on a trade than out in the black with no options."

"Fierra, the freshly terraformed world below us, was an appealing offer," Terrance added. "But if they all know about the picotech, then that world would just be a pretty cage at best."

Sera snorted. "That's so like Bollam's."

The captain picked up the story. "We were negotiating with their ambassador when the first of the pirate fleets showed up. Before we could blink, a full-scale battle was playing out around us. We deployed our fleet—much to their surprise, I might add—and we entered into the current stalemate."

"There was that move when you tapped into the jovian's magnetic field with our ramscoop and used it to smash the shields on a dozen of those pirate corvettes," Joe said to Earnest. "It was pure genius."

Earnest chuckled. "It's amazing the effect a finely focused beam of gamma rays can have on someone's level of caution. Didn't really damage anyone, but I could tell that whatever they were shielding themselves with had to expend a lot of power to protect them. Now that I know its graviton based, it makes sense."

He pulled his glasses off and cleaned them—a strange gesture, and an even stranger, archaic method of eyesight correction. "Why they don't have stasis shields is beyond me. If they can generate cheap gravitons, then antimatter is less expensive than air. Every ship could have stasis shields and could fly through a star if they wanted with no damage."

Silence fell at his words.

"I'm guessing by the expression on your face that no one is able to do that in the ninetieth century?" Terrance asked.

"If they can, they aren't sharing," Sera said slowly, the implications racing through her mind. "Now you understand why the *Intrepid* is so valuable and why none of these factions will let the others get a hold of this ship or its personnel. Whoever captures *Intrepid* will rule space for a hundred light-years in every direction. That is not something we can allow to happen."

"We'd better get to it, then," the captain said. "What do we need to do to get started?"

"My AI, Helen, can work with your engineering chief to achieve a full implementation."

"You'll also want to interface with *Sabrina* to get her scan and targeting packages," Tanis added. "The algorithms for tracking and hitting ships that can jink like our friends out there are no simple thing. Luckily, I bought the best."

Several small conversations broke out as plans were laid and issues discussed. Captain Andrews cocked his head as a message was passed to him, then he raised his hand.

"It would appear that we have a message from the Bollam's World Fleet. Chief, Earnest, I'm certain you have things you'd rather be doing. If everyone else would like to remain, let's see what they have to say."

The far end of the conference table lit up with a holo projection of a bridge on another ship. The image was entirely lifelike; it was as though the *Intrepid* ended and another ship began half way down the table.

"Admiral Argon, how good for you to call on us again," Captain Andrews said.

"Captain Andrews, we see that you are increasing your offensive capabilities, and stealing our resources to do it."

Sera guessed that the admiral was referring to the asteroid she saw a tug pulling to the *Orkney* on their way in.

The Bollam's admiral continued, "This cannot be allowed within our sovereign system. We require that you cease your increase in armament and resume talks with us."

"Admiral, we were in the midst of talks when you made a series of impossible demands in exchange for the world we orbit. You know as well as I that what you were willing to give us wasn't much different than being your indentured servants. You also seem to be having issues with a few pirates and outside interferences from the core worlds. Perhaps we should be treating with them instead of you."

The admiral on the Bollam's World ship turned a very curious shade of red. "It would seem you already have been, as you now possess information you did not when we last spoke."

"Not so, Admiral. Rather, one of our crew, who had been abducted by pirates while in your system, managed to escape and get back to us. It's a pity you can't seem to keep your system free of such elements. They seem to cause you no end of trouble."

Sera noted that the captain seemed to be enjoying playing the Bollam's World admiral. It was perhaps a bit petty, but she probably would have done the same.

"We'll deal with them and with you. The *Intrepid* is the property of the sovereign system of Bollam's World and we will have it."

With that, the transmission was cut.

"Well, that certainly was presumptuous," Terrance laughed.

"Who names their system 'Bollam's World', anyway?" asked Joe. "It's a system, not a world. It's rather confusing."

"Having just come from Kapteyn's Star, I suspect it's our curse," Tanis said with a laugh.

"I think we should call them the Bollers," Brandt volunteered. "It would make this a lot simpler."

"Seconded," Tanis said with a smile.

"So shall it be," Joe announced. "They are the Bollers, and their star is The Boll."

PREPARATIONS

STELLAR DATE: 10.27.8927 (Adjusted Years)
LOCATION: ISS *Intrepid,* Orbiting Fierra
REGION: Bollam's World System, Bollam's World Federation

Following a brief meal, where she was impressed to see Tanis consume three BLTs, Sera provided them with a breakdown of the types of weapons and tactics they could expect to face.

The *Intrepid's* leadership listened intently to her recitation of the pirate ships' abilities as well as those of the Bollam's World fleet. She also imparted what she knew of the weapons capabilities and arsenals of the AST dreadnaughts.

<*Please, be straight with me, Sera,*> Tanis finally said as Sera was discussing the current types of focusing mechanisms used to track and focus on objects fifty thousand kilometers away moving near the speed of light.

<*You've gone past the point of no return now. The fact you won't share how you attained all this information is the only thing hurting your credibility. If you don't share soon, Bob will figure it out, if he hasn't already.*>

<*It's not top of my list,*> Bob interjected himself into their communication. <*But it will be soon. Nice to meet you, by the way, Sera.*>

Sera was stunned by Bob's mental presence.

She looked at Tanis to see the general smiling. <*Now you get why we use Amanda and Priscilla, if for no other reason than it's impossible to concentrate when he talks directly to you like that.*>

<*That's your AI?*> Sera's voice was a whisper. <*He's not in the history books…but there are legends about AI like him.*>

<*Massive, multi-nodal AI are legendary?*> Tanis asked.

<*Gods are legendary,*> Sera replied.

Tanis didn't reply—either she agreed, or didn't know what to say.

<*I'll…I just need to work out one detail—make sure it pans out, then I'll share everything,*> Sera said after several moments.

<*Work it out soon,*> Tanis replied ominously.

The conversation continued around them, and Sera found herself increasingly curious about Captain Andrews. She tapped into the ship's archives and pulled up his public dossier.

Captain Jason Andrews had been commanding starships for almost a thousand years of relative time when he landed the job as the *Intrepid's* captain. From what she could see, it was in no small part due to a longstanding relationship with Terrance.

His temporal age was just shy of four hundred years—perhaps that explained the grey hair, though she knew many men far older than he who didn't look a day over thirty. Yet, somehow the aging suited Andrews.

She wondered what sort of personal relationships he would have had given all that interstellar travel. There was no record of a wife, or even rumor of a dalliance on the ship. Was he the sort of man who took what love he could get, or did he hold out for long-term, quality relationships? There was just something about him and his bearing that she found intriguing.

<Liar, you find him irresistible, not intriguing,> Helen broke into her reverie.

<Stop eavesdropping on my thoughts.>

<If you stopped broadcasting them in our shared neural net I wouldn't have to listen to you go on about him,> Helen said with the insufferable smugness.

Sera knew she was being baited, but replied before she could stop herself. <I know you can tune it out. You are soooo superior, after all.>

<Yes, yes I am,> Helen said with an air of finality. Sera could tell she had lost that battle of wits.

"I know you don't want to say before you've contacted them, but how certain are you that the FGT has a world we can colonize?" Terrance asked for what had to be the third time.

"I'm positive," Sera replied. "Almost every time someone goes out beyond the current sphere of human colonization to a G spectrum star, they find that it already has terraformed worlds. I'm betting the FGT will want to trade some technology for the location of an out-of-the-way system, but that will most likely be the only caveat."

"I wonder what tech that might be," Joe said and coughed into his hand.

"So, somehow you'll send a message to the FGT and they'll meet with us for this trade?" Captain Andrews asked.

"Yes, I'll tell them to meet us spin-ward of the Ascella system. It's uninhabited, so we shouldn't have any visitors."

"And they'll be there?" Terrance asked. "This is a mighty big gamble we're taking."

Sera smiled. "You and your ship are the largest human curiosity in the known universe. No one will be able to resist its lure."

"And what if they decide to simply take it by force as our friends out there have?" Admiral Sanderson asked, apparently less than convinced that they'd find a warm welcome anywhere.

"They won't. There has never been a recorded instance of an FGT-instigated battle."

"At least the FGT is a known quantity," Tanis sighed. "Better than pirates and power-hungry star systems."

"Agreed. I've always found them to be quite noble," Brandt added.

"A lot can change in five thousand years," Terrance warned. "The FGT we left was in open communication with the rest of humanity."

"Speaking of five-thousand years," Joe asked Sera, "why do you think it was so hard for us to pinpoint the year when we got here? It shouldn't have been that hard to figure out."

<I've been conversing with Sabrina about that,> Priscilla said. <She is a thoroughly pleasant little ship. She's informed me that some of the stellar shift has been greater than expected—most of it due to the supernova of Betelgeuse. It was far more massive than predicted, with dark matter, from what I've learned, accounting for much of that. There is now a rather nice nebula where it used to be.

<The dark matter which escaped the nova broke apart several of the nearby stars, scattered the Orion dust cloud and even shifted Rigel a touch.>

"So, I'm guessing that that region of space is pretty much off limits," Captain Andrews said.

"Yeah, the dark matter is everywhere, so no one can pass through in FTL. Not to mention that it's still rife with radiation from the explosion."

<I have a preliminary estimate,> Earnest broke into their conversation. <Helen has supplied us with the specs and we're adapting

them for our ship. There are some promising applications—some I think that no one in the ninetieth century has sorted out yet, either.>

"The estimate?" Captain Andrews asked aloud.

<Four days, five at the most. We won't have artificial gravity or inertial dampeners, but we can get the systems in place for an FTL transition. It's really not that hard once you know some of the tricks.>

"Damn, that's fast," Sera said.

<We're equipped to build a colony, plus we left Victoria with a lot of spare parts. We didn't want to end up in a situation like we did after Estrella de la Muerte again.>

Earnest signed off and Sera gave a soft laugh. "I can't believe it was you guys that named that star. Do you realize it stuck?"

<Yes!> Priscilla exclaimed.

"I suppose I had better send that message to the FGT," Sera said and rose from the table. "Plus, it's been a really long day."

Everyone agreed that they had dallied long enough and that there was work demanding their attention and the meeting broke up. In the corridor, Tanis stopped Sera.

"Any chance I can sit in on your call to the FGT?" Tanis asked.

Sera grimaced. "Look…I know your curiosity burns eternal, but I have to do this alone."

Tanis's expression soured. "A lot is riding on your prediction."

"Earnest says my FTL specs are good. Even if I can't hold up my end of the deal, you can get out of here and fly to the edge of space and make a colony where no one will find you," Sera replied coldly. "It's what you want, right? To get away from everything? To hide and hoard your technology and not share it with humanity?"

She could see Tanis was taken aback by the vehemence of her statement. Joe and Flaherty both watched with raised eyebrows, sharing a look between them.

"Send your message, then," Tanis said coldly. "But you should know that it would be a lot easier to relate to you if you weren't hiding so much."

"C'mon," Joe said, taking Tanis's arm. "There's a lot you need to do." He looked over his shoulder to Sera and Flaherty. "It was nice meeting you, I imagine you'll want to get back to your ship. The nav NSAI can guide you."

With that, he whisked Tanis away, leaving Sera and Flaherty standing alone.

"Well, that was unexpected," Sera said with a sigh.

"It really wasn't," Flaherty replied. "I'm surprised she didn't give that to you with both barrels in the meeting with the captain."

Sera looked at him in surprise. "Really? I didn't think it was bothering her that much."

"On the way here, she had no way of knowing what she was up against, so she compartmentalized her worry about her people and focused only on the task at hand—you remember compartmentalization, right?" Flaherty said with a frown. "Now that she's back here, the two and a half million lives on this ship are her biggest concern, and you are her biggest unknown. To Tanis, you've become the definition of risk in human form. The fact that you saved her life is likely all that's keeping her from kicking you off the *Intrepid*."

<I doubt she'd be that rash,> Helen added. *<But I bet it's crossed her mind.>*

Sera stared at Flaherty and Helen's virtual presence in surprise.

"You know why it's so hard for me. I don't want to go down that road."

"You're already going down that road," Flaherty said. "You're taking me and Helen with you, I might add, but I swore on my life that I would keep you safe. You need to grow up and take charge of your destiny. The first part of that is coming clean with Tanis...and your crew, for that matter."

They walked in silence past Priscilla who didn't speak, but sent a greeting into their minds. At the end of the corridor, they boarded a maglev car and gave it their destination.

<Who do you think that they'll send to meet us?> Sera finally asked.

<With our luck it will be Florence,> Flaherty replied dourly.

<Unlikely,> Helen added. *<They'll send Greg. You can count on it.>*

<Ugh. I shouldn't have gotten up that day we left Coburn. Nothing is worth having to deal with Greg,> Sera sighed

Flaherty chuckled.

<Acceptance of your destiny is the first step.>

The rest of the trip back passed in silence. The maglev eventually stopped at a large station labeled "A1 Docking Bay".

The corridor to the bay itself was short, and when they arrived, there was a corporal waiting for them with a groundcar.

"Ma'am, sir, I'm to take you to your ship," she said.

"Glad to hear it," Sera replied. "It looks like it's a kilometer away."

"A bit more," the corporal—Nair, by her uniform's tag—said.

The groundcar took off and Sera closed her eyes for the trip, working up what she would say in her message. Before they arrived, she was interrupted by a call from Cargo.

<Sera, are you coming back soon?> Cargo asked, a hint of panic in his voice.

<Yeah, I'll be there in about a minute, what's up?>

<Oh nothing, there's just a platoon of bios out there that want to come onboard and further investigate some new pathogens they detected on us during our little tour. They want to inspect all the freight, as well.>

<Okay, hold them off, I'll deal with them.>

Cargo thanked her and Sera accessed Priscilla via the return path from her last greeting. *<Priscilla, can you Link me to Tanis? I can't seem to reach her.>*

<She asked not to be disturbed unless the ship is under attack,> Priscilla said. *<Overzealous bios are close, but I don't think they quite qualify. I can put you in touch with the captain, though. Will he do?>*

<Uh, sure. I just need to speak with him for a moment.>

<Will do, but just so you know, go easy on the bios. They were let down at Victoria by not waking to their real destination, and now they've learned that New Eden was snagged up long ago. Your ship, however, is providing them with a very interesting distraction. >

<Specialists with nothing special to do,> Helen added. *<The most dangerous kind.>*

<Well hello!> Priscilla said to Helen. *<We didn't make contact before. You're…different from the other AI on Sabrina.>*

Sera smiled to herself. Every now and then an advanced intelligence would detect that Helen was no regular AI. It was interesting to be privy to the meeting of those minds.

<I'm Helen,> the AI replied. *<I must admit that between the two of us, you are far more unusual.>*

<*I'm not so sure about that,*> Priscilla said. Sera was now an afterthought, left in the loop of the conversation purely out of courtesy. <*You aren't an AI at all!*>

Sera opted out of the conversation. No other intelligence had ever made that observation of Helen, and, as much as she wanted to see how Helen handled it, the conversation was bound to begin flowing so fast that she wouldn't be able to follow it.

Suddenly, she was Linked with Captain Andrews and she focused her attention on him.

<*Captain Sera, what can I do for you?*> His tone was warm and welcoming, something that was impressive to hear from a man who probably had thousands of things demanding his attention.

<*I just wanted to check in with you regarding your gaggle of bios I see up ahead. Do you think they are totally necessary? It's not quite as good as your time, but disease is all but unknown in the ninetieth century.*>

<*I just got to their request in my backlog,*> the captain said. <*They apparently didn't wait for my approval before besieging you. I've chastised them for it. However, would you mind letting them do their bit? It'll make them feel better, and save me days of sorting through their requests—which I fully intend to pass to Tanis once she's had some time to herself.*>

Sera sent him a mental chuckle. <*Only because you played both the Tanis and the paperwork card. Sorry to bother you, I'll let you get back to your various troubles.*>

Captain Andrews laughed in response and closed the connection.

Ahead, *Sabrina* came into view, tucked in a corner behind a massive pile of equipment; she checked in on Helen and found that her AI was still in a deep conversation with Priscilla. She'd never considered it before, but she wondered if her and Helen's secret would finally get out. The thought was both exhilarating and terrifying. She put that thought from her mind as the groundcar pulled up to her ship.

She thanked the corporal for the ride and approached the throng of bios.

"Hello, I'm Captain Sera. I've been informed you'd like to do an inspection of my crew and any possible health issues?"

An officious-looking man, there was always one in every group, pushed through the other bios—seven in total.

"Yes. I'm Dr. Philips. We demand that we be allowed to inspect your ship and its cargo to ascertain any possible health concerns. The fact that you have been allowed access to the *Intrepid* without being screened first is unconscionable. You could be spreading some sickness against which we have no defense!"

"As I understand it, we were screened when we first boarded the *Andromeda*," Sera said with a smile. "Some very impressive systems you have on this ship of yours."

"Well, not physically examined, though, and your ship could be harboring contaminants."

Sera sighed. "Don't you think that if there were some highly communicable and deadly sickness rampant amongst us that Tanis would have caught it?"

"Not necessarily…" the man said as he looked around her, seeing only Flaherty. "Where is Mrs. Richards, anyway?" he asked.

"Don't you mean General Richards?" Sera asked.

"Yes, yes, Priscilla won't tell me where she is. We should check her, too."

"I believe she is taking a few hours of personal time with Joseph," Sera said.

The man blanched and Sera had to suppress a smile. He nodded to one of the bios with him. The man grabbed a case from the pile near the airlock and dashed toward their groundcar.

He looked at his other associates. "I suppose there is no point in us suiting up. We've probably already been contaminated and that may just concentrate it." He then turned back to Sera. "You will grant us access to your ship now."

The man was really starting to get on her nerves. She swished her head, tossing her hair over her shoulder, and placed her hands on her waist. The desired effect was achieved; the man took a moment before his eyes returned to hers, at which point her glower was severe, causing him to flinch.

"What's the magic word?" Sera asked.

"What?"

"The magic word, what is it?"

"Magic?" He grew flustered and Sera's glower twitched, threatening to turn into a smile.

Everyone else in the group looked exasperated with Dr. Philips. One of the women leaned over and smacked him in the shoulder. "It's please, you dolt."

"Oh, er, please."

Sera's glower disappeared and she beamed. "Cargo," she said over the Link and audibly for the bios benefit. "Assemble the crew in the galley so these medical folks can check us over to make sure we're not carrying the plague."

With that, she slipped past the bios, Flaherty following, and stepped through *Sabrina's* airlock. The bios quickly picked up their equipment and followed her down the freight deck's main corridor. Perversely, she took the ladders and enjoyed hearing them struggle to pull their equipment up after her to the crew deck.

Cargo, Cheeky, and Thompson were already in the galley and Nance indicated over the ship's audible comm that she would arrive in a minute. Three of the bios set up their equipment while two began taking air and surface samples from around the wardroom. Dr. Philips was overseeing everything while casting dark looks at the bowl of fruit on the table.

Flaherty walked to the coffee machine and poured himself cup full of their strongest black brew before sitting down beside Thompson. He looked like he was considering putting his feet up on the table, but Sera shot him a look that contained an entire paragraph about how she felt about feet on her maple and walnut table.

"So, how'd things go in your big meeting, Captain?" Cargo asked, ignoring everything going on around them.

"Very well, they've begun implementing the grav systems they'll need to make FTL transition."

"That going to take long?" Thompson asked. "I don't relish sitting here in this exceptionally large target—even though it is amazing—while we wait and see if one of those folks out there decides to end the party and send an RM our way."

"Don't worry. Helen is helping them modify the spec for this ship. It's going quite well. I wouldn't worry too much about RMs. Apparently there have been no small number of missiles sent this ship's way and it's still here."

"For real?" Cheeky asked. "That's got to be some story."

"Who's Helen?" Dr. Philips asked.

"Don't worry yourself," Cheeky drawled. "She's an AI. She won't spread any germs."

"Fine," Dr. Philips sighed. "I want to inspect your cargo, as well."

"Once you clear Thompson here, he can show you around. You'll not open anything without his permission, and if a door's locked, it stays locked. Our environmental systems are the same ship-wide, so you don't need to look in every corner to find out if anything is amiss."

Dr. Philips looked unhappy but accepted that. "Where's your last crew member?"

Sera smiled as Nance stepped into the wardroom. "Here she is."

Nance was in her full getup. Her isolated air supply was hooked up and her facial filter totally sealed. She held several sealed containers with what Sera assumed were her blood and tissue samples.

"What is this?" Dr. Philips asked, clearly alarmed. "Is she sick? Is it contagious?"

"Yes, very. We usually don't let her out, but you demanded that we all assemble," Sera said, working to retain a straight face.

She glanced across the table at Cheeky, who was snickering behind her hand.

Dr. Philips followed her gaze and scowled at Nance.

"This is serious. Give me those," he said and snatched the samples from Nance.

"This is Nance. She's our bio," Sera said with a grin. "It would seem that she feels about you the same way that you feel about us."

<Joking aside, they are far more likely to have something that we can catch than the other way around,> Nance said.

"She's right, you know, Mark," one of the women in the group said to Dr. Philips. "At least some of the diseases they have may require biological specifics that we haven't evolved to allow for yet, while everything that we have in our systems they can probably catch."

"And none of which occurred with Tanis, I'd like to remind you," Sera pointed out. "Our basic nano is that good, at least." Nance sat at the table, her back ramrod straight. "Besides," Sera continued. "She always dresses like this; it's not really that much of a statement about your chances of infecting her, but of anyone's."

The *Intrepid's* medics took Thompson's sample first, then Dr. Philips took one of his party with the super and left to go over the ship. Sera turned to Cargo.

"Bridge and all crew quarters are sealed, right?"

"It's not my first inspection," Cargo smiled. "Gonna make 'em say please for every little thing."

The woman who had come to Nance's defense smiled at them as she took samples from some of the foodstuffs in the wardroom. "Don't blame Dr. Philips, he's just ferociously bored. He spent the whole time on Victoria out of stasis, only because he wholly expected to wake up to a colony next time. It's starting to wear his personality thin."

Sera laughed. "That much is apparent."

The woman smiled. "I'm Terry, and this is Anne and Sam." She gestured to the woman and man still with her in the wardroom who nodded in response. "We just got thawed last week. It's hard to believe we ended up in the ninetieth century!"

"Alive and well," Cargo replied with a smile.

"They're not going to let us settle that moon down there, are they?" Terry asked.

"I'd say the chances of that happening now are between zero and nil," Sera agreed. "The *Intrepid* out-values it about a million to one, but newly terraformed worlds are very rare in this region. Bollam's World is in the midst of a heavily settled space; they have no expansion available, so this is their only option."

"So, where are we going to go, then?" Anne asked.

"Once we get your ol' girl FTL capable, we'll head out to rendezvous with the FGT. They'll set you up with a nice colony well out of the way."

A quick check informed Sera that Helen and Priscilla were still lost in a deep conversation. Great, this was going to give her a headache whether she paid attention to it or not. She asked Helen at least to keep the blood vessels in her head from swelling.

"FTL?" Terry asked. "So that rumor was true."

"You bet," Sera replied. "We provided the details for the technology. If your Reddings are all history says they are cracked up to be, then the *Intrepid* should be ready to make the jump in less than a week."

Terry blushed and the other two looked guilty. "Here you are doing all of this for us and we're treating you like some sort of quarantine violators. I'm really sorry about that." She looked over at Nance. "If you don't mind, I wouldn't mind seeing the environmental systems on this ship after we're done here. I used to be a bio on some small transports. I'd like to see what's changed in the last couple of thousand years."

Sera was surprised that Nance nodded in agreement.

A half an hour later, the inspection was over. The preliminary examinations showed that *Sabrina* posed no threats and Terry promised to see if there was anything that the crew of the *Intrepid* could inadvertently pass to them. Dr. Philips wanted to take more samples, but his med techs managed to convince him that they should spend time reviewing what they knew to catch any possible issues fast. If anything suspicious turned up, they would do a more thorough investigation later. The way Terry winked at Sera when they left, she was certain that nothing would come to Dr. Philip's attention unless it was a truly serious problem. She also set a time to come back and see the environmental systems with Nance.

"I thought they'd never leave," Thompson said as he closed the inner airlock.

"Good times," Sera smiled.

* * * * *

The bridge was empty when Sera stepped onto it. Cargo was off duty, and Jessica asked Cheeky to join her in reviewing the specs of the ISF fighters and how the Intrepid would stack up against the enemy fleets.

<Sabrina, secure Link.>

<Link is secure,> Sabrina responded after a moment.

<You know that system I informed you to forget about?> Sera asked.

<Access pass?> Sabrina's mental tone was entirely free of emotion.

<Fina and Uncle Mandy,> Sera replied.

<That's the one,> Sabrina said. <Are you finally going to use this thing?>

<Yup. No one has ever discovered it, have they?>

<How would they? It's linked to the power system in your shower. Not many people go in there.>

<Someone may have noticed that my shower's grav system is powered by a superconductor cable as thick as my wrist.>

<If they did, they must have just thought you had some sort of kinky sex system set up in your cabin.>

Sera laughed. *<What, like the one Cheeky has?>*

<Thompson has one, too.>

<Now that I didn't know.> Sera shook her head and smiled to herself. *<Anything else like that I don't know about?>*

<Yes.>

Sera felt her ire rise for a moment, but forced herself to let it go. She knew enough not to attempt to control everything. That road ultimately led to total loss of control.

<Let's get this message sent; its burning a hole in my brain.>

<You're going to need to jack in for the connection. Helen is using almost all of your wireless bandwidth, and from what I understand, the control circuitry for this transmitter is inside you. You really don't want to max your throughput.>

Sera reached behind her headrest and pulled the hardlink cable out and connected it to the port at the base of her skull.

When *Sabrina* confirmed the hardlink, she activated the U-layer transmitter secreted away in her shower. She set the coordinates for the message and called up the script she had pre-recorded. Sera paused for a moment and listened to her words, wondering how they would be received, what the FGT would require of her in return. She pushed aside her indecision and sent the message.

The ship's power usage meters rose and the reactor increased its burn to cover the discharge she had pulled from the SC batteries.

<All systems show a successful transmission,> Sabrina said as she powered down the U transmitter.

<Same here. I'm going to hit the hay. Wake me if anything interesting happens.>

<Yes, Captain,> Sabrina responded as Sera rose and retreated to her cabin, more than ready to sleep off the anxiety that message had caused her.

THE LAKE HOUSE

STELLAR DATE: 10.27.8927 (Adjusted Years)
LOCATION: ISS *Intrepid*, Orbiting Fierra
REGION: Bollam's World System, Bollam's World Federation

"Think you were a little hard on her?" Joe asked as he led Tanis to the maglev station.

Tanis let out a long sigh. "Maybe…I don't know. It's not like she can have any secret so mind-blowing that we can't handle it. We're going to figure it out; she should just tell already."

"Reminds me of how eager you were to share the details of your mission at Toro," Joe replied.

"That was different," Tanis said. "Those records were sealed. I couldn't talk about it."

"Don't play games with me," Joe locked eyes with Tanis as they stopped and waited for a train. "You may not have felt any of your decisions on Toro were wrong, but you felt shame for how it was handled, how you were treated—by the military, your father, and your husband."

Tanis broke eye contact. Even after all the years, thinking back to those days hurt more than she cared to admit.

"OK, point taken."

<I got worried when you were talking about what you went through…the torture, getting your chest half blown off again…are you sure our little girl's OK?> Joe asked privately.

<I'm sorry,> Tanis replied, her eyes filled with compassion. *<I should have reassured you right away. The stasis field protected her very well—Angela moved heaven and earth to make sure she's OK…but…>*

<But?> Joe asked, worry flooding his features.

<When I got shot up, Angela couldn't keep the stasis field intact while fixing me back up, so she pulled our little girl out. After all the surgery was done, I had her put back in…but out of stasis.>

Joe's face split into a smile so bright Tanis almost had to look away. He grabbed her by the waist and spun her around.

<Stars, yes! No point in waiting for New Eden anymore!>

Tanis laughed and he set her back on the deck plate.

"Let's get out of here and enjoy our reunion," he said. "All that unpleasant saving everyone's skin stuff will come crashing back on you soon enough."

"Gee," Tanis said with a chuckle. "You sure know how to take a load off my mind."

A maglev car pulled up beside them, and they stepped on, along with several other passengers—more than a few were whispering about seeing the general.

Tanis sat and rested her head on Joe's shoulder, blocking out the worry and all the distractions around her. There was no doubt in her mind that they would come out on top of this challenge.

Joe was right. She needed to take this time and relax and rebuild her reserves.

They didn't speak for the rest of the ride to Old Sam, neither verbally, nor over the Link.

The maglev made several stops, and passengers came and went, but Tanis barely noticed. Eventually, the train came to rest at their stop, a station half a kilometer from their cabin.

They disembarked and walked down the long, wooded path, arm in arm.

In the woods around them, birds sang and the sounds of small animals going about their business could be heard. Tanis saw a mother deer and her fawn in a clearing as they neared their destination.

"It's good to be home," she said with a contented sigh.

They rounded the bend and her breath caught. She expected to see the cabin and its grounds overrun by weeds and debris—after all, with the time in stasis after leaving Kapteyn's Star combined with the months following her abduction, neither of them had been to the cabin in years.

But there it stood, the yard clean, what appeared to be a fresh coat of paint on the walls, and the garden overflowing with fruits and vegetables.

"Did Bob arrange this?" Tanis asked as they approached.

"No, I did," a voice said from behind them.

Tanis turned to see Ouri stepping out from behind a tree. Her shipsuit was covered in dirt and a pair of work gloves hung from her belt.

"Ouri!" Tanis cried out and rushed to embrace the woman. "Thank you so much for this. You have no idea what it means…I guess that's why you ducked out of our meeting early."

"And had Priscilla make your train take longer," the colonel grinned. "It hasn't all been me. A lot of us from the SOC, command crew, and no small number of Marines have been down here. Even Amanda was here not long ago weeding your strawberry patch, but she had to run and prep to trade off with Priscilla."

"Come inside," Tanis said and took Ouri's arm. "I'll make coffee—I imagine there's coffee."

Ouri chuckled. "Your larder is fully stocked. I would come in, but you have no idea the workload I'm shielding you from right now. I came down here because I wanted to see the look on your face, but I need to get back to the grind."

"Are you sure?" Tanis asked. "I know your boss; he works for me."

"I seem to recall that, yes," Ouri replied. "But if I stay, Sanderson is going to start calling both of us, and I want you to enjoy yourself for a few more hours at least."

"OK," Tanis agreed. "But we have to sit down before long, you'll really want to hear about my little trip, especially New Eden."

"New Eden?" Ouri gasped. "You were there? Is it as beautiful as we hoped?"

"You'll just have to wait and see," Tanis said replied with a wink.

"Are we sure this is our Tanis?" Ouri asked Joe. "She seems far too easygoing."

"I think the smuggler crew she spent the last few months with has rubbed off on her," Joe replied.

"Stars, I really do wish I could stay," Ouri said, a frown clouding her expression. "But duty calls. I'll see the two of you soon enough."

Ouri turned and walked back up the path, leaving Tanis and Joe to spend a last moment admiring their home before stepping inside.

* * * * *

Later that afternoon, as they relaxed in front of the dying embers of their fire, Tanis suddenly reached out and grasped Joe's arm.

"You resigned your commission for me?"

Joe chuckled. "Just got to that place in your queue, eh?"

She sat up and turned to him.

"What were you thinking? How could you…" her voice trailed and she let a slow smile creep over her face.

"You and your belief that the mission is *everything*," Joe chuckled. "I thought you were beyond that."

"I am," Tanis said with a sigh. "It was a momentary relapse. What I meant to say was 'thank you'."

"You're welcome," Joe said pulled her close for a long kiss, which Tanis returned.

Suddenly she pulled back, her piercing eyes locked onto his. "Wait. If you resigned and/or went AWOL, how is it that you were in command of the *Andromeda* when you scooped us up?"

"It turns out, Bob forced Jason to back down. My resignation never hit the official record," Joe said with a shrug.

"It's nice to have your friendly neighborhood AI-god on your side," Tanis said with a laugh.

<Not you, too,> Bob said with a sigh.

<Sorry, I couldn't resist,> Tanis laughed in response.

"The next thing in your queue is likely a note from Jason telling you that my punishment is up to you," Joe said with a wink.

"Oh, is it now?" Tanis asked as she leaned back and pulled him on top of her. "I wonder what we should do about that?"

AN UNEXPECTED INVITATION

STELLAR DATE: 10.28.8927 (Adjusted Years)
LOCATION: ISS Intrepid, Orbiting Fierra
REGION: Bollam's World System, Bollam's World Federation

<Sera.> The sound broke into her dreams. *<Sera.>* It repeated. *<Wake up Sera, you've got a call.>*

Sera tried to swat away Helen's voice. "Lemme 'lone…sleeping."

<I know that, Fina, but its Captain Andrews. I thought you'd want to take it.>

Sera snorted and turned over, fighting the voice that was telling her she should wake.

<Come on, Fina. Wake up.>

"Kay, kay." Sera knew from decades of experience that when Helen thought it was time to wake up, there was no fighting it. *<Patch me through.>*

<He called you,> Helen reminded her.

*<Oh, yeah, patch **him** through, then.>* Sera waited a moment and then her HUD showed that the captain was connected. *<Good morning, Captain, what can I do for you?>*

Captain Andrew's warm chuckle filled her mind. *<I guess we're on different clocks. What time is it there?>*

Sera checked and grimaced. *<Oh four hundred.>*

<I'm sorry about that, it's only oh fifteen here. I was going to invite you and your crew to our officer's wardroom at eighteen hundred hours for our evening dinner. Sort of an eve before battle meal, but if the timing is bad…>

Sera tried to compose her mind, this sort of thing was important, probably not to be missed. *<No, no, we'd be honored to come. Eighteen hundred, you said?>*

<Yes, I'll have someone meet you and bring you up at a quarter to.>

<Sounds good, we'll be ready.> Sera fought the urge to yawn. For some reason, she was one of those people who couldn't hear both audibly and mentally when she did.

<We'll likely all be in our dress uniforms for the occasion,> Captain Andrews said. *<But you can wear whatever is your custom—you looked quite beautiful in what you had on today.>*

Sera almost laughed—she had been wearing a short jacket and nothing else. If only he knew. Then again, she considered, he had probably seen a lot in his years. Perhaps he did know.

<Thank you, Captain Andrews. So, we're all welcome to come?>

<Of course, I would love to meet your crew.>

<Eighteen hundred hours, then,> Sera said.

<Looking forward to it,> Captain Andrews replied.

The captain closed the connection and Sera heard Helen chuckle softly.

<I'm guessing he noticed.>

Sera held a hand up and turned it over slowly. Her glossy black skin was a thing of beauty, but it would be nice to change its color.

<Your level of self-appreciation would be considered unhealthy in some circles,> Helen said quietly.

<They'd probably be right,> Sera thought in response.

The play of light across her fingers began to lull her mind back to sleep when the realization struck her that the dinner was in three hours. Cheeky was going to kill her! She quickly connected to *Sabrina's* shipnet and messaged her crew.

<We've been invited to a formal dinner with the Intrepid's *officers,>* Sera said to an immediate squeal of delight from Cheeky, and a delayed pair of groans from Thompson and Cargo. *<Someone will have to stay behind and keep an eye on things, and keep Sabrina company.>*

<I wish I could eat. It must be fun,> Sabrina said.

<It is fun,> Cheeky replied. *<I wish we could show you.>*

Thompson and Cargo were already arguing about who was going to get to stay behind and determined that a combat sim would be the decision maker. Sera was surprised that she didn't hear Nance arguing with them about whose turn it was. Usually she hated these sorts of things.

Instead, the bio asked, *<When is it?>*

Sera was stunned. Even Cheeky stopped her food-related discussion with Sabrina.

<What?> Sera asked stupidly.

<How long 'til the dinner?> Nance asked again.

<It's at eighteen hundred Intrepid time. Someone will be here to pick us up in just under three hours.>

<What?> Cheeky yelled. *<How are we supposed to get ready for a formal dinner that fast?>*

Sera groaned inwardly and was about to tell Cheeky to deal with it, when she heard what sounded like a mental sob come from Nance. She had never heard anything but stoicism from her bio and was out of bed and in the corridor in moments. Cheeky emerged from her cabin at the same time and they met at the door to Nance's cabin.

Cheeky gave Sera a long look, neither sure what to say.

<Are you okay, Nance?> Sera eventually asked.

<I…I'm…no, I'm not okay.>

<Can we come in?> Cheeky asked.

There was no response, but after a long moment the door opened and the two women stepped inside. Neither had ever entered the bio's cabin and they were both taken aback by what they saw.

The walls were colored a soft pink and lined with shelves that held row upon row of dolls. They ranged from replicas of holo stars to ancient china dolls. It was both cute and a little bit eerie at the same time with dozens upon dozens of eyes following their every move.

Nance was sitting on her bed in a long shift, tears streaming down her face. Sera looked at Cheeky. A bet or two would be settled over this. Nance, as it turned out, did not sleep in her hazsuit. They quickly sat down on either side of their crewmate, wrapping their arms around her.

"What's wrong, Nance?" Cheeky asked softly.

"There's not enough time to get ready," Nance replied around a sniffle.

"You want to go to the dinner?" Sera asked.

"I always want to go," Nance said. "I just can't because of that damn suit." She pointed to the hazsuit that was draped over a chair.

"I don't understand," Cheeky frowned. "You could have just taken the suit off and come to any of the dinners and parties we've been to over the last few years."

Nance shook her head. "No, I couldn't have. To be around strangers and all their germs and filth without protection? I would have had no appetite…I probably would have gotten sick and thrown up on someone."

The fact that Nance was irrationally terrified of germs was no surprise to Sera and she mouthed *see, not a fetish,* to Cheeky, over Nance's head.

"What changed?" Sera asked. "How come you aren't worried about germs on the *Intrepid*?"

"It was that med-tech, Terry. She said she used to be—still is actually—terrified of germs and sickness and infection. She tried everything to stop it, but she couldn't stop thinking about all the bacteria and microbes that live in and around us. She had the perfect solution though."

Nance looked up as she spoke, a glimmer of hope in her eyes.

"Not something mental I hope," Sera said. "Those quick fix mental alterations always have unpleasant side-effects."

"No, nothing like that, I'm still terrified of germs, but she has nano and systems that monitor it all and show her exactly what is living in and on her body as well as the ability to remove anything she doesn't want there. She recognized me as someone with similar issues and shared her nano with me and helped me upgrade my AI with the monitoring systems." Nance gave a happy smile. "I don't have to be afraid anymore."

"That's great, Nance!" Cheeky hugged her. "So, what's the problem?"

"I don't have anything to wear! All I have is that damn suit!"

Sera laughed and Cheeky giggled.

"Anywhere else that may be a problem, but you have Cheeky here. I've got everything you need," the pilot said.

"And probably more than you want," Sera added.

Cheeky stood and pulled Nance up after her. The two women left and Sera following them out into the corridor; Cheeky cast a grin back at Sera as she guided Nance into her cabin. Cheeky always loved a project.

Cargo passed through the corridor and into his cabin, grumbling that Thompson must have cheated to win so fast, and that he didn't even know where his nice shoes were.

<*Oh, I almost forgot to mention,*> Helen paused in her conversation with the AI aboard the *Intrepid*. <*Bob whipped up a solution for your skin problem, it's in a package waiting in our airlock.*>

<*Bob* whipped it up?> Sera asked incredulously. <*I didn't even know he knew about my skin.*>

<*I mentioned it to Priscilla—who has her own special skin, you may have noticed. Anyway, the nano package will solve your problems. At least that's what he said.*>

Sera had to admit that the prospect piqued her interest. She reached the airlock in less than a minute where she found a ubiquitous silver cylinder.

<*Unscrew the end and touch it to your palm,*> Helen supplied.

Sera did as instructed and felt the distinct tingle of a large volume of nanobots passing into her body.

Her arm began to feel full as the canister emptied. From the weight difference, she guessed that almost two kilograms worth of nano were flooding her. A prompt appeared from the bots, requesting access to her core brain to nano interface—apparently to upgrade it.

<*Accept it,*> Helen said. <*You'll be glad you did.*>

<*Why not,*> Sera shrugged. <*When has acquiescing to the wishes of a god ever gone wrong?*>

Despite slight misgivings, she accepted, curiosity winning out over trepidation.

Her interface programming was updated and Sera immediately felt greater clarity regarding to the state of her body. She had always thought that her implants gave her very fine-tuned control over physical state, but now she realized that it had always been a blurry image at best. She could now introspect and adjust every muscle, every gland, even her individual cells down to their DNA.

<*Don't get carried away,*> Helen advised. <*Let it do its thing.*>

Sera felt her skin begin to tingle and then itch. It wasn't like the searing pain when she first tripped Rebecca's DNA-based trap, but she held her breath, afraid it would get there. The feeling worked its way from her toes up her body. It didn't stop at her neck—where her glossy black skin ended—but crept up her face and over her head.

She peered at herself in the airlock's glass window. Her entire head was now also covered in the glossy black skin. She could even feel it on the inside of her cheeks.

<*Thanks, Helen, I fail to see how this is an improvement—though at least it didn't hurt, or try to kill me.*>

<Wait for it...> Helen replied.

A second later a new interface appeared in her mental HUD. She explored its options, realizing that she now had full control over both the color, sheen and texture of her skin.

"This is incredible..." she whispered to herself. "Cheeky is going to be so jealous!"

She changed her flesh from black, to a pewter grey, to a light pink, and then realized it didn't all have to be the same color. She experimented with dozens of combinations before changing her skin back to something near her original coloring, though still more reflective.

<You're welcome,> Bob's deep tone filled her mind.

<Thank you,> Sera said effusively. <Though I really didn't expect it to change all of my skin.>

<Why not?> Bob asked. <Your biological epidermis was quite inferior. I assumed—and by that, I mean I divined—that you would prefer all your flesh gone in favor of this superior coating.>

Sera's thoughts bunched up as she wondered what Bob meant by 'divined'.

<He's teasing you,> Helen said. <He overhears pretty much all the conversations on the ship's public net. Your comment to Tanis was out there for him to pick up.>

<An AI with a sense of humor about his godhood? I guess all is not lost,> Sera said to Helen before addressing Bob.

<You know...you're right. Thanks.>

<The least I can do. You returned my Tanis to me—I am in your debt.>

His wording was curious, but Sera pushed it from her mind. She had dallied long enough and still had to find the right outfit.

THE CALM BEFORE

STELLAR DATE: 10.28.8927 (Adjusted Years)
LOCATION: ISS *Intrepid*, Orbiting Fierra
REGION: Bollam's World System, Bollam's World Federation

Two and a half hours later, Sera was standing in the galley preparing a cup of coffee when Flaherty and Cargo came in. Cargo wore his formal grey suit, which he often used for more important trade meetings, and Flaherty wore the high-collared, black suit she remembered him sporting several times before their exile.

"I didn't know you still had that," she said softly.

Flaherty shrugged. "I figured it would come in handy someday."

As he spoke, his eyes settled on her and he joined Cargo in an appreciative stare before shaking his head and moving to the counter and busying himself with a drink.

She had changed the color of her skin to something approximating a natural tone, but from her jawline down it gleamed and sparkled. Above it was as close in texture and shine to real skin as she could manage.

The gown she wore was a deep red, ankle-length, armless sheath with a plunging neckline. An embossed white polymer vine—complete with flowers—ran up her right side, around her waist and ending under her breasts. Long, red gloves, which reached her armpits, finished the look.

Her hair was pulled up into a knot on the back of her head, from which it cascaded down her back in long curls. Several wisps framed her face, which bore light, yet well-accentuated makeup.

"Do you like the dress, guys?" she asked while moving forward to sit down at the table. Her left leg completely exposed with each step.

"Looks great," Cargo grunted and joined Flaherty at the counter.

"Why does the boss have to be so sexy?" he asked Flaherty quietly.

"You're lucky," Flaherty grunted. "I'm practically her uncle."

A minute later, Thompson walked in to grab a drink and stopped dead in his tracks.

"Holy cow, Captain. That's quite the dress. Plan on seducing the *Intrepid's* captain or something?"

Sera laughed. "That would be quite the twist, wouldn't it?"

*<Twist? I'm pretty sure it **is** your plan,>* Helen said privately.

"Be a good laugh," Cargo chuckled. "I wonder what Tanis would think?"

A wave of guilt and frustration washed over Sera at the thought of Tanis, but she pushed it from her mind.

Thompson sat down at the table and grinned at the other two men in their suits. "You guys ready to go be bored?"

Cargo gave Thompson a rather undignified hand gesture and Flaherty simply grunted as he sat and took a drink from his mug. Sera caught Thompson stealing a glance at her breasts as they gleamed in the light, before his attention was grabbed by cough from the entrance. They all looked up to see Cheeky enter the wardroom, followed by Nance.

Thompson rose to his feet, his eyes wide as he took in Nance. Without a word, he ran from the room.

<Winner's choice, Cargo, I'm going to the dinner,> he called over the ship-net.

<What?> Cargo retorted. *<I'm already all dressed up!>*

<Too bad, I'm going.>

<Be quick about it,> Sera said, laughing softly. *<Our escort will be here in fifteen minutes.>*

She hadn't taken her eyes off the two women, and neither had Cargo, nor even Flaherty, though he was hiding much of his face behind his coffee cup. Sera had been expecting Cheeky to wear something that would require a shawl to cover, but her pilot had surprised her yet again.

Cheeky wore a long, silk dress in a shade of light gold that played off her hair. Sleeveless and cut deeply, it displayed her ample cleavage. It was tight across her body and down to her knees, where it fell loosely in a shimmering cascade. She spun slowly after entering the room and the whole dress seemed to slide and dance on her skin.

Her hair was swept up in an elaborate configuration that caused small tendrils to spill down on the sides of her face, the rest seemingly suspended above her head in a gravity defying display.

Nance was equally stunning in a light blue silk dress, also sleeveless, with a tight bodice and swaths of silk draped artfully across her stomach. From there, it fell nearly straight, its satin folds reflecting the light as she moved side to side, causing the fabric to sway and caress her hips. Her hair was down—its soft, even curls flowing down her back—with light blue hair clips holding it back from her face. She wore several bracelets and a pair of high heels fastened by thin straps.

"Wow," Cargo finally said aloud.

"Wow is right!" Sera exclaimed. "Suddenly I feel like I may be underdressed. You girls going to a dance I didn't know about?"

"A girl doesn't get much of a chance to dress up in this line of work," Cheeky said as she spun again. "Besides, after what Nance picked out I couldn't be outdone." She beckoned for Sera to stand up. "You don't quite match though; you're all glossy while we're all shimmery."

"You'll have to shine as best you can next to my radiance," Sera grinned. "I rather like this look."

Nance pointed to the slit running up to Sera's hip. "You've been around Cheeky for too long. That's not exactly formal."

Sera laughed. "You'd be surprised how many worlds would consider this too much clothing for formal." Even so, she ran her finger down the seam, lowering the slit to mid-thigh. "Better? Any lower and I'll only be able to take four inch steps"

Nance nodded.

They waited several more minutes for Thompson to return wearing his deep blue naval uniform from his days in the Scipio military, and his hair was actually brushed nicely and pulled behind his ears. He was blushing furiously as he entered the wardroom, with everyone's eyes on him.

"I…uh…" he stammered as he stopped in front of Nance. "I was wondering if you'd let me escort you."

Nance flushed as well. "Me?"

"Yeah. If I'd known you were going, I would have lost to Cargo. I'd really like to take you."

The smile that spread across Nance's face transformed her from the slightly nervous looking woman she had been a minute ago to a radiant beauty. "I'd love for you to escort me."

<Aw…kids,> Helen said to Sera.

<Just what we need, a legitimate shipboard romance.>

"We should go," Flaherty rose and extended his arm for Sera. She slipped hers into his, and a happy memory of the first time she had done that came back to her.

"Oh, what is this?" Cheeky said as Thompson and Nance filed out past her into the lift. "Since when am I the only one without a date?"

Cargo looked like he really didn't want to be left out, and Sera shrugged. Why not, if *Sabrina* wasn't safe here, where could she be?

<Will you be alright alone?> Sera asked Sabrina.

<Of course!> the ship's AI replied brightly. *<Corsia and Bob are teaching me so much!>*

<That's going to be a problem,> Helen said privately to Sera. *<The crew's AI are all going to start getting ideas.>*

<Maybe we should have helped liberate them sooner,> Sera said with a sigh. *<They may not be happy when they realized we could have.>*

"Cargo," she called from the corridor. "Sabrina says she'll be fine. Come on with us."

He almost ran out of the wardroom and joined them in the lift. When it disgorged them onto the ship's main deck, he took Cheeky's arm and the group exited the airlock onto the *Intrepid's* deck.

Their escort turned out to be Tanis, who stood waiting beside a groundcar in a crisp blue uniform. Her left breast was nearly covered with service ribbons and medals while no small number of foreign service medals adorned her right.

"Wow, that's one chest full of metal!" Cheeky said with a grin as they approached. "The ship's been a bit too quiet without you around."

She embraced Tanis, and then it was the general's turn to stare in wonder.

"Nance?" she asked. "I didn't recognize you at first. You look amazing!"

Nance smiled, a beautiful expression that filled her eyes with happiness. "Thanks. One of your bios helped me with my phobia—I don't know if you knew I'm terrified of germs. I can now go out without that damn suit."

"I had my suspicions; I'm really glad to hear someone helped you out. Who was it?"

"Her name is Terry, she works with a rather odious man named Dr. Philips," Nance replied.

"I see her on the roster, though I've never had the opportunity to meet her," Tanis said. "I'll see if I can do something nice for her sometime."

Tanis looked to Sera and an awkward moment passed between them before Tanis held out her hand.

<I'm sorry for what I said earlier,> Tanis spoke first.

<I'm sorry I put you in the position I have,> Sera replied. <I got the message out, I'm sorting out how to share my story.>

<No rush,> Tanis responded. <Bob has figured out your backstory and tells me there's nothing to worry about. I'm still curious, but no longer anxious.>

Sera's breath caught. <What do you mean, he's figured it out?>

<Bob has crafted an…algorithm, which allows him to predict past, present, and future events with near perfect accuracy—given a base level of information. He worked out your backstory—and whatever is preventing you from sharing it,> Tanis said with a smile playing at the edges of her mouth.

<That's…that's both incredible and hard to believe,> Sera replied.

"Come," Tanis gestured for everyone to enter the groundcar. "We'd best not keep Earl waiting."

The car ride was short and brought them back to the maglev station from which Sera had disembarked yesterday. They boarded the train and rocked in their seats as it accelerated rapidly down the line.

"Whoah!" Cheeky exclaimed as the car left the *Intrepid's* hull and raced across one of the structural arcs.

"The train we took yesterday didn't do this," Thompson added. "You guys are nuts," he said to Tanis.

The general chuckled. "You should take one to the stasis bays sometime. There's no track for the last hundred meters to the cylinders. You just line up and shoot into a moving hole."

"You realize this is supposed to be a starship, not a high-risk amusement park, right?" Thompson said while shaking his head.

"Was pretty common back in our time," Tanis said with a shrug. "We didn't have inertial dampeners, so speed and finesse didn't always go hand in hand. On a ship this big—and most stations, for that matter—you want to get places? That's how it's done."

"I really want to see that stuff someday," Nance said wistfully. "Even if it means going to Sol."

"I've had my fill," Tanis said quietly. "I'll never go back there."

No one spoke for the rest of the ride, and Sera saw that the train stopped one station further from the bridge than it had the day before.

The platform was wildly different than any of the stops she had seen yet. It appeared to be more of a food bazaar than a maglev station. A huge ring of vendor's stands and restaurant facades surrounded the platform. Servers—both robotic and human—walked amongst the throngs, offering samples and hawking their menus.

"Your...starship has a food court," Sera stated the obvious.

"It has several dozen. This one is left over from construction. Some companies bid for the rights to set up restaurants in the ship, and when we left we didn't bother removing the facilities. It makes for an interesting forward mess." Tanis threaded her way through the tables and Sera followed with her crew.

"Slow down a bit, these heels are not made for this type of maneuvering," Nance called from behind.

Tanis obliged, slowing her pace.

"I thought it would be more formal than this," Sera said, half expecting to see a couple of tables pushed together with the captain at their head.

"Don't worry, it is. We're just taking the back way in."

They passed the crush of tables and slipped between a pair of short-order restaurants. From there, Tanis led them into a long corridor. The smells in the food court were pleasant, but the smells coming down this hall were nothing short of delectable. She held open a door and everyone filed through into a large, well-appointed kitchen.

Within, directing battalions of chefs, was the largest man Sera had ever seen. She considered he had to be at least one-hundred and fifty kilograms. She had seen a lot of heavy worlders—or mod freaks—who were large, or strong, but this man was not like that. She could only think of him as a jovial mountain of jelly.

"Tanis!" He rushed toward the general and Sera worried for a moment that he would simply bowl her over. He managed to stop short and wrapped her in his massive embrace. "Tanis! I am so glad you are back. When Priscilla told me, I was beside myself with joy." He looked over her shoulder. "And who are these beautiful people gracing my kitchen? The ladies all look good enough to eat if—I weren't so full from sampling this evening's meal." With that, he wrapped he arms around his belly and laughed.

"I thought you were never full, Earl," Tanis replied with a warm smile. "This is Captain Sera; she's here helping us out with our current little problem. The others are her crew—the people who helped save me." Tanis introduced them all in turn, and the chef cast his smiling gaze over the throng.

"Welcome to my kitchen, Captain Sera and *Sabrina's* crew!" he bellowed as he slipped around Tanis with a grace Sera would never expect a man so large to possess, and wrapped her in an embrace, as well. "It is good to meet you. I had despaired that we had entered a time of ruffians and evil men with those ungrateful wretches out there."

Sera wondered if he meant outside the *Intrepid*, or just anywhere outside of his kitchen.

"Sera's not evil, perhaps just mischievous," Tanis said with a wry smile.

"Just the right amount then, I'm sure," Earl said and slapped Sera's ass.

"Um… yes," Sera almost squeaked in startlement.

<Is he always like this?> she said to Tanis over the Link.

<Yeah, it's just his way. His food is so good he gets away with anything he wants. Just smile and tell him you look forward to his meal.>

"Tanis tells me you are the best chef within a dozen light-years," Sera smiled winningly. "I look forward to sampling it myself."

"Oh ho! You'll do more than sample. I expect to see that slim stomach of yours plump and full when you are done."

"Earl's not happy if people eating his food don't have to unbuckle their belts," Tanis added. "But we really must be going Earl, the captain is waiting."

"But of course, we mustn't keep his majesty waiting." Earl bowed and swept his arm as they stepped passed him. Tanis led the way through the kitchen and into the dining room with Earl's calls of what to eat ringing out behind them.

They were smiling and laughing as they stepped into the officer's wardroom where the captain and Terrance were already seated. The room was dominated by a long wooden table, its surface inscribed with intricate patterns. Placed around it were wooden chairs and even the walls were covered with wood. Chandeliers made of natural crystal hung from the ceiling.

Sera took in the opulence, glad she dressed up for the occasion.

"Welcome," Captain Andrews said as he and Terrance rose. "You ladies look stunning," he said, though Sera could tell his eyes lingered longer on her.

"Was Earl pelting you with dinner suggestions?" Terrance asked.

"I think he just told us to sample at least forty separate dishes," Sera replied with a laugh.

"That would be the first course," Captain Andrews chuckled. "He's quite excited to have you back, Tanis."

"Of course he is. He's gotten to stuff me with different creations for a hundred years and I've loved each one—it's like having your biggest fan back."

"He stayed out of stasis that long?" Sera asked.

"All great chefs are control freaks," Tanis said with a shrug. "None can bear the thought of their kitchen in other people's hands for too long."

"But then he's spent half his life in there…" Nance said.

"And he wouldn't have it any other way," Terrance replied.

The captain indicated that Tanis and Sera should sit at the head of the table with him, Sera on his right and Tanis on his left. "You are, after all, the guest of honor," he said to Sera.

The rest of the crew sat down the sides of the table, getting settled just as Joseph entered through the kitchen, wiping his mouth with a napkin.

"I barely escaped with my life!" he laughed as he planted a kiss on Tanis's cheek and sat at her side.

Conversation fell mainly to the events of the last five thousand years, Sera filling in some interesting details of the history they missed. A topic everyone was especially interested in were the initial

FTL wars of the forty-sixth century and the conflicts of the eight millennia, which had very nearly brought an end to the human race.

The other diners filtered in over the next fifteen minutes, more than a few taking a moment to welcome Tanis back. Small conversations picked up around the table as everyone pelted Sera and her crew with questions.

"I have to ask," Cargo said to Tanis at one point. "How is it that we're even having this fancy dinner? Shouldn't we be preparing for a battle? It's a miracle we haven't been attacked yet."

"No miracle," Tanis replied. "No one can win out there, especially considering that they all fear our picotech. Everyone is waiting for reinforcements, and when those reinforcements arrive, it'll still be a stalemate. By that time, our FTL drive will be ready and we'll leave them in the dust. In the meantime—unless they all decide to ally against us, we can hold them off."

The serving staff appeared shortly thereafter, leading carts of appetizers. They were adorned in pristine white hats and jackets—Earl would allow nothing less. With no small amount of poise and decorum, they set plates of everything from finger foods to soups in the center of the table.

Sera didn't hesitate to select a bevy of meat-filled pastries and half a dozen different types of cheeses. The servers quickly replaced empty dishes, and—after her third helping—Sera wondered what could possibly be next.

She did not have wait long before the staff returned with an array of pasta salads, sprinkled with the finest olive oil infused with garlic and oregano. It didn't stop there, as they returned with more food arranged on elegant platters, on which the garnishes even looked good enough to eat.

Sera sampled just a little bit of everything and Cheeky made several vocal sounds of pleasure that were on the verge of embarrassing. Nance and Thompson seemed absorbed in their own private conversation while they shared a meatloaf—purportedly sourced from the ship's own farms.

Sera thought they had reached the height of the banquet, but was mistaken. After their glasses were refilled with red wine, half a dozen chefs came from the kitchen and stood behind a table she had assumed was decorative. A fire roared to life and spread across the table's surface. They watched, completely captivated as vegetables and thin slices of steak mixed with mushrooms were cooked in woks.

The chefs knew their business, spinning the utensils in their hands while dropping marinade into their pans. They served the dish with potatoes and a mixture of rice covered in a delicate cream sauce.

<*I'm ruined for food for the rest of my life,*> Cheeky said privately to Sera.

<*I know! If I wasn't able to tell, I'd think they were drugging us,*> Sera replied.

While the food was the most exquisite she had ever tasted, Sera still couldn't keep from watching the *Intrepid's* captain, even when he wasn't addressing her. Her glances were innocent, but when she peered at him out the corner of her eye she was completely unaware that the look was highly seductive.

Delicate, cream-filled pastries and cakes finished the delectable dinner off perfectly, but it was the conversation and laughter from her crew that gave her the most enjoyment.

As the desert forks were being licked clean, a breathless Earnest Redding burst into the room and raced to the captain's side.

"We…I…You'll…" he gasped.

"Easy Earnest, catch your breath, what's wrong?"

"Nothing's wrong, Captain," he managed after taking a gulp of air. "It's what's right! We've had a breakthrough."

"Really?" Sera asked. "Something beyond the information I provided?"

"Oh yes, very much so, and no. Though we wouldn't have been able to manage it without your graviton systems and all those research studies you provided, as well."

"So, what is it, then?" Terrance asked, his eyes gleaming with anticipation.

"We've discovered how to use the graviton emission systems that Captain Sera provided us with—emissions that work in matter repulsion and photon redirection in directional and focused beams and waves—to create a generalized and consistent suspension wave in the form of a massive halo upon which we were able to successfully place a McPherson generality focus layer tuned to a specific area of space, while altering the gravitational waves supporting it to form a hard shell of non-focused space underneath it." He said without taking a single breath.

"OK, I'm no slouch when it comes to physics, but you've gone levels beyond what I knew existed," Tanis said.

"It's a stasis shield," Sera said, feeling as though the breath had been sucked from her. "He figured out how to make a gods damned stasis shield."

"Does it work as people have always envisioned?" Captain Andrews asked.

Earnest was catching his breath again after his long explanation so Sera responded to him.

"From the description, it's the holy grail—maybe more so than even your picotech."

Earnest nodded emphatically and everyone fell silent, not a single piece of cutlery moved, not a single mouth chewed. The only sound was Earnest taking one last breath before he said. "That's exactly right. And we can have it in place in two days."

Silence reigned again until Terrance stood and raised his glass of wine in the air. "I propose a toast. To our good friends from *Sabrina* and our great and dedicated Edeners. We've proved it before and we're proving it again: there is nothing we can't do, no chasm that can't be crossed, and no wall that can't be breached. We're living legends, people. We're going to make history."

"Make more history, that is," Joe said with a laugh.

Everyone at the table stood and glasses clinked as the toast was repeated down the table, then everyone took a long draught. With wild abandon, Terrance threw his glass at the fireplace where it shattered against the tile. In a moment, everyone followed his lead with laughter and loud calls for more wine.

ESCALATION

STELLAR DATE: 10.29.8927 (Adjusted Years)
LOCATION: ISS *Intrepid*, Orbiting Fierra
REGION: Bollam's World System, Bollam's World Federation

The cocoon of the new Arc-6 fighter drew Jessica into its womb and she felt the ship's systems connect with her mind.

Once more into the breach, she thought to herself.

Cordy, the squadron AI, addressed the pilots.

<Don't skim the preflight checks; these birds haven't seen black before. You're the first to take them out.>

<As if we need reminding,> Cary groused.

<You've read the specs,> Rock said. *<They're just Arc-5s with stasis shields and inertial dampeners. Same thrust and power, just well-nigh indestructible.>*

Jessica smiled at the squadron's banter. Despite her near-death experience battling the Sirian scout ships, she had kept up her pilot's credentials. She had not flown any active combat missions since that fateful battle, but had taken part in several training exercises with the Black Death—as the squadron had become known.

Rock and Cary were old guard; they had flown against the Sirian scouts, as well, but many of the pilots on that fateful mission had been Victorians who stayed behind when the *Intrepid* left The Kap.

Still, she recognized many of the pilots and had exchanged warm greetings in the ready room. The one person she missed was Carson, who had gone on to lead his own squadron—currently out patrolling the space around Fierra's southern hemisphere.

<You ready for this?> she asked Jerry, her wingman.

<More than ready,> Jerry replied. *<Gonna show these bastards they can't mess with the* Intrepid*!>*

<That's the spirit,> Jessica replied with a laugh.

Her preflight checklist showed green, and, while waiting for the squadron to drop down their ladders, she ran it again for good measure.

On cue, she felt movement and turned her vision outward, looking around the bay with the ship's sensors. They confirmed that the suspension field had picked up her Arc-6 and was moving it to her ladder.

The *Intrepid* now sported a dozen fighter bays—a number necessary to store and service the vessel's eight-hundred fighters. This bay held racks for over a hundred ships, though nearly all were currently deployed. On the far side of the bay, techs and automatons worked tirelessly around a cluster of Arc-5s, upgrading them into Arc-6s.

Her ship slipped onto its ladder, along with the other twenty-four fighters in the squadron, and a thirty second countdown appeared on her HUD.

No one spoke, every member of the Black Death likely following whatever rituals they performed alone before a combat drop. Jessica sent a thought to Trist in what she hoped was a glorious afterlife.

This is for you, babe.

There was almost no physical sensation as the fighters slid down their ladders, the new inertial dampeners removing all feelings of motion.

<*This is almost too smooth,*> Jason said. <*I can't even tell which way I'm moving.*>

<*Enable the feedback system,*> Cary advised. <*It'll give you the sensations you're used to, without actually putting the pressure on your body.*>

<*I know,*> Jason replied. <*I read the manual, too, I was just saying…*>

<*Cut the chatter,*> Rock interrupted. <*I want complete shakedown reports by our first pass around Fierra.*>

Jessica complied, and in sequence with the other fighters, applied a 30*g* burn toward the moon below. She didn't even feel a single *g* on her body, and the fighter spun and pivoted like it was on rails.

Amazing, she thought to herself.

The other pilots were also putting the ships through their paces, and Jessica watched the squadron dance and spin as they began to break into a slow polar orbit. Their patrol path called for a half-dozen polar loops before slowing to hold position five-thousand kilometers above the south pole, creating a buffer between the pirate Padre's fleet and the *Intrepid* and its fleet.

The moon below was a welcoming blue and green, with white cumulous clouds dotting its skies. A thick layer of water vapor high in the world's stratosphere blurred the surface, but she could still make out oceans, green lands, deserts, and icy poles.

Worlds like this one—distant from their star and orbiting massive jovians—were not self-sustaining. The less-luminous light of their host star did not impart enough energy to the world to keep it warm with a more natural atmosphere. Combined with the gravity of its parent planet constantly tearing at its skies, the world would ultimately lose most of its air. It would take constant upkeep to remain habitable.

Still, for people who loved green grass and open spaces, it was hard to beat the real deal. Jessica found that she still missed Athabasca, and though it had been nice to visit Victoria from time to time, its brown forests and fields never sated her desire for a more terrestrial world.

She used her sensors to probe the world as much as she could. The mission report held true. No settlements had been constructed, but the moon wasn't uninhabited either. The terraforming crews were still there; her dataset told her it was mostly biologists monitoring their work. A flotilla of tugs and cargo ships hung in low orbit where they had taken refuge from their work constructing a space elevator after the battle broke out between the Bollam's World Space Force and the pirates.

With any luck, this would be over soon and they could go back to their tasks unharmed.

<Good to see some more friendly faces,> a welcoming voice came over the Link.

<Carson! How are you?> Jessica responded.

<Oh, you know, the usual.>

<Anything we should be aware of?> Rock asked.

<The folks up north seem to be keeping to themselves, but these guys down here keep feinting and trying to draw us in. Poor tactics, if you ask me. Whoever starts this fight is going to come out the worst,> Carson replied. <You guys take care. My girls and boys have been out here for three days now and we're heading in to get some sack and have our birds upgraded.>

<You'll love it,> Cary said. <Smooth as butter. You won't ache for days after a ride in these.>

<Now that's an advancement I'm glad to hear about,> Carson laughed. <These old bones of mine aren't so happy about pulling seventy anymore.>

Carson's squadron dropped into a polar orbit, passing the Black Death as they did a quick loop around Fierra to reach the *Intrepid's* elevation.

Four other squadrons patrolled the southern hemisphere, and on their final loop, Jessica's squadron adjusted their trajectory to fit into their place in the pattern—when their final deceleration was interrupted by an exclamation from Cary.

<Oh shit, oh shit, this isn't good!>

<Report, lieutenant, what's going on?> Rock asked calmly.

<Attitude control is gone wonky; I can't rotate my drive for final braking. I tried spinning the whole ship, but I can't hold it steady…I'm tumbling out here.>

Jessica's scan confirmed Cary's words. Her fighter was moving like a dog trying to screw a football, still travelling at over fifty-thousand kilometers per-hour.

<I confirm,> Cordy said. *<Something is messed up in the sensor interface. It can't get good data, and with the dampeners it can't get readings off the fallback gyros.>*

<Turn off the dampeners,> another pilot suggested. *<Won't be fun, but you can take it.>*

<Trying that,> Cary replied. *<Now the system won't take input from the gyros and I think I'm going to hurl.>*

Jessica laughed at the humor. It wasn't possible to vomit in a shoot suit, but that didn't stop a person's body from trying. The data from her scan showed Cary's Arc-6 now spinning wildly as attitude control thrusters fired inaccurately, working off bad data as they tried to right the ship. Cary would be experiencing forces over thirty gs in constant, random vectors.

<Kill your attitude control,> Rock said. *<You're not helping yourself out at all.>*

<I've tried all the tricks I can think of,> Cordy said. *<Something got screwed up in the sensor interfaces. You're going to have to reset and restore from crystal.>*

Cary groaned and then signaled affirmative.

Her fighter ceased its sporadic motion and settled into a relatively consistent vector—one aimed straight for the pirate fleet.

<Uh…Commander?> Cary asked.

<We'll cover you,> Rock replied. <The restore should only take a few minutes.>

<And what if it doesn't work?> Cary asked.

The squadron's combat net was silent for a moment.

<Then we get to see how good these shields really are,> Rock replied.

ENGAGEMENT

STELLAR DATE: 10.29.8927 (Adjusted Years)
LOCATION: ISS *Intrepid,* Orbiting Fierra (6*Mj* Jovian)
REGION: Bollam's World System, Bollam's World Federation

Sera waved a greeting as she walked past Amanda, who was now ensconced in the bridge's foyer and followed the corridor past the conference room to the bridge itself.

She stood in the room's entrance and stared for a full minute.

<OK, now it really does feel like home,> she said to Helen.

The *Intrepid's* bridge was more like a colony command and control center than simply the helm and ship duty stations most vessels possessed.

For starters, it was almost a quarter the volume of *Sabrina*; nearly thirty meters across, and twice as many deep. A large holo tank dominated the center of the room, and beside it stood Tanis, frowning at what she saw. Surrounding her, in concentric circles, were rows and rows of consoles, smaller holo displays, and department liaisons and automatons.

It bustled like a beehive with its queen at the center.

<It's a strange relationship she has with the captain,> Helen observed. *<Almost as though she is the colony leader and he is just a captain under her command.>*

<Almost,> Sera agreed.

Tanis looked up and locked eyes with her. *<Come with me.>*

<Why do I feel like I'm being called into my father's office?> Sera asked Helen with a mental sigh.

<You know why. It's time you told them your story—they need to know.>

Tanis threaded her way through the consoles and bridge personnel, moving toward a doorway on Sera's right. They stepped through the portal into a small, utilitarian office. Behind a desk covered in holo displays sat Captain Andrews.

She caught him glance at her body, something that certainly was understandable given the shimmering silver skin tone she had selected for the day.

<It's sad, really,> Helen observed privately.

<Let me be. I'm a frail organic, subject to my chemically induced whims.>

Helen gave the mental equivalent of a snort in response.

"Good afternoon," he addressed both women. "Tanis, did you see the latest message from the AST ships?"

"I did," the general replied with a chuckle. "Claiming that they own this ship due to late interest payments on loans is pretty weak—especially given that the loans, small as they were, were handled through the GSS, not the Sol Space Federation."

"Well, they did absorb the GSS before they shut it down," Sera said. "It was part of an attempt to stop the exodus of the brightest and most adventurous people from Sol. After you left, Sol started to get pretty stagnant. People had no drive or ambition. Even their birthrate almost hit zero."

"Trust me," Tanis said while shaking her head. "That trend started long before we left."

"Either way," Sera replied with a shrug. "They wrote off all their GSS-related debt millennia ago."

"That's good," Captain Andrews replied. "The only thing worse than enemy fleets chasing you across the stars are bureaucrats who want their money."

"It seems they'll even chase you across millennia," Sera added.

"Do you have the details on that write-off?" Tanis asked. "It would be nice to send a response for them to chew on. Keeping the dialog going never hurts."

"I'm pulling up what we have on *Sabrina*," Sera said as she accessed her ship's archives. "Here it is. After the breakup of the SSF and the eventual formation of the AST, the new government performed a century-long audit of all the assets and debts they possessed.

"Somewhere along the line, someone realized that the government had an ownership stake in several dozen colonies, and colony ships, that no one had heard from in nearly a millennium. They didn't like the potential liability, so they simply wrote off the whole lot and passed legislation that any property the AST would have owned, or had a lien, on was transferred to whoever possessed it at the time of the law's passing."

The captain ran a hand through his hair. "How…indiscreet of them."

Tanis laughed, and Sera passed the relevant information to her.

"Great, I'll have the comm officer organize a response and send it to our friends out there. Should shut them up for a bit."

Tanis turned to Sera, her expression carefully schooled. "You sent your message. The captain and I would finally like to—ah, shit."

"What is it?" Sera asked as Tanis turned toward door.

"One of the fighters is having a malfunction and heading straight for Padre's ships."

They rushed out to the main holo tank, which already displayed the situation at the Fierra's south pole.

"It's the Black Death," a duty officer supplied. "One of their Arc-6s is acting up; they're trying a system restore from crystal backup."

"And if it doesn't finish in time?" Sera asked.

"Then they'll pass right through the middle of Padre's formation," Tanis replied.

"Sorry, my story will have to wait for another time, this could be the start of things," Sera looked from Tanis to Captain Andrews. "I need to get out there."

She could see Tanis and the captain exchange thoughts over the Link before Tanis nodded.

<Amanda, give her priority on a maglev. How is the shield upgrade on her ship going?>

<Finished ten minutes ago, they're just doing final tests.>

<Tell them to step on it. Sabrina is undocking in ten minutes.>

FIRESTORM

STELLAR DATE: 10.29.8927 (Adjusted Years)
LOCATION: Near Kithari, South of Fierra
REGION: Bollam's World System, Bollam's World Federation

<Max burn,> Rock addressed his squadron. *<I want a protective cocoon around Cary.>*

Jessica goosed her fighter to match Cary's vector with several quick burns she barely noticed.

<Five enemy ships are moving to intercept,> Cordy advised.

C'mon, Cary, Jessica thought to herself. *Get that thing fixed.*

She counted down the seconds it should take for a system restore to complete and Cary's silence continued after her count completed. The pilot did not come back on the squadron's combat net.

Another minute passed and Rock's voice broke the silence.

<We're going to punch her through their picket line and one of our pushers is going to grab her. Just need to get past all those bastards down there.>

The pilots silently signaled their acknowledgement, coordinated their flight paths, and selected targets from the five corvettes closing in on Cary.

<How's it look out there?> Colonel Pearson's voice broke the strained silence on the squadron's combat net.

<If the shields, hold we'll be OK. Just make sure Excelsior Nova *is ready to play catch on the far side,>* Rock replied to the group commander.

<Nuwen has his ship ready to catch her, I'm patching him into your net now. The Enterprise *and* Defiance *are dropping lower to provide supporting fire if the whole mess down there swarms you.* Andromeda *sneaking by now to silently drop off some RMs.>*

<Roger that,> Rock replied. *<You heard that,>* he said to his pilots. *<Things are about to get real out here. We could be facing the whole effing galaxy before the day is done, so don't blow your loadout on maybes. Sure, tactical strikes.>*

Jessica nodded to herself and signaled her acknowledgement of the order.

The relative velocity between Cary's fighter and the five pirate corvettes put intercept in twelve minutes. Jessica kept an eye on her NSAI's estimation of lethal range—just under ten thousand kilometers—which they would reach in five minutes.

<Watch the corrections,> Cordy advised the pilots.

Space close to Fierra was full of dust from mined asteroids and no small amount of swirling gas from the jovian it orbited. It was far from empty, and a dust, or hydrogen cloud could make all the difference when it came to striking a lethal blow.

Jessica checked the updated scan. Though the five corvettes had accelerated rapidly to reach Cary, they were now breaking, attempting to match v to snatch her up.

The maneuver made little sense to Jessica. With the rest of the squadron surrounding Cary, the pirate ships would become stationary targets—relatively speaking—if they attempted to grab the disabled fighter.

<From what Helen and Sabrina have shared, there are few one-man fighters in this time—certainly none used in fleet combat. They can't generate strong enough grav shielding to hold out against antimatter-powered weapons,> Cordy said.

<So, what you're saying is…these bastards are in for a surprise,> Jessica said, her avatar displaying a wicked grin.

<Except at that range, they'll have no problem destroying Cary, even with the squadron flying close support. All it will take is one low-yield nuke.>

Rock seemed to have the same thought. <Jason, Jessica, Sam, Trinity. Take your wingmen and boost hard and beat those assholes senseless before they get here. Make them think twice about getting up-close and personal with our Arcs.>

They acknowledged the order and eight Arc-6 fighters accelerated toward the pirate corvettes.

They split into two formations, each targeting one of the pirate vessels and none firing until they were well within beam range. It was deemed best to save their power for maximum effectiveness in this stellar soup.

The corvettes were still slowing to match v with the rest of the squadron, and their prey, Cary's ship, when the eight Arc-6s flashed past them, laying withering beam fire on the two lead vessels.

Jessica spun her engine and applied full thrust, the now pointless readout telling her that without the dampeners she would be crushed under a 100gs of acceleration. Scan showed that the enemy corvettes had returned fire at the fighters, a salvo of over seventy beams, and two rail slugs.

The slugs knocked their target Arcs around, but none of the fighters showed any damage.

<Status!> Rock called out.

<Shields show no change. I got hit by one of those slugs and didn't feel a thing. We're coming for another pass,> Jason reported.

<They're spooling their AP drives,> Cordy said. <I advise that you come around and fire right up their funnels. It should punch right through their antimatter containment.>

Jessica sent an affirmative response, feeling giddy as the adrenaline coursed through her body. It was going to be like shooting fish in a barrel. The fighters slowed, and then stopped before their engines drove them back toward the pirate corvettes. Almost lazily, they drifted over their enemy, shrugging off the beams and rails before dropping directly into the stream of gamma rays that flowed at light speed from the AP engines.

It took conscious effort to drop her ship into the engine wash— normally such action would result in certain death, but the stasis shields brushed off the luminal impacts with ease.

In unison, five of the eight fighters lanced streams of protons into the pirate ship's engines.

As predicted, the beams penetrated the antimatter containment and the pirate ships exploded in tremendous displays of plasma and shrapnel.

<There's the one time we get to do that,> Jessica said.

<The rest of their fleet has already started jinking more erratically,> Jason chuckled.

<They're also moving to engage us,> Cordy added. <They'll be in range in four minutes.>

Rock gave the order for the eight fighters to form up with the rest of the squadron. Jessica adjusted her relative v to zero with a quick burst from her AP engine.

<I could get used to this,> she commented to Jerry.

<No kidding,> Jerry replied. <It's going to be a cake walk.>

<Don't get too cocky,> Jessica replied. <We may have been able to brush off the beams from five ships, but it's about to get a lot hotter.>

* * * * *

"That's amazing," Tanis commented from beside the bridge's main holo tank. "It's like the enemy wasn't even firing."

"It's a game changer, alright," Sanderson observed.

"The bulk of their fleet is engaging," Tanis cautioned as the tank lit up with an explosion of energy surrounding Black Death's position. Nearly two hundred corvettes and four cruisers focused every beam and railgun in their fleet on the fighter squadron's tight cocoon around Cary's disabled vessel.

She tasted blood and realized that she was biting her lip.

<What have I done to them,> she whispered to Angela. <Jessica is in there…fuck…if anyone is still in there.>

Angela had no response, though concern flowed from her into Tanis's mind.

The salvo lasted only seven seconds, but it felt like an eternity to Tanis.

The assault ceased as if a switch had been flipped. Scan took a moment to clear and then the bridge erupted with cheers. The squadron was still there, surrounding their comrade's ship, all undamaged.

<Squadron leader, status,> Tanis queried.

<General! Wow…that was…sorry. We're all OK. Our reactors are running about as hot as they go, though—we can't withstand another one of those barrages.>

<You won't have to,> Tanis replied.

The pirate fleet had passed the fighters and split into two groups, each looping around to re-engage the squadron, a maneuver they were executing while taking great care not to expose their engines to the Arc6's.

Tanis watched trajectory estimates and corrections scroll down a secondary holo. It was going to be a direct hit.

She finally let out her breath.

Both groups of Padre's armada passed right through dense fields of grapeshot courtesy of the *Enterprise* and *Defiance*. The lead ships were torn to ribbons under the barrage and even one of the cruisers blossomed into a cloud of hot gas and jets of fire.

Seconds later, twenty-two new signatures lit up on the display. The relativistic missiles seeded by the *Andromeda* came to life and sought their targets with ruthless efficiency. The enemy fleet was completely obscured by the nuclear fireballs, their explosions just far enough from the squadron of Arc-6s that they evaded everything but the light from the blast.

When scan was finally able to get a clear picture, less than a hundred enemy ships remained and only fifty of those appeared to be operational.

Calls of surrender flooded the comm channels while two cruisers and a dozen of the corvettes altered course, pushing for a tight loop around Kithari to gain an outsystem vector.

<*Take them out,*> Tanis ordered. <*Padre was on one of those ships.*> She was not going to let him continue to roam the galaxy.

On her command, the 42nd squadron, consisting of newly deployed Arc-6s, broke from their approach to Fierra's northern hemisphere and pursued the fleeing ships, beams flashing and missiles flying from both formations.

Tanis turned her attention back to Jessica's squadron. The *Excelsior Nova* was matching velocity with Cary's fighter to effect the pickup, and the Black Death squadron was maintaining a protective shield, should any of the remaining pirate vessels get any ideas.

"What happens when everyone gets shields like these?" Captain Andrews asked softly. "What level of destructive power will two ships need to level against one another?"

Tanis cast the captain a sidelong glance. He had never opposed it, but she knew he had never been comfortable with the military buildup of the *Intrepid* and its fleet. Though, on deeper refection, she had to admit that he was right. If fleets could no longer do battle with conventional weapons, what would they resort to? Planetary destruction? Stellar destruction?

<*Sera's right,*> Angela whispered. <*This is a bigger game changer than the picotech.*>

Tanis took a moment to consider her feelings on the matter before replying.

"You're right, Captain. I'm passing orders to ensure that the keys to this technology never leave Bob and Earnest's minds," Tanis said to Captain Andrews. "It's too dangerous to ever let loose."

The captain nodded slowly, and Admiral Sanderson gave her an evaluating look before inclining his head in agreement.

During the battle with Padre's ships, Tanis had observed The Mark fleet repositioning itself. Rebecca's ships were now five-thousand kilometers beyond the effective beam range of the Arc-5s in position north of Fierra.

<What do you think her play is?> Amanda asked. <She can't tell the difference between our Arc-5s and 6s to be sure that they all don't have stasis shields.>

<She'll find out soon enough,> Tanis replied. <When are the next batch of 6s ready for deployment?>

<Thirty minutes,> came the avatar's reply.

Tanis was beginning to think she shouldn't have been so rash in sending her other Arc-6s after the remnants of Padre's fleet. They had destroyed or disabled the fleeing ships, but now needed to pass around Kithari before coming back into range.

With Padre's fleet taken care of, Jessica's squadron could fill the gap, but the Boller fleet had also shifted to a more aggressive stance.

<Move squadrons eleven through thirty-one to bolster the northern hemisphere,> Tanis directed. <I want the Dresden and Orkney, along with the Pike and Andromeda, on station between the Intrepid and the Boller ships.>

She addressed the ISF over the general fleet net.

<We've kicked the hornet's nest, for sure,> she began. <But it's not anything we haven't been up against before. They fear us. They fear our picotech, and now they fear our stasis shields. Use that to our advantage. Be bold, don't show hesitation, and they'll wonder what else we have up our sleeves.>

Tanis looked around the bridge, every crewmember's eyes were on her. She took a deep breath and continued.

<Many of you may have heard rumors—yes, we've sent a message to the FGT, and we're going to rendezvous with them soon. In thirty hours, we'll have FTL capability and leave these greedy bastards behind. The FGT has terraformed systems far beyond known space, and we'll be able to build our new world in peace!>

Tanis felt her mental tone waver at the last word. She hoped it didn't detract from her speech—though from the expressions on the faces of those around her, it seemed to have had a positive effect.

There was a moment's pause after her words, and then another round of cheers erupted across the bridge.

"Ok, ok, back to work," Tanis said with her hands raised and a small smile. "We still have go survive the next thirty hours."

* * * * *

Sabrina boosted away from the *Intrepid*, Cheeky threading the arcs of the colony ship's super structure like it was something she did every day. Once in open space, she spun out the AP nozzle and boosted toward Fierra's northern hemisphere.

Sera smiled to herself. No one needed to ask where she wanted to go. She had a score to settle with Rebecca.

<*Think it was a mistake to leave her alive?*> Helen asked.

<*I don't know…maybe. I had to hope that mercy would get me some consideration.*>

<*Who knows, maybe it has—but it wouldn't stop her from wanting to get her hands on the* Intrepid. *Especially after you stole back the CriEn module.*>

"Incoming signal," Flaherty announced from the new scan and weapons console.

He turned to look Sera in the eyes. "You'll never guess who it is."

Sera stood. "Put her on."

The holo shifted its display of the space around the moon to a secondary tank and Rebecca appeared on the bridge, as clear as though she were really there.

The pirate leader's eyebrows rose and she smiled. "I see you've appropriated some of my style."

Sera looked down at her gleaming crimson skin and shrugged. "If I'm going to kick your ass, I'm going to do it in style."

"We'll see about that," Rebecca smiled. "I have to admit; I'm pleased to have both prizes in one place. My new ship out there, *and* the power module you stole from me. It's going to be a good day."

"What about me?" Sera asked with a faux pout. "I thought I was your prize?"

"There'll be time enough for you, I promise," Rebecca stepped close to Sera, her holographically projected hand tracing down Sera's breast, along her side and to her hip. "I am very curious how you survived stealing my clothing—though you don't seem to have escaped unscathed."

"I wanted to thank you for that," Sera replied. "You may be the dumbest bitch in the galaxy, but you do have a sense of style—I'll grant you that. If your flagship survives, I may raid the rest of your wardrobe. There were some shoes in there I'd kill for."

<Dear god, you're killing me! Are you going to get her to tip her hand or what?> Cargo asked.

<Wait for it; she's getting all bent out of shape. If there ever was a woman who had vanity as her weakness, it's Rebecca,> Sera answered.

<I can think of someone else, too,> Cargo replied sourly.

"If you think you're going to take out even *one* of my ships, you have another thing coming," Rebecca spat back. "I'm not just going to sit there and take it like that moron Padre did. By the way, thank your friends on the *Intrepid* for me. It'll be good business taking over all his operations."

"You can thank her yourself," Sera said as Tanis joined the conversation.

"Nice to see you again, Rebecca," Tanis said with a smile.

A look of confusion washed across Rebecca's face. "No! You're that navigator woman on Sera's hunk of junk…who are you really?"

"General Tanis Richards, XO of the ISS *Intrepid*, at your service," Tanis replied with a nod. "It's really time for you to go now. You saw what we did to Padre's fleet. You don't stand a chance."

"It doesn't matter," Rebecca said with a swipe of her hand. "We know a few tricks that fool Padre never even dreamed of. I'll be sleeping in your quarters tonight, *General* Richards."

Rebecca cut the communication and Tanis looked Sera.

"What do you think she has up her sleeve?"

Sera raced through the possibilities, of which there were many. One, however, stood out.

"She said that we wouldn't damage even one of her ships. I think they may try a shield lock."

"No!" Cheeky shouted. "She wouldn't be so stupid. This close to a mass like Kithari? She's just as likely to create a singularity."

"What does that mean?" Tanis asked.

"With some skill—and guts—it's possible to merge the shields of multiple ships into a multi-layered, shifting shell of protection. If she can pull it off with her fleet, it's going to be pretty hard to punch through."

Tanis glanced away. "Damn, that Boller admiral is calling, and he seems upset—you'd think they'd be happy we took out Padre." The general paused and frowned, thinking for a moment. "The *Thracia* and *Babylon* are already on their way to the moon's northern hemisphere. I'm sending the *Enterprise as* well—show her we mean business. Amanda will get you onto their tactical net. You're the only one with a stasis shield till the 42nd squadron gets back into play, so use it wisely."

"Wise is my middle name," Sera replied with a roguish grin.

Tanis laughed in response and cut the holo connection.

<Push her buttons, don't let her push yours,> the general passed a parting thought.

Count on it, Sera thought to herself.

She sat back in her chair and connected to the tactical net Amanda had opened to her.

A virtual space opened up in her mind and she saw the captains of the four capital ships, as well as three fighter group commanders.

<Welcome, Captain Sera,> Captain Espensen of the *Enterprise* said. *<Glad to have you in our ranks today.>*

<Happy to be on the team,> Sera replied. *<What's our plan?>*

<Our orders are to contain The Mark's fleet and keep them out of effective range of the Intrepid*—that means no closer than seventy-thousand kilometers,>* Sheeran, captain of the Babylon, replied.

<If they lock shields, that will be no simple task,> Sera replied.

<Amanda briefed us on that. Is it really as effective as she said?> Captain Espensen asked.

<It is,> Sera replied. *<It's going to take everything we have to break a shield powered by that many ships—if she can construct it.>*

<How likely is that?> Colonel Pearson asked.

<Normally I'd say not likely at all,> Sera replied. *<But the Hand operated a base within the dark layer for years. They know things about the DL that gave them an edge. I should warn you, though, it's just as likely that*

she's going to create a black hole that will suck in the moon below and Kithari, too.>

<Well shit,> Sheeran exclaimed. *<Should we hit her first?>*

<The general gave us orders not to start anything,> Captain Espensen said with a raised eyebrow. *<We can't overcommit. There are two other fleets still out there.>*

Sheeran shrugged. *<Going to be worse if they do their shield mojo after the Bollers attack.>*

<I'm with the general on this,> Sera replied. *<After what we did to Padre, you can bet she'll start with RMs—I don't know that even our stasis shields can withstand a hundred or more of those. I say we wait and see if she can actually pull her trick off. Like I said, she stands a greater chance of killing herself than us.>*

<I endorse the self-immolation of my enemies,> Captain Espensen said.

<Then we wait,> Colonel Pearson agreed.

* * * * *

"That's definitely an unfriendly posture," Tanis sighed.

The Bollam's World Space Force was upping the ante as the minutes ticked by. Their initial blockade of fifty-two ships had ballooned to nearly four-hundred. More took up positions in a defensive grid near the AST dreadnaughts than the *Intrepid* and The Mark fleet.

Even with the Black Death's demonstration of near invincibility, it appeared that the Bollam's World Space Force was more concerned about the AST ships.

<It makes sense,> Angela said. *<They still think—or hope—that we intend to stay and treat with them. They know the AST intends only to take our ship and leave—or worse, take it and stay.>*

<They probably also think that we'll take out The Mark's fleet and save them the trouble—which is how I bet things will play out,> Tanis agreed. *<We're more likely to do that if they're not threatening us as much.>*

"The nano probes we shot out of the rails earlier have started to send in some interesting data. So far we've picked up seventy-two rail platforms in the system—more than Sera thought there would be. They're all pointed at us and the AST ships," the scan officer reported.

<Two of them are on a pair of Kithari's smaller moons,> Amanda added.

Tanis nodded and added every rail platform within thirty light minutes to the priority target list. The second the Bollers turned hostile, half-ton slugs would be fired at each of those platforms. They probably wouldn't all hit, but it was better than leaving them there to fire on the ISF fleet.

For added insurance, the *Andromeda* was quietly seeding relativistic missiles throughout potential paths of approach for enemy ships. If there was one thing no one objected to after the Battle for Victoria, it was an oversupply of RMs.

<Bollam's ambassador has just requested permission for his pinnace to undock,> Amanda announced.

"Well, if that's not a clear sign, I don't know what is," Captain Andrews said. "What's the latest on our stasis shield?"

"Abby reported that they're working through some kinks. She wouldn't give me a time, but based on her level of surliness I don't think that we should count on it right now."

<She was cursing Earnest's ship design at one point,> Amanda added. *<Something about 'stupid irregular protrusions'.>*

If the pressure stemming from the overwhelming force encircling the *Intrepid* wasn't so great, Tanis would have laughed.

<At least a lot of the Boller ships aren't much bigger than the pirate corvettes,> Angela supplied. *<Their relative isolation doesn't require them to have a large space force—especially with New Eden shielding them from the AST.>*

<Thank the stars for small miracles,> Tanis responded.

"There," scan pointed out. "Three of their ships just slid over three kilometers."

Tanis began mapping trajectories, but Amanda beat her to it.

<Trajectory lines up with a rail one light minute out and the Orkney's *position in five minutes.>*

Tanis sent the signal across the fleet for all ships to institute gamma-pattern jinking.

<Helm, bring us around to Fierra's L1 with Kithari, then execute gamma pattern. I don't want us to be in the same spot more than once every ten minutes.>

The *Intrepid's* helm and ships fleet-wide signaled their acknowledgement and Tanis settled in to wait. If a shot passed through the *Orkney's* former path, then she would not wait for further provocation.

Barely a word was uttered on the bridge as the five minutes passed. Then, right on cue, scan picked up a three hundred kilogram slug travelling at a quarter the speed of light.

<ISF Fleet, this is General Richards. All batteries assigned non-ship-mounted priority targets, send a five-shot salvo.>

Across the fleet, fifty-two rail guns opened fire, sending half-ton slugs hurling into the black. In less than a minute, two hundred and sixty kinetic rounds were en route to their targets. Scan showed Boller ships changing position, attempting to intercept and lase the slugs before they reached their targets.

Several fired rails at the ISF slugs, hoping to impact and deflect the incoming projectiles.

"I bet they didn't think we knew about quite so many of those," the admiral chuckled.

"I read a dozen slugs passing through positions our ships would have been occupying right now," scan reported.

"Well done in seeing the significance on that ship movement," Tanis said. "Your team just saved the fleet."

The scan officer sat up straighter and smiled in acknowledgement before turning back to his console and the never-ending streams of information being fed from the NSAIs, which handled the raw sensor data. He gave a word of encouragement over the Link to the humans and AI on scan.

"Incoming from the Boller fleet admiral," the comm officer said. "Should I put it on the main tank?"

"What the hell?" Tanis sighed. "I expect we could all use a good laugh."

The figure on the display was a woman this time, and her expression was less than pleased.

"You've just sentenced thousands of Bollam's citizens to death," she said in soft, icy tones. "There will be no more treaties. We will reclaim our new world, take your ship—whole or in pieces—and crush your pathetic little fleet."

Tanis turned to Terrance. "At least when we were dealing with the Sirians they had proper megalomaniacs. This pales in comparison."

The woman grew even more enraged, her face turning red.

"Our ancestors were from Sirius! They were caught in Kapteyn's Streamer hundreds of years before you. They earned these worlds."

"Sirians…that explains a lot," Tanis shook her head before turning back to the admiral. "You say that we killed hundreds, but thousands would have died on our ships had your kinetic rounds connected."

"They would not have!" the woman exclaimed. "You have advanced shielding, what we fired was merely a shot across the bow."

Tanis couldn't believe what she was hearing. "Are you seriously going to attempt to paint us as the aggressors? Until your unmistakable act of war, we have only taken defensive actions. You are brigands, you attempt to seize whatever drifts past your system to better yourselves. You're nothing more than well-established interstellar bandits."

Tanis hadn't even finished speaking her final words before the woman was yelling so loudly that the bridge's audio systems lowered her output.

"You sanctimonious, dusty old bitch! Our people built this system out of nothing. We worked for millennia to create what you see. You would come here and pick our best worlds for yourselves in trade for trinkets. No one will have your tech. Not those pirates, not those core-world bastards, and certainly not you. I'll—"

Tanis cut the connection.

<Fleet division one, prepare for incoming assault,> Tanis advised her captains and fighter group commanders.

"She seems excitable," Captain Andrews said. "Though you may not have needed to goad her quite so much."

"'Needed' is just the word," Tanis replied. "It was clear that she opposed any sort of deal with us—but that cannot be the case across the entire system. I've just made her look the fool in front of her fleet. When the time comes for hard choices, it may be that not all of her people make the wrong ones."

Tanis reviewed the battlefield. One squadron of Arc-5s patrolled the field of destroyed and disabled ships that was Padre's fleet. The other twenty-two squadrons in the fleet's first wing had formed two picket lines, one leading Kithari and the other trailing the gas giant.

The *Pike* and *Gilese* anchored the first group, and the *Condor* anchored the second with the *Andromeda* lurking nearby. Closer to the *Intrepid* lay the *Orkney* and *Dresden*, with their own fighter shields deployed around them.

Armed with deadly antimatter and fusion engines, the *Intrepid's* eighteen heavy tugs provided the final layer of protection.

Scan called out impacts on the first rail gun emplacements, an event that kicked off the Boller assault.

"Looks like a quarter of their force," Sanderson commented. "Thirty-six cruisers, forty destroyers and a mess of corvettes. No fighters, though."

"From what Sera says, no one uses fighters anymore…though I wonder if that might change after they saw what our Arcs can do."

"The odds look worse than when the Sirians invaded," Terrance said softly. "And we had three times the ships we have now."

"Like the admiral said," Tanis replied. "Our fighters count for a lot—especially given that there are nearly five hundred of them between us and the Bollers. Seventy-two are Arc-6s, as well. They can park right in the engine wash of any of those cruisers and lance their ships to pieces."

I just hope it will be enough, she thought.

"Hell, they can probably fly through those ships if they had to," Sanderson grunted.

There's a tactic no one will ever put in the books, Tanis thought to herself, worried that they would ultimately have to resort to just such an attack.

"Sirs? The Mark's ships are doing something," the scan officer reported.

* * * * *

<There they go,> Sera said. <We'll know in a minute if they can pull this off.>

<Wouldn't this be the best time to attack?> Captain Sheeran asked. <If we can disrupt them and make them destroy themselves...>

<Not unless you fancy getting sucked into a black hole that's drawing mass and energy from the dark layer,> Sera replied. <Like Captain Espensen said, if there weren't two other fleets out there, we'd have smoked them half an hour ago.>

Sera looked to Cheeky, Cargo, and Flaherty. "God, I hope this was the right play," she said softly.

"There is no right play, here," Flaherty replied.

The Mark ships shifted into a large sphere with the three cruisers at the center. *Sabrina's* scan showed streams of gravitons flowing from the center ships to the corvettes on the perimeter. Those gravitons where harnessed and amplified by the corvettes and a kilometer-thick shield snapped into place around the armada.

"Well I'll be damned," Sera whispered. "She totally nailed that."

<Well, so much for destroying themselves,> Captain Sheeran said. <What now?>

<We have to wear that shell down,> Captain Espensen ordered. <They're already boosting for the *Intrepid*.>

"They're going to wrap their shield around the *Intrepid* and storm the ship," Flaherty said.

"I believe you're right," Sera nodded in agreement.

The ISF ships were engaging The Mark's shield bubble with little effect. Even the near-luminal impacts of relativistic missiles only slightly altered the trajectory of the sphere—movement that was quickly corrected as The Mark ships accelerated toward the *Intrepid*.

The fighters darted close to the enemy fleet, lancing out with lasers and missiles, but the beams did no damage and few of the missiles even reached the shields. The cruisers did what they could from a distance, but without stasis shields, it was certain death to approach The Mark ships and their thousands of beams.

Only the single squadron of Arc-6s dared dance close to the enemy, but even at less than a kilometer away, their weapons had no measurable effect on the armada's super shield.

A desperate pilot arched away from the battle, taking a long loop around Fierra before coming back at a hundredth the speed of light, smashing his ship into the pirate fleet's shield.

"That had an effect," Flaherty said, a small measure of excitement slipping into his voice. "The umbrella in that section lost a layer when the fighter hit."

"How is the fighter, though?" Sera asked.

"Looks like its disabled," Flaherty replied. "Though the dampeners did keep the pilot alive."

<*I have a plan,*> Sera said to the fleet captains. <*Keep them as focused on you as you can.*>

<*What are you going to do?*> Captain Espensen asked.

<*Something like that fighter just did, just on a larger scale.*>

She outlined what she would need to the captains and left their virtual conference.

"Cheeky, set this course, maximum acceleration."

Cheeky's eyes grew wide. She looked up at Sera. "Are you serious?"

"I am. *Sabrina* can take it. I know this will work."

"This isn't like the rest of your super-secret special knowledge!" Cargo turned, his eyes filled with fear and worry. "The *Intrepid's* scientists just invented stasis shields two days ago! This is our shakedown run, for star's sakes!"

"You can get out and walk if you want to," Sera replied to Cargo without breaking eye contact with Cheeky. "Do it now."

Cheeky nodded and turned to her work. As *Sabrina* began to turn away from the battle, a call came in from Rebecca. Sera put it on the tank.

"Running away already?" Rebecca asked, her expression haughty as Sera had expected.

"I know when to cut my losses," Sera replied. "Good luck storming a ship with a hundred thousand square kilometers of deck with your rag-tag band of miscreants. That is, before the AST comes in and exterminates you."

"I'm not afraid of those core-worlders," Rebecca replied. "I'll have that ship, and I'll use it to hunt you down and crush you. You'll be back under my tender ministrations before you know what happened."

"Sure, whatever," Sera replied and cut the connection.

She let out a deep sigh.

"Let's hope that riles her up enough."

No one on *Sabrina's* bridge replied as Kithari grew larger in the forward view.

Sabrina flashed past the jovian and raced out into the space beyond, Cheeky altering course until the planet obscured her from The Mark's fleet.

The fusion engines were running at full bore, singing with the pure helium-3 the *Intrepid* had supplied. Between them, the AP nozzle was spun out to its maximum focal length, and at the ship's bow, the grav drives were parting the thick interstellar medium before pushing it back together behind *Sabrina* for the other drives to react against.

After seven minutes, Cheeky cut the thrust and spun the ship, reversing burn and bringing their velocity, relative to Kithari, to zero.

She locked eyes with Sera, who nodded slowly.

Directly ahead, a tenth of an AU distant, the gas giant rotated slowly, its space lanes mostly clear, except for a cluster of ships around the orbital habitation.

Cheeky brought all engines to full, hurling the ship toward the planet.

Sabrina's collision detection systems blared warnings, and Sera shut them off, only to see the comm board light up with calls from system traffic control warning of an impending impact. Defensive beams, meant to prevent asteroid impacts with the gas giant peppered the ship, but the stasis shield shrugged them off.

The seven minutes it took to travel the distance back to the planet seemed to take forever. Then, in the last few seconds, Kithari grew rapidly, and at a pre-programmed time, *Sabrina* twitched, sliding to the side of the planet, brushing past the jovian's swirling clouds.

"Correcting!" Cheeky called out as she aimed the ship at The Mark's armada as it chased the *Intrepid* around Fierra.

<*Brace!*> Sera called over the Link, though she didn't know why. If the stasis shield and the dampeners didn't compensate, no amount of bracing was going to help.

For a second, The Mark's armada was visible as a small dot closing on the *Intrepid*, and then everything went black.

* * * * *

Nothing they threw at The Mark's shield bubble had any effect. The pirate fleet just kept coming. At least it was moving slowly—relatively speaking—as it matched speeds with the *Intrepid* so they could envelop and board the colony ship.

Tanis had pulled the *Dresden, Orkney*, and their fighters closer to the *Intrepid*. If Rebecca was going to seal them inside her armada's shields, she would enclose a lot of enemy ships in with her.

The Mark ships seemed to realize this, and were doing their best to neutralize the ISF cruisers before they made their final approach.

Given enough time, the enemy's plan might work, but for the moment, refractive clouds of chaff kept their beams at bay, and the *Intrepid's* scoop-turned-MDC tore the enemy's missiles apart while a punishing barrage of rail slugs kept the enemy focusing much of their energy on their super-shield.

Tanis had to admit that Rebecca's plan was not too bad—right up until the part where she thought that boarding the *Intrepid* could actually work.

Perhaps they really didn't understand how large the ship was, or anticipate the four thousand Marines in powered armor who stood ready to repel any boarders.

"She hasn't come through yet," the scan officer reported.

"I don't care. Get those tugs in position," Tanis replied. "When she shows, they'll need to grab that bubble and toss it high, or we're going to be wearing a fleet's worth of shrapnel.

Tanis glanced to the other tank where the battle between Bollam's ships and her two defensive lines raged. Dozens of ISF fighters had been disabled, but so far her capital ships had not taken any serious hits.

The two squadrons of Arc-6s were making all the difference. The ships had destroyed half a dozen destroyers and two cruisers, even though the ISF ships had to continually retreat, lest they face overwhelming weapons fire.

"Just a little longer," Tanis whispered.

"There!" the scan officer cried out.

Tanis felt the bridge slow down around her as she watched the events unfold one millisecond at a time.

Sabrina exploded from high in Kithari's clouds, traveling at over ten thousand kilometers per second, on a course that would take it only a kilometer over the *Intrepid's* stern.

At the same time, two of the heavy pusher tugs boosted hard, their stasis grapples reaching out and grabbing The Mark's shield bubble. Fusion engines capable of nudging small worlds out of orbit fired on full burn and The Mark armada was pushed up, above the *Intrepid.*

The maneuver took only three seconds and then the tugs accelerated away from pirate fleet.

Sabrina lanced across the shrinking distance, perfectly aligned with her target.

A split second later, holo emitters dimmed their output as a blinding explosion flared. The Mark's shield bubble, along with the armada within, was gone.

A subdued cheer sounded across the bridge at the apparent destruction of Rebecca and her entire fleet while scan searched for *Sabrina.*

"There!" the scan officer called out and this time the bridge really did erupt in cheers. "Their entire ship appears to be in stasis. No, wait, it's out, it's decelerating and turning around."

"Going to take them a bit to get back here. They're already a quarter million kilometers away," Tanis said to herself, then aloud, "Any sign of our pirate friends?"

"No," scan replied. "Unless you consider a field of pebble-sized debris a sign."

Tanis expected the incredible show of power to cause the Boller fleet to draw back, but the rain of debris falling on Fierra's northern hemisphere seemed to incense them all the more.

"They're committing nearly half their fleet," the scan officer announced, worry lacing his voice.

"So they are," Tanis said softly, sharing a significant look with Admiral Sanderson and Captain Andrews.

* * * * *

Jessica gave a mental cry of victory as she punched through a cruiser's shields and sent a missile into its engines.

<Another one bites the dust,> she called out over the squadron's combat net.

<Don't get cocky,> Rock replied.

Jessica schooled her emotions as she surveyed the battlefield, searching for her and Jerry's next target. The *Pike* and *Gilese* were falling back behind a cloud of dust and gravel that Kithari had collected while orbiting its star. The cover kept the enemy ships from advancing too quickly, but, with no inertial dampening, the ISF cruisers were sitting ducks when in range of the enemy's beams.

The Arc-5s were also having only limited success.

While they couldn't jink anywhere near as fast as the 6s—or the enemy's capital ships, for that matter—their pilots had discovered two key weaknesses in the enemy's targeting algorithms.

The first was that they were not used to tracking such small targets at high relative *v*. The second was that when a ship jinked, they expected it to move a lot further. To the Boller targeting AIs, every move the fighters made looked like a feint. Given that a high percentage of their movements *were* feints, it was rare that an enemy beam fired at a location actually occupied by a fighter.

The erratic movement of the fighters was causing the Boller ships to continually tighten their ranks. Initially, they were spread out over more than six million cubic kilometers of space. That had tightened to just over a million cubic kilometers.

The fighters flitted through the region, creating enticing targets and placing themselves between enemy ships as often as possible. Entire fields of fire became unavailable to the enemy cruisers and destroyers, and ships that did not update their view of the battlefield fast enough contributed to an increasing amount of friendly fire incidents.

The ISF Arcs had no such issue. The squadron AIs were linked, providing an accurate view of the battlefield drawn from millions of sensors. Above that, Jessica could feel the combined hand of Tanis and Angela, guiding the ships in her fleet with lightning reflexes no human should possess.

<She's doing it again,> Jason spoke softly over the combat net.

<She is, now shut up about it,> Rock responded.

Jessica knew what they were talking about, but had never experienced it first-hand. Several times since the first defense against the relativistic battle when the STR had attacked with in Sol, Tanis had spread her consciousness out across the ship's tactical nets coaxing and guiding all the vessels under her command with one omniscient hand.

It was a thing that only AI could do, and even few of them could manage such a large network. Many believed it was actually Bob and not Tanis guiding them—that he put a friendly face on his actions, but anyone who had Linked with Tanis knew better. This had her touch—hers and Angela's.

Jessica knew those two had been paired too long—everyone knew it, but no one spoke of it. Many had asked Amanda or Priscilla if Tanis was a full merge, and the avatars always responded in the negative.

Jessica had even queried Bob extensively and he emphatically stated that Tanis and Angela were two distinct entities.

Two entities that shouldn't be able to spread their minds over a net like they had during every space battle since that first.

Every pilot in the fleet knew it was unnatural, that it probably violated the Phobos Accords, but no one cared. To them, Tanis was their savior, their guiding hand in the dark.

That hand directed Jessica to another target of opportunity, and she saw her entire squadron following the same path. They arched over one of the enemy cruisers, jinking and spinning at their pilot's thresholds, before simultaneously firing proton beams at the ship, penetrating its grav shield in a dozen locations.

Then the squadron's fighters rotated weapons and picked off three of the cruisers' close-support destroyers.

Four ships taken out in seconds. Only a few hundred more to go.

She saw another cruiser go up as three squadrons of Arc-5s overwhelmed its shields.

The tactics and coordination would likely go down in the history books as one of the most brilliantly fought battles in hundreds of years.

But they were still losing.

Despite the small victories of the ISF fighters, the Bollam's ships pushed forward; there were just too many for them to hold back.

The Arc-5s fell back to provide cover for the *Pike* and *Gilese* as the ISF capital ships pulled further back toward their mother ship, now only five-hundred thousand kilometers distant.

A flash of light washing over her sensors, momentarily blinded Jessica. She reset her instruments and pulled in an update, amazed at what she saw. *Sabrina* had hit The Mark fleet with astounding kinetic energy, and completely obliterated the entire armada.

<Sweet stars above,> one of the Black Death pilots whispered.

<Having the wrong effect on the Bollers, though,> Jessica said. <Looks like they're going to double down.>

<Well, that freighter did just ruin a perfectly good moon. It's getting pummeled with debris, > Jason said.

The pilots carried out the conversation as they streaked across the enemy fleet, peppering ships with beam fire and missiles.

<Conserve your missiles,> Cordy advised. <Squadron armament is down to twenty percent.>

The pilots acknowledged and worked to get as many engine shots as possible, a maneuver that was becoming increasingly difficult as the Boller targeting and evasion AI adapted to the fighter's tactics.

<Disengage, move out and take on the next wave,> Tanis's voice came over the combat net with a strange echo.

<What about the rest of our wing?> Jessica asked.

<They're going to fall back for close support. We need you to slow the advance of that second wave.>

Rock signaled his acknowledgement. The Black Death broke into a wide formation and boosted past the Boller ships they had been engaging. Jessica saw that the other two squadrons of Arc-6s fighting on the far side of Kithari were doing the same.

If Jessica could have moved her jaw, she would have gritted her teeth with determination. She knew better, but it still felt like Tanis was sending the squadron on a suicide run.

Their stasis shields appeared to be nearly invincible, but every pilot could see their reactor temperatures spike whenever the shields had to deflect a heavy barrage. Each time they did, they didn't quite cool to their previous level.

There was a limit to how much punishment the Arc-6s could take.

The next wave of enemy ships was approaching fast, only a hundred thousand kilometers distant. Cordy began flagging potential targets and Rock spotted one he liked.

<Target of opportunity here, that big ship there must be one of their flags and it has two cruisers way too close—only a thousand meters to either side.>

<Plan?> Jason asked.

<We'll do a spearhead and see if we can slam our birds right through its shields. The wings can rake it deep and we'll drop a few bombs into its engines. If the blast hits fast enough, it could weaken its escorts and we'll take them down, too.>

<Agreed,> Cordy said, updating ship plots and providing trajectories for the pilots to follow.

Jessica calmed herself, thinking of that porch she and Tanis would sit on one day as they remembered the old days.

Once more into the breach.

* * * * *

"What's your plan?" Admiral Sanderson asked as Tanis directed her ships to fall back.

"The cruisers used the cover of battle to seed those asteroid clusters with RMs. When those ships advance past, they're going to get a hundred nuclear fireballs up their asses."

Sanderson nodded slowly, but still frowned. "Some ships will survive. Over half by tactical's estimation."

Tanis nodded. "We're going to pull the same trick you guys did while I was flying across the galaxy. After what Sera did, the Van Allen belts on Kithari are going nuts. We're going to syphon that radiation with the scoop and lance it out at them again. It'll weaken their shields just before we pelt them with grapeshot."

<This should disable much of their fleet,> Bob interjected. <But what about the second wave they are sending in?>

"If they come in range, we'll do it again to them. I'm betting that it will re-instate the stalemate and buy us time to get our stasis shield up," Tanis replied, her brow furrowed as she spun the main holo view, testing various strategies.

She looked up at the captain and admiral, both standing with her at the holo tank.

"There's no good plan here, no sure win. We just have to hold them off and buy time. Honestly, it's a damned miracle we've taken only the minor losses we have."

<Sabrina *is docking*,> Amanda added. <*Their reactor overheated and went into emergency shutdown.*>

<*Get repair on that right away*,> Tanis replied. <*Is everyone OK?*>

<*They are. A bit shaken still after the flash stasis their entire ship went through, though.*>

<*I bet.*>

Tanis really wanted to talk to Sera, she felt the woman would have some knowledge that could help out—keep her from using her weapon of last resort. But first she had to mollify the captain and admiral.

"What if the AST ships engage?" Sanderson asked.

"Then I'll dance for joy," Tanis replied. "That's what I'm counting on."

"The Boller ships will pass the asteroid fields in one minute," the scan officer announced.

Tanis nodded in acknowledgement and took a deep breath, spreading her mind across all the ships and fighters in her fleet, accounting for each one and ensuring none would be caught in the attack.

The killing field was clear of ISF ships, every vessel cruising on their assigned trajectories.

She watched with her mind as much as eyes, witnessing the RMs come to life and streak out of their cover, driving toward the rear of the enemy fleet. The missiles jinked and shifted, using every trick their onboard NSAI could muster to avoid the defensive measures of their prey.

Not that there was much time to do so. The relativistic missiles were traveling at half the speed of light in less than a minute, leaving a thousand kilometers of hot plasma in their wake.

Both arms of the enemy fleet were obscured as the RMs nuclear warheads detonated. When the scan cleared, most of the enemy ships were still intact and operational, but their shields were either weakened or gone entirely.

Then the grapeshot hit.

It wasn't the devastating swaths that the rail platforms in the Kapteyn's system delivered, but it was enough. The unshielded vessels were torn apart, and many of the ships, whose shields survived the RMs saw them fail under the high-velocity kinetic impacts.

<Stars, I've come to hate this,> Tanis said privately to Angela. <System after system, we deploy unthinkable weapons to keep thieves and tyrants at bay…for what? To watch another fleet filled with men and women die? Some days I think I would have seen less death and war if we had stayed in Sol.>

<Then who would have saved these people?> Angela asked. <Who would have stopped Myrrdan? You may not have lived under it, but your children would have seen his return as the owner of the most powerful technology in existence.>

<Are we doing so much better with it?> Tanis asked.

<We are, trust me, we are.>

Bravely, remnants of the Boller fleet pressed forward, though many ships turned back.

Fifty ships advanced, now only a hundred thousand kilometers from the *Intrepid*. This form of warfare was strange to Tanis. The ships were moving slowly, fighting as though they were taking a two-dimensional battlefield, yet they flickered from position to position, moving erratically to avoid beam fire.

It was entirely unlike the high-velocity battles she had fought in Sol or over Victoria, where an engagement was measured in seconds.

She issued a final warning to the advancing fleet. Turn back, or be destroyed.

Ten ships did. Subsequently—over the next sixty seconds—two events occurred. One Tanis enacted, and the other she anticipated.

Firstly, the *Intrepid* altered course, pulling away from the moon Fierra and flew toward a strong band in the gas giant's Van Allen belts, drawing in the radiation with one side of its ES scoop and funning it out the other in a focused stream of solar radiation.

More powerful than the beams of a hundred starships, the stream of radiation sliced through the weakened shields of the last forty ships.

Then, the second event occurred far across the battlefield: the eleven AST cruisers began to break their distant orbits.

* * * * *

<What do you think they're going to do?> Jerry asked.

<I think that they have waited for the Intrepid to play out its hand. They have to suspect that we're low on RMs and energy reserves. We've taken out over half the opposition,> Jessica replied.

<Easy pickins for them now,> Jason added.

<They're punching right through the Boller blockade,> Jessica observed.

Unlike the Intrepid, the AST dreadnaughts were built exclusively for war. Moreover, they were built to stop wars from ever happening. Each vessel supported hundreds of laser batteries, and dozens of rail guns.

Forming up in a loose line, roughly eight thousand kilometers across, the core-worlder ships pushed through the Boller ships with little resistance. As far as the pilots of the Black Death squadron could tell, not a single beam or missile broke through their shields.

<Each one of those things is a match for the entire ISF,> Jessica said with morbid appreciation. <What can we do against them?>

<We could do what Sabrina did to the Mark armada,> a pilot suggested.

<They'd see us coming and jink faster than we could correct,> Rock replied. <Plus, I don't think our reactors could sustain the shield like Sabrina's could. Especially not the way we've been running them.>

The pilots of the Black Death pulled back from their harassment of the Boller Space Force's second wave, letting the ships defend against the AST dreadnaughts. After just a few minutes, it became apparent that the core-world ships were not going to be slowed by any force thrown at them.

<We made the Boller fleet into perfect targets,> Jason observed. <They're too weak and spread out to mount a successful defense against those dreadnaughts. They just can't bring enough fire to bear on them.>

Tanis's voice entered the minds of the twenty-three pilots.

<I'm enacting omega protocol,> she said. *<Each of your vessels carries a picobomb. It is now available in your arsenal. Punch through the shields of those dreadnaughts and deliver your packages.>*

No one responded for several seconds until Rock remembered himself and flagged acknowledgement on behalf of the squadron.

<Picobombs?> Jerry asked. *<We're carrying pico?>*

<Stow it,> Rock grunted. *<We have our orders. Form up and pour on that throttle.>*

* * * * *

Sera stepped onto the *Intrepid's* bridge and approached the holo tank where Tanis stood with the captain and admiral.

As she threaded the consoles, a whistle sounded, then a congratulatory shout, and a moment later, the entire bridge crew was cheering.

"I'm not sure that's deserved," Sera said, once the noise died down.

"I'm pretty sure it is," Captain Andrews replied.

"One ship taking out two-hundred? Yes, that will go down in the history books for sure," Admiral Sanderson said with a rare smile.

Sera looked over the holo projection of the battlefield.

"Quite the mess you guys have made—though it's a miracle you've not lost any capital ships."

Tanis nodded. "Keeping them out of range is key."

"You can bet that a lot of systems will be considering the creation of single pilot fighters after this. Even the ones without stasis shields are nothing to sneeze at."

"I can't believe they ever fell out of fashion," Tanis replied.

"A lot was lost, or discarded over the years," Sera said with a sigh. "So what's your plan for those AST ships? They've always been the real threat. Everything else was just a warmup."

Tanis turned back to the holo tank, her expression grim. "Watch and see."

* * * * *

Jessica and Jerry maintained a pattern of evasive maneuvers as they raced past the Boller ships, though little heed was paid to them as the fleet desperately defended against the AST dreadnaughts.

They passed into the vacant space surrounding their target, the massive warship looming large as they pushed their fighters with everything they had. Cordy had programmed the ship's onboard NSAI to drop the picobombs during the short time the fighters would be within the dreadnaught's shields.

There was barely a moment to think as the enemy vessel filled her vision and then, following a brief shudder as her fighter smashed through the dreadnaught's shields, she was out in space again.

Jessica spun her vision, looking at her target, when she realized that Jerry wasn't where he was supposed to be. Her sensor log showed that his ship entered the dreadnaught's shields, but didn't come out.

<It shifted,> Cordy said, her voice filled with sadness. <He drove right into the dreadnaught.>

<It shouldn't matter, his shield should have held,> Jessica said, knowing her insistence was irrational.

<It should have,> Cordy agreed solemnly. <But you know how strained your reactors are. His flared at the last millisecond. I don't have data beyond that.>

Jessica watched in mixed horror and sadness as the picobomb's swarm became visible and began to consume the enemy ship. She hoped that Jerry hadn't survived his collision. No one should die watching their body dissolve.

All the fighters struck their targets within seconds of each other, and, as the first dreadnaughts began to disintegrate and crumble into clouds of dust, escape pods began to pour out of all the AST vessels. Most made it free in time, but some dissolved even as they launched.

<Come home,> Tanis's voice came into their minds; sounding sad and tired. <Come home and let us leave this place forever.>

The Black Death squadron arched stellar north over the remnants of the Boller fleet, watching in horror as the system's military shot down every last one of the AST escape pods.

<Why are they doing that?> a pilot asked, her voice incredulous.

<They fear the pico contamination,> Jessica replied. *Now they fear us as much.*

REVELATIONS

STELLAR DATE: 10.29.8927 (Adjusted Years)
LOCATION: ISS *Intrepid*, Orbiting Fierra (6*Mj* Jovian)
REGION: Bollam's World System, Bollam's World Federation

Murmurs filled the bridge as the crew watched the AST ships disintegrate and the Boller fleet take up their grizzly task. No one cheered, though there were worn smiles while what remained of the enemy fleet pulled back and began rescue and recovery operations.

"Are you going to rescue any of Padre's fleet?" Sera asked Tanis.

Tanis shook her head. "I will not. Though I sent a message to whoever is running the Bollam's World fleet now that I won't hinder any of their rescue operations."

<It's ready!> Earnest's voice broke into their conversation.

<The stasis shield?> Tanis asked.

<Yes, we can activate it whenever you want.>

<Standby,> Tanis replied. <We need to recall our fleet.>

"Better late than never," Captain Andrews gave a soft chuckle.

<What about the FTL drive?> Sanderson asked. <I think we may have worn out our welcome here.>

<Now that we have the shield up, I can focus on the final aspects of the grav drive. Twelve hours at the least.>

Tanis gave orders to recall the rest of the fleet and took a seat, trying her best not to wince at the pain in her head.

<You may have overreached a bit,> Angela said.

<Me? You were right there with me, pushing to touch every part of the fleet. And we did it.>

<We did,> Angela was smiling in Tanis's mind. <The headache is heat related, it'll pass in a minute or two. It didn't reach a dangerous level.>

<Glad to hear it,> Tanis replied.

"We're going to need to refuel before we make the jump," Captain Andrews said. "The entire fleet is nearly dry."

"You're also going to need to get halfway across the system," Sera added. She looked to Tanis, who nodded in response, and expanded the view in the holo tank to encompass the system. "The jump point we need to exit through is here," she said and pointed to a location stellar north, beyond the bloated gas giant, Aurora.

"Well, that works out," Andrews replied. "I wasn't too excited about scooping around Kithari after you smashed through its upper clouds and we messed up its Van Allen belts." He smiled in Sera's direction. "Not that I mind overmuch—though the Bollers weren't too happy about it."

Tanis glanced at a holo display nearby. It showed the moon Fierra covered in dark clouds as fires caused by the debris from The Mark fleet spread across its northern hemisphere.

"Did the bios get off the world?" she asked; it was something she didn't even bother to check in the heat of battle.

Sanderson nodded. "They evac'd less than two minutes after Sera did her little light show."

"Smart," Sera replied.

"So it's decided then," Tanis said as she stood. "We'll scoop at Aurora—which is what I think they made it for anyway…I think."

"Make sure you fill up your tanks—or whatever this ship uses— all the way," Sera said. "If we scoop there, then run hard to the jump point, this monster can hit what… a tenth the speed of light before we drop to FTL?"

"That's about right," Captain Andrews replied with a nod. "What is your concern?"

"Well, the first is that FTL is a speed multiplier. If we hit at only $0.10c$ you're looking at over two years to get to Ascella. The second is that we have a lot of work to do to cover our tracks."

"I was thinking the same thing," Tanis said with a sigh.

Sera nodded. "The AST isn't going to just let you go. They'll send fleets along your departure trajectory, skipping across space, looking for where we drop out. Then they're going to extrapolate destinations and spread out the search."

"Given their resources, and the half-life of the isotopes in our engine wash, we may need to course correct a dozen times," Andrews said with a frown.

"Yes, hence the need to top off your tanks," Sera replied. "Don't forget, those AST ships can hit FTL at over $0.9c$. That means they can also get to any destination way faster than we can. It's going to be a hell of a race if they find our trail."

"Captain, sirs," the comm officer interrupted. "We have heavy communications between the Boller ships. They've word that there are more AST ships coming. A full battle fleet."

"That doesn't sound good." Captain Andrews ran a hand through his hair. "Any idea what that entails, Sera?"

Sera resisted the urge to mimic his gesture and run her own hand through her hair. "Depends on what they could muster up this far out, but I'd bet it will be a few dozen more of those dreadnaughts; plus they'll bring cruisers this time—a couple hundred at least."

Tanis whistled appreciatively. "It's a good thing we're invincible now." Sanderson frowned and she shrugged in response. "Well, let's hope we are."

"Comm, let the folks in the Boller Space Force know that we're leaving, and tell them sorry about their moon."

The comm officer paused. "Should I really tell them that?"

"If you don't, I will," Sera grinned.

No one else provided any direction and the comm officer bent to her task.

"Wow, they are *really* unhappy," she said partway through her transmission.

"Serves them right," Tanis muttered, to which Sera nodded emphatically.

Helm began to ease the *Intrepid* away from Kithari, on a course to pick up the last of the Arc-6s on the way to Aurora, while Tanis spun the holo display to show a wider view of the space they were traversing.

"You're sure the FGT will get your message?" the captain asked as he watched the Boller ships work through the wreckage of their fleet. Though the search and rescue ships were careful to offer no threat, several of their larger cruisers also shadowed the *Intrepid* from a hundred thousand kilometers.

"They'll have it in a month," Sera replied.

"That fast? I thought that they were likely over a thousand light-years out."

"They probably are," Sera nodded.

"You're not going to share how a message can make it a thousand light-years in thirty days are you? That's over twelve thousand times the speed of light," Captain Andrews asked.

"It's actually closer to fifteen thousand. The message will have to pass through a few relays," Sera smiled enigmatically.

The captain ran his hand through his hair again and looked to Tanis.

"Both of you, come to my office, please. Admiral, you have the conn."

"Aye," Sanderson replied, looking very much like he would like to hear what was to be discussed.

Inside his office, Andrews closed the door and stood, arms akimbo and head down for a long minute before speaking.

"Sera, I want to thank you for what you've done for us. You returned Tanis to our ship, and brought us tech that, without a doubt, has saved the lives of every person on the *Intrepid*."

"Tha—" Sera began, but the captain held up his hand.

"But this cloak and dagger shit has to stop. We've laid our secrets bare to you, and been forthcoming and transparent at every turn. Hell, we even gave you stasis shielding—something that, while I'm glad we did in this case, I am now certain is a tech that we should never share."

"Uh...thanks..." Sera replied awkwardly.

"Look at this from our point of view," Tanis said, while leaning against the bulkhead. "You are, more or less, the only person in the ninetieth century that has treated with us fairly. That makes you an anomaly. You have tech no one else has—not even the AST from the looks of it. Anomaly. You can communicate with the FGT. Anomaly. We're not stupid. There's a pretty narrow list of possibilities for who you are. Bob says he knows and will tell us if you don't." She raised her hands, palms outward. "So just tell us already."

Sera took a deep breath, and her eyes danced between Tanis and Andrews.

<Tell them,> Helen said. <**They** have to know. **You** need to tell it.>

"OK, OK, I was planning to tell you earlier. You know, before we got interrupted by all the fleets in the galaxy," Sera said and gestured for Tanis and Andrews to take a seat. She sat across from them and placed her hands on her knees.

She decided not to pussy-foot around.

"Humanity is in the dark—manipulated, and kept that way by design."

"Manipulated?" Tanis sat up straight. "By who?"

"The FGT."

"The FGT manipulates humanity?" Andrews asked with uncertainty.

"Not with the deftest of hands, but for all intents and purposes, they run the show. Let me start from the beginning."

Andrews gestured for Sera to proceed.

"Back in the fourth millennia, before this ship even left Earth, the FGT realized that the core worlds of humanity would be too self-centered to be a positive force in the expansion of mankind. They would develop greater levels of technology and lord it over colonies. Colony worlds would become little more than slaves to the core.

"Unfortunately, they didn't have the means to do anything about this. While the various terraforming flotillas did communicate with one another, they were, for the most part, islands in the dark; messages took centuries to pass between all the terraformers and there was no cohesion.

"Still, they began to craft a solution to counter the core world strength.

"As with everything else, FTL changed their plans—granted, the FGT was probably the last group to become aware of the technology—it wasn't until the end of the fourth millennia that they acquired it.

"By then, humanity had already started to fall. The first true interstellar wars had already occurred and the Great Dark Age settled in. But, because of their remote and often unknown locations, the worldships retained their advanced levels of technology."

Sera paused and smiled at Tanis and Andrews. "Mind you, the last FGT ship left Sol in the late third millennia. You have nearly five-hundred years of technological advances over them—sure the FGT scientists have made some brilliant breakthroughs, but you lived in the Golden Age. Even without your picotech—and what I suspect Earnest has discovered beneath it—you still possess thousands, maybe millions, of advances that no one else has."

"We know this," Andrews grunted. "You're getting off track."

Sera nodded. "Right. I was using it illustrate the state of the human sphere in the beginning of the fifth millennia."

She cleared her throat and continued. "Many in the FGT's ranks wanted to help. They sent rescue and assistance missions back into the settled stars and...well, things didn't go as they'd hoped. Three FGT ships ran into situations like the *Intrepid* has. Two were destroyed, one managed to come out victorious.

"Following those encounters, they pulled back, left terraforming projects half-complete, abandoned their works. They created a buffer between themselves and the rest of humanity—they became isolationists."

"Wait," Tanis held up her hand. "Are you saying that there is a second human civilization in the Milky Way? One that is distant enough from the known human sphere of expansion that the bulk of humanity isn't even aware of it?"

"That is exactly what I'm saying," Sera nodded. "Mostly. There's more to tell."

"Then do tell," Andrews said.

"While the rest of humanity fell into war and chaos, the FGT advanced—a lot. There were still many elements that wished to help, but no one deemed it wise to attempt a full-scale uplift of humanity. The result was a corps which infiltrates and guides major political entities within what the FGT calls the Inner Stars.

"That corps is what brought humanity back from the brink. Without them, all the Inner Stars would be desolate wastelands, with the remnants of human civilization scratching out a meager existence on ruined worlds."

"You are a part of that corps," Tanis said simply.

Sera cast her eyes to the deck and nodded. "I was."

<How close were you, Bob?> Tanis asked.

<So far, nearly perfect,> he replied. <We'll see how the details hold up. Her proximity to you has made her...less predictable.>

"I have to admit, this FGT you describe seems sinister, yet the FGT of our time contained the most altruistic and benevolent of all people—people who were giving their lives to create a home for humanity amongst the stars," Andrews said.

"Those people are still there, and they still hold to those core values...they've just...soured," Sera replied.

"Wait," Tanis interrupted. "When you say 'those people are still there', do you mean the *same exact* people? As in the original crews?"

"Well, they've grown a lot, yes, but most of the original crews—at least from the fourth millennia ships—are still out there, still working."

Tanis whistled. "That's incredible. They're immortal now aren't they? Are they still mostly biological?"

Sera chuckled. "Yes they are immortal, yet still more biological than you, I'd dare say."

"I'm still human," Tanis said, her words sounding more defensive than she had intended.

Sera fixed her with a penetrating stare. "Some might disagree with that assessment, but I'll accept it."

"I assume that a part of your reticence to share has to do with how you came to leave this corps you spoke of," Andrews changed the subject.

"It has a big fancy name, but those of us in its ranks just call it The Hand," Sera replied. "And yes, I was sort of kicked out and exiled."

<Self-imposed exile,> Helen added.

"Better that than the eternal humiliation—or being bailed out by my father," Sera retorted.

<This is where the story gets good, I bet,> Angela interjected.

"Juicy, perhaps," Sera replied. "Though not what I'd call *good*."

She stood and walked to the small bar in Andrews' office and poured herself a glass of whisky before returning to her seat.

Tanis was leant forward, elbows on her knees while Captain Andrews reclined. Though his posture was relaxed, of the two he appeared more concerned. Tanis looked…almost excited.

"I lost something. Something very valuable that should never have fallen into Inner Stars hands. It's called a CriEn module."

"Aha! That's what you were carrying on the *Regal Dawn*, wasn't it?" Tanis asked triumphantly.

"It was," Sera nodded. "It's a zero-point energy module."

"I don't gather what is so special about that," Tanis said. "We use zero-point energy for backup systems on the *Intrepid*."

"You create pocket dimensions and draw energy from those," Sera replied with a shake of her head. "A CriEn draws power from this universe, and it can operate in both normal space and the dark layer—in fact, I've advised Earnest not to utilize your zero-point energy systems while in the dark layer—at least while I'm not within a light-year of you."

"So somehow you lost that to Kade, and that's what you've been doing in your exile, getting in close to him so you could steal it back," Tanis said with a smug smile, and leaned back in her seat.

"More or less," Sera nodded. "At first I had to figure out who had it. There are a lot of unsavory factions in the Inner Stars, so I decided that becoming a smuggler was the best way to get my feelers into a lot of groups. I eventually tracked it down to Kade. The events you set in motion created the perfect scenario for getting to his base—though it wasn't in a fashion I would have chosen.

"Though now I can return the CriEn to the corps and...I don't know...I don't think I really want to rejoin their ranks again."

"You can always settle with us," Tanis replied.

"Speaking of that," Andrews said. "I assume this world will be in the separate FGT area of space."

Sera nodded. "They do terraform some worlds closer to the Inner Stars—part of their grand schemes—but neither you, nor they, will want the *Intrepid* colony to settle on one of those. Too close to this mess."

"What do they call the...the not-inner-stars?" Tanis asked.

"FGT space is a bubble—well, more of a donut—that wraps around the Inner Stars." Sera replied. "There are a lot of different regions, but on the whole, it's called The Transcend. Its outer reaches stretch beyond the Orion arm of the galaxy, both spin and core-ward."

Tanis whistled. "Given that most of the Inner Stars fit within a thousand light year-wide bubble around Sol, the Transcend must have way more territory."

"Yes, but it's much less densely populated," Sera said. "Though you wouldn't be the first refugee group to take shelter out there."

"Orion is only about three-thousand light-years wide," Andrews said with a frown. "From what I understand about FTL, an average multiplier is five hundred times. That means a three-thousand light-year journey should only take six years. How is it that the bulk of humanity hasn't spread into the Transcend already?"

Sera coughed. "People do stumble into it from time to time, but it doesn't happen as often as you'd think. Partly because we foster conflict around the edges of the Inner Stars, which tends to stall exploration. A few proxy nations around the fringes also keep the core contained. Galactic north and south, we don't control many systems and that's where we let expansion occur.

"At some point we'll reveal ourselves. We're just trying to gently uplift the rest of humanity first—we're trying to prevent another full-scale war."

Tanis couldn't help but notice how Sera's use of "they" had long since turned to "we".

"So, will you rejoin them, then?" Tanis asked, her forehead wrinkling into a frown. "You and Flaherty, I assume."

"That obvious, is it?" Sera asked.

"Well, he does have the whole 'protector of the young woman obligation' thing going on," Tanis replied. "It's only logical that he has joined you in your self-imposed exile."

Sera nodded and was silent for a moment. "I don't know if I'll even be wanted—though if I know my father, I'm likely to be summoned before the throne. The fact that he hasn't sent anyone to take me home—recently, mind you—is almost surprising."

She looked to Andrews, and then to Tanis.

"So there you have it, my big secret. Given that I'm on a ship that has picotech and stasis shields, it doesn't seem like such a big deal anymore."

Tanis stood and stretched. "I don't even know what it would take for anything to feel like a big deal anymore." She paused. "Wait...what was that about your father and a throne?"

REPERCUSSIONS

STELLAR DATE: 11.03.8927 (Adjusted Years)
LOCATION: ISS *Intrepid*, Outer System
REGION: Bollam's World System, Bollam's World Federation

Sera and Tanis were taking a break from staring at scan updates—wondering when the new AST fleet would show up—in the officer's wardroom. Tanis was working her way through her second BLT and Sera was enjoying a bowl of strawberries.

"I don't know how you eat the same thing over and over again," Sera said with a chuckle.

Tanis shrugged. "When you find a winner, stick with it. Besides, you're the one who has only eaten strawberries for three days now."

"No one has had a strawberry in four-thousand years! Damn skippy I'm going to eat them. I'm going to eat a bowl of strawberries every day for the rest of my life," Sera said with a laugh.

"Well, then at least you'll lose the high ground for mocking me over my BLTs."

"For such interesting people, you have the most boring palettes," Terrance said with a smile as he sat.

His plate was filled with a cornucopia of foods; more than any one person should even conceive of enjoying in one sitting.

Sera popped another strawberry in her mouth and smiled, showing off her red teeth. "Mock me all you want. I'm in heaven."

Terrance shook his head and addressed Tanis. "I hear the FTL systems are nearly in place."

Tanis nodded. "Abby has people working like machines, and the machines working like…well…better machines. She's already done a few simulations and has just a few more tweaks to make before we'll be good to go."

<She and her husband are incredible,> Helen added. <I don't think that an FGT engineering team could have given this ship FTL capability in a month. Already Earnest may have the best understanding of the technology in the galaxy.>

"This," Terrance said around a mouthful of salad. "This is not something that surprises me at all. That man doesn't even know *about* the word 'impossible', let alone that it means he couldn't do a thing."

Tanis laughed and nodded.

"So, what do you think is up with Aurora?" Sera asked. "Why would they combine two gas giants and then not start up a brown dwarf?"

Terrance nodded. "Just one sufficiently large comet strike and that thing will light right up—and this system is brimming with comets."

"You know your stellar physics," Sera nodded appreciatively.

"I did fund a colony ship to travel to another star—though these days I guess just about anyone who could afford to start a small business could get a starship and travel to more stars than I ever imagined seeing…"

Tanis smiled. Every now and then, Terrance showed that he was really just a romantic underneath. She was pretty certain that he was enjoying the *Intrepid's* grand adventure.

<For whatever reason, they're keeping it from starting deuterium fusion,> Helen interjected. *<Amanda just reported that the* Intrepid's *sensors have picked up a web of defensive satellites around the planet—most likely to protect it from any impacts.>*

<The remains of the Boller fleet is also pretty emphatic that we stay away from it—though they haven't actually made a move to stop us,> Amanda added.

<Sera,> Helen said, her tone suddenly serious. *<Sabrina says you'd better get down to the ship.>*

* * * * *

"Doesn't it seem suspicious," Thompson said as he picked an apple from the fruit basket, tossed it in the air and then took a bite, "that the captain just happens to have the right tools at exactly the right time to get the job done?"

"What do you mean?" Cheeky said after she had set her plate down at the table and popped a strawberry into her mouth. "These will never get old. Nothing on the *Intrepid* is worth as much as the fact that they have the only strawberry plants in the universe."

"Do you ever think of anything other than sex and food?" Thompson asked.

"Of course I do. You haven't died in a space accident, so I suppose I must think of piloting from time to time."

"Touché." Nance grinned at Thompson.

"So, what do you mean about the captain?" Cheeky asked.

"I dunno, seems like some things are just a bit too tidy. Like, who has the plans to outfit a ship the size of the *Intrepid* with grav shields. Do any of you even have the slightest idea how to build a graviton emitter?"

<*I do,*> Sabrina offered.

"Besides you," Thompson said.

<*I'm excluded because I don't support your theory? Or because I'm an AI?*> Sabrina asked crossly.

"Would you have been able to just whip out the plans for an FTL and grav shield system for a ship like the *Intrepid?*" Thompson asked.

Sabrina gave the mental equivalent of a shrug. <*Well no...until Sera said otherwise, I didn't think it was possible. But in my defense, everyone said it couldn't be done, and I didn't exactly have a reason to try to devise one.*>

"Exactly my point. No one has a need for those specs. There aren't any ships this big. No ships, thus no specs for things non-existent ships would have," Thompson said.

<*They were bigger,*> Sabrina added.

"What was bigger?" Nance asked.

<*The specs, they were for a ship bigger than the* Intrepid. *Being the only ship available with the grav drives, I helped with their work. They had to adjust the designs for the FTL drive because it was made for something with almost double this ship's mass.*>

"Are you kidding me?" Cheeky asked. "Sera had plans for grav systems for a ship twice the size of the *Intrepid*? You sure there aren't ships that big?" she asked Thompson.

"Not that I've ever seen, and I've been around," Thompson replied. "Worked on an ore hauler or two that are larger, but those don't go FTL—they can't, based on what we all thought we knew. Trust me, if the AST could make bigger warships, they would. *Intrepid's* the biggest interstellar ship there is."

No one spoke and Cheeky grabbed a few more strawberries.

"You know," Nance said eventually, "I overheard Sera say on more than one occasion that the *Intrepid* was the most valuable *available* ship in known space. I wonder what she meant by that."

"Combine that with the fact that she just happened to know how to get a hold of the FGT," Thompson added. "How did she pull that off?"

"Probably with whatever she has in her quarters that need that massive power line she has run up there," Nance said.

"That doesn't mean anything," Thompson said, his cheeks reddening slightly.

"It's able to handle a lot more load than yours," Nance gave a coy smile, which caused Thompson's blush to deepen. "And for the first time since I've been on the ship, it actually made a draw from the reactor."

"When?" Cheeky asked around a strawberry.

"A few days ago," Nance said. "It shifted the base frequency in our mains and I had a pump go all squirrely."

"Around when she was supposedly sending a message to the FGT?" Thompson said.

"Well, she had to transmit it somehow," Cheeky shrugged. "Good to know she actually did it."

"You're missing the point," Thompson said.

"You have a point?" Cheeky responded with a lewd gesture and was surprised to see Nance blush before darting her eyes to Thompson. Cheeky passed Nance an impressed look.

Thompson missed the exchange of expressions. "Haven't you been listening? She contacted the FGT with her super-secret radio! No one contacts the FGT. If it weren't for newly terraformed planets showing up every now and then, no one would even believe they still existed."

"Okay, so you've got a point," Cheeky grinned. "But we've always know that Sera is a little more than just some freighter captain."

"We have?" Thompson's expression skewed from anger to confusion.

"Yeah, I mean, there was that time that she got the Pavnan government to pardon her on what should have been murder charges, and then grant her the license to export their rare blue diamonds," Cheeky said.

"And the time that she refused to pay 'protection' money on that station out in the Targes Dominion, then ended up discovering systemic corruption through the entire station and exposed the whole thing," Nance added.

"Didn't she get a commendation from the planetary government for that?" Cheeky asked.

"*That* I remember," Thompson said.

"And don't forget about Helen," Cheeky continued and Sabrina made an affirmative sound.

"What do you mean?" Nance asked.

"You and Thompson may not have noticed 'cause you don't work with Helen very much, but she is super evolved. A lot more than any other AI on this ship," Cheeky said.

"Hey!" Sabrina said audibly.

"I hate to say it, Sabrina, but you know it's true," Cheeky said.

<I know,> Sabrina replied sullenly. <It's not right how an AI in such a small body can be smarter than me. Smarter than nearly any other AI I've ever met, for that matter.>

"Even smarter than Angela?" Nance asked.

<Angela is weird,> Sabrina said. <I have no idea how smart she is. On the Link it's hard to tell her and Tanis apart. But Helen is certainly above AI like Corsia on the Andromeda. Though she's not even noticeable next to Bob, but he's a whole different thing,> Sabrina said with no small amount of adoration in her voice.

"Is anyone seeing the nav points here?" Cheeky asked.

Everyone gave her blank looks and then Nance's eyes began to widen. "No, it can't be. They severed all contact with the rest of humanity."

"Maybe they haven't," Cheeky said with a hint of smugness as she took a bite of a large strawberry. "It all adds up. She took a way bigger interest in Tanis than made sense—you said so, too, that night when…" Cheeky stopped for a moment. "When I was helping you with that thing. Anyways, we should have just given her a ride. Instead, we head out to Bollam's World and dive right into a war. Not that I really mind; taking out The Mark was awesome. On top of that, she whips out plans for stuff no one has ever seen before and contacts the FGT. What else could it be?"

"Very little else," Flaherty said from the doorway.

"We uh…we were just…" Cheeky stammered as everyone in the galley shifted uncomfortably.

Flaherty moved silently to the counter where he poured himself a cup of coffee, his back to the three silent crewmembers around the table. Once he had finished adding condiments and stirring carefully, he turned to face them.

"So you think that Sera is from the FGT? A freighter captain from the FGT?" Flaherty asked.

"She's not your usual freighter captain," Nance said. "There are some discrepancies."

Flaherty nodded. "A few, yeah. She can hold secrets pretty well, but when she doesn't really want to, they tend to slip out."

<Are you confirming she is with the FGT?> Sabrina asked. <Are you? You've always been with her, ever since the beginning.>

"It's not my place to say such things," Flaherty replied.

Nance looked angry, her brown eyes sparking. "If she is, then she has a lot to answer for. We've been little puppets in her schemes while she risks our lives for god knows what!"

"You all knew the risk when you signed up," Flaherty replied calmly.

"Like hell we did," Thompson said. "I don't remember anyone telling me that we'd be hurling ourselves into other ships."

"Not specifically, no. No one can predict the exact course of the future, but she did inform all of you that this was not a regular freighter, that we would be doing things that didn't make sense, and that there would be a lot of danger involved."

"Yeah, but this is different."

"Is it?" Flaherty asked. "If Sera were FGT, do you know how dangerous that knowledge would be? What if someone let it slip?" He let that sink in as they all contemplated the value and danger of that knowledge. "Not that I am confirming, nor denying it. I am just promoting rational thought."

"What's all the noise in here?" Cargo asked. "I could hear you guys hollering all the way up on the bridge and Sabrina seems upset about something."

Cheeky cast an accusing glance at Flaherty. "We're discussing whether or not Sera is FGT."

Cargo walked over to the table and picked up a strawberry. "Oh, that."

"What do you mean 'oh, that'?" Nance asked. "She's been lying to us this whole time."

"Not telling you her life story is lying?" Cargo asked around his mouthful of strawberry. "I don't recall her ever lying about her past. She just never talks about it."

"So when did she tell you?" Cheeky asked. "How long have you been keeping this from us?"

"She never told me. I figured it out on my own about two months ago."

"Just how did you manage that?" Thompson asked.

"She was talking with Tanis on the bridge. They had the holo showing the *Intrepid* from Tanis's Link. Tanis asked if it would be possible to get a ship that large to transition to FTL and Sera said that she had heard of bigger ships managing it."

"What ships are bigger that can go FTL?" Cheeky asked.

"Exactly," Cargo said. "I thought about that long and hard and came up with just one answer: FGT worldships. They are the only thing I could dig up that were larger than the *Intrepid*. I've never known Sera to lie, so I assumed that the FGT was the only possible answer."

"And you didn't share it with the rest of us?" Cheeky asked. "Why would you keep that to yourself?"

"Because Sera didn't want it known, and I respect her too much to go sharing her secrets without her permission. Besides," Cargo continued after a moment, "that's some pretty dangerous knowledge."

The strawberries were all gone from the basket so he grabbed one from Cheeky's plate, before continuing under her glare. "It's also possible she has some personal reason for not sharing, as well. God knows I have enough stuff in my past that I don't want to talk about. I bet she has her share, as well."

"I appreciate your consideration," Sera said from the entrance to the room. "Sorry for barging in on your discussion like this, but Sabrina reached out to Helen and I."

Sera stepped into the room, revealing Tanis standing behind her.

"What is she doing here?" Thompson asked. "This is crew business."

"Tanis was crew on this ship for almost four months," Sera replied. "She also saved my life; and this *is* my ship, after all."

Thompson sat back in his chair and crossed his arms. He looked like he was going to speak for a moment, but then thought better of it.

"Does she already know, too?" Nance asked. "Are we the last to know?"

Sera took a deep breath. "She does know; I told her and Captain Andrews about it a few days ago—although, in my defense, Bob had already figured it all out and was going to tell them if I didn't."

"I already figured it out, too," Cargo said with a smile from behind his cup of coffee."

"So how come Flaherty knows?" Cheeky asked. "I've been on this ship almost as long as he has."

"Because I was born on an FGT worldship, just like the captain," Flaherty grunted. "Kinda hard to unknow that."

"Oh," Cheeky replied and sat back. "I guess we're all just a bunch of stooges, then."

"You lied to us," Nance accused.

"I…I don't think I lied. I just didn't share." Sera's knuckles were white as she gripped the back of a chair. She took a breath before continuing. "I didn't leave the FGT on what you could call good terms. I displayed a little more of my classic attitude than they were prepared to accept and it…" She swallowed deeply. "It caused some problems. I left the FGT and tried to fix what I'd broken. My recklessness had lost something valuable that Kade eventually got hold of. It's why I started smuggling, to find what I'd lost and eventually get it back."

"So that's why you got so focused on just working with Kade after a while," Cargo said with a nod.

"Yes, though that is done now. I recovered the device from The Mark's station before I destroyed it. When we meet with the FGT, I will return it to them and my exile will be over—I…I don't know if they'll let me stay with you."

"What do you mean?" Cheeky's anger had lessened, though there was still a hint of it behind her eyes.

<Will you take us with you?> Sabrina asked. *<I would love to see a worldship.>*

"What will happen to us?" Thompson asked at the same time. "We're just going to be left high and dry?"

Sera forced a smile. "*If.* If I am forced. I may be able to squeeze my way out of their grasp. I've done it before, I can do it again." She looked to Flaherty, who nodded.

"You don't have to come along to the rendezvous," Tanis said. "I'm sure that whether you're there or not, they will still work with us and give us a colony."

"I imagine so," Sera replied. "But they'll treat you more fairly with me there. I know who they're likely..." Sera stopped, tears welling in her eyes. She took a deep breath and brought herself under control. "If I end up going with them, the ship is yours, Cargo." She nodded to her first mate. "Or, if you all decide that you've had enough of me and what I've put you through, you can separate. Drop out of the dark layer while we are in transit. I won't stop you from either course of action."

No one spoke for several moments; everyone appeared to be giving deep consideration to what their captain had said.

"I know you don't want my opinion..."

"Correct, we really don't," Thompson responded.

Tanis turned her gaze to Thompson and held his eyes until he looked away. "Sera has worked tirelessly to make the galaxy a safer place, she's put her life on the line to help a lot of people. She's one of the good ones and I'd stick by her, were I you."

<Tanis, you and Sera are needed on the Intrepid's *bridge,>* Angela broke into the conversation.

"Keep things tight," Sera said to them all. "If this goes badly, we may never have to worry about what will happen when we meet the FGT."

AURORA

STELLAR DATE: 11.03.8927 (Adjusted Years)
LOCATION: ISS *Intrepid*, Approaching Aurora (12*Mj* Jovian)
REGION: Bollam's World System, Bollam's World Federation

The atmosphere was tense on the bridge as Tanis and Sera entered.

"Our friends have arrived," Captain Andrews said from beside the main holo tank.

The display of the Bollam's World system was expanded to show their destination, the planet Aurora; the *Intrepid*, still three hours away; and the newly arrived AST fleet.

It was even larger and more intimidating than expected.

One hundred and twenty dreadnaughts, and over five-hundred cruisers were highlighted on the holo display. The AST ships were spread out, having arrived at half a dozen jump points. Based on their velocity, only a quarter of their fleet would arrive while the *Intrepid* was filling its tanks at Aurora.

"That's a lot of ships," Sera whispered.

"You can say that again," Tanis said.

"That's a—" Sera stopped when Tanis shot her a look.

"Thoughts?" Captain Andrews asked as Tanis took up her place beside him.

"It really comes down to whether or not they got the message about our picotech. If they did, I imagine they will exercise some caution."

Sera chuckled. "You can bet that if they didn't hear they're still going to be cautious—given how there is no sign of the eleven dreadnaughts they sent ahead—not to mention the debris of half the Boller fleet."

Tanis nodded. "It would make me think twice about rushing in."

"Maintain course," the captain directed helm. "We'll see how this plays out."

* * * * *

The *Intrepid's* leadership stood around the holo tank, Tanis with her arm around Joe's waist while his was around her shoulders. Across from her, Ouri scowled at the display of Aurora, while Brandt and Jessica whispered about the chance of a fight with the new AST fleet.

Terrance and Captain Andrews were also speaking—though more optimistically about the elections they would hold upon arrival at their colony world. Admiral Sanderson was discussing fighter design with Sera and Amanda, the trio growing increasingly animated over small details and improvements to the Arc-6s

An alert sounded and the holo showed the *Intrepid* closing within ten-thousand kilometers of Aurora's surface. As though a switch had been flipped, the disparate conversations ceased. All eyes fixed upon the display before them.

The gas giant's unnatural existence meant that it didn't possess atmospheric strata typical for a planet of its size. To capture enough deuterium and lithium-7 to fill the *Intrepid's* tanks, the colony ship would have to drop below the planet's upper clouds for its scoop to reach the denser layers below.

"So that's what they're doing! For being so behind on tech, these Bollers have something pretty ingenious going on here," Earnest said, his holographic image appearing on the bridge.

"You finally figured out what the heck they're doing with this planet?" Tanis asked.

"I have indeed—well, Bob did most of it. They're using graviton emitters—pretty large ones, at that—to emit a negative gravity field around the planet. But that field only goes so far. Then it reverses and increases pressure. Basically, the whole thing is a helium-3 generator. It's the biggest gas station you ever saw. If they didn't have the graviton emitters, it would collapse into a brown dwarf star."

He walked around the holo display, peering intently at the world into which they were descending.

"If they focus the energy coming off it, they could probably use it as a heat source for orbiting dwarf planets, too. It's like having a second star without all the problems a second star causes."

"Nice of them to leave it here for us, then," Tanis said. "Saves us having to turn protium and deuterium into helium-3 ourselves."

"I wonder if they'll try to bill us," Joe chuckled.

The *Intrepid* slipped past the graviton emitter web and into the atmosphere of the planet, while above, scan showed that the leading ships in the AST fleet were now within a hundred thousand kilometers of Aurora

"I wonder if they have any idea what we're doing?" Sera asked.

"There's nothing to see here, go back to your homes," Tanis chuckled.

"Gods, I wish they would," Sera replied.

The *Intrepid* dipped beneath the swirling clouds and deployed its scoop. Like a straw, it reached deep into the planet and began to draw the denser deuterium and helium-3 into the ship. The process proceeded quickly, and thirty minutes later the colony ship's tanks were full and Captain Andrews directed helm to bring the ship out of the clouds, timing their ascent for a vector toward their desired jump point.

They broke free of Aurora's atmosphere to see the world ringed by AST ships.

Scan called out an alert. "They're launching something—a lot of somethings!"

"RMs," Tanis swore. "They're targeting the graviton emitters."

"Oh, that's bad, very bad," Earnest shook his head with dismay.

"Helm, full thrust. Get us out of here!" the captain called out.

"Why very bad?" Tanis asked. "The mass is the same, the planet will just collapse."

"You don't understand," Earnest said. "One of two things will happen. The first is that the planet just collapses. Except things like this don't happen naturally, you don't get nice spherical balls of heavy hydrogen and helium isotopes that can collapse under their own gravity *in minutes*. This thing is a planet-sized fusion bomb just waiting to happen."

Tanis frowned, watching as concern showed on the bridge crew's faces.

"What's the other option?" Tanis asked.

"Graviton emitters don't just make gravitons out of vacuum," Earnest replied. "They get them from somewhere. That somewhere is the dark layer. They tap into dark matter for mass and energy."

"Seriously?" Tanis asked.

Sera and Earnest nodded together.

"Sooo?" Tanis asked.

<Black hole,> Angela supplied.

"The Bollers are really going to hate us," Terrance commented. "I have to admit, I feel bad for them."

"They did try to kill us," Andrews frowned. "I don't feel so bad. Besides, we're not taking out their big H-bomb of a planet, the AST is."

"I can see why it *might* create a singularity, but why do you think it's probable?" Tanis asked Earnest.

"When a ship transitions into the dark layer to achieve FTL, it does so by slipping through the fabric of space-time into that sub-dimension—graviton emitters do something very similar.

"A better description of what a ship does is to say that it cuts open a portal into the dark layer. That portal self-heals, because no energy is being used to keep it open. But if there was an energy source nearby—say an exploding planet, it could be used to keep the portal open. It's why systems enforce the use of their jump points, and it's also why people don't just blind-jump into unexplored systems—at least I would imagine they don't."

"You are correct," Sera nodded. "People who do that usually aren't heard from again."

Tanis took a deep, calming breath. "To the case at hand, Earnest. What do you think?"

"I think we need to push our engines harder than we have ever pushed them before," Earnest replied.

<Which we're already doing,> Amanda added. <We can walk and chew gum here—well, I can't, but you get the picture.>

Everyone fell silent as scan updated, showing graviton emitter platforms exploding in a wave across the planet.

"Oh!" Earnest said.

All eyes turned to him.

"There's a lot more tritium in this planet than I expected. My money is on black hole. Given how much dark matter is clustered around this world, we're looking at a significant increase in mass."

The *Intrepid* was pulling past the last of the planet's clouds, even as the gasses began to rush past them, drawn down into the deep gravity well that the graviton emitters had kept them from for so long.

"Neutron storm incoming!" scan called out, and Amanda announced that full shielding was in place. Stasis layered over grav, layered over electro-static.

On the holo, the AST ships began to veer off, apparently also realizing the full enormity of what their actions caused.

"They really didn't think this through," Earnest said through gritted teeth.

"Or maybe they considered it worth the risk to destroy us," Joe replied. "Think about it. We have an invincible shield and our pico could wipe them out. What better way to deal with an unimaginable threat than to drop it into a black hole."

"Makes sense," Tanis scowled.

"Too damn much sense," Anderson agreed.

The *Intrepid* had reached an altitude of twenty-five thousand kilometers above the previous surface of Aurora—though the radius of the planet had decreased by fifty-thousand kilometers.

Earnest began whispering a countdown to himself, and then a moment after he reached zero, the planet's collapse stopped and a massive explosion of light, matter, and energy flared out from its compressed core.

As Earnest predicted, compression won. After that initial explosion, the visible light all but snapped off and the pull of gravity began to increase, slowing the *Intrepid's* progress.

On the scan Tanis saw that two of the AST ships had moved to pursue the *Intrepid*, likely intent on ensuring that the colony ship fell back into the world below. Their course put them too close to the world when the explosion occurred. The ships were pushed outward by the blast, but then, as the mass of the world collapsed into a black hole and drew matter from the dark layer, they began to fall in.

The shockwave passed over the *Intrepid*, sending a violent shudder through the ship.

"Will she hold?" Terrance asked.

"Earnest nodded. "She'll hold. We don't have the dampeners that those other ships, have, but our stacked decking was designed to handle lateral thrust."

Tanis tightened her arm around Joe as she wondered if this is how the crew felt when they passed close to Estrella de la Muerte and were hit by a solar flare. There was nothing to do but wait and pray to whatever gods or stars you believed held sway.

Sera spun the view on the main holo and some of the bridge crew gasped as several of Aurora's moons appeared to stretch, and then disintegrated, falling back into the dark, roiling mass below. Above the *Intrepid* an icy moon was pulled out of its orbit and the ship altered course with a lurch to avoid the debris as it crumbled and fell.

"This is amazing," Earnest whispered.

Tanis looked at the rapt expression on Earnest's face and shook her head. "For some definition of amazing, perhaps."

"Oh, come on!" Earnest gestured at the display. "How often do you see the death of a planet and the birth of a black hole. If they're lucky they can stabilize it. It's a far better source of energy than what they had."

"If they can keep the rest of their planets in stable orbits," Sera said. "There are already reports of earthquakes on one of their inhabited worlds and solar flares are bound to let lose across their star."

"I never said it was going to be an enjoyable transition," Earnest replied.

No one responded as a new vibration began beneath their feet.

"OK, are you still sure she'll hold?" Earnest asked.

<*Yes,*> Bob replied.

On scan, the two AST ships lost their battle and disappeared into the black hole, around which now swirled a glowing accretion disk.

Scan highlighted three other enemy ships, which were also struggling to pull free of the deepening gravity well. Tanis marveled as they began to detonate nuclear warheads behind their ships in a desperate attempt to pull free.

Joe cast Tanis a worried look. "They got a lot more bang for their buck than they expected."

The gravity well swelled, growing faster than anyone had anticipated and more of the AST fleet began to fall into it. The vibration in the *Intrepid's* hull increased and the ship began to lose velocity relative to the monster growing beneath them.

She returned Joe's concerned look, unable to find any words to voice the fear she began to feel in her heart.

The bridge crew also began to look anxious, though no one spoke, everyone attempting to focus on finding a way to improve the ship's chances of survival.

Earnest appeared calm, just as he always did when facing some insurmountable problem. "We're reversing the polarity of the scoop, sweeping it behind us. It will give us a bubble of reverse polarized ions to slip through."

The captain nodded his approval and a minute later the vibration in the deck ceased and the ship began to move forward once more.

"Two hundred thousand kilometers," someone announced with a note of nervous jubilation in their voice—and then Tanis felt everything stop.

"Wha—?" she began to ask when she saw that the ship's clocks had jumped by eleven minutes.

"Status!" the captain called out.

<I enacted safety protocols,> Bob replied. <The black hole began to spin and hit us with its relativistic jet. I put the entire ship in stasis.>

"Handy trick," Joe said softly.

Reports rolled in; helm responded, scan was operational. Engines were online, the scoop team indicated the emitter was damaged, but they could repair it in a few hours. Stasis shields were down, but only needed a reset of their control systems. The ship's position was updated on scan and everyone gasped.

"Wow, it really gave us a boost," Sera whistled.

The blast of plasma from the fledgling black hole had flung them over fifteen million kilometers. They were nearly at the jump point and helm reported they could adjust course and be in position for FTL transition in just over an hour.

"Well, that's a rapid change in fortune," Terrance observed.

Behind them, a large number of the AST ships were gone, but those which remained were boosting after the *Intrepid* in a furious attempt to catch their prey.

"Jump early," Sera said softly.

"What?" Tanis asked.

Scan updated again, revealing so many relativistic missiles that scan could not reliably separate their signatures and simply estimated the count to be over a thousand. They were spread out like an arrow of death arching toward the *Intrepid*.

"Jump early. Jump as soon as you can. Jump now if you can manage it!" Sera insisted.

"She's right," Earnest nodded. "The dark matter maps for this entire system are useless now. No one knows where it's safe to jump—it doesn't matter where we do it. Once the stasis shields are up, we need to go."

"Time on stasis shields?" the captain asked.

<Three minutes,> Amanda replied.

<All crew,> The captain announced ship-wide. <Prepare for FTL transition.>

A deep quiet settled over the bridge as everyone watched the swarm of relativistic missiles slash their way toward the *Intrepid*. Everyone prayed to their gods and stars that the transition would go smoothly as the time to impact and the countdown for FTL transition spun down in near unison.

Then, a minute early, Bob's voice rang out in their minds.

<Shields are up. Initiating transition.>

"Well, here we go," Tanis whispered to Joe.

THE END

* * * * *

Tanis and the *Intrepid*'s adventures in the Orion Arm of the galaxy are just getting started. With the colony system of New Eden no longer available, they must now meet with the ancient terraforming group, the FGT to trade technology for a place to settle.

Dive into **New Canaan**, the second book in the Orion War series. However, before you do, you may wish to read **Set the Galaxy on Fire**, an anthology of short stories that occur in the final days of Destiny Lost and the months following.

While reading Set the Galaxy on Fire does not have to be read before New Canaan, it will add color, and introduce you to some of the new players in the Orion Arm.

Also, to receive the short story, *To Fly Sabrina*, sign up for my mailing list at www.aeon14.com/signup. You'll learn the story of when Sera first hired Cheeky on as pilot of *Sabrina*.

* * * * *

Reviews are the lifeblood of a book. Amazon promotes books that get reviews and it keeps them at the top of lists without authors having to spend money on ads and promotions.

If you liked this book, and are enjoying the adventures of Jessica and *Sabrina*, please leave a review, it means a lot to me.
Also, if you want more Aeon 14, plus some exclusive perks, you can support me on Patreon (www.patreon.com/mdcooper), or join the Facebook Fan Group (facebook.com/groups/aeon14fans)

Thank you for taking the time to read *Destiny Lost*, and I look forward to seeing you again in the next book!

THE BOOKS OF AEON 14

Keep up to date with what is releasing in Aeon 14 with the free Aeon 14 Reading Guide.

The Intrepid Saga (The Age of Terra)
- Book 1: Outsystem
- Book 2: A Path in the Darkness
- Book 3: Building Victoria

- The Intrepid Saga Omnibus – *Also contains Destiny Lost, book 1 of the Orion War series*

- Destiny Rising – *Special Author's Extended Edition comprised of both Outsystem and A Path in the Darkness with over 100 pages of new content.*

The Orion War
- Book 1: Destiny Lost
- Book 2: New Canaan
- Book 3: Orion Rising
- Book 4: The Scipio Alliance
- Book 5: Attack on Thebes
- Book 6: War on a Thousand Fronts
- Book 7: Fallen Empire (2018)
- Book 8: Airtha Ascendancy (2018)
- Book 9: The Orion Front (2018)
- Book 10: Starfire (2019)
- Book 11: Race Across Time (2019)
- Book 12: Return to Sol (2019)

Tales of the Orion War
- Book 1: Set the Galaxy on Fire
- Book 2: Ignite the Stars
- Book 3: Burn the Galaxy to Ash (2018)

Perilous Alliance (Age of the Orion War – w/Chris J. Pike)
- Book 1: Close Proximity
- Book 2: Strike Vector
- Book 3: Collision Course
- Book 4: Impact Imminent
- Book 5: Critical Inertia (2018)

Rika's Marauders (Age of the Orion War)
- Prequel: Rika Mechanized
- Book 1: Rika Outcast
- Book 2: Rika Redeemed
- Book 3: Rika Triumphant
- Book 4: Rika Commander
- Book 5: Rika Infiltrator (2018)
- Book 6: Rika Unleashed (2018)
- Book 7: Rika Conqueror (2019)

Perseus Gate (Age of the Orion War)
Season 1: Orion Space
- Episode 1: The Gate at the Grey Wolf Star
- Episode 2: The World at the Edge of Space
- Episode 3: The Dance on the Moons of Serenity
- Episode 4: The Last Bastion of Star City
- Episode 5: The Toll Road Between the Stars
- Episode 6: The Final Stroll on Perseus's Arm
- Eps 1-3 Omnibus: The Trail Through the Stars
- Eps 4-6 Omnibus: The Path Amongst the Clouds

Season 2: Inner Stars
- Episode 1: A Meeting of Bodies and Minds
- Episode 3: A Deception and a Promise Kept
- Episode 3: A Surreptitious Rescue of Friends and Foes (2018)
- Episode 4: A Trial and the Tribulations (2018)
- Episode 5: A Deal and a True Story Told (2018)
- Episode 6: A New Empire and An Old Ally (2018)

Season 3: AI Empire
- Episode 1: Restitution and Recompense (2019)

- Five more episodes following…

The Warlord (Before the Age of the Orion War)
- Book 1: The Woman Without a World
- Book 2: The Woman Who Seized an Empire
- Book 3: The Woman Who Lost Everything

The Sentience Wars: Origins (Age of the Sentience Wars – w/James S. Aaron)
- Book 1: Lyssa's Dream
- Book 2: Lyssa's Run
- Book 3: Lyssa's Flight
- Book 4: Lyssa's Call
- Book 5: Lyssa's Flame (June 2018)

Enfield Genesis (Age of the Sentience Wars – w/Lisa Richman)
- Book 1: Alpha Centauri
- Book 2: Proxima Centauri (2018)

Hand's Assassin (Age of the Orion War – w/T.G. Ayer)
- Book 1: Death Dealer
- Book 2: Death Mark (August 2018)

Machete System Bounty Hunter (Age of the Orion War – w/Zen DiPietro)
- Book 1: Hired Gun
- Book 2: Gunning for Trouble
- Book 3: With Guns Blazing (June 2018)

Vexa Legacy (Age of the FTL Wars – w/Andrew Gates)
- Book 1: Seas of the Red Star

Building New Canaan (Age of the Orion War – w/J.J. Green
- Book 1: Carthage (2018)

Fennington Station Murder Mysteries (Age of the Orion War)
- Book 1: Whole Latte Death (w/Chris J. Pike)
- Book 2: Cocoa Crush (w/Chris J. Pike)

The Empire (Age of the Orion War)
- The Empress and the Ambassador (2018)
- Consort of the Scorpion Empress (2018)
- By the Empress's Command (2018)

Tanis Richards: Origins (The Age of Terra)
- Prequel: Storming the Norse Wind (At the Helm Volume 3)
- Book 1: Shore Leave (in Galactic Genesis)
- Book 2: The Command (July 2018)
- Book 3: Infiltrator (July 2018)

The Sol Dissolution (The Age of Terra)
- Book 1: Venusian Uprising (2018)
- Book 2: Scattered Disk (2018)
- Book 3: Jovian Offensive (2019)
- Book 4: Fall of Terra (2019)

The Delta Team Chronicles (Expanded Orion War)
- A "Simple" Kidnapping (Pew! Pew! Volume 1)
- The Disknee World (Pew! Pew! Volume 2)
- It's Hard Being a Girl (Pew! Pew! Volume 4)
- A Fool's Gotta Feed (Pew! Pew! Volume 4)
- Rogue Planets and a Bored Kitty (Pew! Pew! Volume 5)

APPENDICES

Be sure to check www.aeon14.com for the latest information on the Aeon 14 universe.

TERMS & TECHNOLOGY

AI (SAI, NSAI) – Is a term for Artificial Intelligence. AI are often also referred to as non-organic intelligence. They are broken up into two sub-groups: Sentient AI and Non-Sentient AI.

c – Represented as a lower case c in italics, this symbol stands for the speed of light and means constant. The speed of light in a vacuum is constant at 670,616,629 miles per hour. Ships rate their speed as a decimal value of c with c being 1. Thus a ship traveling at half the speed of light will be said to be traveling at 0.50 c.

Casimir effect – The Casimir effect is a small attractive force that acts between two close parallel uncharged conducting plates. It is due to quantum vacuum fluctuations of the electromagnetic field.

CriEn – A CriEn module is a device which taps into the base energy of the universe, also known as zero-point, or vacuum energy. Unlike more common zero-point energy modules, which pull energy from artificial bubble dimensions, the CriEn module is capable of pulling energy from normal space-time, and can even do so while in the dark layer.

Cryostasis (cryogenics) – See also, 'stasis'.

Older methods of slowing down organic aging and decay involve cryogenically freezing the organism (usually a human) through a variety of methods. The person would then be thawed through a careful process when they were awakened.

Cryostasis is risky and has a higher failure rate, but one that makes few people consider it as an option. When true stasis was discovered, it became the de-facto method of slowing organic decay over long periods.

Dark Layer – The Dark Layer is a special sub-layer of space where dark matter possesses physical form. The dark layer is also frictionless and reactionless. It is not fully understood, but it also seems to possess many of the attributes of a universal frame of reference.

Deuterium – D2 (2H) is an isotope of hydrogen where the nucleus of the atom is made up of one proton and one neutron as opposed to a single proton in regular hydrogen (protium). Deuterium is naturally occurring and is found in the oceans of planets with water and is also created by fusion in stars and brown dwarf sub stars. D2 is a stable isotope that does not decay.

Edgeworth Kuiper Belt (EK Belt) – The EK belt is a circumstellar disk of dust, rocks, and small planetoids which extends from Neptune's orbit to 50 AU from Sol (in humanity's home system).

Many other star systems possess belts similar to Sol's EK Belt and the term fell into common usage to describe the first belt beyond the last major planet in a star system.

Electrostatic shields/fields – Not to be confused with a faraday cage, electrostatic shield's technical name is static electric stasis field. By running a conductive grid of electrons through the air and holding it in place with a stasis field the shield can be tuned to hold back oxygen, but allow solid objects to pass through, or to block solid objects. Fields are used in objects such as ramscoops and energy conduits.

Modified versions also see use as ship's shields where they are used to bleed off energy from beam weapons, or slow the impact of kinetic weapons.

EMF – Electro Magnetic Fields are given off by any device using electricity that is not heavily shielded. Using sensitive equipment, it is possible to tell what type of equipment is being used, and where it is by its EMF signature. In warfare it is one of the primary ways to locate an enemy's position.

EMP – Electro Magnetic Pulses are waves of electromagnetic energy that can disable or destroy electronic equipment. Because so many people have electronic components in their bodies, or share their minds with AI, they are susceptible to extreme damage from an EMP. Ensuring that human/machine interfaces are hardened against EMPs is of paramount importance.

FGT – The Future Generation Terraformers is a program started in 2352 with the purpose of terraforming worlds in advance of colony ships being sent to the worlds. Because terraforming of a world could take hundreds of years the FGT ships arrive and begin the process.

Once the world(s) being terraformed reached stage 3, a message was sent back to the Sol system with an 'open' date for the world(s) being terraformed. The GSS then handles the colony assignment.

A decade after the *Destiny Ascendant* left the Sol system in 3728 the FGT program was discontinued by the SolGov, making it the last FGT ship to leave. Because the FGT ships are all self-sustaining none of them came home after the program was discontinued—most of the ship's crews had spent generations in space and had no reason to return to Sol.

After the discontinuation FGT ships continued on their primary mission of terraforming worlds, but only communicated with the GSS and only when they had worlds completed.

Fission – Fission is a nuclear reaction where an atom is split apart. Fission reactions are simple to achieve with heavier, unstable elements such as Uranium or Plutonium. In closed systems with extreme heat and pressure it is possible to split atoms of much more stable elements, such as Helium. Fission of heavier elements typically produces less power and far more waste matter and radiation than Fusion.

FTL (Faster Than Light) – Refers to any mode of travel where a ship or object is able to travel faster than the speed of light (c). According to Einstein's theory of Special Relativity nothing can travel faster than the speed of light. As of the year 4123 no technology has been devised to move a physical object faster than the speed of light.

Fusion – Fusion is a nuclear reaction where atoms of one type (Hydrogen for example) are fused into atoms of another type (Helium in the case of Hydrogen fusion). Fusion was first discovered and tested in the H-Bombs (Hydrogen bombs) of the twentieth century. Fusion reactors are also used as the most common source of ship power from roughly the twenty fourth century on.

***g* (gee, gees, g-force)** – Represented as a lower case g in italics, this symbol stands for gravity. On earth, at sea-level, the human body experiences 1*g*. A human sitting in a wheeled dragster race-car will achieve 4.2*g*s of horizontal g-force. Arial fighter jets will impose g-forces of 7-12*g*s on their pilots. Humans will often lose consciousness around 10*g*s. Unmodified humans will suffer serious injury or death at over 50*g*s. Starships will often impose burns as high as 20*g*s and provide special couches or beds for their passengers during such maneuvers. Modified starfighter pilots can withstand g-forces as high as 70*g*s.

Graviton – These are small massless particles that are emitted from objects with large mass, or by special generators capable of creating them without large masses. There are also negatively charged gravitons which push instead of pull. These are used in shielding systems in the form of Gravitational Waves. The *GSS Intrepid* uses a new system of channeled gravitons to create the artificial gravity in the crew areas of the ship.

GSS – The Generational Space Service is a quasi-federal organization that handles the assignment of colony worlds. In some cases, it also handles the construction of the colony ships.

After the discontinuation of federal support and funding for the FGT project in 3738, the GSS became self-funded, by charging for the right to gain access to a colony world. While SolGov no longer funded the GSS the government supported the GSS's position and passed law ensuring that all colony assignment continued through the GSS.

Helium-3 – This is a stable, non-radioactive isotope of Helium, produced by T3 Hydrogen decay, and is used in nuclear fusion reactors. The nucleus of the Helium-3 atom contains two protons, but only one neutron as opposed to the two neutrons in regular Helium. Helium-3 Can also be created by nuclear reactions that create Lithium-4 which decays into Helium-3.

HUD – Stands for Heads Up Display. It refers to any type of display where information about surroundings and other data is directly overlaid on a person's vision.

Link – Refers to an internal connection to computer networks. This connection is inside of a person and directly connects their brain to what is essentially the Internet in the fourth millennia. Methods of accessing the Link vary between retinal overlays to direct mental insertion of data.

Maglev – A shorthand term for magnetic levitation. First used commercially in 1984, most modern public transportation uses maglev to move vehicles without the friction caused by axles, rails and wheels. The magnetic field is used to both support the vehicle and accelerate it. The acceleration and braking is provided by linear induction motors which act on the magnetic field provided by the maglev 'rail'. Maglev trains can achieve speeds of over one thousand kilometers per hour with very smooth and even acceleration.

MDC (molecular decoupler) – These devices are uses to break molecules bonds to one another. This technology was first discovered in the early nineteenth century—by running electric current through water, William Nicholson was able to break water into its hydrogen and oxygen components. Over the following centuries this process was used to discover new elements such as potassium and sodium. When mankind began to terraform planets the technology behind electrostatic projectors was used to perform a type of electrolysis on the crust of a planet. The result was a device that could break apart solid objects. MDC's are massive, most over a hundred kilometers long and require tremendous energy to operate.

Mj – Refers to the mass of the planet Jupiter as of the year 2103. If something is said to have 9MJ that means it has nine times the mass of Jupiter.

Nano (nanoprobes, nanobots, etc…) – Refers to very small technology or robots. Something that is nanoscopic in size is one thousand times smaller than something that is microscopic in size.

Pico (picotech, picobots, etc…) – Refers to technology on a pico-scale—one thousand times smaller than nanotech.

After a series of accidents that nearly consumed an entire dwarf world, picotech research was banned in the Sol system.

Railgun – Railguns fire physical rounds, usually small pellets at speeds up to 10 kilometers per second by pushing the round through the barrel via a magnetic field. The concept is similar to that of a maglev train, but to move a smaller object much faster. Railguns were first conceived of in 1918 and the first actual magnetic particle accelerator was built in 1950. Originally railguns were massive, sometimes kilometers in size. By the twenty-second century reliable versions as small as a conventional rifle had been created.

Larger versions take the form of orbital railgun platforms which can fire sabot rounds or grapeshot at speeds over a hundred-thousand kilometers per second.

Ramscoop – A type of starship fuel collection system and engine. They are sometimes also referred to as Bussard ramscoops or ramjets. Ramscoops were considered impractical due to the scarcity of interstellar hydrogen until electrostatic scoops were created that can capture atoms at a much more distant range and funnel them into a starship's engine.

Scattered Disc – Beyond a star system's EK Belt lies a region filled with comets, asteroids, and dwarf worlds. In the Sol System this region begins roughly 50 AU from Sol and extends to the edge of the Oort cloud. While it contains the least mass of a system, a system's scattered disc typically contains hundreds of dwarf planets and fills an area nearly half a cubic light year.

Stasis – Early stasis systems were invented in the year 2541 as a method of 'cryogenically' freezing organic matter without using extreme cold (or lack of energy) to do so. The effect is similar in that all atomic motion is ceased, but not by the removal of energy by gradual cooling, but by removing the ability of the surrounding space to accept that energy and motion. There are varying degrees of effectiveness of stasis systems. The FGT and other groups possess the ability to put entire planets in stasis, while other groups only have the technology to put small items, such as people, into stasis. Personal stasis is often still referred to as cryostasis, though there is no cryogenic process involved.

Tritium – T3 (3H) is an isotope of hydrogen where the nucleus of the atom is made up of one proton and two neutrons as opposed to just a single proton and no neutrons in regular hydrogen (protium). T3 is radioactive and has a half-life of 12.32 years. It decays into Helium-3 through this process.

v – Represented as a lower case v in italics, this symbol stands for velocity. If a ship is increasing its speed it will be said that it is increasing *v*.

Van Allen belts – A radiation belt of energetic charged particles that is held in place around a magnetized planet, such as the Earth, by the planet's magnetic field. The Earth has two such belts and sometimes others may be temporarily created. The discovery of the belts is credited to James Van Allen, and as a result the Earth's belts are known as the Van Allen belts.

Vector – Vectors used are spatial vectors. Vector refers to both direction and rate of travel (speed or magnitude). Vector can be changed (direction) and increased (speed or magnitude).

PLACES

Aurora – The seventh planet in the Bollam's World System used to be two separate planets (the 7th and 8th), but was combined into one world in the late 89th century. The mass of the planet is 12*Mj,* which places it above the limit for sustained nuclear fusion. This is stopped by the use of massive antigravity fields around the world which hold it apart.

Ayrea (41 Arae 2) – An independent system centered a pair of binary stars, both cool dwarf stars with a well populated, stable stellar population. The stars lie only 28 light-years from Sol, but have managed to avoid being forced into the AST as of the 90th century.

Bollam's World – Bollam's World is the name of the fourth planet from 82 Eridani, in the Bollam's World System.

Bollam's World System (58 Eridani) – Independent system known as "Bollam's World". The system was settled in 5123 by the colonists of the GSS *Yewing* which left Sirius in the year 3814.

Coburn Station – Located above Trio in the Trio System of the Silstrand Alliance, this system is connected to its host world by the system's only space elevator.

Fierra – The seventh moon of the planet Kithari in the Bollam's World System. Fierra is in the late stages of terraforming when the *Intrepid* arrives intending to trade their tech for the world.

Gedri – A system on the core-ward fringe of the Silstrand Alliance. The Gedri System is the most corrupt and lawless of the worlds in the alliance and is rife with pirates and smugglers.

Kithari – The sixth major planet in the Bollam's World System, Kithari is a 6*Mj* gas giant with jovian characteristics. It has a multitude of stations and inhabited worlds surrounding it.

New Eden (82 Eridani) – This stellar system was terraformed by the FGT in the late forty-first and early forty-second centuries. The stellar primary is a Sol-like star with two Earth-like planets in orbit.

"New Eden" also is the name the colonists gave to the first of the two Earth-like worlds in the system.

Silstrand (HR-5279 / HD 122862) – The seat of the Silstrand Alliance government and the center of the Alliance's trade and commerce, the Silstrand System boasts three terraformed worlds, one with a ring and space elevators.

Silstrand Alliance – The Silstrand Alliance is a collection of worlds located roughly 90 light-years from Sol, which have banded together under an elected representative parliamentary government. The alliance consists of 10 major star systems.

Sol – This is the name of the star which in antiquity was simply referred to as 'The Sun'. Because humans call the star that lights up their daytime sky 'the sun' in every system it became common practice to refer to Sol by its proper name.

Trio – The fourth world from Trio Prime, the world is a terrestrial planet with a single space elevator which reaches Coburn Station. Though the world has a space elevator, the system is not well populated due to prior wars with the Scipio Federation.

Trio Prime (CP-67 2079 / HD 111232) – Trio lies on the core-ward edge of the Silstrand Alliance. It has one terraformed world known as Trio.

PEOPLE

Abby Redding – Engineer responsible for building the *Intrepid*.

Amanda – One of the two human AI interfaces for the *Intrepid*.

Angela – A military intelligence sentient AI embedded within Tanis.

Bob – Bob is the name Amanda gave to the *Intrepid's* primary AI after she was installed as its human avatar. She chose the name because she claims it suits him, though only she and Priscilla understand why. Bob is perhaps the most advanced AI ever created. He is the child of seventeen very unique and well regarded AIs. He also has portions of his neural network reflecting the minds of the Reddings. He is the first AI to be multi-nodal, to have each of those nodes be as powerful as the largest NSAI, and to remain sane and cogent.

Brandt – Initially the commander of the first Marine Battalion aboard the *Intrepid*, Brandt eventually became the commandant of the Marine forces in the ISF.

Cargo – The first mate of *Sabrina* bears a strange name as it was the first he was ever given after being found as a stowaway on a freighter as a child. He has lived on freighters in space ever since.

Carson – A fighter pilot from Sol, Carson is with the *Andromeda* when it battles the three Sirian scout ships.

Cary – Pilot in the Black Death squadron.

Cheeky – Biologically modified human who is capable of releasing heavy doses of pheromones and would be described as a nymphomaniac in some circles. She is also the pilot of the starship, *Sabrina*.

Cordy – AI of the Black Death fighter squadron.

Corsia – The AI operating the *ISF Andromeda*.

Earnest Redding – Engineer responsible for much of the *Intrepid's* design. Earnest is one of the leading scientific minds in the Sol system and was responsible for much of Terrance Enfield's success.

Flaherty – Long-time friend of Sera and muscle on *Sabrina*.

Helen – The AI embedded in Sera's mind. Helen is an ancient AI, well over six-thousand years in age. She was a ship AI on one of the first FGT worldships to leave Sol in the 4th millennia. Helen was Sera's caretaker as a child, and late her mentor. Before the events that led Sera to be exiled from the FGT, Helen had herself embedded in Sera's mind.

Helen harbors a deep secret and mysterious background. Her origins date back to Sol's AI wars.

Jason Andrews – An old spacer who has completed several interstellar journeys. Captain of the *Intrepid*.

Jerry – Jessica's wingman in the Black Death squadron during the Battle of Bollam's World.

Jessica Keller – A TBI (Terran Bureau of Investigations) officer who was chasing after Myrrdan, Jessica was found by Tanis in a stasis pod with no record of how she got there.

Jessica's experience with police procedure was useful in setting up the Victorian police force and academy. She also became an accomplished pilot in the ISF.

Joseph Evans – ISF Colonel, Joseph Evans is one of the ISF's top pilots and goes on to found the Victorian Space Academy.

Kade – Leader of The Mark pirate organization until he is killed by Rebecca on *Sabrina*.

Nance – The ship's bio on *Sabrina* who also handles many of the ship's engineering duties. Nance is a germaphobe who never goes out in public without a hazsuit.

Ouri – ISF Colonel responsible for the *Intrepid's* security.

Pearson – Commander of the *Andromeda's* fighter wings.

Petrov – Pilot on the *Andromeda*.

Priscilla – One of the two human AI interfaces for the *Intrepid*.

Rebecca – Second in command of The Mark's pirate organization, and eventual leader after she murdered Kade.

Rock – Leader of the Black Death squadron.

Sabrina – The AI of the starship *Sabrina*. Sabrina has chosen the same name as her ship and identifies very deeply with it. She has neurotic tendencies due to a long period spent alone in a salvage yard.

Seraphina – Commonly known as just Sera, though Helen refers to her as "Fina", Sera is the captain of the starship *Sabrina* and a former member of the FGT organization known as The Hand.

Sue – Originally partnered with Trist, Sue went on to become the ship's AI on the Dresden.

Tanis Richards – Former TSF counterinsurgency officer, Tanis has held the ranks of major, lieutenant colonel, and general on the *Intrepid*. She was born on February 29th, 4052 on Mars.

Terrance Enfield – Financial backer for the *Intrepid*.

Thompson – *Sabrina's* supercargo and muscle. Thompson is a surly man who doesn't like much of anything and takes pleasure in being angry.

ABOUT THE AUTHOR

Michael Cooper likes to think of himself as a jack of all trades (and hopes to become master of a few). When not writing he can be found writing software, working in his shop at his latest carpentry project, or likely reading a book.

He shares his home with a precocious young girl, his wonderful wife (who also writes), two cats, a never-ending list of things he would like to build, and ideas...

Find out what's coming next at www.aeon14.com

Made in the USA
Middletown, DE
12 June 2019